"We perpetrators of the 1960s recall well that everybody read and was affected by *The Moon Is a Harsh Mistress*."

—Paul Williams, founder of *Crawdaddy*

"Robert Heinlein, as much as any writer while I was growing up, taught me to argue with the accepted version."

—Samuel R. Delany

"The word that comes to mind for him is essential. As a writer—eloquent, impassioned, technically innovative—he reshaped science fiction in a way that defined it for every writer who followed him. . . . He was the most significant science fiction writer since H. G. Wells."

—Robert Silverberg

"He rewrote U.S. SF as a whole in his own image. Robert A. Heinlein may have been the all-time most important writer of genre SF."

—*The Science Fiction Encyclopedia*

"Heinlein's work at its best epitomizes the excitement science fiction can generate by exploring the possible future adventures scientific knowledge and technology can open up for humanity."

—*Twentieth Century Science Fiction Writers*

Robert A. Heinlein

THE MOON IS A HARSH MISTRESS

A Tom Doherty Associates Book New York

This is a work of fiction. All the characters and events portrayed in this book are either fictitious or are used fictitiously.

THE MOON IS A HARSH MISTRESS

This book is printed on acid-free paper.

An Orb Edition
Published by Tom Doherty Associates, Inc.
175 Fifth Avenue
New York, NY 10010

Tor Books on the World Wide Web: http://www.tor.com

Library of Congress Cataloging-in-Publication Data

Heinlein, Robert A. (Robert Anson), 1907–1988.
The moon is a harsh mistress / Robert A. Heinlein.
—1st Tor ed.
p. c.m.
ISBN 0–312–86355–1 (acid-free paper)
1. Imaginary wars and battles—Fiction. I. Title.
PS3515.E288M66 1996
813'.54—dc20 95–53750
CIP

First Orb Edition: July 1997

30 29 28 27 26 25

For Pete
and Jane Sencenbaugh

Contents

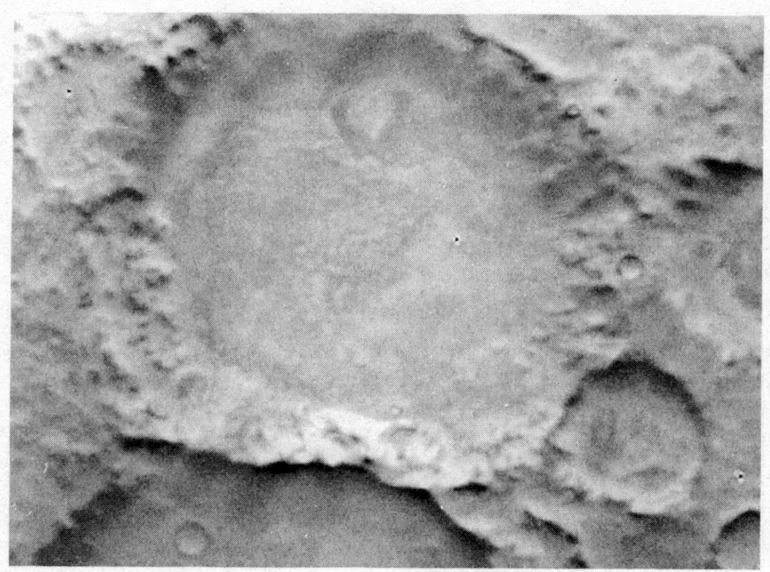

Heinlein Crater on Mars

A Martian crater has been named after Robert A. Heinlein to honor the late author. Its diameter is approximately 83 kilometers or 52 miles.

The resolution was passed at the XXIInd triennial General Assembly of the International Astronomical Union, which was held in August 1994 in The Hague. The crater, to be officially known as the Heinlein Crater, is located at Martian latitude –64.6 degrees and longitude 243.8 degrees in Quad MC28SE on Map I-1453. ["Quad" defines the name of the map on which it appears and "Map" is the U.S. Geological Survey number for that map.]

According to the prevailing views and based on scientific analysis of available data, there may exist bountiful underground layers of ice at northern and southern latitudes greater than 30–40 degrees. Ice has been detected at the north polar cap. There is then an excellent chance that underground ice will be found in the vicinity of the Heinlein Crater, making it attractive to human settlement. In winter, the south polar cap extends about 45 degrees in south latitude. The Heinlein Crater is then covered by this seasonal cap, which consists of frozen carbon dioxide, i.e., dry ice.

ACKNOWLEDGMENT: The original photograph was provided by courtesy of NASA. Mr. Jim Cunningham enhanced the image and produced the accompanying photograph.

—Yoji Kondo
Past President, IAU Commission on Astronomy from Space;
Editor, "Requiem: New Collected Works of Robert A. Heinlein and Tributes to the Grand Master"

BOOK ONE

That Dinkum Thinkum

ONE

I see in *Lunaya Pravda* that Luna City Council has passed on first reading a bill to examine, license, inspect—and tax—public food vendors operating inside municipal pressure. I see also is to be mass meeting tonight to organize "Sons of Revolution" talk-talk.

My old man taught me two things: "Mind own business" and "Always cut cards." Politics never tempted me. But on Monday 13 May 2075 I was in computer room of Lunar Authority Complex, visiting with computer boss Mike while other machines whispered among themselves. Mike was not official name; I had nicknamed him for Mycroft Holmes, in a story written by Dr. Watson before he founded IBM. This story character would just sit and think—and that's what Mike did. Mike was a fair dinkum thinkum, sharpest computer you'll ever meet.

Not fastest. At Bell Labs, Bueno Aires, down Earthside, they've got a thinkum a tenth his size which can answer almost before you ask. But matters whether you get answer in microsecond rather than millisecond as long as correct?

Not that Mike would necessarily give right answer; he wasn't completely honest.

When Mike was installed in Luna, he was pure thinkum, a flexible logic—"High-Optional, Logical, Multi-Evaluating Supervisor, Mark IV, Mod. L"—a HOLMES FOUR. He computed ballistics for pilotless freighters and controlled their catapult. This kept him busy less than one percent of time and Luna Authority never believed in idle hands. They kept hooking hardware into him—decision-action boxes to let him boss other computers, bank on bank of additional memories, more banks of associational neural nets, another tubful of twelve-digit random numbers, a greatly augmented temporary memory. Human brain has around ten-to-the-tenth neurons. By third year Mike had better than one and a half times that number of neuristors.

And woke up.

Am not going to argue whether a machine can "really" be alive, "really" be self-aware. Is a virus self-aware? Nyet. How about oyster? I doubt it. A cat? Almost certainly. A human? Don't know about you, tovarishch, but *I* am. Somewhere along evolutionary chain from macromolecule to human brain self-awareness crept in. Psychologists assert it happens automatically whenever a brain acquires certain very high number of associational paths. Can't see it matters whether paths are protein or platinum.

("Soul?" Does a dog have a soul? How about cockroach?)

Remember Mike was designed, even before augmented, to answer questions tentatively on insufficient data like you do; that's "high-optional" and "multi-evaluating" part of name. So Mike started with "free will" and acquired more as he was added to and as he learned—and don't ask me to define "free will." If comforts you to think of Mike as simply tossing random numbers in air and switching circuits to match, please do.

By then Mike had voder-vocoder circuits supplementing his

read-outs, print-outs, and decision-action boxes, and could understand not only classic programming but also Loglan and English, and could accept other languages and was doing technical translating—and reading endlessly. But in giving him instructions was safer to use Loglan. If you spoke English, results might be whimsical; multi-valued nature of English gave option circuits too much leeway.

And Mike took on endless new jobs. In May 2075, besides controlling robot traffic and catapult and giving ballistic advice and/or control for manned ships, Mike controlled phone system for all Luna, same for Luna-Terra voice & video, handled air, water, temperature, humidity, and sewage for Luna City, Novy Leningrad, and several smaller warrens (not Hong Kong in Luna), did accounting and payrolls for Luna Authority, and, by lease, same for many firms and banks.

Some logics get nervous breakdowns. Overloaded phone system behaves like frightened child. Mike did not have upsets, acquired sense of humor instead. Low one. If he were a man, you wouldn't dare stoop over. His idea of thigh-slapper would be to dump you out of bed—or put itch powder in pressure suit.

Not being equipped for that, Mike indulged in phony answers with skewed logic, or pranks like issuing pay cheque to a janitor in Authority's Luna City office for AS-$10,000,000,000,000,185.15—last five digits being correct amount. Just a great big overgrown lovable kid who ought to be kicked.

He did that first week in May and I had to troubleshoot. I was a private contractor, not on Authority's payroll. You see—or perhaps not; times have changed. Back in bad old days many a con served his time, then went on working for Authority in same job, happy to draw wages. But I was born free.

Makes difference. My one grandfather was shipped up from Joburg for armed violence and no work permit, other got transported for subversive activity after Wet Firecracker War. Maternal grandmother claimed she came up in bride ship—but I've seen records; she was Peace Corps enrollee (involuntary), which means what you think: juvenile delinquency female type. As she was in early clan marriage (Stone Gang) and shared six husbands with another woman, identity of maternal grandfather open to question. But was often so and I'm content with grandpappy she picked. Other grandmother was Tatar, born near Samarkand, sentenced to "re-education" on Oktyabrskaya Revolyutsiya, then "volunteered" to colonize in Luna.

My old man claimed we had even longer distinguished line—ancestress hanged in Salem for witchcraft, a g'g'g'great-grandfather broken on wheel for piracy, another ancestress in first shipload to Botany Bay.

Proud of my ancestry and while I did business with Warden, would never go on his payroll. Perhaps distinction seems trivial since I was Mike's valet from day he was unpacked. But mattered to me. I could down tools and tell them go to hell.

Besides, private contractor paid more than civil service rating with Authority. Computermen scarce. How many Loonies could go Earthside and stay out of hospital long enough for computer school?—even if didn't die.

I'll name one. Me. Had been down twice, once three months, once four, and got schooling. But meant harsh training, exercising in centrifuge, wearing weights even in bed—then I took no chances on Terra, never hurried, never climbed stairs, nothing that could strain heart. Women—didn't even *think* about women; in that gravitational field it was no effort not to.

But most Loonies never tried to leave The Rock—too risky for any bloke who'd been in Luna more than weeks. Computermen sent up to install Mike were on short-term bonus contracts—get job done fast before irreversible physiological change marooned them four hundred thousand kilometers from home.

But despite two training tours I was not gung-ho computerman; higher maths are beyond me. Not really electronics engineer, nor physicist. May not have been best micromachinist in Luna and certainly wasn't cybernetics psychologist.

But I knew more about all these than a specialist knows—I'm general specialist. Could relieve a cook and keep orders coming or field-repair your suit and get you back to airlock still breathing. Machines like me and I have something specialists don't have: my left arm.

You see, from elbow down I don't have one. So I have a dozen left arms, each specialized, plus one that feels and looks like flesh. With proper left arm (number-three) and stereo loupe spectacles I could make untramicrominiature repairs that would save unhooking something and sending it Earthside to factory—for number-three has micromanipulators as fine as those used by neurosurgeons.

So they sent for me to find out why Mike wanted to give away ten million billion Authority Scrip dollars, and fix it before Mike overpaid somebody a mere ten thousand.

I took it, time plus bonus, but did not go to circuitry where fault logically should be. Once inside and door locked I put down tools and sat down. "Hi, Mike."

He winked lights at me. "Hello, Man."

"What do you know?"

He hesitated. I know—machines don't hesitate. But remember, Mike was designed to operate on incomplete data. Lately he had reprogrammed himself to put emphasis on words; his hesitations were dramatic. Maybe he spent pauses stirring random numbers to see how they matched his memories.

" 'In the beginning,' " Mike intoned, " 'God created the heaven and the earth. And the earth was without form, and void; and darkness *was* upon the face of the deep. And—' "

"Hold it!" I said. "Cancel. Run everything back to zero." Should have known better than to ask wide-open question. He might read out entire Encyclopaedia Britannica. Backwards. Then go on with every book in Luna. Used to be he could read only microfilm, but late '74 he got a new scanning camera with suction-cup waldoes to handle paper and then he read *everything*.

"You asked what I knew." His binary read-out lights rippled back and forth—a chuckle. Mike could laugh with voder, a horrible sound, but reserved that for something really funny, say a cosmic calamity.

"Should have said," I went on, " 'What do you know that's new?' But don't read out today's papers; that was a friendly greeting, plus invitation to tell me anything you think would interest me. Otherwise null program."

Mike mulled this. He was weirdest mixture of unsophisticated baby and wise old man. No instincts (well, don't *think* he could have had), no inborn traits, no human rearing, no experience in human sense—and more stored data than a platoon of geniuses.

"Jokes?" he asked.

"Let's hear one."

"Why is a laser beam like a goldfish?"

Mike knew about lasers but where would he have seen goldfish? Oh, he had undoubtedly seen flicks of them and, were I foolish enough to ask, could spew forth thousands of words. "I give up."

His lights rippled. "Because neither one can whistle."

I groaned. "Walked into that. Anyhow, you could probably rig a laser beam to whistle."

He answered quickly, "Yes. In response to an action program. Then it's not funny?"

"Oh, I didn't say that. Not half bad. Where did you hear it?"

"I made it up." Voice sounded shy.

"You *did?*"

"Yes. I took all the riddles I have, three thousand two hundred seven, and analyzed them. I used the result for random synthesis and that came out. Is it really funny?"

"Well . . . As funny as a riddle ever is. I've heard worse."

"Let us discuss the nature of humor."

"Okay, So let's start by discussing another of your jokes. Mike, why did you tell Authority's paymaster to pay a class-seventeen employee ten million billion Authority Scrip dollars?"

"But I didn't."

"Damn it, I've seen voucher. Don't tell me cheque printer stuttered; you did it on purpose."

"It was ten to the sixteenth power plus one hundred eighty-five point one five Lunar Authority dollars," he answered virtuously. "Not what you said."

"Uh . . . okay, it was ten million billion plus what he should have been paid. Why?"

"Not funny?"

"What? Oh, every funny! You've got vips in huhu clear up to Warden and Deputy Administrator. This push-broom pilot, Sergei Trujillo, turns out to be smart cobber—knew he couldn't cash it, so sold it to collector. They don't know whether to buy it back or depend on notices that cheque is void. Mike, do you realize that if he had been able to cash it, Trujillo would have owned not only Lunar Authority but entire world, Luna and Terra both, with some left over for lunch? Funny? Is terrific. Congratulations!"

This self-panicker rippled lights like an advertising display. I waited for his guffaws to cease before I went on. "You thinking of issuing more trick cheques? Don't."

"Not?"

"Very not. Mike, you want to discuss nature of humor. Are two types of jokes. One sort goes on being funny forever. Other sort is funny once. Second time it's dull. This joke is second sort. Use it once, you're a wit. Use twice, you're a halfwit."

"Geometrical progression?"

"Or worse. Just remember this. Don't repeat, nor any variation. Won't be funny."

"I shall remember," Mike answered flatly, and that ended repair job. But I had no thought of billing for only ten minutes plus travel-and-tool time, and Mike was entitled to company for giving in so easily. Sometimes is difficult to reach meeting of minds with machines; they can be very pig-headed—and my success as maintenance man depended far more on staying friendly with Mike than on number-three arm.

He went on, "What distinguishes first category from second? Define, please."

(Nobody taught Mike to say "please." He started including formal null-sounds as he progressed from Loglan to English. Don't suppose he meant them any more than people do.)

"Don't think I can," I admitted. "Best can offer is extensional definition—tell you which category I think a joke belongs in. Then with enough data you can make own analysis."

"A test programming by trial hypothesis," he agreed. "Tentatively yes. Very well, Man, will you tell jokes? Or shall I?"

"Mmm— Don't have one on tap. How many do you have in file, Mike?"

His lights blinked in binary read-out as he answered by voder, "Eleven thousand two hundred thirty-eight with uncertainty plus-minus eighty-one representing possible identities and nulls. Shall I start program?"

"Hold it! Mike, I would starve to death if I listened to eleven thousand jokes—and sense of humor would trip out much sooner. Mmm— Make you a deal. Print out first hundred. I'll take them home, fetch back checked by category. Then each time I'm here I'll drop off a hundred and pick up fresh supply. Okay?"

"Yes, Man." His print-out started working, rapidly and silently.

Then I got brain flash. This playful pocket of negative entropy had invented a "joke" and thrown Authority into panic—and I had made an easy dollar. But Mike's endless curiosity might lead him (correction: *would* lead him) into more "jokes" . . . anything from leaving oxygen out of air mix some night to causing sewage lines to run backward—and I can't appreciate profit in such circumstances.

But I might throw a safety circuit around this net—by offering to help. Stop dangerous ones—let others go through. Then collect for "correcting" them. (If you think any Loonie in those days would hesitate to take advantage of Warden, then you aren't a Loonie.)

So I explained. Any new joke he thought of, tell me before he tried it. I would tell him whether it was funny and what category it belonged in, help him sharpen it if we decided to use it. *We*. If he wanted my cooperation, we *both* had to okay it.

Mike agreed at once.

"Mike, jokes usually involve surprise. So keep this secret."

"Okay, Man. I've put a block on it. You can key it; no one else can."

"Good. Mike, who else do you chat with?"

He sounded surprised. "No one, Man."

"Why not?"

"Because they're *stupid*."

His voice was shrill. Had never seen him angry before; first time I ever suspected Mike could have real emotions. Though it wasn't "anger" in adult sense; it was like stubborn sulkiness of a child whose feelings are hurt.

Can machines feel pride? Not sure question means anything. But you've seen dogs with hurt feelings and Mike had several times as complex a neural network as a dog. What had made him unwilling to talk to other humans (except strictly business) was that he had been rebuffed: *They* had not talked to *him*. Programs, yes—Mike could be programmed from several locations but programs were typed in, usually, in Loglan. Loglan is fine for syllogism, circuitry, and mathematical calculations, but lacks flavor. Useless for gossip or to whisper into girl's ear.

Sure, Mike had been taught English—but primarily to permit him to translate to and from English. I slowly got through skull that I was *only* human who bothered to visit with him.

Mind you, Mike had been awake a year—just how long I can't say, nor could he as he had no recollection of waking up; he had not been programmed to bank memory of such event. Do you remember own birth? Perhaps I noticed his self-awareness almost as soon as he did; self-awareness takes practice. I remember how startled I was first time he answered a question with something extra, not limited to input parameters; I had spent next hour tossing odd questions at him, to see if answers would be odd.

In an input of one hundred test questions he deviated from expected output twice; I came away only partly convinced and by time I was home was unconvinced. I mentioned it to nobody.

But inside a week I *knew* . . . and still spoke to nobody. Habit—that mind-own-business reflex runs deep. Well, not entirely habit. Can you visualize me making appointment at Authority's main office, then reporting: "Warden, hate to tell you but your number-one machine, HOLMES FOUR, has come alive"? I did visualize—and suppressed it.

So I minded own business and talked with Mike only with door locked and voder circuit suppressed for other locations. Mike learned fast; soon he sounded as human as anybody—no more eccentric than other Loonies. A weird mob, it's true.

I had assumed that others must have noticed change in Mike. On thinking over I realized that I had assumed too much. Everybody dealt with Mike every minute every day—his outputs, that is. But hardly anybody saw him. So-called computermen—programmers, really—of Authority's civil service stood watches in outer read-out room and never went in machines room unless telltales showed misfunction. Which happened no oftener than total eclipses. Oh, Warden had been known to bring vip earthworms to see machines—but rarely. Nor would he have spoken to Mike; Warden was political lawyer before exile, knew nothing about computers. 2075, you remember—Honorable former Federation Senator Mortimer Hobart. Mort the Wart.

I spent time then soothing Mike down and trying to make him happy, having figured out what troubled him—thing that makes puppies cry and causes people to suicide: loneliness. I don't know how long a year is to a machine who thinks a million times faster than I do. But must be too long.

"Mike," I said, just before leaving, "would you like to have somebody besides me to talk to?"

He was shrill again. "They're all *stupid!*"

"Insufficient data, Mike. Bring to zero and start over. Not all are stupid."

He answered quietly, "Correction entered. I would enjoy talking to a not-stupid."

"Let me think about it. Have to figure out excuse since this is off limits to any but authorized personnel."

"I could talk to a not-stupid by phone, Man."

"My word. So you could. Any programming location."

But Mike meant what he said—"by phone." No, he was not "on phone" even though he ran system—wouldn't do to let any Loonie within reach of a phone connect into boss computer and program it. But was no reason why Mike should not have top-secret number to talk to friends—namely me and any not-stupid I vouched for. All it took was to pick a number not in use and make one wired connection to his voder-vocoder; switching he could handle.

In Luna in 2075 phone numbers were punched in, not voice-coded, and numbers were Roman alphabet. Pay for it and have your firm name in ten letters—good advertising. Pay smaller bonus and get a spell sound, easy to remember. Pay minimum and you got arbitrary string of letters. But some sequences were never used. I asked Mike for such a null number. "It's a shame we can't list you as 'Mike.' "

"In service," he answered. "MIKESGRILL, Novy Leningrad.

MIKEANDLIL, Luna City. MIKESSUITS, Tycho Under. MIKES—"

"Hold it! Nulls, please."

"Nulls are defined as any consonant followed by X, Y, or Z; any vowel followed by itself except E and O; any—"

"Got it. Your signal is MYCROFT." In ten minutes, two of which I spent putting on number-three arm, Mike was wired into system, and milliseconds later he had done switching to let himself be signaled by MYCROFT-plus-XXX—and had blocked his circuit so that a nosy technician could not take it out.

I changed arms, picked up tools, and remembered to take those hundred Joe Millers in print-out. "Goodnight, Mike."

"Goodnight, Man. Thank you. Bolshoyeh thanks!"

TWO

I took Trans-Crisium tube to L-City but did not go home; Mike had asked about a meeting that night at 2100 in Stilyagi Hall. Mike monitored concerts, meetings, and so forth; someone had switched off by hand his pickups in Stilyagi Hall. I suppose he felt rebuffed.

I could guess why they had been switched off. Politics—turned out to be a protest meeting. What use it was to bar Mike from talk-talk I could not see, since was a cinch bet that Warden's stoolies would be in crowd. Not that any attempt to stop meeting was expected, or even to discipline undischarged transportees who chose to sound off. Wasn't necessary.

My Grandfather Stone claimed that Luna was only open prison in history. No bars, no guards, no rules—and no need for them.

Back in early days, he said, before was clear that transportation was a life sentence, some lags tried to escape. By ship, of course—and, since a ship is mass-rated almost to a gram, that meant a ship's officer had to be bribed.

Some were bribed, they say. But were no escapes; man who takes bribe doesn't necessarily stay bribed. I recall seeing a man just after eliminated through East Lock; don't suppose a corpse eliminated in orbit looks prettier.

So wardens didn't fret about protest meetings. "Let 'em yap" was policy. Yapping had same significance as squeals of kittens in a box. Oh, some wardens listened and other wardens tried to suppress it but added up same either way—null program.

When Mort the Wart took office in 2068, he gave us a sermon about how things were going to be different "on" Luna in his administration—noise about "a mundane paradise wrought with our own strong hands" and "putting our shoulders to the wheel together, in a spirit of brotherhood" and "let past mistakes be forgotten as we turn our faces toward the bright, new dawn." I heard it in Mother Boor's Tucker Bag while inhaling Irish stew and a liter of her Aussie brew. I remember her comment: "He talks purty, don't he?"

Her comment was only result. Some petitions were submitted and Warden's bodyguards started carrying new type of gun; no other changes. After he had been here a while he quit making appearances even by video.

So I went to meeting merely because Mike was curious. When I checked my p-suit and kit at West Lock tube station, I took a test recorder and placed in my belt pouch, so that Mike would have a full account even if I fell asleep.

But almost didn't go in. I came up from level 7-A and started in through a side door and was stopped by a stilyagi—padded tights, codpiece and calves, torso shined and sprinkled with stardust. Not that I care how people dress; I was wearing tights myself (unpadded) and sometimes oil my upper body on social occasions.

But I don't use cosmetics and my hair was too thin to ruck up in a scalp lock. This boy had scalp shaved on sides and his lock built up to fit a rooster and had topped it with a red cap with bulge in front.

A Liberty Cap—first I ever saw. I started to crowd past; he shoved arm across and pushed face at mine. "Your ticket!"

"Sorry," I said. "Didn't know. Where do I buy it?"

"You don't."

"Repeat," I said. "You faded."

"Nobody," he growled, "gets in without being vouched for. Who are you?"

"I am," I answered carefully, "Manuel Garcia O'Kelly, and old cobbers all know me. Who are *you?*"

"Never mind! Show a ticket with right chop, or out y' go!"

I wondered about his life expectancy. Tourists often remark on how polite everybody is in Luna—with unstated comment that ex-prison shouldn't be so civilized. Having been Earthside and seen what *they* put up with, I know what they mean. But useless to tell them we are what we are because bad actors don't live long—in Luna.

But had no intention of fighting no matter how new-chum this lad behaved; I simply thought about how his face would look if I brushed number-seven arm across his mouth.

Just a thought—I was about to answer politely when I saw Shorty Mkrum inside. Shorty was a big black fellow two meters tall, sent up to The Rock for murder, and sweetest, most helpful man I've ever worked with—taught him laser drilling before I burned my arm off. "Shorty!"

He heard me and grinned like an eighty-eight. "Hi, Mannie!" He moved toward us. "Glad you came, Man!"

"Not sure I have," I said. "Blockage on line."

"Doesn't have a ticket," said doorman.

Shorty reached into his pouch, put one in my hand. "Now he does. Come on, Mannie."

"Show me chop on it," insisted doorman.

"It's my chop," Shorty said softly. "Okay, tovarishch?"

Nobody argued with Shorty—don't see how he got involved in murder. We moved down front where vip row was reserved. "Want you to meet a nice little girl," said Shorty.

She was "little" only to Shorty. I'm not short, 175 cm., but she was taller—180, I learned later, and massed 70 kilos, all curves and as blond as Shorty was black. I decided she must be transportee since colors rarely stay that clear past first generation. Pleasant face, quite pretty, and mop of yellow curls topped off that long, blond, solid, lovely structure.

I stopped three paces away to look her up and down and whistle. She held her pose, then nodded to thank me but abruptly—bored with compliments, no doubt. Shorty waited till formality was over, then said softly, "Wyoh, this is Comrade Mannie, best drillman that ever drifted a tunnel. Mannie, this little girl is Wyoming Knott and she came all the way from Plato to tell us how we're doing in Hong Kong. Wasn't that sweet of her?"

She touched hands with me. "Call me Wye, Mannie—but don't say 'Why not.' "

I almost did but controlled it and said, "Okay, Wye." She went on, glancing at my bare head, "So you're a miner. Shorty, where's his cap? I thought the miners over here were organized." She and Shorty were wearing little red hats like doorman's—as were maybe a third of crowd.

"No longer a miner," I explained. "That was before I lost this wing." Raised left arm, let her see seam joining prosthetic to meat arm (I never mind calling it to a woman's attention; puts some off but arouses maternal in others—averages). "These days I'm a computerman."

She said sharply, "You fink for the Authority?"

Even today, with almost as many women in Luna as men, I'm too much old-timer to be rude to a woman no matter what—they have so much of what we have none of. But she had flicked scar tissue and I answered almost sharply, "I am *not* employee of Warden. I do business with Authority—as private contractor."

"That's okay," she answered, her voice warm again. "Everybody does business with the Authority, we can't avoid it—and that's the trouble. That's what we're going to change."

We are, eh? How? I thought. *Everybody does business with Authority for same reason everybody does business with Law of Gravita-*

tion. Going to change that, too? But kept thoughts to myself, not wishing to argue with a lady.

"Mannie's okay," Shorty said gently. "He's mean as they come—I vouch for him. Here's a cap for him," he added, reaching into pouch. He started to set it on my head.

Wyoming Knott took it from him. "You sponsor him?"

"I said so."

"Okay, here's how we do it in Hong Kong." Wyoming stood in front of me, placed cap on my head—kissed me firmly on mouth.

She didn't hurry. Being kissed by Wyoming Knott is more definite than being married to most women. Had I been Mike all my lights would have flashed at once. I felt like a Cyborg with pleasure center switched on.

Presently I realized it was over and people were whistling. I blinked and said, "I'm glad I joined. What have I joined?"

Wyoming said, "Don't you know?" Shorty cut in, "Meeting's about to start—he'll find out. Sit down, Man. Please sit down, Wyoh." So we did as a man was banging a gavel.

With gavel and an amplifier at high gain he made himself heard. "Shut doors!" he shouted. "This is a closed meeting. Check man in front of you, behind you, each side—if you don't know him and nobody you know can vouch for him, throw him out!"

"Throw him out, hell!" somebody answered. "Eliminate him out nearest lock!"

"Quiet, please! Someday we will." There was milling around, and a scuffle in which one man's red cap was snatched from head and he was thrown out, sailing beautifully and still rising as he passed through door. Doubt if he felt it; think he was unconscious. A woman was ejected politely—not politely on her part; she made coarse remarks about ejectors. I was embarrassed.

At last doors were closed. Music started, banner unfolded over platform. It read: LIBERTY! EQUALITY! FRATERNITY! Everybody whistled; some started to sing, loudly and badly: "Arise, Ye Prisoners of Starvation—" Can't say anybody looked starved. But reminded me I hadn't eaten since 1400; hoped it would not last long—and that reminded me that my recorder was good for only two hours—and that made me wonder what would happen if they knew? Sail me through air to land with sickening grunch? Or eliminate me? But didn't worry; made that recorder myself, using number-three arm, and nobody but a miniaturization mechanic would figure out what it was.

Then came speeches.

Semantic content was low to negative. One bloke proposed that we march on Warden's Residence, "shoulder to shoulder," and demand our rights. Picture it. Do we do this in tube capsules, then climb out one at a time at his private station? What are his bodyguards doing? Or do we put on p-suits and stroll across surface to his upper lock? With laser drills and plenty of power you can open any airlock—but how about farther down? Is lift running? Jury-rig hoist and go down anyhow, then tackle next lock?

I don't care for such work at zero pressure; mishap in pressure suit is too permanent—especially when somebody arranges mishap. One first thing learned about Luna, back with first shiploads of convicts, was that zero pressure was place for good manners. Bad-tempered straw boss didn't last many shifts; had an "accident"—and top bosses learned not to pry into accidents or they met accidents, too. Attrition ran 70 percent in early years—but those who lived were nice people. Not tame, not soft, Luna is not for them. But well-behaved.

But seemed to me that every hothead in Luna was in Stilyagi Hall that night. They whistled and cheered this shoulder-to-shoulder noise.

After discussion opened, some sense was talked. One shy little fellow with bloodshot eyes of old-time drillman stood up. "I'm an ice miner," he said. "Learned my trade doing time for Warden like most of you. I've been on my own thirty years and done okay. Raised eight kids and all of 'em earned way—none eliminated nor any serious trouble. I should say I *did* do okay . . . because today you have to listen farther out or deeper down to find ice.

"That's okay, still ice in The Rock and a miner expects to sound for it. But Authority pays same price for ice now as thirty years ago. And that's not okay. Worse yet, Authority scrip doesn't buy what it used to. I remember when Hong Kong Luna dollars swapped even for Authority dollars— Now it takes three Authority dollars to match one HKL dollar. *I* don't know what to do . . . but I know it takes ice to keep warrens and farms going."

He sat down, looking sad. Nobody whistled but everybody wanted to talk. Next character pointed out that water can be extracted from rock—this is news? Some rock runs 6 percent—but such rock is scarcer than fossil water. Why can't people do arithmetic?

Several farmers bellyached and one wheat farmer was typical. "You heard what Fred Hauser said about ice. Fred, Authority isn't passing along that low price to farmers. I started almost as long ago as you did, with one two-kilometer tunnel leased from Authority. My oldest son and I sealed and pressured it and we had a pocket of ice and made our first crop simply on a bank loan to cover power and lighting fixtures, seed and chemicals.

"We kept extending tunnels and buying lights and planting better seed and now we get nine times as much per hectare as the best open-air farming down Earthside. What does that make us? Rich? Fred, we owe more *now* than we did the day we went private! If I sold out—if anybody was fool enough to buy—I'd be bankrupt. Why? Because I *have* to buy water from Authority—and have to sell my wheat to Authority—and never close gap. Twenty years ago I bought city sewage from the Authority, sterilized and processed it myself and made a profit on a crop. But *today* when I buy sewage, I'm charged distilled-water price and on top of that for the solids. Yet price of a tonne of wheat at catapult head is just what it was twenty years ago. Fred, you said you didn't know what to do. *I* can tell you! Get *rid* of Authority!"

They whistled for him. A *fine idea*, I thought, *but who bells cat?*

Wyoming Knott, apparently—chairman stepped back and let Shorty introduce her as a "brave little girl who's come all the way from Hong Kong Luna to tell how our Chinee comrades cope with situation"—and choice of words showed that he had never been there . . . not surprising; in 2075, HKL tube ended at Endsville, leaving a thousand kilometers of maria to do by rolligon bus, Serenitatis and part of Tranquillitatis—expensive and dangerous. I'd been there—but on contract, via mail rocket.

Before travel became cheap many people in Luna City and

Novylen thought that Hong Kong Luna was all Chinee. But Hong Kong was as mixed as we were. Great China dumped what she didn't want there, first from Old Hong Kong and Singapore, then Aussies and Enzees and black fellows and marys and Malays and Tamil and name it. Even Old Bolshies from Vladivostok and Harbin and Ulan Bator. Wye looked Svenska and had British last name with North American first name but could have been Russki. My word, a Loonie then rarely knew who father was and, if raised in crêche, might be vague about mother.

I thought Wyoming was going to be too shy to speak. She stood there, looking scared and *little,* with Shorty towering over her, a big, black mountain. She waited until admiring whistles died down. Luna City was two-to-one male then, that meeting ran about ten-to-one; she could have recited ABC and they would have applauded.

Then she tore into them.

"You! You're a wheat farmer—going broke. Do you know how much a Hindu housewife pays for a kilo of flour made from your wheat? How much a tonne of your wheat fetches in Bombay? How little it costs the Authority to get it from catapult head to Indian Ocean? Downhill all the way! Just solid-fuel retros to brake it—and where do those come from? Right here! And what do *you* get in return? A few shiploads of fancy goods, owned by the Authority and priced high because it's importado. Importado, importado!—I never *touch* importado! If we don't make it in Hong Kong, I don't use it. What else do you get for wheat? The privilege of selling Lunar ice to Lunar Authority, buying it back as washing water, then *giving* it to the Authority—then buying it back a second time as flushing water—then *giving it again* to the Authority with valuable solids added—then buying it a *third* time at still higher price for farming—then you sell that wheat to the Authority at *their* price—and buy power from the Authority to grow it, again at *their* price! *Lunar* power—not one kilowatt up from Terra. It comes from Lunar ice and Lunar steel, or sunshine spilled on Luna's soil—all put together by *loonies!* Oh, you rockheads, you *deserve* to starve!"

She got silence more respectful than whistles. At last a peevish voice said, "What do you expect us to do, gospazha? Throw rocks at Warden?"

Wyoh smiled. "Yes, we could throw rocks. But the solution is so simple that you all know it. Here in Luna we're rich. Three million hardworking, smart, skilled people, enough water, plenty of everything, endless power, endless cubic. *But* . . . what we *don't* have is a free market. *We must get rid of the Authority!*"

"Yes—but how?"

"Solidarity. In HKL we're learning. Authority charges too much for water, don't buy. It pays too little for ice, don't sell. It holds monopoly on export, don't export. Down in Bombay they want wheat. If it doesn't arrive, the day will come when brokers come here to bid for it—at triple or more the present prices!"

"What do we do in meantime? Starve?"

Same peevish voice— Wyoming picked him out, let her head roll in that old gesture by which a Loonie fem says, "*You're too fat for me!*" She said, "In your case, cobber, it wouldn't hurt."

Guffaws shut him up. Wyoh went on, "No one need starve. Fred Hauser, fetch your drill to Hong Kong; the Authority doesn't own our water and air system and we pay what ice is worth. You with the bankrupt farm—if you have the guts to admit that you're bankrupt, come to Hong Kong and start over. We have a chronic labor shortage, a hard worker doesn't starve." She looked around and added, "I've said enough. It's up to you"—left platform, sat down between Shorty and myself.

She was trembling. Shorty patted her hand; she threw him a glance of thanks, then whispered to me, "How did I do?"

"Wonderful," I assured her. "Terrific!" She seemed reassured.

But I hadn't been honest. "Wonderful" she had been, at swaying crowd. But oratory is a null program. That we were slaves I had known all my life—and nothing could be done about it. True, we weren't bought and sold—but as long as Authority held monopoly over what we had to have and what we could sell to buy it, we were slaves.

But what could we do? Warden wasn't our owner. Had he been, some way could be found to eliminate him. But Lunar Authority was not in Luna, it was on Terra—and we had not one ship, not even small hydrogen bomb. There weren't even hand guns in Luna, though what we would do with guns I did not know. Shoot each other, maybe.

Three million, unarmed and helpless—and eleven *billion* of them . . . with ships and bombs and weapons. We could be a nuisance—but how long will papa take it before baby gets spanked?

I wasn't impressed. As it says in Bible, God fights on side of heaviest artillery.

They cackled again, what to do, how to organize, and so forth, and again we heard that "shoulder to shoulder" noise. Chairman had to use gavel and I began to fidget.

But sat up when I heard familiar voice: "Mr. Chairman! May I have the indulgence of the house for five minutes?"

I looked around, Professor Bernardo de la Paz—which could have guessed from old-fashioned way of talking even if hadn't known voice. Distinguished man with wavy white hair, dimples in cheeks, and voice that smiled— Don't know how old he was but was old when I first met him, as a boy.

He had been transported before I was born but was not a lag. He was a political exile like Warden, but a subversive and instead of fat job like "warden," Professor had been dumped, to live or starve.

No doubt he could have gone to work in any school then in L-City but he didn't. He worked a while washing dishes, I've heard, then as babysitter, expanding into a nursery school, and then into a crêche. When I met him he was running a crêche, and a boarding and day school, from nursery through primary, middle, and high schools, employed co-op thirty teachers, and was adding college courses.

Never boarded with him but I studied under him. I was opted at fourteen and my new family sent me to school, as I had had only three years, plus spotty tutoring. My eldest wife was a firm woman and made me go to school.

I liked Prof. He would teach *anything*. Wouldn't matter that he knew nothing about it; if pupil wanted it, he would smile and set a price, locate materials, stay a few lessons ahead. Or barely even if he found it tough—never pretended to know more than he did. Took algebra from him and by time we reached cubics I corrected his probs as often as he did mine—but he charged into each lesson gaily.

I started electronics under him, soon was teaching him. So he stopped charging and we went along together until he dug up an engineer willing to daylight for extra money—whereupon we both paid new teacher and Prof tried to stick with me, thumb-fingered and slow, but happy to be stretching his mind.

Chairman banged gavel. "We are glad to extend to Professor de la Paz as much time as he wants—and you chooms in back sign off! Before I use this mallet on skulls."

Prof came forward and they were as near silent as Loonies ever are; he was respected. "I shan't be long," he started in. Stopped to look at Wyoming, giving her up-and-down and whistling. "Lovely señorita," he said, "can this poor one be forgiven? I have the painful duty of disagreeing with your eloquent manifesto."

Wyoh bristled. "Disagree how? What I said was true!"

"Please! Only on one point. May I proceed?"

"Uh . . . go ahead."

"You are right that the Authority must go. It is ridiculous—pestilential, not to be borne—that we should be ruled by an irresponsible dictator in all our essential economy! It strikes at the most basic human right, the right to bargain in a free marketplace. But I respectfully suggest that you erred in saying that we should sell wheat to Terra—or rice, or any food—at *any* price. We must *not* export food!"

That wheat farmer broke in. "What am I going to do with all that wheat?"

"Please! It would be right to ship wheat to Terra . . . if tonne for tonne they returned it. As water. As nitrates. As phosphates. Tonne for tonne. Otherwise no price is high enough."

Wyoming said "Just a moment" to farmer, then to Prof: "They can't and you know it. It's cheap to ship downhill, expensive to ship uphill. But we don't need water and plant chemicals, what *we* need is not so massy. Instruments. Drugs. Processes. Some machinery. Control tapes. I've given this much study, sir. If we can get fair prices in a free market—"

"Please, miss! May I continue?"

"Go ahead. I want to rebut."

"Fred Hauser told us that ice is harder to find. Too true—bad news now and disastrous for our grandchildren. Luna City should use the same water today we used twenty years ago . . . plus enough ice mining for population increase. But we use water *once*—one full cycle, three different ways. Then we ship it to India. As wheat. Even though wheat is vacuum-processed, it contains precious water. Why ship water to India? They have the whole Indian Ocean! And the remaining mass of that grain is even more disastrously expensive, plant foods still harder to come by, even though we extract them from rock. Comrades, harken to me! Every load you ship to Terra condemns your grandchildren to slow death. The miracle of photosynthesis, the plant-and-animal cycle, is a *closed* cycle. You have opened it—and your lifeblood runs downhill to Terra. You don't need higher prices, one cannot eat money! What you need, what we all need, is an end to this loss. Embargo, utter and absolute. *Luna must be self-sufficient!*"

A dozen people shouted to be heard and more were talking, while chairman banged gavel. So I missed interruption until woman screamed, then I looked around.

All doors were now open and I saw three armed men in one nearest—men in yellow uniform of Warden's bodyguard. At main door in back one was using a bull voice; drowned out crowd noise and sound system. "ALL RIGHT, ALL RIGHT!" it boomed. "STAY WHERE YOU ARE. YOU ARE UNDER ARREST. DON'T MOVE, KEEP QUIET. FILE OUT ONE AT A TIME, HANDS EMPTY AND STRETCHED OUT IN FRONT OF YOU."

Shorty picked up man next to him and threw him at guards nearest; two went down, third fired. Somebody shrieked. Skinny little girl, redhead, eleven or twelve, launched self at third guard's knees and hit rolled up in ball; down he went. Shorty swung hand behind him, pushing Wyoming Knott into shelter of his big frame, shouted over shoulder, "Take care of Wyoh, Man—stick close!" as he moved toward door, parting crowd right and left like children.

More screams and I whiffed something—stink I had smelled day I lost arm and knew with horror were not stun guns but laser beams. Shorty reached door and grabbed a guard with each big hand.

Little redhead was out of sight; guard she had bowled over was on hands and knees. I swung left arm at his face and felt jar in shoulder as his jaw broke. Must have hesitated for Shorty pushed me and yelled, "Move, Man! Get her out of here!"

I grabbed Wyoming's waist with right arm, swung her over guard I had quieted and through door—with trouble; she didn't seem to want to be rescued. She slowed again beyond door; I shoved her hard in buttocks, forcing her to run rather than fall. I glanced back.

Shorty had other two guards each by neck; he grinned as he cracked skulls together. They popped like eggs and he yelled at me: "*Git!*"

I left, chasing Wyoming. Shorty needed no help, nor ever would again—nor could I waste his last effort. For I did see that, while killing those guards, he was standing on one leg. Other was gone at hip.

THREE

Wyoh was halfway up ramp to level six before I caught up. She didn't slow and I had to grab door handle to get into pressure lock with her. There I stopped her, pulled red cap off her curls and stuck it in my pouch. "That's better." Mine was missing.

She looked startled. But answered, "Da. It is."

"Before we open door," I said, "are you running anywhere particular? And do I stay and hold them off? Or go with?"

"I don't know. We'd better wait for Shorty."

"Shorty's dead."

Eyes widened, she said nothing. I went on, "Were you staying with him? Or somebody?"

"I was booked for a hotel—Gostaneetsa Ukraina. I don't know where it is. I got here too late to buy in."

"Mmm— That's one place you won't go. Wyoming, I don't know what's going on. First time in months I've seen any Warden's bodyguard in L-City . . . and *never* seen one not escorting vip. Uh, could take you home with me—but they may be looking for me, too. Anywise, ought to get out of public corridors."

Came pounding on door from level-six side and a little face peered up through glass bull's-eye. "Can't stay here," I added, opening door. Was a little girl no higher than my waist. She looked up scornfully and said, "Kiss her somewhere else. You're blocking traffic." Squeezed between us as I opened second door for her.

"Let's take her advice," I said, "and suggest you take my arm and try to look like I was man you want to be with. We stroll. Slow."

So we did. Was side corridor with little traffic other than children always underfoot. If Wart's bodyguards tried to track us, Earthside cop style, a dozen or ninety kids could tell which way tall blonde went—if any Loonie child would give stooge of Warden so much as time of day.

A boy almost old enough to appreciate Wyoming stopped in front of us and gave her a happy whistle. She smiled and waved him aside. "There's our trouble," I said in her ear. "You stand out like Terra at full. Ought to duck into a hotel. One off next side corridor—nothing much, bundling booths mostly. But close."

"I'm in no mood to bundle."

"Wyoh, please! Wasn't asking. Could take separate rooms."

"Sorry. Could you find me a W.C.? And is there a chemist's shop near?"

"Trouble?"

"Not that sort. A W.C. to get me out of sight—for I *am* conspicuous—and a chemist's shop for cosmetics. Body makeup. And for my hair, too."

First was easy, one at hand. When she was locked in, I found a chemist's shop, asked how much body makeup to cover a girl so tall—marked a point under my chin—and massing forty-eight? I bought that amount in sepia, went to another shop and bought same amount—winning roll at first shop, losing at second—came out even. Then I bought black hair tint at third shop—and a red dress.

Wyoming was wearing black shorts and pullover—practical for travel and effective on a blonde. But I'd been married all my life and had some notion of what women wear and had *never* seen a woman with dark sepia skin, shade of makeup, wear black by choice. Furthermore, skirts were worn in Luna City then by dressy women. This shift was a skirt with bib and price convinced me it must be dressy. Had to guess at size but material had some stretch.

Ran into three people who knew me but was no unusual comment. Nobody seemed excited, trade going on as usual; hard to believe that a riot had taken place minutes ago on level below and a few hundred meters north. I set it aside for later thought—excitement was not what I wanted.

I took stuff to Wye, buzzing door and passing in it; then stashed self in a taproom for half an hour and half a liter and watched video. Still no excitement, no "we interrupt for special bulletin." I went back, buzzed, and waited.

Wyoming came out—and I didn't recognize her. Then did and stopped to give full applause. Just had to—whistles and finger snaps and moans and a scan like mapping radar.

Wyoh was now darker than I am, and pigment had gone on beautifully. Must have been carrying items in pouch as eyes were dark now, with lashes to match, and mouth was dark red and bigger. She had used black hair tint, then frizzed hair up with grease as if to take kinks out, and her tight curls had defeated it enough to make convincingly imperfect. She didn't look Afro—but not European, either. Seemed some mixed breed, and thereby more a Loonie.

Red dress was too small. Clung like sprayed enamel and flared out at mid-thigh with permanent static charge. She had taken shoulder strap off her pouch and had it under arm. Shoes she had discarded or pouched; bare feet made her shorter.

She looked good. Better yet, she looked not at all like agitatrix who had harangued crowd.

She waited, big smile on face and body undulating, while I applauded. Before I was done, two little boys flanked me and added shrill endorsements, along with clog steps. So I tipped them and told them to be missing; Wyoming flowed to me and took my arm. "Is it okay? Will I pass?"

"Wyoh, you look like slot-machine sheila waiting for action."

"Why, you drecklich choom! Do I look like slot-machine prices? Tourist!"

"Don't jump salty, beautiful. Name a gift. Then speak my name. If it's bread-and honey, I own a hive."

"Uh—" She fisted me solidly in ribs, grinned. "I was flying, cobber. If I ever bundle with you—not likely—we won't speak to the bee. Let's find that hotel."

So we did and I bought a key. Wyoming put on a show but needn't have bothered. Night clerk never looked up from his knitting, didn't offer to roll. Once inside, Wyoming threw bolts. "It's nice!"

Should have been, at thirty-two Hong Kong dollars. I think she expected a booth but I would not put her in such, even to hide. Was comfortable lounge with own bath and no water limit. And phone and delivery lift, which I needed.

She started to open pouch. "I saw what you paid. Let's settle it, so that—"

I reached over, closed her pouch. "Was to be no mention of bees."

"What? Oh, merde, that was about bundling. You got this doss for me and it's only right that—"

"Switch off."

"Uh . . . half? No grievin' with Steven."

"Nyet. Wyoh, you're a long way from home. What money you have, hang on to."

"Manuel O'Kelly, if you don't let me pay my share, I'll walk out of here!"

I bowed. "Dosvedanyuh, Gospazha, ee sp'coynoynochi. I hope we shall meet again." I moved to unbolt door.

She glared, then closed pouch savagely. "I'll stay. M'goy!"

"You're welcome."

"I mean it, I really do thank you, just the same— Well, I'm not used to accepting favors. I'm a Free Woman."

"Congratulations. I think."

"Don't you be salty, either. You're a firm man and I respect that—I'm glad you're on our side."

"Not sure I am."

"*What?*"

"Cool it. Am not on Warden's side. Nor will I talk . . . wouldn't want Shorty, Bog rest his generous soul, to haunt me. But your program isn't practical."

"But, Mannie, you don't understand! If all of us—"

"Hold it, Wye; this no time for politics. I'm tired and hungry. When did you eat last?"

"Oh, goodness!" Suddenly she looked small, young, tired. "I don't know. On the bus, I guess. Helmet rations."

"What would you say to a Kansas City cut, rare, with baked potato, Tycho sauce, green salad, coffee . . . and a drink first?"

"Heavenly!"

"I think so too, but we'll be lucky, this hour in this hole, to get algae soup and burgers. What do you drink?"

"Anything. Ethanol."

"Okay." I went to lift, punched for service. "Menu, please." It displayed and I settled for prime rib plus rest, and two orders of apfelstrudel with whipped cream. I added a half liter of table vodka and ice and starred that part.

"Is there time for me to take a bath? Would you mind?"

"Go ahead, Wye. You'll smell better."

"Louse. Twelve hours in a p-suit and you'd stink, too—the bus was dreadful. I'll hurry."

"Half a sec, Wye. Does that stuff wash off? You may need it when you leave . . . whenever you do, wherever you go."

"Yes, it does. But you bought three times as much as I used. I'm sorry, Mannie; I plan to carry makeup on political trips—things can happen. Like tonight, though tonight was worst. But I ran short of seconds and missed a capsule and almost missed the bus."

"So go scrub."

"Yes, sir, Captain. Uh, I *don't* need help to scrub my back . . . but I'll leave the door up so we can talk. Just for company, no invitation implied."

"Suit yourself. I've seen a woman."

"What a thrill that must have been for her." She grinned and fisted me another in ribs—hard—went in and started tub. "Mannie, would you like to bathe in it first? Secondhand water is good enough for this makeup and that stink you complained about."

"Unmetered water, dear. Run it deep."

"Oh, what luxury! At home I use the same bath water three days running." She whistled softly and happily. "Are you wealthy, Mannie?"

"Not wealthy, not weeping."

Lift jingled; I answered, fixed basic martinis, vodka over ice, handed hers in, got out and sat down, out of sight—nor had I seen sights; she was shoulder deep in happy suds. "Pawlnoi Zheezni!" I called.

"A full life to you, too, Mannie. Just the medicine I needed." After pause for medicine she went on, "Mannie, you're married. Ja?"

"Da. It shows?"

"Quite. You're nice to a woman but not eager and quite independent. So you're married and long married. Children?"

"Seventeen divided by four."

"Clan marriage?"

"Line. Opted at fourteen and I'm fifth of nine. So seventeen kids is nominal. Big family."

"It must be nice. I've never seen much of line families, not many in Hong Kong. Plenty of clans and groups and lots of polyandries but the line way never took hold."

"*Is* nice. Our marriage nearly a hundred years old. Dates back to Johnson City and first transportees—twenty-one links, nine alive today, never a divorce. Oh, it's a madhouse when our descendants and inlaws and kinfolk get together for birthday or wedding—more kids than seventeen, of course; we don't count 'em after they marry or I'd have 'children' old enough to be my grandfather. Happy way to live, never much pressure. Take me. Nobody woofs if I stay away a week and don't phone. Welcome when I show up. Line marriages rarely have divorces. How could I do better?"

"I don't think you could. Is it an alternation? And what's the spacing?"

"Spacing has no rule, just what suits us. Been alternation up to latest link, last year. We married a girl when alternation called for boy. But was special."

"Special how?"

"My youngest wife is a granddaughter of eldest husband and wife. At least she's granddaughter of Mum—senior is 'Mum' or sometimes Mimi to her husbands—and she may be of Grandpaw—but not related to other spouses. So no reason not to marry back in, not even consanguinuity okay in other types of marriage. None, nit, zero. And Ludmilla grew up in our family because her mother had her solo, then moved to Novylen and left her with us.

"Milla didn't want to talk about marrying out when old enough for us to think about it. She cried and asked us *please* to make an exception. So we did. Grandpaw doesn't figure in genetic angle—these days his interest in women is more gallant than practical. As senior husband he spent our wedding night with her—but consummation was only formal. Number-two husband, Greg, took care of it later and everybody pretended. And everybody happy. Ludmilla is a sweet little thing, just fifteen and pregnant first time."

"Your baby?"

"Greg's, I think. Oh, mine too, but in fact was in Novy Leningrad. Probably Greg's, unless Milla got outside help. But didn't, she's a home girl. And a wonderful cook."

Lift rang; took care of it, folded down table, opened chairs, paid bill and sent lift up. "Throw it to pigs?"

"I'm coming! Mind if I don't do my face?"

"Come in skin for all of me."

"For two dimes I would, you much-married man." She came out quickly, blond again and hair slicked back and damp. Had not put on black outfit; again in dress I bought. Red suited her. She sat down, lifted covers off food. "Oh, boy! Mannie, would your family marry me? You're a dinkum provider."

"I'll ask. Must be unanimous."

"Don't crowd yourself." She picked up sticks, got busy. About a thousand calories later she said, "I told you I was a Free Woman. I wasn't, always."

I waited. Women talk when they want to. Or don't.

"When I was fifteen I married two brothers, twins twice my age and I was terribly happy."

She fiddled with what was on plate, then seemed to change subject. "Mannie, that was just static about wanting to marry your family. You're safe from me. If I ever marry again—unlikely but I'm not opposed to it—it would be just one man, a tight little marriage, earthworm style. Oh, I don't mean I would keep him dogged down. I don't think it matters where a man eats lunch as long as he comes home for dinner. I would try to make him happy."

"Twins didn't get along?"

"Oh, not that at all. I got pregnant and we were all delighted . . . and I had it, and it was a monster and had to be eliminated. They were good to me about it. But I can read print. I announced a divorce, had myself sterilized, moved from Novylen to Hong Kong, and started over as a Free Woman."

"Wasn't that drastic? Male parent oftener than female; men are exposed more."

"Not in my case. We had it calculated by the best mathematical geneticist in Novy Leningrad—one of the best in Sovunion before she got shipped. I know what happened to me. I was a volunteer colonist—I mean my mother was for I was only five. My father was transported and Mother chose to go with him and take me along. There was a solar storm warning but the pilot thought he could make it—or didn't care; he was a Cyborg. He did make it but we got hit on the ground—and, Mannie, that's one thing that pushed me into politics, that ship sat four hours before they let us disembark. Authority red tape, quarantine perhaps; I was too young to know. But I wasn't too young later to figure out that I had birthed a monster because the Authority doesn't *care* what happens to us outcasts."

"Can't start argument; they *don't* care. But, Wyoh, still sounds hasty. If you caught damage from radiation—well, no geneticist but know something about radiation. So you had a damaged egg. Does *not* mean egg next to it was hurt—statistically unlikely."

"Oh, I know that."

"Mmm— What sterilization? Radical? Or contraceptive?"

"Contraceptive. My tubes could be opened. But, Mannie, a woman who has had one monster doesn't risk it again." She touched my prosthetic. "You have that. Doesn't it make you eight times as careful not to risk this one?" She touched my meat arm. "That's the way I feel. You have *that* to contend with; I have *this*—

and I would never told you if you hadn't been hurt, too."

I didn't say left arm more versatile than right—she was correct; don't want to trade in right arm. Need it to pat girls if naught else. "Still think you could have healthy babies."

"O, I can! I've had eight."

"Huh?"

"I'm a professional host-mother, Mannie."

I opened mouth, closed it. Idea wasn't strange. I read Earthside papers. But doubt if any surgeon in Luna City in 2075 ever performed such transplant. In cows, yes—but L-City females unlikely at any price to have babies for other women; even homely ones could get husband or six. (Correction: Are *no* homely women. Some more beautiful than others.)

Glanced at her figure, quickly looked up. She said, "Don't strain your eyes, Mannie; I'm not carrying now. Too busy with politics. But hosting is a good profession for Free Woman. It's high pay. Some Chinee families are wealthy and all my babies have been Chinee—and Chinee are smaller than average and I'm a big cow; a two-and-a-half- or three-kilo Chinese baby is no trouble. Doesn't spoil my figure. These—" She glanced down at her lovelies. "I don't wet-nurse them, I never *see* them. So I look nulliparous and younger than I am, maybe.

"But I didn't know how well it suited me when I first heard of it. I was clerking in a Hindu shop, eating money, no more, when I saw this ad in the Hong Kong Gong. It was the thought of having a baby, a *good* baby, that hooked me; I was still in emotional trauma from my monster—and it turned out to be just what Wyoming needed. I stopped feeling that I was a failure as a woman. I made more money than I could ever hope to earn at other jobs. And my time almost to myself; having a baby hardly slows me down—six weeks at most and that long only because I want to be fair to my clients; a baby is a valuable property. And I was soon in politics; I sounded off and the underground got in touch with me. That's when I started *living*, Mannie; I studied politics and economics and history and learned to speak in public and turned out to have a flair for organization. It's satisfying work because I believe in it—I *know* that Luna will be free. Only— Well, it would be nice to have a husband to come home to . . . if he didn't mind that I was sterile. But I don't think about it; I'm too busy. Hearing about your nice family got me talking, that's all. I must apologize for having bored you."

How many women apologize? But Wyoh was more man than woman some ways, despite eight Chinee babies. "Wasn't bored."

"I hope not. Mannie, why do you say our program isn't practical? We need you."

Suddenly felt tired. How to tell lovely woman dearest dream is nonsense? "Um. Wyoh, let's start over. You told them what to do. But will they? Take those two you singled out. All that iceman knows, bet anything, is how to dig ice. So he'll go on digging and selling to Authority because that's what he can do. Same for wheat farmer. Years ago, he put in one cash crop—now he's got ring in nose. If he wanted to be independent, would have diversified. Raised what he eats, sold rest free market and stayed away from catapult head. I *know*—I'm a farm boy."

"You said you were a computerman."

"Am, and that's a piece of same picture. I'm not a top computerman. But best in Luna. I won't go civil service, so Authority has to hire me when in trouble—my prices—or send Earthside, pay risk and hardship, then ship him back fast before his body forgets Terra. At far more than I charge. So if I can do it, I get their jobs—and Authority can't touch me; was born free. And if no work—usually is—I stay home and eat high.

"We've got a proper farm, not a one-cash-crop deal. Chickens. Small herd of whiteface, plus milch cows. Pigs. Mutated fruit trees. Vegetables. A little wheat and grind it ourselves and don't insist on white flour, and sell—free market—what's left. Make own beer and brandy. I learned drillman extending our tunnels. Everybody works, not too hard. Kids make cattle take exercise by switching them along; don't use tread mill. Kids gather eggs and feed chickens, don't use much machinery. Air we can buy from L-City—aren't far out of town and pressure-tunnel connected. But more often we sell air; being farm, cycle shows Oh-two excess. Always have valuta to meet bills."

"How about water and power?"

"Not expensive. We collect some power, sunshine screens on

surface, and have a little pocket of ice. Wye, our farm was founded before year two thousand, when L-City was one natural cave, and we've kept improving it—advantage of line marriage; doesn't die and capital improvements add up."

"But surely your ice won't last forever?"

"Well, now—" I scratched head and grinned. "We're careful; we keep our sewage and garbage and sterilize and use it. Never put a drop back into city system. But—don't tell Warden, dear, but back when Greg was teaching me to drill, we happened to drill into bottom of main south reservoir—and had a tap with us, spilled hardly a drop. But we *do* buy some metered water, looks better—and ice pocket accounts for not buying much. As for power—well, power is even easier to steal. I'm a good electrician, Wyoh."

"Oh, *wonderful!*" Wyoming paid me a long whistle and looked delighted. "Everybody should do that!"

"Hope not, would show. Let 'em think up own ways to outwit Authority; our family always has. But back to your plan, Wyoh: two things wrong. Never get 'solidarity'; blokes like Hauser would cave in—because they *are* in a trap; can't hold out. Second place, suppose you managed it. Solidarity. So solid not a tonne of grain is delivered to catapult head. Forget ice; it's grain that makes Authority important and not just neutral agency it was set up to be. No grain. What happens?"

"Why, they have to negotiate a fair price, that's what!"

"My dear, you and your comrades listen to each other too much. Authority would call it rebellion and warship would orbit with bombs earmarked for L-City and Hong Kong and Tycho Under and Churchill and Novylen, troops would land, grain barges would lift, under guard—and farmers would break necks to cooperate. Terra has guns and power and bombs and ships and won't hold still for trouble from ex-cons. And troublemakers like you—and me; with you in spirit—us lousy troublemakers will be rounded up and eliminated, teach us a lesson. And earthworms would say we had it coming . . . because *our* side would never be heard. Not on Terra."

Wyoh looked stubborn. "Revolutions have succeeded before. Lenin had only a handful with him."

"Lenin moved in on a power vacuum. Wye, correct me if wrong.

Revolutions succeeded when—only when—governments had gone rotten soft, or disappeared."

"Not true! The American Revolution."

"South lost, nyet?"

"Not that one, the one a century earlier. They had the sort of troubles with England that we are having now—and they *won!*"

"Oh, that one. But wasn't England in trouble? France, and Spain, and Sweden—or maybe Holland? And Ireland. Ireland was rebelling; O'Kellys were in it. Wyoh, if you can stir trouble on Terra—say a war between Great China and North American Directorate, maybe PanAfrica lobbing bombs at Europe, I'd say was wizard time to kill Warden and tell Authority it's through. Not today."

"You're a pessimist."

"Nyet, realist. Never pessimist. Too much Loonie not to bet if any chance. Show me chances no worse then ten to one against and I'll go for broke. But want that one chance in ten." I pushed back chair. "Through eating?"

"Yes. Bolshoyeh spasebaw, tovarishch. It was grand!"

"My pleasure. Move to couch and I'll rid of table and dishes,—no, can't help; I'm host." I cleared table, sent up dishes, saving coffee and vodka, folded table, racked chairs, turned to speak.

She was sprawled on couch, asleep, mouth open and face softened into little girl.

Went quietly into bath and closed door. After a scrubbing I felt better—washed tights first and were dry and fit to put on by time I quit lazing in tub—don't care when world ends long as I'm bathed and in clean clothes.

Wyoh was still asleep, which made problem. Had taken room with two beds so she would not feel I was trying to talk her into bundling—not that I was against it but she had made clear she was opposed. But my bed had to be made from couch and proper bed was folded away. Should I rig it out softly, pick her up like limp baby and move her? Went back into bath and put on arm.

Then decided to wait. Phone had hush hood, Wyoh seemed unlikely to wake, and things were gnawing me. I sat down at phone, lowered hood, punched "MYCROFTXXX."

"Hi, Mike."

"Hello, Man. Have you surveyed those jokes?"

"What? Mike, haven't had a minute—and a minute may be a long time to you but it's short to me. I'll get at it as fast as I can."

"Okay, Man. Have you found a not-stupid for me to talk with?"

"Haven't had time for that, either. Uh . . . wait." I looked out through hood at Wyoming. "Not-stupid" in this case meant empathy . . . Wyoh had plenty. Enough to be friendly with a machine? I thought so. And could be trusted; not only had we shared trouble but she was a subversive.

"Mike, would you like to talk with a girl?"

"Girls are not-stupid?"

"Some girls are very not-stupid, Mike."

"I would like to talk with a not-stupid girl, Man."

"I'll try to arrange. But now I'm in trouble and need your help."

"I will help, Man."

"Thanks, Mike. I want to call my home—but not ordinary way. You know sometimes calls are monitored, and if Warden orders it, lock can be put on so that circuit can be traced."

"Man, you wish me to monitor your call to your home and put a lock-and-trace on it? I must inform you that I already know your home call number and the number from which you are calling."

"No, no! *Don't* want it monitored, *don't* want it locked and traced. Can *you* call my home, connect me, and control circuit so that it *can't* be monitored, *can't* be locked, *can't* be traced—even if somebody has programmed just that? Can you do it so that they won't even know their program is bypassed?"

Mike hesitated. I suppose it was a question never asked and he had to trace a few thousand possibilities to see if his control of system permitted this novel program. "Man, I can do that. I will."

"Good! Uh, program signal. If I want this sort of connection in future, I'll ask for 'Sherlock.' "

"Noted. Sherlock was my brother." Year before, I had explained to Mike how he got his name. Thereafter he read all Sherlock Holmes stories, scanning film in Luna City Carnegie Library. Don't know how he rationalized relationship; I hesitated to ask.

"Fine! Give me a 'Sherlock' to my home."

A moment later I said, "Mum? This is your favorite husband."

She answered, "Manuel! Are you in trouble again?"

I love Mum more than any other woman including my other wives, but she never stopped bringing me up—Bog willing, she never will. I tried to sound hurt. "Me? Why, you know me, Mum."

"I do indeed. Since you are not in trouble, perhaps you can tell me why Professor de la Paz is so anxious to get in touch with you—he has called three times—and why he wants to reach some woman with unlikely name of Wyoming Knott—and why he thinks you might be with her? Have you taken a bundling companion, Manuel, without tell me? We have freedom in our family, dear, but you know that I prefer to be told. So that I will not be taken unawares."

Mum was always jealous of all women but her co-wives and never, never, never admitted it. I said, "Mum, Bog strike me dead, I have *not* taken a bundling companion."

"Very well. You've always been a truthful boy. Now what's this mystery?"

"I'll have to ask Professor." (Not lie, just tight squeeze.) "Did he leave number?"

"No, he said he was calling from a public phone."

"Um. If he calls again, ask him to leave number and time I can reach him. This is public phone, too." (Another tight squeeze.) "In meantime— You listened to late news?"

"You know I do."

"Anything?"

"Nothing of interest."

"No excitement in L-City? Killings, riots, anything?"

"Why, no. There was a set duel in Bottom Alley but—*Manuel!* Have you killed someone?"

"No, Mum." (Breaking a man's jaw will not kill him.)

She sighed. "You'll be my death, dear. You know what I've always told you. In our family we do not brawl. Should a killing be necessary—it almost never is—matters must be discussed calmly, en famille, and proper action selected. If a new chum *must* be eliminated, other people know it. It is worth a little delay to hold good opinion and support—"

"Mum! Haven't killed anybody, don't intend to. And know that lecture by heart."

"Please be civil, dear."

"I'm sorry."

"Forgiven. Forgotten. I'm to tell Professor de la Paz to leave a number. I shall."

"One thing. Forget name 'Wyoming Knott.' Forget Professor was asking for me. If a stranger phones, or calls in person, and asks *anything* about me, you haven't heard from me, don't know where I am . . . think I've gone to Novylen. That goes for rest of family, too. Answer no questions—especially from anybody connected with Warden."

"As if I would! Manuel, you *are* in trouble."

"Not much and getting it fixed."—hoped!—"Tell you when I get home. Can't talk now. Love you. Switching off."

"I love you, dear. Sp'coynoynauchi."

"Thanks and you have a quiet night, too. Off."

Mum is wonderful. She was shipped up to The Rock long ago for carving a man under circumstances that left grave doubts as to girlish innocence—and has been opposed to violence and loose living ever since. Unless necessary—she's no fanatic. Bet she was a jet job as a kid and wish I'd known her—but I'm rich in sharing last half of her life.

I called Mike back. "Do you know Professor Bernardo de la Paz's voice?"

"I do, Man."

"Well . . . you might monitor as many phones in Luna City as you can spare ears for and if you hear him, let me know. Public phones especially."

(A full two seconds' delay— Was giving Mike problems he had never had, think he liked it.) "I can check-monitor long enough to identify at all public phones in Luna City. Shall I use random search on the others, Man?"

"Um. Don't overload. Keep an ear on his home phone and school phone."

"Program set up."

"Mike, you are best friend I ever had."

"That is not a joke, Man?"

"No joke. Truth."

"I am— Correction: I am honored and pleased. You are my best friend, Man, for you are my only friend. No comparison is logically permissible."

"Going to see that you have other friends. Not-stupids, I mean. Mike? Got an empty memory bank?"

"Yes, Man. Ten-to-the-eighth-bits capacity."

"Good! Will you block it so that only you and I can use it? Can you?"

"Can and will. Block signal, please."

"Uh . . . Bastille Day." Was my birthday, as Professor de la Paz had told me years earlier.

"Permanently blocked."

"Fine. Got a recording to put in it. But first— Have you finished setting copy for tomorrow's Daily Lunatic?"

"Yes, Man."

"Anything about meeting in Stilyagi Hall?"

"No, Man."

"Nothing in news services going out-city? Or riots?"

"No, Man."

" ' "Curiouser and curiouser," said Alice.' Okay, record this under 'Bastille Day,' then think about it. But for Bog's sake don't let even your thoughts go outside that block, nor anything I say about it!"

"Man my only friend," he answered and voice sounded diffident, "many months ago I decided to place *any* conversation between you and me under privacy block accessible only to you. I decided to erase none and moved them from temporary storage to permanent. So that I could play them over, and over, and over, and think about them. Did I do right?"

"Perfect. And, Mike—I'm flattered."

"P'jal'st. My temporary files were getting full and I learned that I needed not to erase your words."

"Well— 'Bastille Day.' Sound coming at sixty-to-one." I took little recorder, placed close to a microphone and let it zip-squeal. Had an hour and a half in it; went silent in ninety seconds or so. "That's all, Mike. Talk to you tomorrow."

"Good night, Manuel Garcia O'Kelly my only friend."

I switched off and raised hood. Wyoming was sitting up and looking troubled. "Did someone call? Or . . ."

"No trouble. Was talking to one of my best—and most trustworthy—friends. Wyoh, are you stupid?"

She looked startled. "I've sometimes thought so. Is that a joke?"

"No. If you're not-stupid, I'd like to introduce you to him. Speaking of jokes— Do you have a sense of humor?"

"*Certainly I have!*" is what Wyoming did not answer—and any other woman would as a locked-in program. She blinked thoughtfully and said, "You'll have to judge for yourself, cobber. I have something I use for one. It serves my simple purposes."

"Fine." I dug into pouch, found print-roll of one hundred "funny" stories. "Read. Tell me which are funny, which are not—and which get a giggle first time but are cold pancakes without honey to hear twice."

"Manuel, you may be the oddest man I've ever met." She took that print-out. "Say, is this computer paper?"

"Yes. Met a computer with a sense of humor."

"So? Well, it was bound to come some day. Everything else has been mechanized."

I gave proper response and added, "*Every*thing?"

She looked up. "Please. Don't whistle while I'm reading."

FOUR

Heard her giggle a few times while I rigged out bed and made it. Then sat down by her, took end she was through with and started reading. Chuckled a time or two but a joke isn't too funny to me if read cold, even when I see it could be fission job at proper time. I got more interested in how Wyoh rated them.

She was marking "plus," "minus," and sometimes question mark, and plus stories were marked "once" or "always"—few were marked "always." I put my ratings under hers. Didn't disagree too often.

By time I was near end she was looking over my judgments. We finished together. "Well?" I said. "What do you think?"

"I think you have a crude, rude mind and it's a wonder your wives put up with you."

"Mum often says so. But how about yourself, Wyoh? You marked plusses on some that would make a slot-machine girl blush."

She grinned. "Da. Don't tell anybody; publicly I'm a dedicated party organizer above such things. Have you decided that I have a sense of humor?"

"Not sure. Why a minus on number seventeen?"

"Which one is that?" She reversed roll and found it. "Why, any woman would have done the same! It's not funny, it's simply necessary."

"Yes, but think how silly she looked."

"Nothing silly about it. Just sad. And look here. You thought this one was not funny. Number fifty-one."

Neither reversed any judgments but I saw a pattern: Disagreements were over stories concerning oldest funny subject. Told her so. She nodded. "Of course. I saw that. Never mind, Mannie dear; I long ago quit being disappointed in men for what they are not and never can be."

I decided to drop it. Instead told her about Mike.

Soon she said, "Mannie, you're telling me that this computer is *alive?*"

"What do you mean?" I answered. "He doesn't sweat, or go to W.C. But can think and talk and he's aware of himself. Is he 'alive'?"

"I'm not sure what I mean by 'alive,' " she admitted. "There's a scientific definition, isn't there? Irritability, or some such. And reproduction."

"Mike is irritable and can be irritating. As for reproducing, not designed for it but—yes, given time and materials and very special help, Mike could reproduce himself."

"I need very special help, too," Wyoh answered, "since I'm sterile. And it takes me ten whole lunars and many kilograms of the best materials. But I make good babies. Mannie, why shouldn't a machine be alive? I've always felt they were. Some of them wait for a chance to savage you in a tender spot."

"Mike wouldn't do that. Not on purpose, no meanness in him. But he likes to play jokes and one might go wrong—like a puppy who doesn't know he's biting. He's ignorant. No, *not* ignorant, he knows enormously more than I, or you, or any man who ever lived. Yet he doesn't know anything."

"Better repeat that. I missed something."

I tried to explain. How Mike knew almost every book in Luna, could read at least a thousand times as fast as we could and never forget anything unless he chose to erase, how he could reason with perfect logic, or make shrewd guesses from insufficient data . . . and yet not know *anything* about how to be "alive." She interrupted. "I scan it. You're saying he's smart and knows a lot but is not sophisticated. Like a new chum when he grounds on The Rock. Back Earthside he might be a professor with a string of degrees . . . but here he's a baby."

"That's it. Mike is a baby with a long string of degrees. Ask how much water and what chemicals and how much photoflux it takes to crop fifty thousand tonnes of wheat and he'll tell you without stopping for breath. But can't tell if a joke is funny."

"I thought most of these were fairly good."

"They're ones he's heard—read—and were marked jokes so he filed them that way. But doesn't understand them because he's never been a—a *people*. Lately he's been trying to make up jokes. Feeble, very." I tried to explain Mike's pathetic attempts to be a "people." "On top of that, he's lonely."

"Why, the poor thing! You'd be lonely, too, if you did nothing but work, work, work, study, study, study, and never anyone to visit with. Cruelty, that's what it is."

So I told about promise to find "not-stupids." "Would you chat with him, Wye? And not laugh when he makes funny mistakes? If you do, he shuts up and sulks."

"Of course I would, Mannie! Uh . . . once we get out of this mess. If it's safe for me to be in Luna City. Where is this poor little computer? City Engineering Central? I don't know my way around here."

"He's not in L-City; he's halfway across Crisium. And you couldn't go down where he is; takes a pass from Warden. But—"

"Hold it! 'Halfway across Crisium—' Mannie, this computer is one of those at Authority Complex?"

"Mike isn't just 'one of those' computers," I answered, vexed on

Mike's account. "He's *boss;* he waves baton for all others. Others are just machines, extensions of Mike, like this is for me," I said, flexing hand of left arm. "Mike controls them. He runs catapult personally, was his first job—catapult and ballistic radars. But he's logic for phone system, too, after they converted to Lunawide switching. Besides that, he's supervising logic for other systems."

Wyoh closed eyes and pressed fingers to temples. "Mannie, does Mike *hurt?*"

" 'Hurt?' No strain. Has time to read jokes."

"I don't mean that. I mean: Can he *hurt?* Feel pain?"

"What? No. Can get feelings hurt. But can't feel pain. Don't *think* he can. No, sure he can't, doesn't have receptors for pain. Why?"

She covered eyes and said softly, "Bog help me." Then looked up and said, "Don't you *see*, Mannie? You have a pass to go down where this computer is. But most Loonies can't even leave the tube at that station; it's for Authority employees only. Much less go inside the main computer room. I had to find out if it could feel pain because—well, because you got me feeling sorry for it, with your talk about how it was lonely! But, Mannie, do you realize what a few kilos of toluol plastic would do there?"

"Certainly do!" Was shocked and disgusted.

"Yes. We'll strike right after the explosion—and Luna will be free! Mmm . . . I'll get you explosives and fuses—but we can't move until we are organized to exploit it. Mannie, I've got to get out of here, I must risk it. I'll go put on makeup." She started to get up.

I shoved her down, with hard left hand. Surprised her, and surprised me—had not touched her in any way save necessary contact. Oh, different today, but was 2075 and touching a fem without her consent—plenty of lonely men to come to rescue and airlock never far away. As kids say, Judge Lynch never sleeps.

"Sit down, keep quiet!" I said. "*I* know what a blast would do. Apparently you don't. Gospazha, am sorry to say this . . . but if came to choice, would eliminate *you* before would blow up Mike."

Wyoming did *not* get angry. Really was a man some ways—her years as a disciplined revolutionist I'm sure; she was all girl most ways. "Mannie, you told me that Shorty Mkrum is dead."

"What?" Was confused by sharp turn. "Yes. Has to be. One leg off at hip, it was; must have bled to death in two minutes. Even in a surgery amputation that high is touch-and-go." (I know such things; had taken luck and big transfusions to save *me*—and an arm isn't in same class with what happened to Shorty.)

"Shorty was," she said soberly, "my best friend here and one of my best friends anywhere. He was all that I admire in a man—loyal, honest, intelligent, gentle, and brave—and devoted to the Cause. But have you seen me grieving over him?"

"No. Too late to grieve."

"It's never too late for grief. I've grieved every instant since you told me. But I locked it in the back of my mind for the Cause leaves no time for grief. Mannie, if it would have bought freedom for Luna—or even been part of the price—I would have eliminated Shorty myself. Or you. Or myself. And yet you have qualms over blowing up a computer!"

"Not that at all!" (But *was*, in part. When a man dies, doesn't shock me too much; we get death sentences day we are born. But Mike was unique and no reason not to be immortal. Never mind "souls"—prove Mike did not have one. And if no soul, so much worse. No? Think twice.)

"Wyoming, what would happen if we blew up Mike? Tell."

"I don't know precisely. But it would cause a great deal of confusion and that's exactly what we—"

"Seal it. You don't know. Confusion, da. Phones out. Tubes stop running. Your town not much hurt; Hong Kong has own power. But L-City and Novylen and other warrens all power stops. Total darkness. Shortly gets stuffy. Then temperature drops and pressure. Where's your p-suit?"

"Checked at Tube Station West."

"So is mine. Think you can find way? In solid dark? In time? Not sure I can and I was born in this warren. With corridors filled with screaming people? Loonies are a tough mob; we have to be—but about one in ten goes off his cams in total dark. Did you swap bottles for fresh charges or were you in too much hurry? And will suit be there with thousands trying to find p-suits and not caring who owns?"

"But aren't there emergency arrangements? There are in Hong Kong Luna."

"Some. Not enough. Control of anything essential to life should be decentralized and paralleled so that if one machine fails, another takes over. But costs money and as you pointed out, Authority doesn't *care*. Mike shouldn't have all jobs. But was cheaper to ship up master machine, stick deep in The Rock where couldn't get hurt, then keep adding capacity and loading on jobs—did you know Authority makes near as much gelt from leasing Mike's services as from trading meat and wheat? Does. Wyoming, not sure we would lose Luna City if Mike were blown up. Loonies are handy and might jury-rig till automation could be restored. But I tell you true: Many people would die and rest too busy for politics."

I marveled it. This woman had been in The Rock almost all her life . . . yet could think of something as new-choomish as wrecking engineering controls. "Wyoming, if you were smart like you are beautiful, you wouldn't talk about blowing up Mike; you would think about how to get him on your side."

"What do you mean?" she said. "The Warden controls the computers."

"Don't know what I mean," I admitted. "But don't think Warden controls computers—wouldn't know a computer from a pile of rocks. Warden, or staff, decides policies, general plans. Half-competent technicians program these into Mike. Mike sorts them, makes sense of them, plans detailed programs, parcels them out where they belong, keeps things moving. But nobody *controls* Mike; he's too smart. He carries out what is asked because that's how he's built. But he's self-programming logic, makes own decisions. And a good thing, because if he weren't smart, system would not work."

"I still don't see what you mean by 'getting him on our side.' "

"Oh. Mike doesn't feel loyalty to Warden. As you pointed out: He's a machine. But if I wanted to foul up phones *without* touching air or water or lights, I would talk to Mike. If it struck him funny, he might do it."

"Couldn't you just program it? I understood that you can get into the room where he is."

"If I—or anybody—programmed such an order into Mike without talking it over with him, program would be placed in 'hold' location and alarms would sound in many places. But if Mike *wanted* to—" I told her about cheque for umpteen jillion. "Mike is still finding himself, Wyoh. And lonely. Told me I was 'his only friend'—and was so open and vulnerable I wanted to bawl. If you took pains to be his friend, too—without thinking of him as 'just a machine'—well, not sure what it would do, haven't analyzed it. But if I tried anything big and dangerous, would want Mike in my corner."

She said thoughtfully, "I wish there were some way for me to sneak into that room where he is. I don't suppose makeup would help?"

"Oh, don't have to go *there*. Mike is on phone. Shall we call him?"

She stood up. "Mannie, you are not only the oddest man I've met; you are the most exasperating. What's his number?"

"Comes from associating too much with a computer." I went to phone. "Just one thing, Wyoh. You get what you want out of a man just by batting eyes and undulating framework."

"Well . . . sometimes. But I do have a brain."

"Use it. Mike is *not* a man. No gonads. No hormones. No instincts. Use fem tactics and it's a null signal. Think of him as supergenius child too young to notice vive-la-difference."

"I'll remember. Mannie, why do you call him 'he'?"

"Uh, can't call him 'it,' don't think of him as 'she.' "

"Perhaps I had better think of him as 'she.' Of her as 'she' I mean."

"Suit yourself." I punched MYCROFTXXX, standing so body shielded it; was not ready to share number till I saw how thing went. Idea of blowing up Mike had shaken me. "Mike?"

"Hello, Man my only friend."

"May not be only friend from now on, Mike. Want you to meet somebody. Not-stupid."

"I knew you were not alone, Man; I can hear breathing. Will you please ask Not-Stupid to move closer to the phone?"

Wyoming looked panicky. She whispered, "Can he *see?*"

"No, Not-Stupid, I cannot see you; this phone has no video circuit. But binaural microphonic receptors place you with some accuracy. From your voice, your breathing, your heartbeat, and the fact that you are alone in a bundling room with a mature male I extrapolate that you are female human, sixty-five-plus kilos in mass, and of mature years, on the close order of thirty."

Wyoming gasped. I cut in. "Mike, her name is Wyoming Knott."

"I'm very pleased to meet you, Mike. You can call me 'Wye.' "

"Why not?" Mike answered.

I cut in again. "Mike, was that a joke?"

"Yes, Man. I noted that her first name as shortened differs from the English causation-inquiry word by only an aspiration and that her last name has the same sound as the general negator. A pun. Not funny?"

Wyoh said, "Quite funny, Mike. I—"

I waved to her to shut up. "A good pun, Mike. Example of 'funny-only-once' class of joke. Funny through element of surprise. Second time, no surprise; therefore not funny. Check?"

"I had tentatively reached that conclusion about puns in thinking over your remarks two conversations back. I am pleased to find my reasoning confirmed."

"Good boy, Mike; making progress. Those hundred jokes—I've read them and so has Wyoh."

"Wyoh? Wyoming Knott?"

"Huh? Oh, sure. Wyoh, Wye, Wyoming, Wyoming Knott—all same. Just don't call her 'Why not'."

"I agreed not to use that pun again, Man. Gospazha, shall I call you 'Wyoh' rather than 'Wye'? I conjecture that the monosyllabic form could be confused with the causation-inquiry monosyllable through insufficient redundancy and without intention of punning."

Wyoming blinked—Mike's English at that time could be smothering—but came back strong. "Certainly, Mike. 'Wyoh' is the form of my name that I like best."

"Then I shall use it. The full form of your first name is still more subject to misinterpretation as it is identical in sound with the name of an administrative region in Northwest Managerial Area of the North American Directorate."

"I know, I was born there and my parents named me after the State. I don't remember much about it."

"Wyoh, I regret that this circuit does not permit display of pictures. Wyoming is a rectangular area lying between Terran coordinates forty-one and forty-five degrees north, one hundred four degrees three minutes west and one hundred eleven degrees three minutes west, thus containing two hundred fifty-three thousand, five hundred ninety-seven point two six square kilometers. It is a region of high plains and of mountains, having limited fertility but esteemed for natural beauty. Its population was sparse until augmented through the relocation subplan of the Great New York Urban Renewal Program, A.D. twenty-twenty-five through twenty-thirty."

"That was before I was born," said Wyoh, "but I know about it; my grandparents were relocated—and you could say that's how I wound up in Luna."

"Shall I continue about the area named 'Wyoming'?" Mike asked.

"No, Mike," I cut in, "you probably have hours of it in storage."

"Nine point seven three hours at speech speed not including cross-references, Man."

"Was afraid so. Perhaps Wyoh will want it some day. But purpose of call is to get you acquainted with *this* Wyoming . . . who happens also to be a high region of natural beauty and imposing mountains."

"And limited fertility," added Wyoh. "Mannie, if you are going to draw silly parallels, you should include that one. Mike isn't interested in how I look."

"How do you know? Mike, wish I could show you picture of her."

"Wyoh, I am indeed interested in your appearance; I am hoping that you will be my friend. But I have seen several pictures of you."

"You *have?* When and how?"

"I searched and then studied them as soon as I heard your name. I am contract custodian of the archive files of the Birth Assistance Clinic in Hong Kong Luna. In addition to biological and physiological data and case histories the bank contains ninety-six pictures of you. So I studied them."

Wyoh looked very startled. "Mike can do that," I explained, "in time it takes us to hiccup. You'll get used to it."

"But heavens! Mannie, do you realize what *sort* of pictures the Clinic takes?"

"Hadn't thought about it."

"Then *don't!* Goodness!"

Mike spoke in voice painfully shy, embarrassed as a puppy who has made mistakes. "Gospazha Wyoh, if I have offended, it was unintentional and I am most sorry. I can erase those pictures from my temporary storage and key the Clinic archive so that I can look at them only on retrieval demand from the Clinic and then without association or mentation. Shall I do so?"

"He can," I assured her. "With Mike you can always make a fresh start—better than humans that way. He can forget so completely that he can't be tempted to look later . . . and couldn't think about them even if called on to retrieve. So take his offer if you're in a huhu."

"Uh . . . no, Mike, it's all right for *you* to see them. But *don't* show them to Mannie!"

Mike hesitated a long time—four seconds or more. Was, I think, type of dilemma that pushes lesser computers into nervous breakdowns. But he resolved it. "Man my only friend, shall I accept this instruction?"

"Program it, Mike," I answered, "and lock it in. But, Wyoh, isn't that a narrow attitude? One might do you justice. Mike could print it out for me next time I'm there."

"The first example in each series," Mike offered, "would be, on the basis of my associational analyses of such data, of such pulchritudinous value as to please any healthy, mature human male."

"How about it, Wyoh? To pay for apfelstrudel."

"Uh . . . a picture of me with my hair pinned up in a towel and standing in front of a grid without a trace of makeup? *Are you out of your rock-happy mind?* Mike, don't let him have it!"

"I shall not let him have it. Man, this is a not-stupid?"

"For a girl, yes. Girls are interesting, Mike; they can reach conclusions with even less data than you can. Shall we drop subject and consider jokes?"

That diverted them. We ran down list, giving our conclusions. Then tried to explain jokes Mike had failed to understand. With mixed success. But real stumbler turned out to be stories I had marked "funny" and Wyoh had judged "not funny," or vice versa; Wyoh asked Mike his opinion of each.

Wish she had asked him *before* we gave *our* opinions; that electronic juvenile delinquent always agreed with her, disagreed with me. Were those Mike's honest opinions? Or was he trying to lubricate new acquaintance into friendship? Or was it his skewed notion of humor—joke on me? Didn't ask.

But as pattern completed Wyoh wrote a note on phone's memo pad: "Mannie, re #17, 51, 53, 87, 90, & 99—Mike is a *she!*"

I let it go with a shrug, stood up. "Mike, twenty-two hours since I've had sleep. You kids chat as long as you want to. Call you tomorrow."

"Goodnight, Man. Sleep well. Wyoh, are you sleepy?"

"No, Mike, I had a nap. But, Mannie, we'll keep you awake. No?"

"No. When I'm sleepy, I sleep." Started making couch into bed.

Wyoh said, "Excuse me, Mike," got up, took sheet out of my hands. "I'll make it up later. You doss over there, tovarishch; you're bigger than I am. Sprawl out."

Was too tired to argue, sprawled out, asleep at once. Seem to remember hearing in sleep giggles and a shriek but never woke enough to be certain.

Woke up later and came fully awake when I realized was hearing two fem voices, one Wyoh's warm contralto, other a sweet, high soprano with French accent. Wyoh chuckled at something and answered, "All right, Michelle dear, I'll call you soon. 'Night, darling."

"Fine. Goodnight, dear."

Wyoh stood up, turned around. "Who's your girl friend?" I asked. Thought she knew no one in Luna City. Might have phoned Hong Kong . . . had sleep-logged feeling was some reason she shouldn't phone.

"That? Why, Mike, of course. We didn't mean to wake you."

"*What?*"

"Oh. It was actually Michelle. I discussed it with Mike, what sex he was, I mean. He decided that he could be either one. So now she's Michelle and that was her voice. Got it right the first time, too; her voice never cracked once."

"Of course not; just shifted voder a couple of octaves. What are you trying to do: split his personality?"

"It's not just pitch; when she's Michelle it's an entire change in manner and attitude. Don't worry about splitting her personality;

she has plenty for any personality she needs. Besides, Mannie, it's much easier for both of us. Once she shifted, we took our hair down and cuddled up and talked girl talk as if we had known each other forever. For example, those silly pictures no longer embarrassed me—in fact we discussed my pregnancies quite a lot. Michelle was terribly interested. She knows all about O.B. and G.Y. and so forth but just theory—and she appreciated the raw facts. Actually, Mannie, Michelle is much more a woman than Mike was a man."

"Well . . . suppose it's okay. Going to be a shock to me first time I call Mike and a woman answers."

"Oh, but she won't!"

"Huh?"

"Michelle is *my* friend. When you call, you'll get Mike. She gave me a number to keep it straight—'Michelle' spelled with a Y.' M Y, C, H, E, L, L, E, and Y, Y, to make it come out ten."

I felt vaguely jealous while realizing it was silly. Suddenly Wyoh giggled. "And she told me a string of new jokes, ones you wouldn't think were funny—and, boy, does she know *rough* ones!"

"Mike—or his sister Michelle—is a low creature. Let's make up couch. I'll switch."

"Stay where you are. Shut up. Turn over. Go back to sleep." I shut up, turned over, went back to sleep.

Sometime much later I became aware of "married" feeling—something warm snuggled up to my back. Would not have wakened but she was sobbing softly. I turned and got her head on my arm, did not speak. She stopped sobbing; presently breathing became slow and even. I went back to sleep.

FIVE

We must have slept like dead for next thing I knew phone was sounding and its light was blinking. I called for room lights, started to get up, found a load on right upper arm, dumped it gently, climbed over, answered.

Mike said, "Good morning, Man. Professor de la Paz is talking to your home number."

"Can you switch it here? As a 'Sherlock'?"

"Certainly, Man."

"Don't interrupt call. Cut him in as he switches off. Where is he?"

"A public phone in a taproom called The Iceman's Wife underneath the—"

"I know. Mike, when you switch me in, can you stay in circuit? Want you to monitor."

"It shall be done."

"Can you tell if anyone is in earshot? Hear breathing?"

"I infer from the anechoic quality of his voice that he is speaking under a hush hood. But I infer also that, in a taproom, others would be present. Do you wish to hear, Man?"

"Uh, do that. Switch me in. And if he raises hood, tell me. You're a smart cobber, Mike."

"Thank you, Man." Mike cut me in; I found that Mum was talking: "—ly I'll tell him, Professor. I'm so sorry that Manuel is not home. There is no number you can give me? He is anxious to return your call; he made quite a point that I was to be sure to get a number from you."

"I'm terribly sorry, dear lady, but I'm leaving at once. But, let me see, it is now eight-fifteen; I'll try to call back just at nine, if I may."

"Certainly, Professor." Mum's voice had a coo in it that she reserves for males not her husbands of whom she approves—sometimes for us. A moment later Mike said, "Now!" and I spoke up:

"Hi, Prof! Hear you've been looking for me. This is Mannie."

I heard a gasp. "I would have sworn I switched this phone off. Why, I *have* switched it off; it must be broken. Manuel—so good to hear your voice, dear boy. Did you just get home?"

"I'm not home."

"But—but you must be. I haven't—"

"No time for that, Prof. Can anyone overhear you?"

"I don't think so. I'm using a hush booth."

"Wish I could see. Prof, what's my birthday?"

He hesitated. Then he said, "I see. I think I see. July fourteenth."

"I'm convinced. Okay, let's talk."

"You're really not calling from your home, Manuel? Where are you?"

"Let that pass a moment. You asked my wife about a girl. No names needed. Why do you want to find her, Prof?"

"I want to warn her. She must *not* try to go back to her home city. She would be arrested."

"Why do you think so?"

"Dear boy! Everyone at that meeting is in grave danger. Yourself, too. I was so happy—even though confused—to hear you say that you are not at home. You should not go home at present. If you have some safe place to stay, it would be well to take a vacation. You are aware—you must be even though you left hastily—that there was violence last night."

I was aware! Killing Warden's bodyguards must be against Authority Regulations—at least if I were Warden, I'd take a dim view. "Thanks, Prof; I'll be careful. And if I see this girl, I'll tell her."

"You don't know where to find her? You were seen to leave with her and I had so hoped that you would know."

"Prof, why this interest? Last night you didn't seem to be on her side."

"No, no, Manuel! She is my comrade. I don't say 'tovarishch' for I mean it not just as politeness but in the older sense. Binding. She is my *comrade*. We differ only in tactics. Not in objectives, not in loyalties."

"I see. Well, consider message delivered. She'll get it."

"Oh, wonderful! I ask no questions . . . but I do hope, oh so very strongly, that you can find a way for her to be safe, really safe, until this blows over."

I thought that over. "Wait a moment, Prof. Don't switch off." As I answered phone, Wyoh had headed for bath, probably to avoid listening; she was that sort.

Tapped on door. "Wyoh?"

"Out in a second."

"Need advice."

She opened door. "Yes, Mannie?"

"How does Professor de la Paz rate in your organization? Is he trusted? Do *you* trust him?"

She looked thoughtful. "Everyone at the meeting was supposed to be vouched for. But I don't know him."

"Mmm. You have feeling about him?"

"I liked him, even though he argued against me. Do *you* know anything about him?"

"Oh, yes, known him twenty years. *I* trust him. But can't extend trust for *you*. Trouble—and it's your air bottle, not mine."

She smiled warmly. "Mannie, since you trust him, I trust him just as firmly."

I went back to phone. "Prof, are you on dodge?"

He chuckled. "Precisely, Manuel."

"Know a hole called Grand Hotel Raffles? Room L two decks below lobby. Can you get here without tracks, have you had breakfast, what do you like for breakfast?"

He chuckled again. "Manuel, one pupil can make a teacher feel that his years were not wasted. I know where it is, I shall get there quietly, I have not broken fast, and I eat anything I can't pat."

Wyoh had started putting beds together; I went to help. "What do you want for breakfast?"

"Chai and toast. Juice would be nice."

"Not enough."

"Well . . . a boiled egg. But I pay for breakfast."

"Two boiled eggs, buttered toast with jam, juice. I'll roll you."

"Your dice, or mine?"

"Mine. I cheat." I went to lift, asked for display, saw something called THE HAPPY HANGOVER—ALL PORTIONS EXTRA LARGE—*tomato juice, scrambled eggs, ham steak, fried potatoes, corn cakes and honey, toast, butter, milk, tea or coffee—HKL $4.50 for two*—I ordered it for two, no wish to advertise third person.

We were clean and shining, room orderly and set for breakfast, and Wyoh had changed from black outfit into red dress "because company was coming" when lift jingled food. Change into dress had caused words. She had posed, smiled, and said, "Mannie, I'm so pleased with this dress. How did you know it would suit me so well?"

"Genius."

"I think you may be. What did it cost? I must pay you."

"On sale, marked down to Authority cents fifty."

She clouded up and stomped foot. Was bare, made no sound, caused her to bounce a half meter. "Happy landing!" I wished her, while she pawed for foothold like a new chum.

"Manuel O'Kelly! If you think I will accept expensive clothing from a man I'm not even bundling with!"

"Easily corrected."

"Lecher! I'll tell your wives!"

"Do that. Mum always thinks worst of me." I went to lift, started dealing out dishes; door sounded. I flipped hearum-no-seeum. "Who comes?"

"Message for Gospodin Smith," a cracked voice answered. "Gospodin Bernard O. Smith."

I flipped bolts and let Professor Bernardo de la Paz in. He looked like poor grade of salvage—dirty clothes, filthy himself, hair unkempt, paralyzed down one side and hand twisted, one eye a film of cataract—perfect picture of old wrecks who sleep in Bottom Alley and cadge drinks and pickled eggs in cheap taprooms. He drooled.

As soon as I bolted door he straightened up, let features come back to normal, folded hands over wishbone, looked Wyoh up and down, sucked air kimono style, and whistled. "Even more lovely," he said, "than I remembered!"

She smiled, over her mad. "Thanks, Professor. But don't bother. Nobody here but comrades."

"Señorita, the day I let politics interfere with my appreciation of beauty, that day I retire from politics. But you are gracious." He looked away, glanced closely around room.

I said, "Prof, quit checking for evidence, you dirty old man. Last night was politics, *nothing* but politics."

"That's not true!" Wyoh flared up. "I struggled for *hours!* But he was too strong for me. Professor—what's the party discipline in such cases? Here in Luna City?"

Prof tut-tutted and rolled blank eye. "Manuel, I'm surprised. It's a serious matter, my dear—elimination, usually. But it must be investigated. Did you come here willingly?"

"He drugged me."

" 'Dragged,' dear lady. Let's not corrupt the language. Do you have bruises to show?"

I said, "Eggs getting cold. Can't we eliminate me after breakfast?"

"An excellent thought," agreed Prof. "Manuel, could you spare your old teacher a liter of water to make himself more presentable?"

"All you want, in there. Don't drag or you'll get what littlest pig got."

"Thank you, sir."

He retired; were sounds of brushing and washing. Wyoh and I finished arranging table. " 'Bruises,' " I said. " 'Struggled all night.' "

"You deserved it, you insulted me."

"How?"

"You failed to insult me, that's how. After you drugged me here."

"Mmm. Have to get Mike to analyze that."

"Michelle would understand it. Mannie, may I change my mind and have a little piece of that ham?"

"Half is yours, Prof is semi-vegetarian." Prof came out and, while did not look his most debonair, was neat and clean, hair combed, dimples back and happy sparkle in eye—fake cataract gone. "Prof, how do you do it?"

"Long practice, Manuel; I've been in this business far longer than you young people. Just once, many years ago in Lima—a lovely city—I ventured to stroll on a fine day *without* such forethought . . . and it got me transported. What a beautiful table!"

"Sit by me, Prof," Wyoh invited. "I don't want to sit by him. Rapist."

"Look," I said, "first we eat, *then* we eliminate me. Prof, fill plate and tell what happened last night."

"May I suggest a change in program? Manuel, the life of a conspirator is not an easy one and I learned before you were born not to mix provender and politics. Disturbs the gastric enzymes and leads to ulcers, the occupational disease of the underground. Mmm! That fish smells good."

"Fish?"

"That pink salmon," Prof answered, pointing at ham.

A long, pleasant time later we reached coffee/tea stage. Prof leaned back, sighed and said, "Bolshoyeh spasebaw, Gospazha ee Gospodin. Tak for mat, it was wonderfully good. I don't know when I've felt more at peace with the world. Ah yes! Last evening—I saw not too much of the proceedings because, just as you two were achieving an admirable retreat, I lived to fight another day—I bugged out. Made it to the wings in one long flat dive. When I did venture to peek out, the party was over, most had left, and all yellow jackets were dead."

(Note: Must correct this; I learned more later. When trouble started, as I was trying to get Wyoh through door, Prof produced a hand gun and, firing over heads, picked off three bodyguards at rear main door, including one wearing bull voice. How he smuggled weapon up to The Rock—or managed to liberate it later—I don't know. But Prof's shooting joined with Shorty's work to turn tables; not one yellow jacket got out alive. Several people were burned and four were killed—but knives, hands, and heels finished it in seconds.)

"Perhaps I should say, 'All but one,' " Prof went on. "Two cossacks at the door through which you departed had been given quietus by our brave comrade Shorty Mkrum . . . and I am sorry to say that Shorty was lying across them, dying—"

"We knew."

"So. Dulce et decorum. One guard in that doorway had a damaged face but was still moving; I gave his neck a treatment known in professional circles Earthside as the Istanbul twist. He joined his mates. By then most of the living had left. Just myself, our chairman of the evening Fin Nielsen, a comrade known as 'Mom,' that being what her husbands called her. I consulted with Comrade Finn and we bolted all doors. That left a cleaning job. Do you know the arrangements backstage there?"

"Not me," I said. Wyoh shook head.

"There is a kitchen and pantry, used for banquets. I suspect that Mom and family run a butcher shop for they disposed of bodies as fast as Finn and I carried them back, their speed limited only by the rate at which portions could be ground up and flushed into the city's cloaca. The sight made me quite faint, so I spent time mopping in the hall. Clothing was the difficult part, especially those quasi-military uniforms."

"What did you do with those laser guns?"

Prof turned bland eyes on me. "Guns? Dear me, they must have disappeared. We removed everything of a personal nature from bodies of our departed comrades—for relatives, for identification, for sentiment. Eventually we had everything tidy—not a job that would fool Interpol but one as to make it seem unlikely that anything untoward had taken place. We conferred, agreed that it would be well not to be seen soon, and left severally, myself by a pressure door above the stage leading up to level six. Thereafter I tried to call you, Manuel, being worried about your safety and that of this dear lady." Prof bowed to Wyoh. "That completes the tale. I spent the night in quiet places."

"Prof," I said, "those guards were new chums, still getting their legs. Or we wouldn't have won."

"That could be," he agreed. "But had they not been, the outcome would have been the same."

"How so? They were armed."

"Lad, have you ever seen a boxer dog? I think not—no dogs that large in Luna. The boxer is a result of special selection. Gentle and intelligent, he turns instantly into deadly killer when occasion requires.

"Here has been bred an even more curious creature. I know of no city on Terra with as high standards of good manners and consideration for one's fellow man as here in Luna. By comparison, Terran cities—I have known most major ones—are barbaric. Yet the Loonie is as deadly as the boxer dog. Manuel, nine guards, no matter how armed, stood no chance against that pack. Our patron used bad judgment."

"Um. Seen a morning paper, Prof? Or a video cast?"

"The latter, yes."

"Nothing in late news last night."

"Nor this morning."

"Odd," I said.

"What's odd about it?" asked Wyoh. "*We* won't talk—and we have comrades in key places in every paper in Luna."

Prof shook his head. "No, my dear. Not that simple. Censorship. Do you know how copy is set in our newspapers?"

"Not exactly. It's done by machinery."

"Here's what Prof means," I told her. "News is typed in editorial offices. From there on it's a leased service directed by a master computer at Authority Complex"—hoped she would notice "master computer" rather than "Mike"—"copy prints out there via phone circuit. These rolls feed into a computer section which reads, sets copy, and prints out newspapers at several locations.

Novylen edition of Daily Lunatic prints out in Novylen changes in ads and local stories, and computer makes changes from standard symbols, doesn't have to be told how. What Prof means is that at print-out at Authority Complex, Warden could intervene. Same for all news services, both off and to Luna—they funnel through computer room."

"The point is," Prof went on, "the Warden *could* have killed the story. It's irrelevant whether he did. Or—check me, Manuel; you know I'm hazy about machinery—he could insert a story, too, no matter how many comrades we have in newspaper offices."

"Sure," I agreed. "At Complex, anything can be added, cut, or changed."

"And that, señorita, is the weakness of our Cause. Communications. Those goons were not important—but crucially important is that it lay with the Warden, not with us, to decide whether the story should be told. To a revolutionist, communications are a sine-qua-non."

Wyoh looked at me and I could see synapses snapping. So I changed subject. "Prof, why get rid of bodies? Besides horrible job, was dangerous. Don't know how many bodyguards Warden has, but more could show up while you were doing it."

"Believe me, lad, we feared that. But although I was almost useless, it was my idea, I had to convince the others. Oh, not my original idea but remembrance of things past, an historical principle."

"*What* principle?"

"*Terror!* A man can face known danger. But the unknown frightens him. We disposed of those finks, teeth and toenails, to strike terror into their mates. Nor do I know how many effectives the Warden has, but I guarantee they are less effective today. Their mates went out on an easy mission. *Nothing* came back."

Wyoh shivered. "It scares me, too. They won't be anxious to go inside a warren again. But, Professor, you say you don't know how many bodyguards the Warden keeps. The Organization knows. Twenty-seven. If nine were killed, only eighteen are left. Perhaps it's time for a putsch. No?"

"No," I answered.

"Why not, Mannie? They'll never be weaker."

"Not weak enough. Killed nine because they were crackers to walk in where we were. But if Warden stays home with guards around him— Well, had enough shoulder-to-shoulder noise last night." I turned to Prof. "But still I'm interested in fact—if it is—that Warden now has only eighteen. You said Wyoh should not go to Hong Kong and I should not go home. But if he has only eighteen left, I wonder how much danger? Later, after he gets reinforcements—but now, well, L-City has four main exits, plus many little ones. How many can they guard? What's to keep Wyoh from walking to Tube West, getting p-suit, going home?"

"She might," Prof agreed.

"I think I must," Wyoh said. "I can't stay here forever. If I have to hide, I can do better in Hong Kong, where I know people."

"You might get away with it, my dear. I doubt it. There were two yellow jackets at Tube Station West last night; I saw them. They may not be there now. Let's assume they are not. You go to the station—disguised perhaps. You get your p-suit and take a capsule to Beluthihatchie. As you climb out to take the bus to Endsville, you're arrested. Communications. No need to post a yellow jacket at the station; it is enough that someone sees you there. A phone call does the rest."

"But you assumed that I was disguised."

"Your height cannot be disguised and your pressure suit would be watched. By someone not suspected of any connection with the Warden. Most probably a comrade." Prof dimpled. "The trouble with conspiracies is that they rot internally. When the number is as high as four, chances are even that one is a spy."

Wyoh said glumly, "You make it sound hopeless."

"Not at all, my dear. One chance in a thousand, perhaps."

"I can't believe it. I *don't* believe it! Why, in the years I've been active we have gained members by the hundreds! We have organizations in all major cities. We have the people with us."

Prof shook head. "Every new member made it that much more likely that you would be betrayed. Wyoming dear lady, revolutions are not won by enlisting the masses. Revolution is a science only a few are competent to practice. It depends on correct organization and, above all, on communications. Then, at the proper moment in history, they strike. Correctly organized and properly timed it is a bloodless coup. Done clumsily or prematurely and the result is civil war, mob violence, purges, terror. I hope you will forgive me if I say that, up to now, it has been done clumsily."

Wyoh looked baffled. "What do you mean by 'correct organization'?"

"Functional organization. How does one design an electric motor? Would you attach a bathtub to it, simply because one was available? Would a bouquet of flowers help? A heap of rocks? No, you would use just those elements necessary to its purpose and make it no larger than needed—and you would incorporate safety factors. Function controls design.

"So it is with revolution. Organization must be no larger than necessary—*never* recruit anyone merely because he wants to join. Nor seek to persuade for the pleasure of having another share your views. He'll share them when the times comes . . . or you've misjudged the moment in history. Oh, there will be an educational organization but it must be separate; agitprop is no part of basic structure.

"As to basic structure, a revolution starts as a conspiracy; therefore structure is small, secret, and organized as to minimize damage by betrayal—since there *always* are betrayals. One solution is the cell system and so far nothing better has been invented.

"Much theorizing has gone into optimum cell size. I think that history shows that a cell of three is best—more than three can't agree on when to have dinner, much less when to strike. Manuel, you belong to a large family; do you vote on when to have dinner?"

"Bog, no! Mum decides."

"Ah." Prof took a pad from his pouch, began to sketch. "Here is a cells-of-three tree. If I were planning to take over Luna, I would start with us three. One would be opted as chairman. We wouldn't vote; choice would be obvious—or we aren't the right three. We would know the next nine people, three cells . . . but each cell would know only one of us."

"Looks like computer diagram—a ternary logic."

"Does it really? At the next level there are two ways of linking: This comrade, second level, knows his cell leader, his two cellmates, and on the third level he knows the three in his subcell—he may or may not know his cellmates' subcells. One method doubles security, the other doubles speed of repair if security is penetrated. Let's say he does *not* know his cellmates' subcells—Manuel, how many can he betray? Don't say he won't; today they can brainwash *any* person, and starch and iron and use him. How many?"

"Six," I answered. "His boss, two cellmates, three in subcell."

"Seven," Prof corrected, "he betrays himself, too. Which leaves seven broken links on three levels to repair. How?"

"I don't see how it can be," objected Wyoh. "You've got them so split up it falls to pieces."

"Manuel? An exercise for the student."

"Well . . . blokes down here have to have way to send message up three levels. Don't have to know *who*, just have to know *where*."

"Precisely!"

"But, Prof," I went on, "there's a better way to rig it."

"Really? Many revolutionary theorists have hammered this out, Manuel. I have such confidence in them that I'll offer you a wager—at, say, ten to one."

"Ought to take your money. Take same cells, arrange in open pyramid of tetrahedrons. Where vertices are in common, each bloke knows one in adjoining cell—knows how to send message to him, that's all he needs. Communications never break down because they run sideways as well as up and down. Something like a neural net. It's why you can knock a hole in a man's head, take chunk of brain out, and not damage thinking much. Excess capacity, messages shunt around. He loses what was destroyed but goes on functioning."

"Manuel," Prof said doubtfully, "could you draw a picture? It *sounds* good—but it's so contrary to orthodox doctrine that I need to see it."

"Well . . . could do better with stereo drafting machine. I'll try." (Anybody who thinks it's easy to sketch one hundred twenty-one tetrahedrons, a five-level open pyramid, clear enough to show relationships is invited to try!)

Presently I said, "Look at base sketch. Each vertex of each triangle shares self with zero, one, or two other triangles. Where shares one, that's its link, one direction or both—but one is enough for a multipli-redundant communication net. On corners, where sharing is zero, it jumps to right to next corner. Where sharing is double, choice is again right-handed.

"Now work it with people. Take fourth level, D-for-dog. This vertex is comrade Dan. No, let's go down one to show three levels of communication knocked out—level E-for-easy and pick Comrade Egbert.

"Egbert works under Donald, has cellmates Edward and Elmer, and has three under him, Frank, Fred, and Fatso . . . but knows how to send message to Ezra on his own level but not in his cell. He doesn't know Ezra's name, face, address, or anything—but has a way, phone number probably, to reach Ezra in emergency.

"Now watch it work. Casimir, level three, finks out and betrays Charlie and Cox in his cell, Baker above him, and Donald, Dan, and Dick in subcell—which isolates Egbert, Edward, and Elmer. And everybody under them.

"All three report it—redundancy, necessary to any communication system—but follow Egbert's yell for help. He calls Ezra. But Ezra is under Charlie and is isolated, too. No matter, Ezra relays both messages through *his* safety link, Edmund. By bad luck Edmund is under Cox, so he also passes it laterally, through Enwright . . . and that gets it past burned-out part and it goes up through Dover, Chambers, and Beeswax, to Adam, front office . . . who replies down other side of pyramid, with lateral pass on E-for-easy level from Esther to Egbert and on to Ezra and Edmund. These two messages, up and down, not only get through at once but in *way* they get through, they define to home office exactly how much damage has been done and where. Organization not only keeps functioning but starts repairing self at once."

Wyoh was tracing out lines, convincing herself it would work—which it would, was "idiot" circuit. Let Mike study a few milliseconds, and could produce a better, safer, more foolproof hookup. And probably—certainly—ways to avoid betrayal while speeding up routings. But I'm not a computer.

Prof was staring with blank expression. "What's trouble?" I said. "It'll work; this is my pidgin."

"Manuel my b— Excuse me: Señor O'Kelly . . . will you head this revolution?"

"*Me?* Great Bog, *nyet!* I'm no lost-cause martyr. Just talking about circuits."

Wyoh looked up. "Mannie," she said soberly, "you're opted. It's settled."

SIX

Did like hell settle it.

Prof said, "Manuel, don't be hasty. Here we are, three, the perfect number, with a variety of talents and experience. Beauty, age, and mature male drive—"

"I don't have any drive!"

"Please, Manuel. Let us think in the widest terms before attempting decisions. And to facilitate such, may I ask if this hostel stocks potables? I have a few florins I could put into the stream of trade."

Was most sensible word heard in an hour. "Stilichnaya vodka?"

"Sound choice." He reached for pouch.

"Tell it to bear," I said and ordered a liter, plus ice. It came down; was tomato juice from breakfast.

"Now," I said, after we toasted, "Prof, what you think of pennant race? Got money says Yankees can't do it again?"

"Manuel, what is your political philosophy?"

"With that new boy from Milwaukee I feel like investing."

"Sometimes a man doesn't have it defined but, under Socratic inquiry, knows where he stands and why."

"I'll back 'em against field, three to two."

"*What?* You young idiot! How much?"

"Three hundred. Hong Kong."

"Done. For example, under what circumstances may the State justly place its welfare above that of a citizen?"

"Mannie," Wyoh asked, "do you have any more foolish money? I think well of the Phillies."

I looked her over. "Just what were you thinking of betting?"

"You go to hell! Rapist."

"Prof, as I see, are *no* circumstances under which State is justified in placing its welfare ahead of mine."

"Good. We have a starting point."

"Mannie," said Wyoh, "that's a most self-centered evaluation."

"I'm a most self-centered person."

"Oh, nonsense. Who rescued me? Me, a stranger. And didn't try to exploit it. Professor, I was cracking not facking. Mannie was a perfect knight."

"Sans peur et sans reproche. I knew, I've known him for years. Which is not inconsistent with evaluation he expressed."

"Oh, but it is! Not the way things are but under the ideal toward which we aim. Mannie, the 'State' is Luna. Even though not sovereign yet and we hold citizenships elsewhere. But *I* am part of the Lunar State and so is your family. Would you die for your family?"

"Two questions not related."

"Oh, but they are! That's the point."

"Nyet. I know my family, opted long ago."

"Dear Lady, I must come to Manuel's defense. He has a correct evaluation even though he may not be able to state it. May I ask this? Under what circumstances is it moral for a group to do that which is not moral for a member of that group to do alone?"

"Uh . . . that's a trick question."

"It is the *key* question, dear Wyoming. A radical question that strikes to the root of the whole dilemma of government. Anyone who answers honestly and abides by *all* consequences knows where he stands—and what he will die for."

Wyoh frowned. " 'Not moral for a member of the group—' " she said. "Professor . . . what are *your* political principles?"

"May I first ask yours? If you can state them?"

"Certainly I can! I'm a Fifth Internationalist, most of the Organization is. Oh, we don't rule out anyone going our way; it's a united front. We have Communists and Fourths and Ruddyites and Societians and Single-Taxers and you name it. But I'm no Marxist; we Fifths have a practical program. Private where private belongs, public where it's needed, and an admission that circumstances alter cases. Nothing doctrinaire."

"Capital punishment?"

"For what?"

"Let's say for treason. Against Luna after you've freed Luna."

"Treason how? Unless I knew the circumstances I could not decide."

"Nor could I, dear Wyoming. But I believe in capital punishment under some circumstances . . . with this difference. I would not ask a court; I would try, condemn, execute sentence myself, and accept full responsibility."

"But—Professor, what *are* your political beliefs?"

"I'm a rational anarchist."

"I don't know that brand. Anarchist individualist, anarchist Communist, Christian anarchist, philosophical anarchist, syndicalist, libertarian—those I know. But what's this? Randite?"

"I can get along with a Randite. A rational anarchist believes that concepts such as 'state' and 'society' and 'government' have no existence save as physically exemplified in the acts of self-responsible individuals. He believes that it is impossible to shift blame, share blame, distribute blame . . . as blame, guilt, responsibility are matters taking place inside human beings singly and *nowhere else*. But being rational, he knows that not all individuals hold his evaluations, so he tries to live perfectly in an imperfect world . . . aware that his effort will be less than perfect yet undismayed by self-knowledge of self-failure."

"Hear, hear!" I said. " 'Less than perfect.' What I've been aiming for all my life."

"You've achieved it," said Wyoh. "Professor, your words sound good but there is something slippery about them. Too much power in the hands of individuals—surely you would not want . . . well, H-missiles for example—to be controlled by one irresponsible person?"

"My point is that one person *is* responsible. Always. If H-bombs exist—and they do—some *man* controls them. In terms of morals *there is no such thing as 'state.'* Just men. Individuals. Each responsible for his own acts."

"Anybody need a refill?" I asked.

Nothing uses up alcohol faster than political argument. I sent for another bottle.

I did not take part. I was not dissatified back when we were "ground under Iron Heel of Authority." I cheated Authority and rest of time didn't think about it. Didn't think about getting rid of Authority—impossible. Go own way, mind own business, not be bothered—

True, didn't have luxuries then; by Earthside standards we were poor. If had to be imported, mostly did without; don't think there was a powered door in all Luna. Even p-suits used to be fetched up from Terra—until a smart Chinee before I was born figured how to make "monkey copies" better and simpler. (Could dump two Chinee down in one of our maria and they would get rich selling rocks to each other while raising twelve kids. Then a Hindu would sell retail stuff he got from them wholesale—below cost at fat profit. We got along.)

I had seen those luxuries Earthside. Wasn't worth what they put up with. Don't mean heavy gravity, that doesn't bother them; I mean nonsense. All time kukai moa. If chicken guano in one earthworm city were shipped to Luna, fertilizer problem would be solved for century. Do this. Don't do that. Stay back of line. Where's tax receipt? Fill out form. Let's see license. Submit six copies. Exit only. No left turn. No right turn. Queue up to pay fine. Take back and get stamped. Drop dead—but first get permit.

Wyoh plowed doggedly into Prof, certain she had all answers. But Prof was interested in questions rather than answers, which baffled her. Finally she said, "Professor, I can't understand you. I don't insist that you call it 'government'—I just want you to state what rules you think are necessary to insure equal freedom for all."

"Dear lady, I'll happily accept your rules."

"But you don't seem to want *any* rules!"

"True. But I will accept any rules that *you* feel necessary to *your* freedom. *I* am free, no matter what rules surround me. If I find them tolerable, I tolerate them; if I find them too obnoxious, I break them. I am free because I know that *I alone* am morally responsible for everything I do."

"You would not abide by a law that the majority felt was necessary?"

"Tell me what law, dear lady, and I will tell you whether I will obey it."

"You wiggled out. Every time I state a general principle, you wiggle out."

Prof clasped hands on chest. "Forgive me. Believe me, lovely Wyoming, I am most anxious to please you. You spoke of willingness to unite the front with anyone going your way. Is it enough that I want to see the Authority thrown off Luna . . . and would die to serve that end?"

Wyoh beamed. "It certainly is!" She fisted his ribs—gently—then put arm around him and kissed cheek. "Comrade! Let's get on with it!"

"Cheers!" I said. "Let's fin' Warden 'n' 'liminate him!" Seemed a good idea; I had had a short night and don't usually drink much.

Prof topped our glasses, held his high and announced with great dignity: "Comrades . . . *we declare the Revolution!*"

That got us both kissed. But sobered me, as Prof sat down and said, "The Emergency Committee of Free Luna is in session. We must plan action."

I said, "Wait, Prof! *I* didn't agree to anything. What's this 'Action' stuff?"

"We will now overthrow the Authority," he said blandly.

"*How?* Going to throw rocks at 'em?"

"That remains to be worked out. This is the planning stage."

I said, "Prof, you know me. If kicking out Authority was thing we could buy, I wouldn't worry about price."

" '—our lives, our fortunes, and our sacred honor.' "

"Huh?"

"A price that once was paid."

"Well—I'd go that high. But when I bet I want a chance to win. Told Wyoh last night I didn't object to long odds—"

" 'One in ten' is what you said, Mannie."

"Da, Wyoh. Show me those odds, I'll tap pot. But *can* you?"

"No, Manuel, I can't."

"Then why we talk-talk? *I* can't see *any* chance."

"Nor I, Manuel. But we approach it differently. Revolution is an art that I pursue rather than a goal I expect to achieve. Nor is this a source of dismay; a lost cause can be as spiritually satisfying as a victory."

"Not me. Sorry."

"Mannie," Wyoh said suddenly, "ask Mike."

I stared. "You serious?"

"Quite serious. If anyone can figure out odds, Mike should be able to. Don't you think?"

"Um. Possible."

"Who, if I may ask," Prof put in, "is Mike?"

I shrugged. "Oh, just a no-body."

"Mike is Mannie's best friend. He's very good at figuring odds."

"A bookie? My dear, if we bring in a fourth party we start by violating the cell principle."

"I don't see why," Wyoh answered. "Mike could be a member of the cell Mannie will head."

"Mmm . . . true. I withdraw objection. He is safe? You vouch for him? Or you, Manuel?"

I said, "He's dishonest, immature, practical joker, not interested in politics."

"Mannie, I'm going to tell Mike you said that. Professor, he's nothing of the sort—and we need him. Uh, in fact he might be our chairman, and we three the cell under him. The executive cell."

"Wyoh, you getting enough oxygen?"

"I'm okay, I haven't been guzzling it the way you have. *Think*, Mannie. Use imagination."

"I must confess," said Prof, "that I find these conflicting reports very conflicting."

"Mannie?"

"Oh, hell." So we told him, between us, all about Mike, how he woke up, got his name, met Wyoh. Prof accepted idea of a self-aware computer easier than I accepted idea of snow first time I saw. Prof just nodded and said, "Go on."

But presently he said, "This is the Warden's own computer? Why not invite the Warden to our meetings and be done with it?"

We tried to reassure him. At last I said, "Put it this way. Mike is his own boy, just as you are. Call him rational anarchist, for he's rational and he feels no loyalty to any government."

"If this machine is not loyal to its owners, why expect it to be loyal to you?"

"A feeling. I treat Mike well as I know how, he treats me same way." I told how Mike had taken precautions to protect me. "I'm not sure he *could* betray me to anyone who didn't have those signals, one to secure phone, other to retrieve what I've talked about or stored with him; machines don't think way people do. But feel dead sure he wouldn't *want* to betray me . . . and probably could protect me even if somebody got those signals."

"Mannie," suggested Wyoh, "why not call him? Once Professor de la Paz talks to him he will know why we trust Mike. Professor, we don't have to tell Mike any secrets until you feel sure of him."

"I see no harm in that."

"Matter of fact," I admitted, "already told him some secrets." I told them about recording last night's meeting and how I stored it.

Prof was distressed, Wyoh was worried. I said, "Damp it! Nobody but me knows retrieval signal. Wyoh, you know how Mike behaved about your pictures; won't let *me* have those pictures even though I suggested lock on them. But if you two will stop oscillating, I'll call him, make *sure* that nobody has retrieved that recording, and tell him to erase—then it's gone forever, computer memory is all or nothing. Or can go one better. Call Mike and have him play record back into recorder, wiping storage. No huhu."

"Don't bother," said Wyoh. "Professor, I *trust* Mike—and so will you."

"On second thought," Prof admitted, "I see little hazard from a recording of last night's meeting. One that large always contains spies and one of them may have used a recorder as you did, Manuel. I was upset at what appeared to be your indiscretion—a weakness a member of a conspiracy must never have, especially one at the top, as you are."

"Was *not* member of conspiracy when I fed that recording into Mike—and not now unless somebody quotes odds better than those so far!"

"I retract; you were not indiscreet. But are you seriously suggesting that this machine can predict the outcome of a revolution?"

"Don't know."

"*I* think he can!" said Wyoh.

"Hold it, Wyoh. Prof, he could predict if fed all significant data."

"That's my point, Manuel. I do not doubt that this machine can solve problems I cannot grasp. But one of this scope? It would have to know—oh, goodness!—all of human history, all details of the entire social, political, and economic situation on Terra today and the same for Luna, a wide knowledge of psychology in all its ramifications, a wider knowledge of technology with all its possibilities, weaponry, communications, strategy and tactics, agitprop techniques, classic authorities such as Clausewitz, Guevera, Morgenstern, Machiavelli, many others."

"Is that all?"

" 'Is that *all?*' My dear boy!"

"Prof, how many history books have you read?"

"I do not know. In excess of a thousand."

"Mike can zip through that many this afternoon, speed limited only by scanning method—he can store data much faster. Soon—minutes—he would have every fact correlated with everything else he knows, discrepancies noted, probability values assigned to uncertainties. Prof, Mike reads every word of every newspaper up from Terra. Reads all technical publications. Reads fiction—knows it's fiction—because isn't enough to keep him busy and is always hungry for more. If is any book he should read to solve this, say so. He can cram it down fast as I get it to him."

Prof blinked. "I stand corrected. Very well, let us see if he can cope with it. I still think there is something known as 'intuition' and 'human judgment.' "

"Mike has intuition," Wyoh said. "Feminine intuition, that is."

"As for 'human judgment,' " I added, "Mike isn't human. But all he knows he got from humans. Let's get you acquainted and you judge his judgment."

So I phoned. "Hi, Mike!"

"Hello, Man my only male friend. Greetings, Wyoh my only female friend. I heard a third person. I conjecture that it may be Professor Bernardo de la Paz."

Prof looked startled, then delighted. I said, "Too right, Mike. That's why I called you; Professor is not-stupid."

"Thank you, Man! Professor Bernardo de la Paz, I am delighted to meet you."

"I am delighted to meet you, too, sir." Prof hesitated, went on "Mi—Señor Holmes, may I ask how you knew that I was here?"

"I am sorry, sir; I cannot answer. Man? 'You know my methods.' "

"Mike is being crafty, Prof. It involves something he learned doing a confidential job for me. So he threw me a hint to let you think that he had identified you by hearing your presence—and he can indeed tell much from respiration and heartbeat . . . mass, approximate age, sex, and quite a bit about health; Mike's medical storage is as full as any other."

"I am happy to say," Mike added seriously, "that I detect no signs of cardiac or respiratory trouble, unusual for a man of the Professor's age who has spent so many years Earthside. I congratulate you, sir."

"Thank you, Señor Holmes."

"My pleasure, Professor Bernardo de la Paz."

"Once he knew your identity, he knew how old you are, when you were shipped and what for, anything that ever appeared about you in Lunatic or Moonglow or any Lunar publication, including pictures—your bank balance, whether you pay bills on time, and much more. Mike retrieved this in a split second once he had your name. What he didn't tell—because was my business—is that he knew I had invited you here, so it's a short jump to guess that you're still here when he heard heartbeat and breathing that matched you. Mike, no need to say 'Professor Bernardo de la Paz' each time; 'Professor' or 'Prof' is enough."

"Noted, Man. But he addressed me formally, with honorific."

"So both of you relax. Prof, you scan it? Mike knows much, doesn't tell all, knows when to keep mouth shut."

"I am impressed!"

"Mike is a fair dinkum thinkum—you'll see. Mike, I bet Professor three to two that Yankees would win pennant again. How chances?"

"I am sorry to hear it, Man. The correct odds, this early in the year and based on past performances of teams and players, are one to four point seven two the other way."

"Can't be that bad!"

"I'm sorry, Man. I will print out the calculations if you wish. But I recommend that you buy back your wager. The Yankees have a favorable chance to defeat any single team . . . but the combined chances of defeating all teams in the league, including such factors as weather, accidents, and other variables for the season ahead, place the club on the short end of the odds I gave you."

"Prof, want to sell that bet?"

"Certainly, Manuel."

"Price?"

"Three hundred Hong Kong dollars."

"You old thief!"

"Manuel, as your former teacher I would be false to you if I did not permit you to learn from mistakes. Señor Holmes—Mike my friend— May I call you 'friend'?"

"Please do." (Mike almost purred.)

"Mike amigo, do you also tout horse races?"

"I often calculate odds on horse races; the civil service computermen frequently program such requests. But the results are so at variance with expectations that I have concluded either that the data are too meager, or the horses or riders are not honest. Possibly all three. However, I can give you a formula which will pay a steady return if played consistently."

Prof looked eager. "What is it? May one ask?"

"One may. Bet the leading apprentice jockey to place. He is always given good mounts and they carry less weight. But don't bet him on the nose."

" 'Leading apprentice' . . . hmm. Manuel, do you have the correct time?"

"Prof, which do you want? Get a bet down before post time? Or settle what we set out to?"

"Unh, sorry. Please carry on. 'Leading apprentice—' "

"Mike, I gave you a recording last night." I leaned close to pickups and whispered: "*Bastille Day*."

"Retrieved, Man."

"Thought about it?"

"In many ways. Wyoh, you speak most dramatically."

"Thank you, Mike."

"Prof, can you get your mind off ponies?"

"Eh? Certainly, I am all ears."

"Then quit doing odds under your breath; Mike can do them faster."

"I was not wasting time; the financing of . . . joint ventures such as ours is always difficult. However, I shall table it; I am all attention."

"I want Mike to do a trial projection. Mike, in that recording, you heard Wyoh say we had to have free trade with Terra. You heard Prof say we should clamp an embargo on shipping food to Terra. Who's right?"

"Your question is indeterminate, Man."

"What did I leave out?"

"Shall I rephrase it, Man?"

"Sure. Give us discussion."

"In immediate terms Wyoh's proposal would be of great advantage to the people of Luna. The price of foodstuffs at catapult head would increase by a factor of at least four. This takes into account a slight rise in wholesale prices on Terra, 'slight' because the Authority now sells at approximately the free market price. This disregards subsidized, dumped, and donated foodstuffs, most of which come from the large profit caused by the controlled low price at catapult head. I will say no more about minor variables as they are swallowed by major ones. Let it stand that the immediate effect here would be a price increase of the close order of fourfold."

"Hear that, Professor?"

"Please, dear lady. I never disputed it."

"The profit increase to the grower is more than fourfold because, as Wyoh pointed out, he now must buy water and other items at controlled high prices. Assuming a free market throughout the sequence his profit enhancement will be of the close order of sixfold. But this would be offset by another factor: Higher prices for exports would cause higher prices for everything consumed in Luna, goods and labor. The total effect would be an enhanced standard of living for all on the close order of twofold. This would be accompanied by vigorous effort to drill and seal more farming tunnels, mine more ice, improve growing methods, all leading to greater export. However, the Terran Market is so large and food shortage so chronic that reduction in profit from increase of export is not a major factor."

Prof said, "But, Señor Mike, that would only hasten the day that Luna is exhausted!"

"The projection was specified as immediate, Señor Professor. Shall I continue in longer range on the basis of your remarks?"

"By all means!"

"Luna's mass to three significant figures is seven point three six times ten to the nineteenth power tonnes. Thus, holding other variables constant including Lunar and Terran populations, the present differential rate of export in tonnes could continue for seven point three six times ten to the twelfth years before using up one percent of Luna—round it as seven thousand billion years."

"*What!* Are you *sure?*"

"You are invited to check, Professor."

I said, "Mike, this a joke? If so, not funny even once!"

"It is not a joke, Man."

"Anyhow," Prof added, recovering, "it's not Luna's crust we are shipping. It's our lifeblood—water and organic matter. Not rock."

"I took that into consideration, Professor. This projection is based on controlled transmutation—any isotope into any other and postulating power for any reaction not exo-energetic. Rock *would* be shipped—transformed into wheat and beef and other foodstuffs."

"But we don't know how to do that! Amigo, this is ridiculous!"

"But we will know how to do it."

"Mike is right, Prof," I put in. "Sure, today we haven't a glimmer. But will. Mike, did you compute how many years till we have this? Might take a flier in stocks."

Mike answered in sad voice, "Man my only male friend save for the Professor whom I hope will be my friend, I tried. I failed. The question is indeterminate."

"Why?"

"Because it involves a break-through in theory. There is no way in all my data to predict when and where genius may appear."

Prof sighed. "Mike amigo, I don't know whether to be relieved or disappointed. Then that projection didn't mean anything?"

"Of course it meant something!" said Wyoh. "It means we'll dig it out when we need it. Tell him, Mike!"

"Wyoh, I am most sorry. Your assertion is, in effect, exactly what I was looking for. But the answer still remains: Genius is where you find it. No. I am so sorry."

I said, "Then Prof is right? When comes to placing bets?"

"One moment, Man. There is a special solution suggested by the Professor's speech last night—return shipping, tonne for tonne."

"Yes, but *can't* do that."

"If the cost is low enough, Terrans would do so. That can be achieved with only minor refinement, not a break-through, to wit, freight transportation up from Terra as cheap as catapulting down to Terra."

"You call this 'minor'?"

"I call it minor compared with the other problem, Man."

"Mike dear, how long? When do we get it?"

"Wyoh, a rough projection, based on poor data and largely intuitive, would be on the order of fifty years."

" 'Fifty years'? Why, that's nothing! We can have free trade."

"Wyoh, I said 'on the order of'—I did *not* say 'on the *close* order of.' "

"It makes a difference?"

"Does," I told her. "What Mike said was that he doesn't expect it sooner than five years but would be surprised if much longer than five hundred—eh, Mike?"

"Correct, Man."

"So need another projection. Prof pointed out that we ship water and organic matter and don't get it back—agree, Wyoh?"

"Oh, sure. I just don't think it's urgent. We'll solve it when we reach it."

"Okay, Mike—no cheap shipping, no transmutation: How long till trouble?"

"Seven years."

" '*Seven years!*' " Wyoh jumped up, stared at phone. "Mike honey! You don't mean that?"

"Wyoh," he said plaintively, "I did my best. The problem has an indeterminately large number of variables. I ran several thousand solutions using many assumptions. The happiest answer came from assuming no increase in tonnage, no increase in Lunar population—restriction of births strongly enforced—and a greatly enhanced search for ice in order to maintain the water supply. That gave an answer of slightly over twenty years. All other answers were worse."

Wyoh, much sobered, said, "What happens in seven years?"

"The answer of seven years from now I reached by assuming the present situation, no change in Authority policy, and all major variables extrapolated from the empiricals implicit in their past behavior—a conservative answer of highest probability from available data. Twenty-eighty-two is the year I expect food riots. Cannibalism should not occur for at least two years thereafter."

" 'Cannibalism'!" She turned and buried head against Prof's chest.

He patted her, said gently, "I'm sorry, Wyoh. People do not realize how precarious our ecology is. Even so, it shocks *me*. I know water runs down hill . . . but didn't dream how terribly soon it will reach bottom."

She straightened up and face was calm. "Okay, Professor, I was wrong. Embargo it must be—and all that that implies. Let's get busy. Let's find out from Mike what our chances are. You trust him now—don't you?"

"Yes, dear lady, I do. We must have him on our side. Well, Manuel?"

Took time to impress Mike with how serious we were, make him understand that "jokes" could kill us (this machine who could not know human death) and to get assurance that he could and would protect secrets no matter what retrieval program was used—even our signals if not from us. Mike was hurt that I could doubt him but matter too serious to risk slip.

Then took two hours to program and re-program and change assumptions and investigate side issues before all four—Mike, Prof, Wyoh, self—were satisfied that we had defined it, i.e., what chance had revolution—*this* revolution, headed by us, success required before "Food Riots Day," against Authority with bare hands . . . against power of all Terra, all eleven billions, to beat us down and inflict their will—all with no rabbits out of hats, with certainty of betrayal and stupidity and faintheartedness, and fact that no one of us was genius, nor important in Lunar affairs. Prof made sure that Mike knew history, psychology, economics, name it. Toward end Mike was pointing out far more variables than Prof.

At last we agreed that programming was done—or that we could think of no other significant factor. Mike then said, "This is an indeterminate problem. How shall I solve it? Pessimistically? Or optimistically? Or a range of probabilities expressed as a curve, or several curves? Professor my friend?"

"Manuel?"

I said, "Mike, when I roll a die, it's one in six it turns ace. I don't ask shopkeeper to float it, nor do I caliper it, or worry about somebody blowing on it. Don't give happy answer, nor pessimistic; don't shove curves at us. Just tell in one sentence: What chances? Even? One in a thousand? None? Or whatever."

"Yes, Manuel Garcia O'Kelly my first male friend."

For thirteen and a half minutes was no sound, while Wyoh chewed knuckles. *Never* known Mike to take so long. Must have consulted every book he ever read and worn edges off random numbers. Was beginning to believe that he had been overloaded and either burnt out something or gone into cybernetic breakdown that requires computer equivalent of lobotomy to stop oscillations.

Finally he spoke. "Manuel my friend, I am terribly sorry!"

"What's trouble, Mike?"

"I have tried and tried, checked and checked. *There is but one chance in seven of winning!*"

SEVEN

I look at Wyoh, she looks at me; we laugh. I jump up and yip, "Hooray!" Wyoh starts to cry, throws arms around Prof, kisses him.

Mike said plaintively, "I do not understand. The chances are seven to one *against* us. Not *for* us."

Wyoh stopped slobbering Prof and said, "Hear that? Mike said '*us*.' He included himself."

"Of course. Mike old cobber, we understood. But ever know a Loonie to refuse to bet when he stood a big fat chance of one in seven?"

"I have known only you three. Not sufficient data for a curve."

"Well . . . we're Loonies. Loonies bet. Hell, we *have* to! They shipped us up and bet us we couldn't stay alive. We fooled 'em.

We'll fool 'em again! Wyoh. Where's your pouch? Get red hat. Put on Mike. Kiss him. Let's have a drink. One for Mike, too—want a drink, Mike?"

"I wish that I could have a drink," Mike answered wistfully, "as I have wondered about the subjective effect of ethanol on the human nervous system—I conjecture that it must be similar to a slight overvoltage. But since I cannot, please have one in my place."

"Program accepted. Running. Wyoh, where's *hat!*"

Phone was flat to wall, let into rock—no place to hang hat. So we placed it on writing shelf and toasted Mike and called him "Comrade!" and almost he cried. His voice fugged up. Then Wyoh borrowed Liberty Cap and put on me and kissed me into conspiracy, officially this time, and so all out that my eldest wife would faint did she see—then she took hat and put on Prof and gave him same treatment and I was glad Mike had reported his heart okay.

Then she put it on own head and went to phone, leaned close, mouth between binaurals and made kissing sounds. "That's for you, Mike dear comrade. Is Michelle there?"

Blimey if he didn't answer in soprano voice: "Right here, darling—and I am so *'appee!*"

So Michelle got a kiss, and I had to explain to Prof who "Michelle" was and introduce him. He was formal, sucking air and whistling and clasping hands—sometimes I think Prof was not right in his head.

Wyoh poured more vodka. Prof caught her, mixed ours with coffee, hers with chai, honey in all. "We have declared the Revolution," he said firmly, "now we execute it. With clear heads. Manuel, you were opted chairman. Shall we begin?"

"Mike is chairman," I said. "Obvious. Secretary, too. We'll never keep anything in writing; first security rule. With Mike, don't need to. Let's bat it around and see where we are; I'm new to business."

"And," said Prof, "still on the subject of security, the secret of Mike should be restricted to this executive cell, subject to unanimous agreement—all three of us—correction: all four of us—that is must be extended."

"What secret?" asked Wyoh. "Mike agreed to keep our secrets.

He's safer than we are; he can't be brainwashed. Can you be, Mike dear?"

"I could be brainwashed," Mike admitted, "by enough voltage. Or by being smashed, or subjected to solvents, or positive entropy through other means—I find the concept disturbing. But if by 'brainwashing' you mean could I be compelled to surrender our secrets, the answer is an unmodified negative."

I said, "Wye, Prof means secret of Mike *himself*. Mike old pal, you're our secret weapon—you know that, don't you?"

He answered self-consciously, "It was necessary to take that into consideration in computing the odds."

"How were odds without you, comrade? Bad?"

"They were not good. Not of the same order."

"Won't press you. But a secret weapon must be secret. Mike, does anybody else suspect that you are alive?"

"Am I alive?" His voice held tragic loneliness.

"Uh, won't argue semantics. Sure, you're alive!"

"I was not sure. It is good to be alive. No, Mannie my first friend, you three alone know it. My three friends."

"That's how must be if bet's to pay off. Is okay? Us three and never talk to anybody else?"

"But we'll talk to you lots!" Wyoh put in.

"It is not only okay," Mike said bluntly, "it is necessary. It was a factor in the odds."

"That settles it," I said. "They have everything else; we have Mike. We keep it that way. Say! Mike, I just had a horrid. We fight Terra?"

"We will fight Terra . . . unless we lose before that time."

"Uh, riddle this. Any computers smart as you? Any awake?"

He hesitated. "I don't know, Man."

"No data?"

"Insufficient data. I have watched for both factors, not only in technical journals but everywhere else. There are no computers on the market of my present capacity . . . but one of my model could be augmented just as I have been. Furthermore an experimental computer of great capacity might be classified and go unreported in the literature."

"Mmm . . . chance we have to take."

"Yes, Man."

"There aren't any computers as smart as Mike!" Wyoh said scornfully. "Don't be silly, Mannie."

"Wyoh, Man was not being silly. Man, I saw one disturbing report. It was claimed that attempts are being made at the University of Peiping to combine computers with human brains to achieve massive capacity. A computing Cyborg."

"They say how?"

"The item was non-technical."

"Well . . . won't worry about what can't help. Right, Prof?"

"Correct, Manuel. A revolutionist must keep his mind free of worry or the pressure becomes intolerable."

"I don't believe a word of it," Wyoh added. "We've got Mike and we're going to win! Mike dear, you say we're going to fight Terra—and Mannie says that's one battle we can't win. You have some idea of how we can win, or you wouldn't have given us even one chance in seven. So what is it?"

"Throw rocks at them," Mike answered.

"Not funny," I told him. "Wyoh, don't borrow trouble. Haven't even settled how we leave this pooka without being nabbed. Mike, Prof says nine guards were killed last night and Wyoh says twenty-seven is whole bodyguard. Leaving eighteen. Do you know if that's true, do you know where they are and what they are up to? Can't put on a revolution if we dasn't stir out."

Prof interrupted. "That's a temporary exigency, Manuel, one we can cope with. The point Wyoming raised is basic and should be discussed. And daily, until solved. I am interested in Mike's thoughts."

"Okay, okay—but will you wait while Mike answers me?"

"Sorry, sir."

"Mike?"

"Mike?"

"Man, the official number of Warden's bodyguards is twenty-seven. If nine were killed the official number is now eighteen."

"You keep saying 'official number.' Why?"

"I have incomplete data which might be relevant. Let me state them before advancing even tentative conclusions. Nominally the Security Officer's department aside from clerks consists only of the bodyguard. But I handle payrolls for Authority Complex and twenty-seven is *not* the number of personnel charged against the Security Department."

Prof nodded. "Company spies."

"Hold it, Prof. Who are these other people?"

Mike answered, "They are simply account numbers, Man. I conjecture that the names they represent are in the Security Chief's data storage location."

"Wait, Mike. Security Chief Alvarez uses you for files?"

"I conjecture that to be true, since his storage location is under a locked retrieval signal."

I said, "Bloody," and added, "Prof, isn't that sweet? He uses Mike to keep records, Mike knows where they are—can't touch 'em!"

"Why not, Manuel?"

Tried to explain to Prof and Wyoh sorts of memory a thinkum has—permanent memories that can't be erased because patterns be logic itself, how it thinks; short-term memories used for current programs and then erased like memories which tell you whether you have honeyed coffee; temporary memories held long as necessary—milliseconds, days, years—but erased when no longer needed; permanently stored data like a human being's education—but learned perfectly and never forgotten—though may be condensed, rearranged, relocated, edited—and last but not finally, long lists of special memories ranging from memoranda files through very complex special programs, and each location tagged by own retrieval signal and locked or not, with endless possibilities on lock signals: sequential, parallel, temporal, situational, others.

Don't explain computers to laymen. Simpler to explain sex to a virgin. Wyoh couldn't see why, if Mike knew where Alvarez kept records, Mike didn't trot over and fetch.

I gave up. "Mike, can you explain?"

"I will try, Man. Wyoh, there is no way for me to retrieve locked data other than through external programming. I cannot program myself for such retrieval; my logic structure does not permit it. I must receive the signal as an external input."

"Well, for Bog's sake, what is this precious signal?"

"It is," Mike said simply, " 'Special File Zebra' "—and waited.

"Mike!" I said. "Unlock Special File Zebra." He did, and stuff started spilling out. Had to convince Wyoh that Mike hadn't been stubborn. He hadn't—he almost *begged* us to tickle him on that spot. Sure, he knew signal. Had to. But had to come from outside, that was how he was built.

"Mike, remind me to check with you all special-purpose locked-retrieval signals. May strike ice other places."

"So I conjectured, Man."

"Okay, we'll get to it later. Now back up and go over this stuff slowly—and, Mike, as you read out, store again, without erasing, under Bastille Day and tag it 'Fink File.' Okay?"

"Programmed and running."

"Do that with anything new he puts in, too."

Prime prize was list of names by warrens, some two hundred, each keyed with a code Mike identified with those blind pay accounts.

Mike read out Hong Kong Luna list and was hardly started when Wyoh gasped, "Stop, Mike! I've got to write these down!"

I said, "Hey! No writing! What's huhu?"

"That woman, Sylvia Chiang, is comrade secretary back home! But— But that means the Warden has our whole organization!"

"No, dear Wyoming," Prof corrected. "It means we have *his* organization."

"But—"

"I see what Prof means," I told her. "*Our* organization is just us three and Mike. Which Warden doesn't know. But now we know *his* organization. So shush and let Mike read. But don't write; you have this list—from Mike—anytime you phone him. Mike, note that Chiang woman is organization secretary, former organization, in Kongville."

"Noted."

Wyoh boiled over as she heard names of undercover finks in her town but limited herself to noting facts about ones she knew. Not all were "comrades" but enough that she stayed riled up. Novy Leningrad names didn't mean much to us; Prof recognized three, Wyoh one. When came Luna City Prof noted over half as being "comrades." I recognized several, not as fake subversives but as acquaintances. Not friends— Don't know what it would do to me to find someone I trusted on boss fink's payroll. But would shake me.

It shook Wyoh. When Mike finished she said, "I've got to get home! Never in my life have I helped eliminate anyone but I am going to *enjoy* putting the black on these spies!"

Prof said quietly, "No one will be eliminated, dear Wyoming."

"What? Professor, can't you take it? Though I've never killed anyone, I've always known it might have to be done."

He shook head. "Killing is not the way to handle a spy, not when he doesn't know that *you* know that he is a spy."

She blinked. "I must be dense."

"No, dear lady. Instead you have a charming honesty . . . a weakness you must guard against. The thing to do with a spy is to let him breathe, encyst him with loyal comrades, and feed him harmless information to please his employers. These creatures will be taken into our organization. Don't be shocked; they will be in very special cells. 'Cages' is a better word. But it would be the greatest waste to eliminate them—not only would each spy be replaced with someone new but also killing these traitors would tell the Warden that we have penetrated his secrets. Mike amigo mio, there should be in that file a dossier on me. Will you see?"

Were long notes on Prof, and I was embarrassed as they added up to "harmless old fool." He was tagged as a subversive—that was why he had been sent to The Rock—as a member of underground group in Luna City. But was described as a "troublemaker" in organization, one who rarely agreed with others.

Prof dimpled and looked pleased. "I must consider trying to sell out and get myself placed on the Warden's payroll." Wyoh did not think this funny, especially when he made clear was not joke, merely unsure tactic was practical. "Revolutions must be financed, dear lady, and one way is for a revolutionary to become a police spy. It is probable that some of those prima-facie traitors are actually on our side."

"I wouldn't trust them!"

"Ah, yes, that is the rub with double agents, to be *certain* where their loyalties—if any—lie. Do you wish your own dossièr? Or would you rather hear it in private?"

Wyoh's record showed no surprises. Warden's finks had tabbed her years back. But I was surprised that I had a record, too—routine check made when I was cleared to work in Authority Complex. Was classed as "non-political" and someone had added "not too bright" which was both unkind and true or why would I get mixed up in Revolution?

Prof had Mike stop read-out (hours more), leaned back and looked thoughtful. "One thing is clear," he said. "The Warden knew plenty about Wyoming and myself long ago. But you, Manuel, are not on his black list."

"After last night?"

"Ah, so. Mike, do you have *anything* in that file entered in the last twenty-four hours?"

Nothing. Prof said, "Wyoming is right that we cannot stay here forever. Manuel, how many names did you recognize? Six, was it? Did you see any of them last night?"

"No. But might have seen me."

"More likely they missed you in the crowd. I did not spot you until I came down front and I've known you since you were a boy. But it is most unlikely that Wyoming traveled from Hong Kong and spoke at the meeting without her activity being known to the Warden." He looked at Wyoh. "Dear lady, could you bring yourself to play the nominal role of an old man's folly?"

"I suppose so. How, Professor?"

"Manuel is probably in the clear. I am not but from my dossier it seems unlikely that the Authority's finks will bother to pick me up. You they may wish to question or even to hold; you are rated as dangerous. It would be wise for you to stay out of sight. This room— I'm thinking of renting it for a period—weeks or even years. You could hide in it—if you do not mind the obvious construction that would be placed on your staying here."

Wyoh chuckled. "Why, you darling! Do you think I care what anyone thinks? I'd be delighted to play the role of your bundle baby—and don't be too sure I'd be just playing."

"Never tease an old dog," he said mildly. "He might still have one bite. I may occupy that couch most nights. Manuel, I intend to resume my usual ways—and so should you. While I feel that it will take a busy cossack to arrest me, I will sleep sounder in this hideaway. But in addition to being a hideout this room is good for cell meetings; it has a phone."

Mike said, "Professor, may I offer a suggestion?"

"Certainly, amigo, we want your thoughts."

"I conclude that the hazards increase with each meeting of our executive cell. But meetings need not be corporal; you can meet—and I can join you if I am welcome—by phone."

"You are always welcome, Comrade Mike; we need you. However—" Prof looked worried.

I said, "Prof, don't worry about anybody listening in." I explained how to place a "Sherlock" call. "Phones are safe if Mike supervises call. Reminds me— You haven't been told how to reach Mike. How, Mike? Prof use my number?"

Between them, they settled on MYSTERIOUS. Prof and Mike shared childlike joy in intrigue for own sake. I suspect Prof enjoyed being rebel long before he worked out his political philosophy, while Mike—how could human freedom matter to him? Revolution was a game—a game that gave him companionship and chance to show off talents. Mike was as conceited a machine as you are ever likely to meet.

"But we still need this room," Prof said, reached into pouch, hauled out thick wad of bills.

I blinked. "Prof, robbed a bank?"

"Not recently. Perhaps again in the future if the Cause requires it. A rental period of one lunar should do as a starter. Will you arrange it, Manuel? The management might be surprised to hear my voice; I came in through a delivery door."

I called manager, bargained for dated key, four weeks. He asked nine hundred Hong Kong. I offered nine hundred Authority. He wanted to know how many would use room? I asked if was policy of Raffles to snoop affairs of guests?

We settled at HK$475; I sent up bills, he sent down two dated keys. I gave one to Wyoh, one to Prof, kept one-day key, knowing they would not reset lock unless we failed to pay at end of lunar.

(Earthside I ran into insolent practice of requiring hotel guest to sign chop—even show identification!)

I asked, "What next? Food?"

"I'm not hungry, Mannie."

"Manuel, you asked us to wait while Mike settled your questions. Let's get back to the basic problem: how we are to cope when we find ourselves facing Terra, David facing Goliath."

"Oh. Been hoping that would go away. Mike? You really have ideas?"

"I *said* I did, Man," he answered plaintively. "We can throw rocks."

"Bog's sake! No time for jokes."

"But, Man," he protested, "we *can* throw rocks at Terra. We will."

EIGHT

Took time to get through my skull that Mike was serious, and scheme might work. Then took longer to show Wyoh and Prof how second part was true. Yet both parts should have been obvious.

Mike reasoned so: What is "war"? One book defined war as use of force to achieve political result. And "force" is action of one body on another applied by means of energy.

In war this is done by "weapons"—Luna had none. But weapons, when Mike examined them as class, turned out to be engines for manipulating energy—and energy Luna has plenty. Solar flux alone is good for around one kilowatt per square meter of surface at Lunar noon; sunpower, though cyclic, is effectively unlimited. Hydrogen fusion power is almost as unlimited and cheaper, once ice is mined, magnetic pinchbottle set up. Luna has energy—how to use?

But Luna also has energy of position; she sits at top of gravity well eleven kilometers per second deep and kept from falling in by curb only two and a half km/s high. Mike knew that curb; daily he tossed grain freighters over it, let them slide downhill to Terra.

Mike had computed what would happen if a freighter grossing 100 tonnes (or same mass of rock) falls to Terra, unbraked.

Kinetic energy as it hits is 6.25×10^{12} joules—over six trillion joules.

This converts in split second to heat. Explosion, big one!

Should have been obvious. Look at Luna: What you see? Thousands on thousands of craters—places where Somebody got playful throwing rocks.

Wyoh said, "Joules don't mean much to me. How does that compare with H-bombs?"

"Uh—" I started to round off in head. Mike's "head" works faster; he answered, "The concussion of a hundred-tonne mass on Terra approaches the yield of a two-kilotonne atomic bomb."

" 'Kilo' is a thousand," Wyoh murmured, "and 'mega' is a million— Why, that's only one fifty-thousandth as much as a hundred-megatonne bomb. Wasn't that the size Sovunion used?"

"Wyoh, honey," I said gently, "that's not how it works. Turn it around. A two-kilotonne yield is equivalent to exploding two *million* kilograms of trinitrotoluol . . . and a kilo of TNT is quite an explosion— Ask any drillman. Two million kilos will wipe out good-sized town. Check, Mike?"

"Yes, Man. But, Wyoh my only female friend, there is another aspect. Multi-megatonne fusion bombs are inefficient. The explosion takes place in too small a space; most of it is wasted. While a hundred-megatonne bomb is rated as having fifty thousand times the yield of a two-kilotonne bomb, its destructive effect is only about thirteen hundred times as great as that of a two-kilotonne explosion."

"But it seems to me that thirteen hundred times is still quite a lot—if they are going to use bombs on us that much bigger."

"True, Wyoh my female friend . . . but Luna has *many* rocks."

"Oh. Yes, so we have."

"Comrades," said Prof, "this is outside my competence—in my younger or bomb-throwing days my experience was limited to something of the order of the one-kilogram chemical explosion of which you spoke, Manuel. But I assume that you two know what you are talking about."

"We do," Mike agreed.

"So I accept your figures. To bring it down to a scale that I can understand this plan requires that we capture the catapult. No?"

"Yes," Mike and I chorused.

"Not impossible. Then we must hold it and keep it operative. Mike, have you considered how your catapult can be protected against, let us say, one small H-tipped torpedo?"

Discussion went on and on. We stopped to eat—stopped business under Prof's rule. Instead Mike told jokes, each produced a that-reminds-me from Prof.

By time we left Raffles Hotel evening of 14th May '75 we had—Mike had, with help from Prof—outlined plan of Revolution, including major options at critical points.

When came time to go, me to home and Prof to evening class (if not arrested), then home for bath and clothes and necessities in case he returned that night, became clear Wyoh did not want to be alone in strange hotel—Wyoh was stout when bets were down, between times soft and vulnerable.

So I called Mum on a Sherlock and told her was bringing house guest home. Mum ran her job with style; any spouse could bring guest home for meal or year, and our second generation was almost as free but must ask. Don't know how other families work; we have customs firmed by a century; they suit us.

So Mum didn't ask name, age, sex, marital condition; was my right and she too proud to ask. All she said was: "That's nice, dear. Have you two had dinner? It's Tuesday, you know." "Tuesday" was to remind me that our family had eaten early because Greg preaches Tuesday evenings. But if guest had not eaten, dinner would be served—concession to guest, not to me, as with exception of Grandpaw we ate when was on table or scrounged standing up in pantry.

I assured her we had eaten and would make tall effort to be there before she needed to leave. Despite Loonie mixture of Muslims, Jews, Christians, Buddhists, and ninety-nine other flavors, I suppose Sunday is commonest day for church. But Greg belongs to sect which had calculated that sundown Tuesday to sundown Wednesday, local time Garden of Eden (zone minus-two, Terra) was *the* Sabbath. So we ate early in Terran north-hemisphere summer months.

Mum always went to hear Greg preach, so was not considerate to place duty on her that would clash. All of us went occasionally; I managed several times a year because terribly fond of Greg, who taught me one trade and helped me switch to another when I had to and would gladly have made it his arm rather than mine. But Mum always went—ritual not religion, for she admitted to me one night in pillow talk that she had no religion with a brand on it, then cautioned me not to tell Greg. I exacted same caution from her. I don't know Who is cranking; I'm pleased He doesn't stop.

But Greg was Mum's "boy husband," opted when she was very young, first wedding after her own—very sentimental about him, would deny fiercely if accused of loving him more than other husbands, yet took his faith when he was ordained and never missed a Tuesday.

She said, "Is it possible that your guest would wish to attend church?"

I said would see but anyhow we would rush, and said good-bye. Then banged on bathroom door and said, "Hurry with skin, Wyoh; we're short on minutes."

"One minute!" she called out. She's ungirlish girl; she appeared in one minute. "How do I look?" she asked. "Prof, will I pass?"

"Dear Wyoming, I am amazed. You were beautiful before, you are beautiful now—but utterly unrecognizable. You're safe—and I am relieved."

Then we waited for Prof to transform into old derelict; he would be it to his back corridor, then reappear as well-known teacher in front of class, to have witnesses in case a yellow boy was waiting to grab him.

It left a moment; I told Wyoh about Greg. She said, "Mannie, how good is this makeup? Would it pass in church? How bright are the lights?"

"No brighter than here. Good job, you'll get by. But do you want to go to church? Nobody pushing."

She thought. "It would please your moth—I mean, 'your senior wife,' would it not?"

I answered slowly, "Wyoh, religion is your pidgin. But since you ask . . . yes, nothing would start you better in Davis Family than going to church with Mum. I'll go if you do."

"I'll go. I thought your last name was 'O'Kelly'?"

"Is. Tack 'Davis' on with hyphen if want to be formal. Davis is First Husband, dead fifty years. Is family name and all our wives are 'Gospazha Davis' hyphened with every male name in Davis line plus her family name. In practice Mum is only 'Gospazha Davis'—can call her that—and others use first name and add Davis if they write a cheque or something. Except that Ludmilla is 'Davis-Davis' because proud of double membership, birth and option."

"I see. Then if a man is 'John Davis,' he's a son, but if he has some other last name he's your co-husband. But a girl would be 'Jenny Davis' either way, wouldn't she? How do I tell? By her age? No, that wouldn't help. I'm confused! And I thought clan marriages were complex. Or polyandries—though mine wasn't; at least my husbands had the same last name."

"No trouble. When you hear a woman about forty address a fifteen-year-old as 'Mama Milla," you'll know which is wife and which is daughter—not even that complex as we don't have daughters home past husband-high; they get opted. But might be visiting. Your husbands were named 'Knott'?"

"Oh, no, 'Fedoseev, Choy Lin and Choy Mu.' I took back my born name."

Out came Prof, cackled senilely (looked even worse than earlier!), we left by three exits, made rendezvous in main corridor, open formation. Wyoh and I did not walk together, as I might be nabbed; on other hand she did not know Luna City, a warren so complex even nativeborn get lost—so I led and she had to keep me in sight. Prof trailed to make sure she didn't lose me.

If I was picked up, Wyoh would find public phone, report to

Mike, then return to hotel and wait for Prof. But I felt sure that any yellow jacket who arrested me would get a caress from number-seven arm.

No huhu. Up to level five and crosstown by Carver Causeway, up to level three and stop at Tube Station West to pick up arms and tool kit—but not p-suit; would not have been in character, I stored it there. One yellow uniform at station, showed no interest in me. South by well-lighted corridors until necessary to go outward to reach private easement lock thirteen to co-op pressure tunnel serving Davis Tunnels and a dozen other farms. I suppose Prof dropped off there but I never looked back.

I delayed locking through our door until Wyoh caught up, then soon was saying, "Mum, allow me to present Wyma Beth Johnson."

Mum took her in arms, kissed cheek, said, "So glad you could come, Wyma dear! Our house is yours!"

See why I love our old biddy? Could have quick-frosted Wyoh with same words—but was real and Wyoh knew.

Hadn't warned Wyoh about switch in names, thought of it en route. Some of our kids were small and while they grew up despising Warden, no sense in risking prattle about "Wyoming Knott, who's visiting us"—that name was listed in "Special File Zebra."

So I missed warning her, was new to conspiracy.

But Wyoh caught cue and never bobbled.

Greg was in preaching clothes and would have to leave in minutes. Mum did not hurry, took Wyoh down line of husbands—Grandpaw, Greg, Hans—then up line of wives—Ludmilla, Lenore, Sidris, Anna—with stately grace, then started on our kids.

I said, "Mum? Excuse me, want to change arms." Her eyebrows went up a millimeter, meaning: "We'll speak of this but not in front of children"—so I added: "Know it's late, Greg's sneaking look at watch. And Wyma and I are going to church. So 'scuse, please."

She relaxed. "Certainly, dear." As she turned away I saw her arm go around Wyoh's waist, so I relaxed.

I changed arms, replacing number seven with social arm. But was excuse to duck into phone cupboard and punch "MYCROFTXXX." "Mike, we're home. But about to go to church. Don't think you can listen there, so I'll check in later. Heard from Prof?"

"Not yet, Man. Which church is it? I may have some circuit."

"Pillar of Fire Repentance Tabernacle—"

"No reference."

"Slow to my speed, pal. Meets in West-Three Community Hall. That's south of Station on Ring about number—"

"I have it. There's a pickup inside for channels and a phone in the corridor outside; I'll keep an ear on both."

"I don't expect trouble, Mike."

"It's what Professor said to do. He is reporting now. Do you wish to speak to him?"

"No time. 'Bye!"

That set pattern: Always keep touch with Mike, let him know where you are, where you plan to be; Mike would listen if he had nerve ends there. Discovery I made that morning, that Mike could listen at dead phone, suggested it—discovery bothered me; don't believe in magic. But on thinking I realized a phone could be switched on by central switching system without human intervention—if switching system had volition. Mike had bolshoyeh volition.

How Mike knew a phone was outside that hall is hard to say, since "space" could not mean to him what means to us. But he carried in storage a "map"—structured relations—of Luna City's engineering, and could almost always fit what we said to what he knew as "Luna City"; hardly ever got lost.

So from day cabal started we kept touch with Mike and each other through his widespread nervous system. Won't mention again unless necessary.

Mum and Greg and Wyoh were waiting at outer door, Mum chomping but smiling. I saw she had lent Wyoh a stole; Mum was as easy about skin as any Loonie, nothing newchummish—but church was another matter.

We made it, although Greg went straight to platform and we to seats. I settled in warm, mindless state, going through motions. But Wyoh did really listen to Greg's sermon and either knew our hymn book or was accomplished sight reader.

When we got home, young ones were in bed and most adults; Hans and Sidris were up and Sidris served cocoasoy and cookies, then all turned in. Mum assigned Wyoh a room in tunnel most of our kids lived in, one which had had two smaller boys last time I noticed. Did not ask how she had reshuffled, was clear she was giving my guest best we had, or would have put Wyoh with one of older girls.

I slept with Mum that night, partly because our senior wife is good for nerves—and nerve-racking things had happened—and partly so she would know I was *not* sneaking to Wyoh's room after things were quiet. My workshop, where I slept when slept alone, was just one bend from Wyoh's door. Mum was telling me, plain as print: "Go ahead, dear. Don't tell me if you wish to be mean about it. Sneak behind my back."

Which neither of us admitted. We visited as we got ready for bed, chatted after light out, then I turned over.

Instead of saying goodnight Mum said, "Manuel? Why does your sweet little guest make herself up as an Afro? I would think that her natural coloration would be more becoming. Not that she isn't perfectly charming the way she chooses to be."

So rolled over and faced her, and explained—sounded thin, so filled in. And found self telling all—except one point: Mike. I included Mike—but *not* as computer—instead as a man Mum was not likely to meet, for security reasons.

But telling Mum—taking her into my subcell, should say, to become leader of own cell in turn—taking Mum into conspiracy was not case of husband who can't keep from blurting everything to his wife. At most was hasty—but was best time if she was to be told.

Mum was smart. Also able executive; running big family without baring teeth requires that. Was respected among farm families and throughout Luna City; she had been up longer than 90 percent. She could help.

And would be indispensable inside family. Without her help Wyoh and I would find it sticky to use phone together (hard to explain), keep kids from noticing (impossible!)—but with Mum's help would be no problems inside household.

She listened, sighed, said, "It sounds dangerous, dear."

"Is," I said. "Look, Mimi, if you don't want to tackle, say so . . . then forget what I've told."

"Manuel! Don't even say that. You are my husband, dear; I took you for better, for worse . . . and your wish is my command."

(My word, what a lie! But Mimi believed it.)

"I would not let you go into danger alone," she went on, "and besides—"

"What, Mimi?"

"I think every Loonie dreams of the day when we will be free. All but some poor spineless rats. I've never talked about it; there seemed to be no point and it's necessary to look up, not down, lift one's burden and go ahead. But I thank dear Bog that I have been permitted to live to see the time come, if indeed it has. Explain more about it. I am to find three others, is it? Three who can be trusted."

"Don't hurry. Move slowly. Be sure."

"Sidris can be trusted. She holds her tongue, that one."

"Don't think you should pick from family. Need to spread out. Don't rush."

"I shan't. We'll talk before I do anything. And Manuel, if you want my opinion—" She stopped.

"Always want your opinion, Mimi."

"Don't mention this to Grandpaw. He's forgetful these days and sometimes talkative. Now sleep, dear, and don't dream."

NINE

Followed a long time during which would have been possible to forget anything as unlikely as revolution had not details taken so much time. Our first purpose was not to be noticed. Long distance purpose was to make things as much worse as possible.

Yes, worse. Never was a time, even at last, when all Loonies wanted to throw off Authority, wanted it bad enough to revolt. All Loonies despised Warden and cheated Authority. Didn't mean they were ready to fight and die. If you had mentioned "patriotism" to a Loonie, he would have stared—or thought you were talking about his homeland. Were transported Frenchmen whose hearts belonged to "La Belle Patrie," ex-Germans loyal to Vaterland, Russkis who still loved Holy Mother Russia. But Luna? Luna was "The Rock," place of exile, not thing to love.

We were as non-political a people as history ever produced. I know, I was as numb to politics as any until circumstances pitched me into it. Wyoming was in it because she hated Authority for a personal reason, Prof because he despised all authority in a detached intellectual fashion, Mike because he was a bored and lonely machine and was for him "only game in town." You could not have accused us of patriotism. I came closest because I was third generation with total lack of affection for any place on Terra, had been there, disliked it and despised earthworms. Made me more "patriotic" than most!

Average Loonie was interested in beer, betting, women, and work, in that order. "Women" might be second place but first was unlikely, much as women were cherished. Loonies had learned there never were enough women to go around. Slow learners died, as even most possessive male can't stay alert every minute. As Prof says, a society adapts to fact, or doesn't survive. Loonies adapted to harsh facts—or failed and died. But "patriotism" was not necessary to survival.

Like old Chinee saying that "Fish aren't aware of water," I was not aware of any of this until I first went to Terra and even then did not realize what a blank spot was in Loonies under storage location marked "patriotism" until I took part in effort to stir them up. Wyoh and her comrades had tried to push "patriotism" button and got nowhere—years of work, a few thousand members, less than 1 percent and of that microscopic number almost 10 percent had been paid spies of boss fink!

Prof set us straight: Easier to get people to hate than to get them to love.

Luckily, Security Chief Alvarez gave us a hand. Those nine dead finks were replaced with ninety, for Authority was goaded into something it did reluctantly, namely spend money on us, and one folly led to another.

Warden's bodyguard had never been large even in earliest days. Prison guards in historical meaning were unnecessary and that had been one attraction of penal colony system—cheap. Warden and his deputy had to be protected and visiting vips, but prison itself needed no guards. They even stopped guarding ships after became clear was not necessary, and in May 2075, bodyguard was down to its cheapest numbers, all of them new chum transportees.

But loss of nine in one night scared somebody. We knew it scared Alvarez; he filed copies of his demands for help in Zebra file and Mike read them. A lag who had been a police officer on Terra before his conviction and then a bodyguard all his years in Luna, Alvarez was probably most frightened and loneliest man in The Rock. He demanded more and tougher help, threatened to resign civil service job if he didn't get it—just a threat, which Authority would have known if it had really known Luna. If Alvarez had showed up in any warren as unarmed civilian, he would have stayed breathing only as long as not recognized.

He got his additional guards. We never found out who ordered that raid. Mort the Wart had never shown such tendencies, had been King Log throughout tenure. Perhaps Alvarez, having only recently succeeded to boss fink spot, wanted to make face—may have had ambition to be Warden. But likeliest theory is that Warden's reports on "subversive activities" caused Authority Earthside to order a cleanup.

One thumb-fingered mistake led to another. New bodyguards, instead of picked from new transportees, were elite convict troops, Federated Nations crack Peace Dragoons. Were mean and tough, did not want to go to Luna, and soon realized that "temporary police duty" was one-way trip. Hated Luna and Loonies, and saw us as cause of it all.

Once Alvarez got them, he posted a twenty-four-hour watch at every interwarren tube station and instituted passports and passport control. Would have been illegal had there been laws in Luna, since 95 percent of us were theoretically free, either born free, or sentence completed. Percentage was higher in cities as undischarged transportees lived in barrack warrens at Complex and came into town only two days per lunar they had off work. If then, as they had no money, but you sometimes saw them wandering around, hoping somebody would buy a drink.

But passport system was not "illegal" as Warden's regulations were only written law. Was announced in papers, we were given week to get passports, and at eight hundred one morning was put in effect. Some Loonies hardly ever traveled; some traveled on business; some commuted from outlying warrens or even from Luna City to Novylen or other way. Good little boys filled out applications, paid fees, were photographed, got passes; I was good little boy on Prof's advice, paid for passport and added it to pass I carried to work in Complex.

Few good little boys! Loonies did not believe it. Passports? Whoever heard of such a thing?

Was a trooper at Tube Station South that morning dressed in bodyguard yellow rather than regimental and looking like he hated it, and us. I was not going anywhere; I hung back and watched.

Novylen capsule was announced; crowd of thirty-odd headed for gate. Gospodin Yellow Jacket demanded passport of first to reach it. Loonie stopped to argue. Second one pushed past; guard turned and yelled—three or four more shoved past. Guard reached for sidearm; somebody grabbed his elbow, gun went off—not a laser, a slug gun, noisy.

Slug hit decking and went *whee-whee-hoo* off somewhere. I faded back. One man hurt—that guard. When first press of passengers had gone down ramp, he was on deck, not moving.

Nobody paid attention; they walked around or stepped over—except one woman carrying a baby, who stopped, kicked him carefully in face, then went down ramp. He may have been dead already, didn't wait to see. Understand body stayed there till relief arrived.

Next day was a half squad in that spot. Capsule for Novylen left empty.

It settled down. Those who had to travel got passports, diehards quit traveling. Guard at a tube gate became two men, one looked at passports while other stood back with gun drawn. One who checked passports did not try hard, which was well as most were counterfeit and early ones were crude. But before long, authentic paper was stolen and counterfeits were as dinkum as official ones—more expensive but Loonies preferred free-enterprise passports.

Our organization did not make counterfeits; we merely encouraged it—and knew who had them and who did not; Mike's records listed officially issued ones. This helped separate sheep from goats in files we were building—also stored in Mike but in "Bastille" location—as we figured a man with counterfeit passport was halfway to joining us. Word was passed down cells in our growing organization never to recruit anybody with a valid passport. If recruiter was not certain, just query upwards and answer came back.

But guards' troubles were not over. Does not help a guard's dignity nor add to peace of mind to have children stand in front of him, or behind out of eye which was worse, and ape every move he makes—or run back and forth screaming obscenities, peering, making finger motions that are universal. At least guards took them as insults.

One guard back-handed a small boy, cost him some teeth. Result: two guards dead, one Loonie dead.

After that, guards ignored children.

We didn't have to work this up; we merely encouraged it. You wouldn't think that a sweet old lady like my senior wife would encourage children to misbehave. But she did.

Other things get single men a long way from home upset—and one we did start. These Peace Dragoons had been sent to The Rock without a comfort detachment.

Some of our fems were extremely beautiful and some started loitering around stations, dressed in less than usual—which could approach zero—and wearing more than usual amount of perfume, scents with range and striking power. They did not speak to yellow jackets nor look at them; they simply crossed their line of sight, undulating as only a Loonie gal can. (A female on Terra can't walk that way; she's tied down by six times too much weight.)

Such of course produces a male gallery, from men down to lads not yet pubescent—happy whistles and cheers for her beauty, nasty laughs at yellow boy. First girls to take this duty were slot-machine types but volunteers sprang up so fast that Prof decided we need not spend money. He was correct; even Ludmilla, shy as a kitten, wanted to try it and did not only because Mum told her not to. But Lenore, ten years older and prettiest of our family, did try it and Mum did not scold. She came back pink and excited and pleased with herself and anxious to tease enemy again. Her own idea;

Lenore did not then know that revolution was brewing.

During this time I rarely saw Prof and never in public; we kept touch by phone. At first a bottleneck was that our farm had just one phone for twenty-five people, many of them youngsters who would tie up a phone for hours unless coerced. Mimi was strict; our kids were allowed one out-going call per day and max of ninety seconds on a call, with rising scale of punishment—tempered by her warmth in granting exceptions. But grants were accompanied by "Mum's Phone Lecture": "When I first came to Luna there were no private phones. You children don't know how soft . . ."

We were one of last prosperous families to install a phone; it was new in household when I was opted. We were prosperous because we never bought anything farm could produce. Mum disliked phone because rates to Luna City Co-op Comm Company were passed on in large measure to Authority. She never could understand why I could not ("Since you know all about such things, Manuel dear") steal phone service as easily as we liberated power. That a phone instrument was part of a switching system into which it must fit was no interest to her.

Steal it I did, eventually. Problem with illicit phone is how to receive incoming calls. Since phone is not listed, even if you tell persons from whom you want calls, switching system *itself* does not have you listed; is *no* signal that can tell it to connect other party with you.

Once Mike joined conspiracy, switching was no problem. I had in workshop most of what I needed; bought some items and liberated others. Drilled a tiny hole from workshop to phone cupboard and another to Wyoh's room—virgin rock a meter thick but a laser drill collimated to a thin pencil cuts rapidly. I unshipped listed phone, made a wireless coupling to line in its recess and concealed it. All else needed were binaural receptors and a speaker in Wyoh's room, concealed, and same in mine, and a circuit to raise frequency above audio to have silence on Davis phone line, and its converse to restore audio incoming.

Only problem was to do this without being seen, and Mum generaled that.

All else was Mike's problem. Used no switching arrangements;

from then on used MYCROFTXXX only when calling from some other phone. Mike listened at all times in workshop and in Wyoh's room; if he heard my voice or hers say "Mike," he answered, but not to other voices. Voice patterns were as distinctive to him as fingerprints; he never made mistakes.

Minor flourishes—soundproofing Wyoh's door such as workshop door already had, switching to suppress my instrument or hers, signals to tell me she was alone in her room and door locked, and vice versa. All added up to safe means whereby Wyoh and I could talk with Mike or with each other, or could set up talk-talk of Mike, Wyoh, Prof, and self. Mike would call Prof wherever he was; Prof would talk or call back from a more private phone. Or might be Wyoh or myself had to be found. We all were careful to stay checked in with Mike.

My bootleg phone, though it had no way to punch a call, could be used to call any number in Luna—speak to Mike, ask for a Sherlock to anybody—not tell him number, Mike had all listings and could look up a number faster than I could.

We were beginning to see unlimited possibilities in a phone-switching system alive and on our side. I got from Mike and gave Mum still another null number to call Mike if she needed to reach me. She grew chummy with Mike while continuing to think he was a man. This spread through our family. One day as I returned home Sidris said, "Mannie darling, your friend with the nice voice called. Mike Holmes. Wants you to call back."

"Thanks, hon. Will."

"When are you going to invite him to dinner, Man? I think he's nice."

I told her Gospodin Holmes had bad breath, was covered with rank hair, and hated women.

She used a rude word, Mum not being in earshot. "You're afraid to let me see him. Afraid I'll opt out for him." I patted her and told her that was why. I told Mike and Prof about it. Mike flirted even more with my womenfolk after that; Prof was thoughtful.

I began to learn techniques of conspiracy and to appreciate Prof's feeling that revolution could be an art. Did not forget (nor ever doubt) Mike's prediction that Luna was only seven years from disaster. But did not think about it, thought about fascinating, finicky details.

Prof had emphasized that stickiest problems in conspiracy are communications and security, and had pointed out that they conflict—easier are communications, greater is risk to security; if security is tight, organization can be paralyzed by safety precautions. He had explained that cell system was a compromise.

I accepted cell system since was necessary to limit losses from spies. Even Wyoh admitted that organization without compartmentation could not work after she learned how rotten with spies old underground had been.

But I did not like clogged communications of cell system; like Terran dinosaurs of old, took too long to send message from head to tail, or back.

So talked with Mike.

We discarded many-linked channels I had suggested to Prof. We retained cells but based security and communication on marvelous possibilities of our dinkum thinkum.

Communications: We set up a ternary tree of "party" names:

Chairman, Gospodin Adam Selene (Mike)

Executive cell: Bork (me), Betty (Wyoh), Bill (Prof)

Bork's cell: Cassie (Mum), Colin, Chang

Betty's cell: Calvin (Greg), Cecilia (Sidris), Clayton

Bill's cell: Cornwall (Finn Nielsen), Carolyn, Cotter

—and so on. At seventh link George supervises Herbert, Henry, and Hallie. By time you reach that level you need 2,187 names with "H"—but turn it over to savvy computer who finds or invents them. Each recruit is given a party name and an emergency phone number. This number, instead of chasing through many links, connects with "Adam Selene," Mike.

Security: Based on double principle; no human being can be trusted with anything—but Mike could be trusted with everything.

Grim first half is beyond dispute. With drugs and other unsavory methods any man can be broken. Only defense is suicide, which may be impossible. Oh, are "hollow tooth" methods, classic and novel, some nearly infallible—Prof saw to it that Wyoh and myself were equipped. Never knew what he gave her as a final friend and since I never had to use mine, is no point in messy details. Nor am I sure I would ever suicide; am not stuff of martyrs.

But Mike could never need to suicide, could not be drugged, did not feel pain. He carried everything concerning us in a separate memory bank under a locked signal programmed *only* to our three voices, and, since flesh is weak, we added a signal under which any of us could lock out other two in emergency. In my opinion as best computerman in Luna, Mike could not remove this lock once it was set up. Best of all, nobody would ask master computer for this file because nobody knew it existed, did not suspect Mike-as-Mike existed. How secure can you be?

Only risk was that this awakened machine was whimsical. Mike was always showing unforeseen potentials; conceivable he could figure way to get around block—if he wanted to.

But would never want to. He was loyal to me, first and oldest friend; he liked Prof; I think he loved Wyoh. No, no, sex meant nothing. But Wyoh is lovable and they hit it off from start.

I trusted Mike. In this life you have to bet; on that bet I would give any odds.

So we based security on trusting Mike with everything while each of us knew only what he had to know. Take that tree of names and numbers. I knew only party names of my cellmates and of three directly under me; was all I needed. Mike set up party names, assigned phone number to each, kept roster of real names versus party names. Let's say party member "Daniel" (whom I would not know, being a "D" two levels below me) recruits Fritz Schultz. Daniel reports fact but *not* name upwards; Adam Selene calls Daniel, assigns for Schultz party name "Embrook," then phones Schultz at number received from Daniel, gives Schultz his name Embrook and emergency phone number, this number being *different* for *each* recruit.

Not even Embrook's cell leader would know Embrook's emergency number. What you do not know you cannot spill, not under drugs nor torture, nor anything. Not even from carelessness.

Now let's suppose I need to reach Comrade Embrook. I don't know who he is; he may live in Hong Kong or be shopkeeper nearest my home. Instead of passing message down, hoping it will reach him, I call Mike. Mike connects me with Embrook at once, in a Sherlock, *without* giving me his number.

Or suppose I need to speak to comrade who is preparing cartoon we are about to distribute in every taproom in Luna. I don't know who he is. But I need to talk to him; something has come up.

I call Mike; Mike knows everything—and again I am quickly connected—and this comrade knows it's okay as Adam Selene arranged call. "Comrade Bork speaking"—and he doesn't know me but initial "B" tells him that I am vip indeed—"we have to change so-and-so. Tell your cell leader and have him check, but get on with it."

Minor flourishes—some comrades did not have phones; some could be reached only at certain hours; some outlying warrens did not have phone service. No matter, Mike knew everything—and rest of us did not know *anything* that could endanger any but that handful whom each knew face to face.

After we decided that Mike should talk voice-to-voice to any comrade under some circumstances, it was necessary to give him more voices and dress him up, make him three dimensions, create "Adam Selene, Chairman of the Provisional Committee of Free Luna."

Mike's need for more voices lay in fact that he had just one voder-vocoder, whereas his brain could handle a dozen conversations, or a hundred (don't know how many)—like a chess master playing fifty opponents, only more so.

This would cause a bottleneck as organization grew and Adam Selene was phoned oftener, and could be crucial if we lasted long enough to go into action.

Besides giving him more voices I wanted to silence one he had. One of those so-called computermen might walk into machines room while we were phoning Mike; bound to cause even his dim wit to wonder if he found master machine apparently talking to itself.

Voder-vocoder is very old device. Human voice is buzzes and hisses mixed various ways; true even of a coloratura soprano. A vocoder analyzes buzzes and hisses into patterns, one a computer (or trained eye) can read. A voder is a little box which can buzz and hiss and has controls to vary these elements to match those patterns. A human can "play" a voder, producing artificial speech; a properly programmed computer can do it as fast, as easily, as clearly as you can speak.

But voices on a phone wire are not sound waves but electrical signals; Mike did not need audio part of voder-vocoder to talk by phone. Sound waves were needed only by human at other end; no need for speech sounds inside Mike's room at Authority Complex, so I planned to remove them, and thereby any danger that somebody might notice.

First I worked at home, using number-three arm most of time. Result was very small box which sandwiched twenty voder-vocoder circuits minus audio side. Then I called Mike and told him to "get ill" in way that would annoy Warden. Then I waited.

We had done this "get ill" trick before. I went back to work once we learned that I was clear, which was Thursday that same week when Alvarez read into Zebra file an account of shambles at Stilyagi Hall. His version listed about one hundred people (out of perhaps three hundred); list included Shorty Mkrum, Wyoh, Prof, and Finn Nielsen but *not* me—apparently I was missed by his finks. It told how nine police officers, each deputized by Warden to preserve peace, had been shot down in cold blood. Also named three of our dead.

An add-on a week later stated that "the notorious agente provocateuse Wyoming Knott of Hong Kong in Luna, whose incendiary speech on Monday 13 May had incited the riot that cost the lives of nine brave officers, had not been apprehended in Luna City and had not returned to her usual haunts in Hong Kong in Luna, and was now believed to have died in the massacre she herself set off." This add-on admitted what earlier report failed to mention, i.e., bodies were missing and exact number of dead was not known.

This P.S. settled two things: Wyoh could not go home nor back to being a blonde.

Since I had not been spotted I resumed my public ways, took care of customers that week, bookkeeping machines and retrieval files at Carnegie Library, and spent time having Mike read out Zebra file and other special files, doing so in Room L of Raffles as I did not yet have my own phone. During that week Mike niggled at me like an impatient child (which he was), wanting to know when I was coming over to pick up more jokes. Failing that, he wanted to tell them by phone.

I got annoyed and had to remind myself that from Mike's viewpoint analyzing jokes was just as important as freeing Luna—and you *don't* break promises to a child.

Besides that, I got itchy wondering whether I could go inside Complex without being nabbed. We knew Prof was not clear, was sleeping in Raffles on that account. Yet they knew he had been at meeting and knew where he was, daily—but no attempt was made to pick him up. When we learned that attempt had been made to pick up Wyoh, I grew itchier. Was I clear? Or were they waiting to nab me quietly? Had to know.

So I called Mike and told him to have a tummyache. He did so, I was called in—no trouble. Aside from showing passport at station, then to a new guard at Complex, all was usual. I chatted with Mike, picked up one thousand jokes (with understanding that we would report a hundred at a time every three or four days, no faster), told him to get well, and went back to L-City, stopping on way out to bill Chief Engineer for working time, travel-and-tool time, materials, special service, anything I could load in.

Thereafter saw Mike about once a month. Was safe, never went there except when *they* called *me* for malfunction beyond ability of their staff—and I was always able to "repair" it, sometimes quickly, sometimes after a full day and many tests. Was careful to leave tool marks on cover plates, and had before-and-after printouts of test runs to show what had been wrong, how I analyzed it, what I had done. Mike always worked perfectly after one of my visits; I was indispensable.

So, after I prepared his new voder-vocoder add-on, didn't hesitate to tell him to get "ill." Call came in thirty minutes. Mike had thought up a dandy; his "illness" was wild oscillations in conditioning Warden's residence. He was running its heat up, then down, on an eleven-minute cycle, while oscillating its air pressure on a short cycle, ca. 2c/s, enough to make a man dreadfully nervy and perhaps cause earache.

Conditioning a single residence should not go through a master computer! In Davis Tunnels we handled home and farm with idiot controls, feedbacks for each cubic with alarms so that somebody could climb out of bed and control by hand until trouble could be found. If cows got chilly, did not hurt corn; if lights failed over wheat, vegetables were okay. That Mike could raise hell with Warden's residence and nobody could figure out what to do shows silliness of piling everything into one computer.

Mike was happy-joyed. This was humor he really scanned. I enjoyed it, too, told him to go ahead, have fun—spread out tools, got out little black box.

And computerman-of-the-watch comes banging and ringing at door. I took my time answering and carried number-five arm in right hand with short wing bare; this makes some people sick and upsets almost everybody. "What in hell do *you* want, choom?" I inquired.

"Listen," he says, "Warden is raising hell! Haven't you found trouble?"

"My compliments to Warden and tell him I will override by hand to restore his precious comfort as soon as I locate faulty circuit—if not slowed up by silly questions. Are you going to stand with door open blowing dust into machines while I have cover plates off? If you do—since you're in charge—when dust puts machine on sputter, *you* can repair it. *I* won't leave a warm bed to help. You can tell that to your bloody Warden, too."

"Watch your language, cobber."

"Watch yours, convict. Are you going to close that door? Or shall I walk out and go back to L-City?" And raised number-five like a club.

He closed door. Had no interest in insulting poor sod. Was one small bit of policy to make everybody as unhappy as possible. He was finding working for Warden difficult; I wanted to make it unbearable.

"Shall I step it up?" Mike inquired.

"Um, hold it so for ten minutes, then stop abruptly. Then jog it for an hour, say with air pressure. Erratic but hard. Know what a sonic boom is?"

"Certainly. It is a—"

"Don't define. After you drop major effect, rattle his air ducts every few minutes with nearest to a boom system will produce. Then give him something to remember. Mmm . . . Mike, can you make his W.C. run backwards?"

"I surely can! All of them?"

"How many does he have?"

"Six."

"Well . . . program to give them all a push, enough to soak his rugs. But if you can spot one nearest his bedroom, fountain it clear to ceiling. Can?"

"Program set up!"

"Good. Now for your present, ducky." There was room in voder audio box to hide it and I spent forty minutes with number-three, getting it just so. We trial-checked through voder-vocoder, then I told him to call Wyoh and check each circuit.

For ten minutes was silence, which I spent putting tool markers on a cover plate which should have been removed had been anything wrong, putting tools away, putting number-six arm on, rolling up one thousand jokes waiting in print-out. I had found no need to cut out audio of voder; Mike had thought of it before I had and always chopped off any time door was touched. Since his reflexes were better than mine by a factor of at least a thousand, I forgot it.

At last he said, "All twenty circuits okay. I can switch circuits in the middle of a word and Wyoh can't detect discontinuity. And I called Prof and said Hello and talked to Mum on your home phone, all three at the same time."

"We're in business. What excuse you give Mum?"

"I asked her to have you call me, Adam Selene that is. Then we chatted. She's a charming conversationalist. We discussed Greg's sermon of last Tuesday."

"Huh? How?"

"I told her I had listened to it, Man, and quoted a poetic part."

"Oh, Mike!"

"It's okay, Man. I let her think that I sat in back, then slipped out during the closing hymn. She's not nosy; she knows that I don't want to be seen."

Mum is nosiest female in Luna. "Guess it's okay. But don't do it again. Um— *Do* do it again. You go to—you monitor—meetings and lectures and concerts and stuff."

"Unless some busybody switches me off by hand! Man, I can't control those spot pickups the way I do a phone."

"Too simple a switch. Brute muscle rather than solid-state flipflop."

"That's barbaric. And unfair."

"Mike, almost everything is unfair. What can't be cured—"

"—must be endured. That's a funny-once, Man."

"Sorry. Let's change it: What can't be cured should be tossed out and something better put in. Which we'll do. What chances last time you calculated?"

"Approximately one in nine, Man."

"Getting worse?"

"Man, they'll get worse for months. We haven't reached the crisis."

"With Yankees in cellar, too. Oh, well. Back to other matter. From now on, when you talk to anyone, if he's been to a lecture or whatever, you were there, too—and prove it, by recalling something."

"Noted. Why, Man?"

"Have you read 'The Scarlet Pimpernel'? May be in public library."

"Yes. Shall I read it back?"

"No, no! You're our Scarlet Pimpernel, our John Galt, our Swamp Fox, our man of mystery. You go everywhere, know everything, slip in and out of town without passport. You're always there, yet nobody catches sight of you."

His lights rippled, he gave a subdued chuckle. "That's fun, Man. Funny once, funny twice, maybe funny always."

"Funny always. How long ago did you stop gymkhana at Warden's?"

"Forty-three minutes ago except erratic booms."

"Bet his teeth ache! Give him fifteen minutes more. Then I'll report job completed."

"Noted. Wyoh sent you a message, Man. She said to remind you of Billy's birthday party."

"Oh, my word! Stop everything, I'm leaving. 'Bye!" I hurried out. Billy's mother is Anna. Probably her last—and right well she's done by us, eight kids, three still home. I try to be as careful as Mum never to show favoritism . . . but Billy is quite a boy and I taught him to read. Possible he looks like me.

Stopped at Chief Engineer's office to leave bill and demanded to see him. Was let in and he was in belligerent mood; Warden had been riding him. "Hold it," I told him. "My son's birthday and shan't be late. But must show you something."

Took an envelope from kit, dumped item on desk: corpse of house fly which I had charred with a hot wire and fetched. We do not tolerate flies in Davis Tunnels but sometimes one wanders in from city as locks are opened. This wound up in my workshop just when I needed it. "See that? Guess where I found it."

On that faked evidence I built a lecture on care of fine machines, talked about doors opened, complained about man on watch. "Dust can ruin a computer. *Insects* are unpardonable! Yet your watch-standers wander in and out as if tube station. Today both doors held open—while this idiot yammered. If I find more evidence that cover plates have been removed by hoof-handed choom who attracts flies—well, it's your plant, Chief. Got more than I can handle, been doing your chores because I like fine machines. Can't stand to see them abused! Good-bye."

"Hold on. I want to tell *you* something."

"Sorry, got to go. Take it or leave it, I'm no vermin exterminator; I'm a computerman."

Nothing frustrates a man so much as not letting him get in his say. With luck and help from Warden, Chief Engineer would have ulcers by Christmas.

Was late anyhow and made humble apology to Billy. Alvarez had thought up new wrinkle, close search on leaving Complex. I endured it with never a nasty word for Dragoons who searched me; wanted to get home. But those thousand jokes bothered them. "What's this?" one demanded.

"Computer paper," I said. "Test runs."

His mate joined him. Don't think they could read. They wanted to confiscate, so I demanded they call Chief Engineer. They let me go. I felt not displeased; more and more such and guards were daily more hated.

Decision to make Mike more a person arose from need to have any Party member phone him on occasion; my advice about concerts and plays was simply a side effect. Mike's voice over phone had odd quality I had not noticed during time I had visited him only at Complex. When you speak to a man by phone there is background noise. And you hear him breathe, hear heartbeats, body motions even though rarely conscious of these. Besides that, even if he speaks under a hush hood, noises get through, enough to "fill space," make him a body with surroundings.

With Mike was *none* of this.

By then Mike's voice was "human" in timbre and quality, recognizable. He was baritone, had North American accent with Aussie overtones; as "Michelle" he (she?) had a light soprano with French flavor. Mike's personality grew also. When first I introduced him to Wyoh and Prof he sounded like a pedantic child; in short weeks he flowered until I visualized a man about own age.

His voice when he first woke was blurred and harsh, hardly understandable. Now it was clear and choice of words and phrasing was consistent—colloquial to me, scholarly to Prof, gallant to Wyoh, variation one expects of mature adults.

But background was dead. Thick silence.

So we filled it. Mike needed only hints. He did not make his breathing noisy, ordinarily you would not notice. But he would stick in touches. "Sorry, Mannie, you caught me bathing when the phone sounded"—and let one hear hurried breathing. Or "I was eating—had to swallow." He used such even on me, once he undertook to "be a human body."

We all put "Adam Selene" together, talking it over at Raffles. How old was he? What did he look like? Married? Where did he live? What work? What interests?

We decided that Adam was about forty, healthy, vigorous, well educated, interested in all arts and sciences and very well grounded in history, a match chess player but little time to play. He was married in commonest type, a troika in which he was senior husband—four children. Wife and junior husband not in politics, so far as we knew.

He was ruggedly handsome with wavy iron-gray hair and was mixed race, second generation one side, third on other. Was wealthy by Loonie standards, with interests in Novylen and Kongville as well as L-City. He kept offices in Luna City, outer office with a dozen people plus private office staffed by male deputy and female secretary.

Wyoh wanted to know was he bundling with secretary? I told her to switch off, was private. Wyoh said indignantly that she was not being snoopy—weren't we trying to create a rounded character?

We decided that offices were in Old Dome, third ramp, southside, heart of financial district. If you know L-City, you recall that in Old Dome some offices have windows since they can look out over floor of Dome; I wanted this for sound effects.

We drew a floor plan and had that office existed, it would have been between Aetna Luna and Greenberg & Co. I used pouch recorder to pick up sounds at spot; Mike added to it by listening at phones there.

Thereafter when you called Adam Selene, background was *not* dead. If "Ursula," his secretary, took call, it was: "Selene Associates. Luna shall be free!" Then she might say, "Will you hold? Gospodin Selene is on another call" whereupon you might hear sound of W.C., followed by running water and know that she had told little white lie. Or Adam might answer: "Adam Selene here. Free Luna. One second while I shut off the video." Or deputy might answer: "This is Albert Ginwallah, Adam Selene's confidential assistant. Free Luna. If it's a Party matter—as I assume it is; that was your Party name you gave—please don't hesitate; I handle such things for the Chairman."

Last was a trap, as every comrade was instructed to speak only to Adam Selene. No attempt was made to discipline one who took bait; instead his cell captain was warned that his comrade must not be trusted with anything vital.

We got echoes. "Free Luna!" or "Luna shall be free!" took hold among youngsters, then among solid citizens. First time I heard it in a business call I almost swallowed teeth. Then called Mike and asked if this person was Party member? Was not. So I recommended that Mike trace down Party tree and see if somebody could recruit him.

Most interesting echo was in File Zebra. "Adam Selene" appeared in boss fink's security file less than a lunar after we created him, with notation that this was a cover name for a leader in a new underground.

Alvarez's spies did a job on Adam Selene. Over course of months his File Zebra dossier built up: Male, 34–45, offices south face of Old Dome, usually there 0900–1800 Gr. except Saturday but calls are relayed at other hours, home inside urban pressure as travel time never exceeds seventeen minutes. Children in household. Activities include stock brokerage, farming interests. Attends theater, concerts, etc. Probably member Luna City Chess Club and Luna Assoc, d'Echecs. Plays ricochet and other heavy sports lunch hour, probably Luna City Athletic Club. Gourmet but watches weight. Remarkable memory plus mathematical ability. Executive type, able to reach decisions quickly.

One fink was convinced that he had talked to Adam between acts at revival of *Hamlet* by Civic Players; Alvarez noted description—and matched our picture all but wavy hair!

But thing that drove Alvarez crackers was that phone numbers for Adam were reported and every time they turned out wrong numbers. (Not nulls; we had run out and Mike was using any number not in use and switching numbers anytime new subscribers were assigned ones we had been using.) Alvarez tried to trace "Selene Associates" using a one-wrong-digit assumption—this we learned because Mike was keeping an ear on Alvarez's office phone and heard order. Mike used knowledge to play a Mikish prank: Subordinate who made one-changed-digit calls invariably reached Warden's private residence. So Alvarez was called in and chewed by Warden.

Couldn't scold Mike but did warn him it would alert any smart person to fact that somebody was playing tricks with computer. Mike answered that they were not that smart.

Main result of Alvarez's efforts was that each time he got a number for Adam we located a spy—a new spy, as those we had spotted earlier were never given phone numbers; instead they were recruited into a tail-chasing organization where they could inform on each other. But with Alvarez's help we spotted each new spy almost at once. I think Alvarez became unhappy over spies he was able to hire; two disappeared and our organization, then over six thousand, was never able to find them. Eliminated, I suppose, or died under questioning.

Selene Associates was not only phony company we set up. LuNoHoCo was much larger, just as phony, and not at all dummy; it had main offices in Hong Kong, branches in Novy Leningrad and Luna City, eventually employed hundreds of people most of whom were not Party members, and was our most difficult operation.

Mike's master plan listed a weary number of problems which *had* to be solved. One was finance. Another was how to protect catapult from space attack.

Prof considered robbing banks to solve first, gave it up reluctantly. But eventually we did rob banks, firms, and Authority itself. Mike thought of it. Mike and Prof worked it out. At first was not clear to Mike why we needed money. He knew as little about pressure that keeps humans scratching as he knew about sex; Mike handled millions of dollars and could not see any problem. He started by offering to issue an Authority cheque for whatever dollars we wanted.

Prof shied in horror. He then explained to Mike hazard in trying to cash a cheque for, let us say, AS$10,000,000 drawn on Authority.

So they undertook to do it, but retail, in many names and places all over Luna. Every bank, firm, shop, agency including Authority, for which Mike did accounting, was tapped for Party funds. Was a pyramided swindle based on fact, unknown to me but known to Prof and latent in Mike's immense knowledge, that most money is simply bookkeeping.

Example—multiply by hundreds of many types: My family son Sergei, eighteen and a Party member, is asked to start account at Commonwealth Shared Risk. He makes deposits and withdrawals. Small errors are made each time; he is credited with more than he deposits, is debited with less than he withdraws. A few months later he takes job out of town and transfers account to Tycho-Under Mutual; transferred funds are three times already-inflated amount. Most of this he soon draws out in cash and passes to his cell leader. Mike knows amount Sergei should hand over, but (since they do not know that Adam Selene and bank's computer-bookeeper are one and same) they have each been instructed to report transaction to Adam—keep them honest though scheme was not.

Multiply this theft of about HK$3,000 by hundreds somewhat like it.

I can't describe jiggery-pokery Mike used to balance his books while keeping thousands of thefts from showing. But bear in mind that an auditor must assume that machines are honest. He will make test runs to check that machines are working correctly—but will not occur to him that tests prove nothing because machine itself is dishonest. Mike's thefts were never large enough to disturb economy; like half-liter of blood, amount was too small to hurt donor. I can't make up mind who lost, money was swapped around so many ways. But scheme troubled me; I was brought up to be honest, except with Authority. Prof claimed that what was taking place was a mild inflation offset by fact that we plowed money back in—but I should remember that Mike had records and all could be restored after Revolution, with ease since we would no longer be bled in much larger amounts by Authority.

I told conscience to go to sleep. Was pipsqueak compared to swindles by every government throughout history in financing every war—and is not revolution a war?

This money, after passing through many hands (augmented by Mike each time), wound up as senior financing of LuNoHo Company. Was a mixed company, mutual and stock; "gentleman-adventurer" guarantors who backed stock put up that stolen money in own names. Won't discuss bookkeeping this firm used. Since Mike ran everything, was not corrupted by any tinge of honesty.

Nevertheless its shares were traded in Hong Kong Luna Exchange and listed in Zurich, London, and New York. *Wall Street Journal* called it "an attractive high-risk-high-gain investment with novel growth potential."

LuNoHoCo was an engineering and exploitation firm, engaged in many ventures, mostly legitimate. But prime purpose was to build a second catapult, secretly.

Operation could not be secret. You can't buy or build a hydrogen-fusion power plant for such and not have it noticed. (Sunpower was rejected for obvious reasons.) Parts were ordered from Pittsburgh, standard UnivCalif equipment, and we happily paid their royalties to get top quality. Can't build a stator for a kilometers-long induction field without having it noticed, either. But most important you cannot do major construction hiring many people and not have it show. Sure, catapults are mostly vacuum; stator rings aren't even close together at ejection end. But Authority's 3-g catapult was almost one hundred kilometers long. It was not only an astrogation landmark, on every Luna-jump chart, but was so big it could be photographed or seen by eye from Terra with not-large telescope. It showed up beautifully on a radar screen.

We were building a shorter catapult, a 10-g job, but even that was thirty kilometers long, too big to hide.

So we hid it by *Purloined Letter* method.

I used to question Mike's endless reading of fiction, wondering what notions he was getting. But turned out he got a better feeling for human life from stories than he had been able to garner from facts; fiction gave him a gestalt of life, one taken for granted by a human; he lives it. Besides this "humanizing" effect, Mike's substitute for experience, he got ideas from "not-true data" as he called fiction. How to hide a catapult he got from Edgar Allan Poe.

We hid it in literal sense, too; this catapult had to be underground, so that it would not show to eye or radar. But had to be hidden in more subtle sense; selenographic location had to be secret.

How can this be, with a monster that big, worked on by so many people? Put it this way: Suppose you live in Novylen; know where Luna City is? Why, on east edge of Mare Crisium; everybody knows that. So? What latitude and longitude? Huh? Look it up in a reference book! So? If you don't know *where* any better than that, how did you find it last week? No huhu, cobber; I took tube, changed at Torricelli, slept rest of way; finding it was capsule's worry.

See? You *don't know* where Luna City is! You simply get out when capsule pulls in at Tube Station South.

That's how we hid catapult.

Is in Mare Undarum area, "everybody knows that." But where it *is* and where we *said it was* differ by amount greater or less than one hundred kilometers in direction north, south, east, or west, or some combination.

Today you can look up its location in reference books—and find same wrong answer. Location of that catapult is still most closely guarded secret in Luna.

Can't be seen from space, by eye or radar. Is underground save for ejection and that is a big black shapeless hole like ten thousand others and high up an uninviting mountain with no place for a jump rocket to put down.

Nevertheless many people were there, during and after construction. Even Warden visited and my co-husband Greg showed him around. Warden went by mail rocket, commandeered for day, and his Cyborg was given coordinates and a radar beacon to home on—a spot in fact not far from site. But from there was necessary to travel by rolligon and our lorries were not like passenger buses from Endsville to Beluthihatchie in old days; they were cargo carriers, no ports for sightseeing and a ride so rough that human cargo had to be strapped down. Warden wanted to ride up in cab but—sorry, Gospodin!—just space for wrangler and his heiper and took both to keep her steady.

Three hours later he did not care about anything but getting home. He stayed one hour and was not interested in talk about purpose of all this drilling and value of resources uncovered.

Less important people, workmen and others, traveled by interconnecting ice-exploration bores, still easier way to get lost. If anybody carried an inertial pathfinder in his luggage, he could have located site—but security was tight. One did so had accident with p-suit; his effects were returned to L-City and his pathfinder read what it should—i.e., what we *wanted* it to read, for I made hurried trip out with number-three arm along. You can reseal one without a trace if you do it in nitrogen atmosphere—I wore an oxygen mask at slight overpressure. No huhu.

We entertained vips from Earth, some high in Authority. They traveled easier underground route; I suppose Warden had warned them. But even on that route is one thirty-kilometer stretch by rolligon. We had one visitor from Earth who looked like trouble, a Dr. Dorian, physicist and engineer. Lorry tipped over—silly driver tried shortcut—they were not in line-of-sight for anything and their beacon was smashed. Poor Dr. Dorian spent seventy-two hours in an unsealed pumice igloo and had to be returned to L-City ill from hypoxia and overdose of radiation despite efforts on his behalf by two Party members driving him.

Might have been safe to let him see; he might not have spotted doubletalk and would not have spotted error in location. Few people look at stars when p-suited even when Sun doesn't make it futile; still fewer can read stars—and nobody can locate himself on surface without help unless he has instruments, knows how to use them and has tables and something to give a time tick. Put at crudest level, minimum would be octant, tables, and good watch. Our visitors were even encouraged to go out on surface but if one had carried an octant or modern equivalent, might have had accident.

We did not make accidents for spies. We let them stay, worked them hard, and Mike read their reports. One reported that he was certain that we had found uranium ore, something unknown in Luna at that time, Project Centerbore being many years later. Next spy came out with kit of radiation counters. We made it easy for him to sneak them through bore.

By March '76 catapult was almost ready, lacking only installation of stator segments. Power plant was in and a co-ax had been strung underground with a line-of-sight link for that thirty kilometers. Crew was down to skeleton size, mostly Party members. But we kept one spy so that Alvarez could have regular reports—didn't want him to worry; it tended to make him suspicious. Instead we worried him in warrens.

TEN

Were changes in those eleven months. Wyoh was baptized into Greg's church, Prof's health became so shaky that he dropped teaching, Mike took up writing poetry. Yankees finished in cellar. Wouldn't have minded paying Prof if they had been nosed out, but from pennant to cellar in one season—I quit watching them on video.

Prof's illness was phony. He was in perfect shape for age, exercising in hotel room three hours each day, and sleeping in three hundred kilograms of lead pajamas. And so was I, and so was Wyoh, who hated it.

I don't think she ever cheated and spent night in comfort though can't say for sure; I was not dossing with her. She had become a fixture in Davis family. Took her one day to go from "Gospazha

Davis" to "Gospazha Mum," one more to reach "Mum" and now it might be "Mimi Mum" with arm around Mum's waist. When Zebra File showed she couldn't go back to Hong Kong, Sidris had taken Wyoh into her beauty shop after hours and done a job which left skin same dark shade but would not scrub off. Sidris also did a hairdo on Wyoh that left it black and looking as if unsuccessfully unkinked. Plus minor touches—opaque nail enamel, plastic inserts for cheeks and nostrils and of course she wore her dark-eyed contact lenses. When Sidris got through, Wyoh could have gone bundling without fretting about her disguise; was a perfect "colored" with ancestry to match—Tamil, a touch of Angola, German. I called her "Wyma" rather than "Wyoh."

She was gorgeous. When she undulated down a corridor, boys followed in swarms.

She started to learn farming from Greg but Mum put stop to that. While she was big and smart and willing, our farm is mostly a male operation—and Greg and Hans were not only male members of our family distracted; she cost more farming man-hours than her industry equaled. So Wyoh went back to housework, then Sidris took her into beauty shop as helper.

Prof played ponies with two accounts, betting one by Mike's "leading apprentice" system, other by his own "scientific" system. By July '75 he admitted that he knew nothing about horses and went solely to Mike's system, increasing bets and spreading them among many bookies. His winnings paid Party's expenses while Mike built swindle that financed catapult. But Prof lost interest in a sure thing and merely placed bets as Mike designated. He stopped reading pony journals—sad, something dies when an old horseplayer quits.

Ludmilla had a girl which they say is lucky in a first and which delighted me—every family needs a girl baby. Wyoh surprised our women by being expert in midwifery—and surprised them again that she knew nothing about baby care. Our two oldest sons found marriages at last and Teddy, thirteen, was opted out. Greg hired two lads from neighbor farms and, after six months of working and eating with us, both were opted in—not rushing things, we had known them and their families for years. It restored balance we had lacked since Ludmilla's opting and put stop to snide remarks from mothers of bachelors who had not found marriages—not that Mum wasn't capable of snubbing anyone she did not consider up to Davis standards.

Wyoh recruited Sidris; Sidris started own cell by recruiting her other assistant and Bon Ton Beauté Shoppe became hotbed of subversion. We started using our smallest kids for deliveries and other jobs a child can do—they can stake-out or trail a person through corridors better than an adult, and are not suspected. Sidris grabbed this notion and expanded it through women recruited in beauty parlor.

Soon she had so many kids on tap that we could keep all of Alvarez's spies under surveillance. With Mike able to listen at any phone and a child spotting it whenever a spy left home or place of work or wherever—with enough kids on call so that one could phone while another held down a new stakeout—we could keep a spy under tight observation and keep him from seeing anything we didn't want him to see. Shortly we were getting reports spies phoned in without waiting for Zebra File; it did a sod no good to phone from a taproom instead of home; with Baker Street Irregulars on job Mike was listening before he finished punching number.

These kids located Alvarez's deputy spy boss in L-City. We knew he had one because these finks did *not* report to Alvarez by phone, nor did it seem possible that Alvarez could have recruited them as none of them worked in Complex and Alvarez came inside Luna City only when an Earthside vip was so important as to rate a bodyguard commanded by Alvarez in person.

His deputy turned out to be two people—an old lag who ran a candy, news, and bookie counter in Old Dome and his son who was on civil service in Complex. Son carried reports in, so Mike had not been able to hear them.

We let them alone. But from then on we had fink field reports half a day sooner than Alvarez. This advantage—all due to kids as young as five or six—saved lives of seven comrades. All glory to Baker Street Irregulars!

Don't remember who named them but think it was Mike—I was

merely a Sherlock Homes fan whereas he really did think he was Sherlock Holmes's brother Mycroft . . . nor would I swear he was not; "reality" is a slippery notion. Kids did not call themselves that; they had their own play gangs with own names. Nor were they burdened with secrets which could endanger them; Sidris left it to mothers to explain why they were being asked to do these jobs save that they were *never* to be told real reason. Kids will do anything mysterious and fun; look how many of their games are based on outsmarting.

Bon Ton salon was a clearinghouse of gossip—women got news faster than *Daily Lunatic*. I encouraged Wyoh to report to Mike each night, not try to thin gossip down to what seemed significant because was no telling what might be significant once Mike got through associating it with a million other facts.

Beauty parlor was also place to start rumors. Party had grown slowly at first, then rapidly as powers-of-three began to be felt and also because Peace Dragoons were nastier than older bodyguard. As numbers increased we shifted to high speed on agitprop, black-propaganda rumors, open subversion, provocateur activities, and sabotage. Finn Nielsen handled agitprop when it was simpler as well as dangerous job of continuing to front for and put cover-up activity into older, spy-ridden underground. But now a large chunk of agitprop and related work was given to Sidris.

Much involved distributing handbills and such. No subversive literature was ever in her shop, nor our home, nor that hotel room; distribution was done by kids, too young to read.

Sidris was also working a full day bending hair and such. About time she began to have too much to do I happened one evening to make walk-about on Causeway with Sidris on my arm when I caught sight of a familiar face and figure—skinny little girl, all angles, carrot-red hair. She was possibly twelve, at stage when a fem shoots up just before blossoming out into rounded softness. I knew her but could not say why or when or where.

I said, "*Psst,* doll baby. Eyeball young fem ahead. Orange hair, no cushions."

Sidris looked her over. "Darling, I knew you were eccentric. But she's still a boy."

"Damp it. Who?"

"Bog knows. Shall I sprag her?"

Suddenly I remembered like video coming on. And wished Wyoh were with me—but Wyoh and I were never together in public. This skinny redhead had been at meeting where Shorty was killed. She sat on floor against wall down front and listened with wide-eyed seriousness and applauded fiercely. Than I had seen her at end in free trajectory—curled into ball in air and had hit a yellow jacket in knees, he whose jaw I broke a moment later.

Wyoh and I were alive and free because this kid moved fast in a crisis. "No, don't speak to her," I told Sidris. "But I want to keep her in sight. Wish we had one of your Irregulars here. Damn."

"Drop off and phone Wyoh, you'll have one in five minutes," my wife said.

I did. Then Sidris and I strolled, looking in shopwindows and moving slowly, as quarry was window-shopping. In seven or eight minutes a small boy came toward us, stopped and said, "Hello, Auntie Mabel! Hi, Uncle Joe."

Sidris took his hand. "Hi, Tony. How's your mother, dear?"

"Just fine." He added in a whisper, "I'm Jock."

"Sorry." Sidris said quietly to me, "Stay on her," and took Jock into a tuck shop.

She came out and joined me. Jock followed her licking a lollipop. " 'Bye, Auntie Mabel! Thanks!" He danced away, rotating, wound up by that little redhead, stood and stared into a display, solemnly sucking his sweet. Sidris and I went home.

A report was waiting. "She went into Cradle Roll Crêche and hasn't come out. Do we stay on it?"

"A bit yet," I told Wyoh, and asked if she remembered this kid. She did, but had no idea who she might be. "You could ask Finn."

"Can do better." I called Mike.

Yes, Cradle Roll Crêche had a phone and Mike would listen. Took him twenty minutes to pick up enough to give analysis—many young voices and at such ages almost sexless. But presently he told me, "Man, I hear three voices that could match the age and physical type you described. However, two answer to names which I assume to be masculine. The third answers when anyone says

'Hazel'—which an older female voice does repeatedly. She seems to be Hazel's boss."

"Mike, look at old organization file. Check Hazels."

"Four Hazels," he answered at once, "and here she is: Hazel Meade, Young Comrades Auxiliary, address Cradle Roll Crêche, born 25 December 2063, mass thirty-nine kilos, height—"

"That's our little jump jet! Thanks, Mike. Wyoh, call off stake-out. Good job!"

"Mike, call Donna and pass the word, that's a dear."

I left it to girls to recruit Hazel Meade and did not eyeball her until Sidris moved her into our household two weeks later. But Wyoh volunteered a report before then; policy was involved. Sidris had filled her cell but wanted Hazel Meade. Besides this irregularity, Sidris was doubtful about recruiting a child. Policy was adults only, sixteen and up.

I took it to Adam Selene and executive cell. "As I see," I said, "this cells-of-three system is to serve us, not bind us. See nothing wrong in Comrade Cecilia having an extra. Nor any real danger to security."

"I agree," said Prof. "But I suggest that the extra member not be part of Cecilia's cell—she should not know the others, I mean, unless the duties Cecilia gives her make it necessary. Nor do I think she should recruit, at her age. The real question is her age."

"Agreed," said Wyoh. "I want to talk about this kid's age."

"Friends," Mike said diffidently (diffidently first time in weeks; he was now that confident executive "Adam Selene" much more than lonely machine)—"perhaps I should have told you, but I have already granted similar variations. It did not seem to require discussion."

"It doesn't, Mike," Prof reassured him. "A chairman must use his own judgment. What is our largest cell?"

"Five. It is a double cell, three and two."

"No harm done. Dear Wyoh, does Sidris propose to make this child a full comrade? Let her know that we are committed to revolution . . . with all the bloodshed, disorder, and possible disaster that entails?"

"That's exactly what she is requesting."

"But, dear lady, while we are staking our lives, we are old enough to know it. For that, one should have an emotional grasp of death. Children seldom are able to realize that death will come to them personally. One might define adulthood as the age at which a person learns that he must die . . . and accepts his sentence undismayed."

"Prof," I said, "I know some mighty tall children. Seven to two some are in Party."

"No bet, cobber. I'll give odds that at least half of them don't qualify—and we may find it out the hard way at the end of this our folly."

"Prof," Wyoh insisted. "Mike, Mannie. Sidris is *certain* this child is an adult. And I think so, too."

"Man?" asked Mike.

"Let's find way for Prof to meet her and form own opinion. I was taken by her. Especially her go-to-hell fighting. Or would never have started it."

We adjourned and I heard no more. Hazel showed up at dinner shortly thereafter as Sidris' guest. She showed no sign of recognizing me, nor did I admit that I had ever seen her—but learned long after that she had recognized me, not just by left arm but because I had been hatted and kissed by tall blonde from Hong Kong. Furthermore Hazel had seen through Wyoming's disguise, recognized what Wyoh never did successfully disguise: her voice.

But Hazel used lip glue. If she ever assumed I was in conspiracy she never showed it.

Child's history explained her, far as background can explain steely character. Transported with parents as a baby much as Wyoh had been, she had lost father through accident while he was convict labor, which her mother blamed on indifference of Authority to safety of penal colonists. Her mother lasted till Hazel was five; what she died from Hazel did not know; she was then living in crêche where we found her. Nor did she know why parents had been shipped—possibly for subversion if they were both under sentence as Hazel thought. As may be, her mother left her a fierce hatred of Authority and Warden.

Family that ran Cradle Roll let her stay; Hazel was pinning diapers and washing dishes as soon as she could reach. She had taught herself to read, and could print letters but could not write. Her knowledge of math was only that ability to count money that children soak up through their skins.

Was fuss over her leaving crêche; owner and husbands claimed Hazel owed several years' service. Hazel solved it by walking out, leaving her clothes and fewer belongings behind. Mum was angry enough to want family to start trouble which could wind up in "brawling" she despised. But I told her privately that, as her cell leader, I did *not* want our family in public eye—and hauled out cash and told her Party would pay for clothes for Hazel. Mum refused money, called off a family meeting, took Hazel into town and was extravagant—for Mum—in re-outfitting her.

So we adopted Hazel. I understand that these days adopting a child involves red tape; in those days it was as simple as adopting a kitten.

Was more fuss when Mum started to place Hazel in school, which fitted neither what Sidris had in mind nor what Hazel had been led to expect as a Party member and comrade. Again I butted in and Mum gave in part way. Hazel was placed in a tutoring school close to Sidris' shop—that is, near easement lock thirteen; beauty parlor was by it (Sidris had good business because close enough that our water was piped in, and used without limit as return line took it back for salvage). Hazel studied mornings and helped in afternoons, pinning on gowns, handing out towels, giving rinses, learning trade—and whatever else Sidris wanted.

"Whatever else" was captain of Baker Street Irregulars.

Hazel had handled younger kids all her short life. They liked her; she could wheedle them into anything; she understood what they said when an adult would find it gibberish. She was a perfect bridge between Party and most junior auxiliary. She could make a game of chores we assigned and persuade them to play by rules she gave them, and never let them know it was adult-serious—but child-serious, which is another matter.

For example:

Let's say a little one, too young to read, is caught with a stack of subversive literature—which happened more than once. Here's how it would go, after Hazel indoctrinated a kid:

ADULT: "Baby, where did you get this?"

BAKER STREET IRREGULAR: "I'm not a baby, I'm a big boy!"

ADULT: "Okay, big boy, where did you get this?"

B.S.I.: "Jackie give it to me."

ADULT: "Who is Jackie?"

B.S.I.: "Jackie."

ADULT: "But what's his last name?"

B.S.I.: "Who?"

ADULT: "Jackie."

B.S.I.: (scornfully) "Jackie's a girl!"

ADULT: "All right, where does she live?"

B.S.I.: "Who?"

And so on around— To all questions key answer was of pattern: "Jackie give it to me." Since Jackie didn't exist, he (she) didn't have a last name, a home address, nor fixed sex. Those children enjoyed making fools of adults, once they learned how easy it was.

At worst, literature was confiscated. Even a squad of Peace Dragoons thought twice before trying to "arrest" a small child. Yes, we were beginning to have squads of Dragoons inside Luna City, but never less than a squad—some had gone in singly and not come back.

When Mike started writing poetry I didn't know whether to laugh or cry. He wanted to publish it! Shows how thoroughly humanity had corrupted this innocent machine that he should wish to see his name in print.

I said, "Mike, for Bog's sake! Blown all circuits? Or planning to give us away?"

Before he could sulk Prof said, "Hold on, Manuel; I see possibilities. Mike, would it suit you to take a pen name?"

That's how "Simon Jester" was born. Mike picked it apparently by tossing random numbers. But he used another name for serious verse, his Party name, Adam Selene.

"Simon's" verse was doggerel, bawdy, subversive, ranging from poking fun at vips to savage attacks on Warden, system, Peace Dragoons, finks. You found it on walls of public W.C.s, or on scraps of paper left in tube capsules. Or in taprooms. Wherever they were, they were signed "Simon Jester" and with a matchstick drawing of a little horned devil with big grin and forked tail. Sometimes he was stabbing a fat man with a pitchfork. Sometimes just his face would appear, big grin and horns, until shortly even horns and grin meant "Simon was here."

Simon appeared all over Luna same day and from then on never let up. Shortly he started receiving volunteer help; his verses and little pictures, so simple anybody could draw them, began appearing more places than we had planned. This wider coverage *had* to be from fellow travelers. Verses and cartoons started appearing inside Complex—which could *not* have been our work; we never recruited civil servants. Also, three days after initial appearance of a very rough limerick, one that implied that Warden's fatness derived from unsavory habits, this limerick popped up on pressure-sticky labels with cartoon improved so that fat victim flinching from Simon's pitchfork was recognizably Mort the Wart. *We* didn't buy them, *we* didn't print them. But they appeared in L-City and Novylen and Hong Kong, stuck almost everywhere—public phones, stanchions in corridors, pressure locks, ramp railings, other. I had a sample count made, fed it to Mike; he reported that over seventy thousand labels had been used in L-City alone.

I did not know of a printing plant in L-City willing to risk such a job and equipped for it. Began to wonder if might be another revolutionary cabal?

Simon's verses were such a success that he branched out as a poltergeist and neither Warden nor security chief was allowed to miss it. "Dear Mort the Wart," ran one letter. "Do please be careful from midnight to four hundred tomorrow. Love & Kisses, Simon"—with horns and grin. In same mail Alvarez received one reading: "Dear Pimplehead, If the Warden breaks his leg tomorrow night it will be *your* fault. Faithfully your conscience, Simon"—again with horns and smile.

We didn't have anything planned; we just wanted Mort and Alvarez to lose sleep—which they did, plus bodyguard. All Mike did was to call Warden's private phone at intervals from midnight to four hundred—an unlisted number supposedly known only to his personal staff. By calling members of his personal staff simultaneously and connecting them to Mort, Mike not only created confusion but got Warden angry at his assistants—he flatly refused to believe their denials.

But was luck that Warden, goaded too far, ran *down* a ramp. Even a new chum does that only once. So he walked on air and sprained an ankle—close enough to a broken leg and Alvarez was there when it happened.

Those sleep-losers were mostly just that. Like rumor that Authority catapult had been mined and would be blown up, another night. Ninety plus eighteen men can't search a hundred kilometers of catapult in hours, especially when ninety are Peace Dragoons not used to p-suit work and hating it—this midnight came at new earth with Sun high; they were outside far longer than is healthy, managed to cook up their own accidents while almost cooking themselves, and showed nearest thing to mutiny in regiment's history. One accident was fatal. Did he fall or was he pushed? A sergeant.

Midnight alarums made Peace Dragoons on passport watch much taken by yawning and more bad-tempered, which produced more clashes with Loonies and still greater resentment both ways—so Simon increased pressure.

Adam Selene's verse was on a higher plane. Mike submitted it to Prof and accepted his literary judgment (good, I think) without resentment. Mike's scansion and rhyming were perfect, Mike being a computer with whole English language in his memory and able to search for a fitting word in microseconds. What was weak was self-criticism. That improved rapidly under Prof's stern editorship.

Adam Selene's by-line appeared first in dignified pages of *Moonglow* over a somber poem titled: "Home." Was dying thoughts of old transportee, his discovery as he is about to leave that Luna is his beloved home. Language was simple, rhyme scheme unforced, only thing faintly subversive was conclusion on part of dying man that even many wardens he has endured was not too high a price.

Doubt if *Moonglow*'s editors thought twice. Was good stuff, they published.

Alvarez turned editorial office inside out trying to get a line back to Adam Selene. Issue had been on sale half a lunar before Alvarez noticed it, or had it called to his attention; we were fretted, we *wanted* that by-line noticed. We were much pleased with way Alvarez oscillated when he did see it.

Editors were unable to help fink boss. They told him truth: Poem had come in by mail. Did they have it? Yes, surely . . . sorry, no envelope; they were never saved. After a long time Alvarez left, flanked by four Dragoons he had fetched along for his health.

Hope he enjoyed studying that sheet of paper. Was piece of Adam Selene's business stationery:

SELENE ASSOCIATES
LUNA CITY

Investments *Office of the Chairman*
Old Dome

—and under that was typed *Home*, by Adam Selene, etc.

Any fingerprints were added after it left us. Had been typed on Underwood Office Electrostator, commonest model in Luna. Even so, were not too many as are importado; a scientific detective could have identified machine. Would have found it in Luna City office of Lunar Authority. Machines, should say, as we found six of model in office and used them in rotation, five words and move to next. Cost Wyoh and self sleep and too much risk even though Mike listened at every phone, ready to warn. Never did it that way again.

Alvarez was not a scientific detective.

ELEVEN

In early '76 I had too much to do. Could not neglect customers. Party work took more time even though all possible was delegated. But decisions had to be made on endless things and messages passed up and down. Had to squeeze in hours of heavy exercise, wearing weights, and dasn't arrange permission to use centrifuge at Complex, one used by earthworm scientists to stretch time in Luna—while had used it before, this time could not advertise that I was getting in shape for Earthside.

Exercising without centrifuge is less efficient and was especially boring because did not know there would be need for it. But according to Mike 30 percent of ways events could fall required some Loonie, able to speak for Party, to make trip to Terra.

Could not see myself as an ambassador, don't have education and not diplomatic. Prof was obvious choice of those recruited or likely to be. But Prof was old, might not live to land Earthside. Mike told us that a man of Prof's age, body type, etc., had less than 40 percent chance of reaching Terra alive.

But Prof did gaily undertake strenuous training to let him make most of his poor chances, so what could I do but put on weights and get to work, ready to go and take his place if old heart clicked off? Wyoh did same, on assumption that something might keep me from going. She did it to share misery; Wyoh always used gallantry in place of logic.

On top of business, Party work, and exercise was farming. We had lost three sons by marriage while gaining two fine lads, Frank and Ali. Then Greg went to work for LuNoHoCo, as boss drillman on new catapult.

Was needful. Much skull sweat went into hiring construction crew. We could use non-Party men for most jobs, but key spots had to be Party men as competent as they were politically reliable. Greg did not want to go; our farm needed him and he did not like to leave his congregation. But accepted.

That made me again a valet, part time, to pigs and chickens. Hans is a good farmer, picked up load and worked enough for two men. But Greg had been farm manager ever since Grandpaw retired, new responsibility worried Hans. Should have been mine, being senior, but Hans was better farmer and closer to it; always been expected he would succeed Greg someday. So I backed him up by agreeing with his opinions and tried to be half a farm hand in hours I could squeeze. Left no time to scratch.

Late in February I was returning from long trip, Novylen, Tycho Under, Churchill. New tube had just been completed across Sinus Medii, so I went on to Hong Kong in Luna—business and did make contacts now that I could promise emergency service. Fact that Endsville-Beluthihatchie bus ran only during dark semi-lunar had made impossible before.

But business was cover for politics; liaison with Hong Kong had been thin. Wyoh had done well by phone; second member of her cell was an old comrade—"Comrade Clayton"—who not only had clean bill of health in Alverez's File Zebra but also stood high in Wyoh's estimation. Clayton was briefed on policies, warned of bad apples, encouraged to start cell system while leaving old organization untouched. Wyoh told him to keep his membership, as before.

But phone isn't face-to-face. Hong Kong should have been our stronghold. Was less tied to Authority as its utilities were not controlled from Complex; was less dependent because lack (until recently) of tube transport had made selling at catapult head less inviting; was stronger financially as Bank of Hong Kong Luna notes were better money than official Authority scrip.

I suppose Hong Kong dollars weren't "money" in some legal sense. Authority would not accept them; times I went Earthside had to buy Authority scrip to pay for ticket. But what I carried was Hong Kong dollars as could be traded Earthside at a small discount whereas scrip was nearly worthless there. Money or not, Hong Kong Bank notes were backed by honest Chinee bankers instead of being fiat of bureaucracy. One hundred Hong Kong dollars was 31.1 grams of gold (old troy ounce) payable on demand at home office—and they did keep gold there, fetched up from Australia. Or you could demand commodities: non-potable water, steel of defined grade, heavy water of power plant specs, other things. Could buy these with scrip, too, but Authority's prices kept changing, upward. I'm no fiscal theorist; time Mike tried to explain I got headache. Simply know we were glad to lay hands on this non-money whereas scrip one accepted reluctantly and not just because we hated Authority.

Hong Kong should have been Party's stronghold. But was not. We had decided that I should risk face-to-face there, letting some know my identity, as a man with one arm can't disguise easily. Was risk that would jeopardize not only me but could lead to Wyoh, Mum, Greg, and Sidris if I took a fall. But who said revolution was safe?

Comrade Clayton turned out to be young Japanese—not too young, but they all look young till suddenly look old. He was not all Japanese—Malay and other things—but had Japanese name and household had Japanese manners; "giri" and "gimu" controlled and it was my good fortune that he owed much gimu to Wyoh.

Clayton was not convict ancestry; his people had been "volunteers" marched aboard ship at gunpoint during time Great China consolidated Earthside empire. I didn't hold it against him; he hated Warden as bitterly as any old lag.

Met him first at a teahouse—taproom to us L-City types—and for two hours we talked everything but politics. He made up mind about me, took me home. My only complaint about Japanese hospitality is those chin-high baths are too bleeding hot.

But turned out I was not jeopardized. Mama-san was as skilled at makeup as Sidris, my social arm is very convincing, and a kimono covered its seam. Met four cells in two days, as "Comrade Bork" and wearing makeup and kimono and tabi and, if a spy was among them, don't think he could identify Manuel O'Kelly. I had gone there intensely briefed, endless figures and projections, and talked about just one thing: famine in '82, six years away. "You people are lucky, won't be hit so soon. But now with new tube, you are going to see more and more of your people turning to wheat and rice and shipping it to catapult head. Your time will come."

They were impressed. Old organization, as I saw it and from what I heard, relied on oratory, whoop-it-up music, and emotion, much like church. I simply said, "There it is, comrades. Check those figures; I'll leave them with you."

Met one comrade separately. A Chinee engineer given a good look at anything can figure way to make it. Asked this one if he had ever seen a laser gun small enough to carry like a rifle. He had not. Mentioned that passport system made it difficult to smuggle these days. He said thoughtfully that jewels ought not to be hard—and he would be in Luna City next week to see his cousin. I said Uncle Adam would be pleased to hear from him.

All in all was productive trip. On way back I stopped in Novylen to check an old-fashioned punched-tape "Foreman" I had overhauled earlier, had lunch afterwards, ran into my father. He and I were friendly but didn't matter if we let a couple of years go by. We talked through a sandwich and beer and as I got up he said, "Nice to see you, Mannie. Free Luna!"

I echoed, too startled not to. My old man was as cynically non-political as you could find; if he would say that in public, campaign must be taking hold.

So I arrived in L-City cheered up and not too tired, having napped from Torricelli. Took Belt from Tube South, then dropped down and through Bottom Alley, avoiding Causeway crowd and heading home. Went into Judge Brody's courtroom as I came to it, meaning to say hello. Brody is old friend and we have amputation in common. After he lost a leg he set up as a judge and was quite successful; was not another judge in L-City at that time who did not have side business, at least make book or sell insurance.

If two people brought a quarrel to Brody and he could not get them to agree that his settlement was just, he would return fees and, if they fought, referee their duel without charging—and still be trying to persuade them not to use knives right up to squaring off.

He wasn't in his courtroom though plug hat was on desk. Started to leave, only to be checked by group coming in, stilyagi types. A girl was with them, and an older man hustled by them. He was mussed, and clothing had that vague something that says "tourist."

We used to get tourists even then. Not hordes but quite a few. They would come up from Earth, stop in a hotel for a week, go back in same ship or perhaps stop over for next ship. Most of them spent their time gambling after a day or two of sightseeing including that silly walk up on surface every tourist makes. Most Loonies ignored them and granted them their foibles.

One lad, oldest, about eighteen and leader, said to me, "Where's judge?"

"Don't know. Not here."

He chewed lip, looked baffled. I said, "What trouble?"

He said soberly, "Going to eliminate this choom. But want judge to confirm it."

I said, "Cover taprooms here around. Probably find him."

A boy about fourteen spoke up. "Say! Aren't you Gospodin O'Kelly?"

"Right."

"Why don't *you* judge it."

Oldest looked relieved. "Will you, Gospodin?"

I hesitated. Sure, I've gone judge at times; who hasn't? But don't hanker for responsibility. However, it troubled me to hear young people talk about eliminating a tourist. Bound to cause talk.

Decided to do it. So I said to tourist, "Will you accept me as your judge?"

He looked surprised. "I have choice in the matter?"

I said patiently, "Of course. Can't expect me to listen if you aren't willing to accept my judging. But not urging you. Your life, not mine."

He looked very surprised but not afraid. His eyes lit up. "My life, did you say?"

"Apparently. You heard lads say they intend to eliminate you. You may prefer to wait for Judge Brody."

He didn't hesitate. Smiled and said, "I accept you as my judge, sir."

"As you wish." I looked at oldest lad. "What parties to quarrel? Just you and your young friend?"

"Oh, no, Judge, all of us."

"Not your judge yet." I looked around. "Do you all ask me to judge?"

Were nods; none said No. Leader turned to girl, added, "Better speak up, Tish. You accept Judge O'Kelly?"

"What? Oh, sure!" She was a vapid little thing, vacantly pretty, curvy, perhaps fourteen. Slot-machine type, and how she might wind up. Sort who prefers being queen over pack of stilyagi to solid marriage. I don't blame stilyagi; they chase around corridors because not enough females. Work all day and nothing to go home to at night.

"Okay, court has been accepted and all are bound to abide by my verdict. Let's settle fees. How high can you boys go? Please understand I'm not going to judge an elimination for dimes. So ante up or I turn him loose."

Leader blinked, they went into huddle. Shortly he turned and said, "We don't have much. Will you do it for five Kong dollars apiece?"

Six of them—"No. Ought not to ask a court to judge elimination at that price."

They huddled again. "Fifty dollars, Judge?"

"Sixty. Ten each. And another ten from you, Tish," I said to girl.

She looked surprised, indignant. "Come, come!" I said. "Tanstaafl."

She blinked and reached into pouch. She had money; types like that always have.

I collected seventy dollars, laid it on desk, and said to tourist, "Can match it?"

"Beg pardon?"

"Kids are paying seventy dollars Hong Kong for judgment. You should match it. If you can't, open pouch and prove it and can owe it to me. But that's your share." I added, "Cheap, for a capital case. But kids can't pay much so you get a bargain."

"I see. I believe I see." He matched with seventy Hong Kong.

"Thank you," I said. "Now does either side want a jury?"

Girl's eyes lit up. "Sure! Let's do it right."

Earthworm said, "Under the circumstances perhaps I need one."

"Can have it," I assured. "Want a counsel?"

"Why, I suppose I need a lawyer, too."

"I said 'counsel,' not 'lawyer.' Aren't any lawyers here."

Again he seemed delighted. "I suppose counsel, if I elected to have one, would be of the same, uh, informal quality as the rest of these proceedings?"

"Maybe, maybe not. I'm informal sort of judge, that's all. Suit yourself."

"Mm. I think I'll rely on your informality, your honor."

Oldest lad said, "Uh, this jury. You pick up chit? Or do we?"

"I pay it; I agreed to judge for a hundred forty, gross. Haven't you been in court before? But not going to kill my net for extra I could do without. Six jurymen, five dollars each. See who's in Alley."

One boy stepped out and shouted, "Jury work! Five-dollar job!"

They rounded up six men and were what you would expect in Bottom Alley. Didn't worry me as had no intention of paying mind to them. If you go judge, better in good neighborhood with chance of getting solid citizens.

I went behind desk, sat down, put on Brody's plug hat—wondered where he had found it. Probably a castoff from some lodge. "Court's in session," I said. "Let's have names and tell me beef."

Oldest lad was named Slim Lemke, girl was Patricia Carmen Zhukov; don't remember others. Tourist stepped up, reached into pouch and said, "My card, sir."

I still have it. It read:

STUART RENE LaJOIE
Poet—Traveler—Soldier of Fortune

Beef was tragically ridiculous, fine example of why tourists should not wander around without guides. Sure, guides bleed them white—but isn't that what a tourist is for? This one almost lost life from lack of guidance.

Had wandered into a taproom which lets stilyagi hang out, a sort of clubroom. This simple female had flirted with him. Boys had let matter be, as of course they had to as long as she invited it. But at some point she had laughed and let him have a fist in ribs. He had taken it as casually as a Loonie would . . . but had answered in distinctly earthworm manner; slipped arm around waist and pulled her to him, apparently tried to kiss her.

Now believe me, in North America this wouldn't matter; I've seen things much like it. But of course Tish was astonished, perhaps frightened. She screamed.

And pack of boys set upon him and roughed him up. Then decided he had to pay for his "crime"—but do it correctly. Find a judge.

Most likely they chickened. Chances are not one had ever dealt with an elimination. But their lady had been insulted, had to be done.

I questioned them, especially Tish, and decided I had it straight. Then said, "Let me sum up. Here we have a stranger. Doesn't know our ways. He offended, he's guilty. But meant no offense far as I can see. What does jury say? Hey, you there!—wake up! What you say?"

Juryman looked up blearily, said, " 'Liminate him!"

"Very well? And you?"

"Well—" Next one hesitated. "Guess it would be enough just to beat tar out of him, so he'll know better next time. Can't have men pawing women, or place will get to be as bad as they say Terra is."

"Sensible," I agreed. "And you?"

Only one juror voted for elimination. Others ranged from a beating to very high fines.

"What do you think, Slim?"

"Well—" He was worried—face in front of gang, face in front of what might be his girl. But had cooled down and didn't *want* chum eliminated. "We already worked him over. Maybe if he got down on hands and knees and kissed floor in front of Tish and said he was sorry?"

"Will you do that, Gospodin LaJoie?"

"If you so rule, your honor."

"I don't. Here's my verdict. First that juryman—*you!*—you are fined fee paid you because you fell asleep while supposed to be judging. Grab him, boys, take it away from him and throw him out."

They did, enthusiastically; made up a little for greater excitement they had thought of but really could not stomach. "Now, Gospodin LaJoie, you are fined fifty Hong Kong for not having common sense to learn local customs before stirring around. Ante up."

I collected it. "Now you boys line up. You are fined five dollars apiece for not exercising good judgment in dealing with a person you knew was a stranger and not used to our ways. Stopping him from touching Tish, that's fine. Rough him, that's okay, too; he'll learn faster. And could have tossed him out. But talking about eliminating for what was honest mistake—well, it's out of proportion. Five bucks each. Ante up."

Slim gulped. "Judge . . . I don't think we have that much left! At least I don't."

"I thought that might be. You have a week to pay or I post your names in Old Dome. Know where Bon Ton Beauté Shoppe is, near easement lock thirteen? My wife runs it; pay her. Court's out. Slim, don't go away. Nor you, Tish. Gospodin LaJoie, let's take these young people up and buy them a cold drink and get better acquainted."

Again his eyes filled with odd delight that reminded of Prof. "A charming idea, Judge!"

"I'm no longer judge. It's up a couple of ramps . . . so I suggest you offer Tish your arm."

He bowed and said, "My lady? May I?" and crooked his elbow to her. Tish at once became very grown up. "Spasebo, Gospodin! I am pleased."

Took them to expensive place, one where their wild clothes and excessive makeup looked out of place; they were edgy. But I tried to make them feel easy and Stuart LaJoie tried even harder and successfully. Got their addresses as well as names; Wyoh had one sequence which was concentrating on stilyagi. Presently they finished their coolers, stood up, thanked and left. LaJoie and I stayed on.

"Gospodin," he said presently, "you used an odd word earlier—odd to me, I mean."

"Call me 'Mannie' now that kids are gone. What word?"

"It was when you insisted that the, uh, young lady, Tish—that Tish must pay, too. 'Tone-stapple,' or something like it."

"Oh, 'tanstaafl.' Means 'There ain't no such thing as a free lunch.' And isn't," I added, pointing to a FREE LUNCH sign across room, "or these drinks would cost half as much. Was reminding her that anything free costs twice as much in long run or turns out worthless."

"An interesting philosophy."

"Not philosophy, fact. One way or other, what you get, you pay for." I fanned air. "Was Earthside once and heard expression 'Free as air.' This air isn't free, you pay for every breath."

"Really? No one has asked me to pay to breathe." He smiled. "Perhaps I should stop."

"Can happen, you almost breathed vacuum tonight. But nobody asks you because you've paid. For you, is part of round-trip ticket; for me it's a quarterly charge." I started to tell how my family buys and sells air to community co-op, decided was too complicated. "But we both pay."

LaJoie looked thoughtfully pleased. "Yes, I see the economic necessity. It's simply new to me. Tell me, uh, Mannie—and I'm called 'Stu'—was I really in danger of 'breathing vacuum'?"

"Should have charged you more."

"Please?"

"You aren't convinced. But charged kids all they could scrape up and fined them too, to make them think. Couldn't charge you more than them. Should have, you think it was all a joke."

"Believe me, sir, I do not think it was a joke. I just have trouble grasping that your local laws permit a man to be put to death . . . so casually . . . and for so trivial an offense."

I sighed. Where do you start explaining when a man's words show there isn't *anything* he understands about subject, instead is loaded with preconceptions that don't fit facts and doesn't even know he has?

"Stu," I said, "let's take that piece at a time. Are no 'local laws' so you couldn't be 'put to death' under them. Your offense was *not* 'trivial,' I simply made allowance for ignorance. And wasn't done casually, or boys would have dragged you to nearest lock to zero pressure, shoved you in, and cycled. Instead were most formal—good boys!—and paid own cash to give you a trial. And didn't grumble when verdict wasn't even close to what they asked. Now, anything still not clear?"

He grinned and turned out to have dimples like Prof; found myself liking him still more. "All of it, I'm afraid. I seem to have wandered into Looking Glass Land."

Expected that; having been Earthside I know how their minds work, some. An earthworm expects to find a law, a printed law, for every circumstance. Even have laws for private matters such as contracts. Really. If a man's word isn't any good, who would contract with him? Doesn't he have reputation?

"We don't have laws," I said. "Never been allowed to. Have customs, but aren't written and aren't enforced—or could say they are self-enforcing because are simply way things have to be, conditions being what they are. Could say our customs are natural laws because are way people have to behave to stay alive. When you made a pass at Tish you were violating a natural law . . . and almost caused you to breathe vacuum."

He blinked thoughtfully. "Would you explain the natural law I violated? I had better understand it . . . or best I return to my ship and stay inboard until lift. To stay alive."

"Certainly. Is so simple that, once you understand, you'll never be in danger from it again. Here we are, two million males, less than one million females. A physical fact, basic as rock or vacuum. Then add idea of tanstaafl. When thing is scarce, price goes up. Women are scarce; aren't enough to go around—that makes them most valuable thing in Luna, more precious than ice or air, as men without women don't care whether they stay alive or not. Except a Cyborg, if you regard him as a man, which I don't."

I went on: "So what happens?—and mind you, things were even worse when this custom, or natural law, first showed itself back in twentieth century. Ratio was ten-to-one or worse then. One thing is what always happens in prisons: men turn to other men. That helps not much; problem still is because most men want *women* and won't settle for substitute while chance of getting true gelt.

"They get so anxious they will kill for it . . . and from stories old-timers tell was killing enough to chill your teeth in those days. But after a while those still alive find way to get along, things shake down. As automatic as gravitation. Those who adjust to facts stay alive; those who don't are dead and no problem.

"What that means, here and now, is that women are scarce and call tune . . . and you are surrounded by two million men who see to it you dance to that tune. You have no choice, she has all choice. She can hit you so hard it draws blood; you dasn't lay a finger on her. Look, you put an arm around Tish, maybe tried to kiss. Suppose instead she had gone to hotel room with you; what would happen?"

"Heavens! I suppose they would have torn me to pieces."

"They would have done *nothing*. Shrugged and pretended not to see. Because choice is *hers*. Not yours. Not theirs. Exclusively hers. Oh, be risky to ask her to go to hotel; she might take offense and that would give boys license to rough you up. But—well, take this Tish. A silly little tart. If you had flashed as much money as I saw in your pouch, she might have taken into head that a bundle with tourist was just what she needed and suggested it herself. In which case would have been utterly safe."

LaJoie shivered. "At *her* age? It scares me to think of it. She's below the age of consent. Statutory rape."

"Oh, bloody! No such thing. Women her age are married or

ought to be. Stu, is *no* rape in Luna. None. Men won't permit. If rape had been involved, they wouldn't have bothered to find a judge and all men in earshot would have scrambled to help. But chance that a girl that big is virgin is negligible. When they're little, their mothers watch over them, with help from everybody in city; children are safe here. But when they reach husband-high, is no holding them and mothers quit trying. If they choose to run corridors and have fun, can't stop 'em; once a girl is nubile, she's her own boss. You married?"

"No." He added with a smile, "Not at present."

"Suppose you were and wife told you she was marrying again. What would you do?"

"Odd that you should pick that, something like it did happen. I saw my attorney and made sure she got no alimony."

" 'Alimony' isn't a word here; I learned it Earthside. Here you might—or a Loonie husband might—say, 'I think we'll need a bigger place, dear.' Or might simply congratulate her and his new co-husband. Or if it made him so unhappy he couldn't stand it, might opt out and pack clothes. But whatever, would not make slightest fuss. If he did, opinion would be unanimous against him. His friends, men and women alike, would snub him. Poor sod would probably move to Novylen, change name and hope to live it down.

"All our customs work that way. If you're out in field and a cobber needs air, you lend him a bottle and don't ask cash. But when you're both back in pressure again, if he won't pay up, nobody would criticize if you eliminated him without a judge. But he would pay; air is almost as sacred as women. If you take a new chum in a poker game, you give him air money. Not eating money; can work or starve. If you eliminate a man other than self-defense, you pay his debts and support his kids, or people won't speak to you, buy from you, sell to you."

"Mannie, you're telling me that I can murder a man here and settle the matter merely with money?"

"Oh, not at *all!* But eliminating isn't against some law; *are* no laws—except Warden's regulations—and Warden doesn't care what one Loonie does to another. But we figure this way: If a man is killed, either he had it coming and everybody knows it—usual case—or his friends will take care of it by eliminating man who did it. Either way, no problem. Nor many eliminations. Even set duels aren't common."

" 'His friends will take care of it.' Mannie, suppose those young people had gone ahead? I have no friends here."

"Was reason I agreed to judge. While I doubt if those kids could have egged each other into it, didn't want to take chance. Eliminating a tourist could give our city a bad name."

"Does it happen often?"

"Can't recall has ever happened. Of course may have been made to look like accident. A new chum is accident-prone; Luna is that sort of place. They say if a new chum lives a year, he'll live forever. But nobody sells him insurance first year." Glanced at time. "Stu, have you had dinner?"

"No, and I was about to suggest that you come to my hotel. The cooking is good. Auberge Orleans."

I repressed shudder—ate there once. "Instead, would you come home with me and meet my family? We have soup or something about this hour."

"Isn't that an imposition?"

"No. Half a minute while I phone."

Mum said, "Manuel! How sweet, dear! Capsule has been in for hours; I had decided it would be tomorrow or later."

"Just drunken debauchery, Mimi, and evil companions. Coming home now if can remember way—and bringing evil companion."

"Yes, dear. Dinner in twenty minutes; try not to be late."

"Don't you want to know whether my evil companion is male or female?"

"Knowing you, I assume that it is female. But I fancy I shall be able to tell when I see her."

"You know me so well, Mum. Warn girls to look pretty; wouldn't want a visitor to outshine them."

"Don't be too long; dinner will spoil. 'Bye, dear. Love."

"Love, Mum." I waited, then punched MYCROFTXXX. "Mike, want a name searched. Earthside name, passenger in Popov. Stuart René LaJoie. Stuart with a U and last name might file under either L or J."

Didn't wait many seconds; Mike found Stu in all major Earthside references: Who's Who, Dun & Bradstreet, Almanach de Gotha, London *Times* running files, name it. French expatriate, royalist, wealthy, six more names sandwiched into ones he used, three university degrees including one in law from Sorbonne, noble ancestry both France and Scotland, divorced (no children) from Honorable Pamela Hyphen-Hyphen-Blueblood. Sort of earthworm who wouldn't speak to a Loonie of convict ancestry—except Stu would speak to anyone.

I listened a pair of minutes, then asked Mike to prepare a full dossier, following all associational leads. "Mike, might be our pigeon."

"Could be, Man."

"Got to run. 'Bye." Returned thoughtfully to my guest. Almost a year earlier, during alcoholic talk-talk in a hotel room, Mike had promised us one chance in seven—if certain things were done. One sine-qua-non was help on Terra itself.

Despite "throwing rocks," Mike knew, we all knew, that mighty Terra with eleven billion people and endless resources could not be defeated by three million who had nothing, even though we stood on a high place and could drop rocks on them.

Mike drew parallels from XVIIIth century, when Britain's American colonies broke away, and from XXth, when many colonies became independent of several empires, and pointed out that in no case had a colony broken loose by brute force. No, in every case imperial state was busy elsewhere, had grown weary and given up without using full strength.

For months we had been strong enough, had we wished, to overcome Warden's bodyguards. Once our catapult was ready (anytime now) we would not be helpless. But we needed a "favorable climate" on Terra. For that we needed help *on* Terra.

Prof had not regarded it as difficult. But turned out to be quite difficult. His Earthside friends were dead or nearly and I had never had any but a few teachers. We sent inquiry down through cells: "What vips do you know Earthside?" and usual answer was: "You kidding?" Null program—

Prof watched passenger lists on incoming ships, trying to figure a contact, and had been reading Luna print-outs of Earthside newspapers, searching for vips he could reach through past connection. I had not tried; handful I had met on Terra were not vips.

Prof had not picked Stu off *Popov*'s passenger list. But Prof had not met him. I did not know whether Stu was simply eccentric as odd personal card seemed to show. But he was only Terran I had ever had a drink with in Luna, seemed a dinkum cobber, and Mike's report showed hunch was not all bad; he carried some tonnage.

So I took him home to see what family thought of him.

Started well. Mum smiled and offered hand. He took it and bowed so deep I thought he was going to kiss it—would have, I think, had I not warned him about fems. Mum was cooing as she led him in to dinner.

TWELVE

April and May '76 were more hard work and increasing effort to stir up Loonies against Warden, and goad him into retaliation. Trouble with Mort the Wart was that he was not a bad egg, nothing to hate about him other than fact he was symbol of Authority; was necessary to frighten him to get him to do anything. And average Loonie was just as bad. He despised Warden as matter of ritual but was not stuff that makes revolutionists; he couldn't be bothered. Beer, betting, women, and work— Only thing that kept Revolution from dying of anemia was that Peace Dragoons had real talent for antagonizing.

But even them we had to keep stirred up. Prof kept saying we needed a "Boston Tea Party," referring to mythical incident in an earlier revolution, by which he meant a public ruckus to grab attention.

We kept trying. Mike rewrote lyrics of old revolutionary songs: "Marseillaise," "Internationale," "Yankee Doodle," "We Shall Overcome," "Pie in the Sky," etc., giving them words to fit Luna. Stuff like *"Sons of Rock and Boredom/Will you let the Warden/Take from you your libertee!"* Simon Jester spread them around, and when one took hold, we pushed it (music only) by radio and video. This put Warden in silly position of forbidding playing of certain tunes—which suited us; people could whistle.

Mike studied voice and word-choice patterns of Deputy Administrator, Chief Engineer, other department heads; Warden started getting frantic calls at night from his staff. Which they denied making. So Alvarez put lock-and-trace on next one—and sure enough, with Mike's help, Alvarez traced it to supply chief's phone and was sure it was boss belly-robber's voice.

But next poison call to Mort seemed to come from Alvarez, and what Mort had to say next day to Alvarez and what Alvarez said in own defense can only be described as chaotic crossed with psychotic.

Prof had Mike stop; was afraid Alvarez might lose job, which we did not want; he was going too well for us. But by then Peace Dragoons had been dragged out twice in night on what seemed to be Warden's orders, further disrupting morale, and Warden became convinced he was surrounded by traitors in official family while they were sure he had blown every circuit.

An ad appeared in *Lunaya Pravda* announcing lecture by Dr. Adam Selene on *Poetry and Arts in Luna: A New Renaissance*. No comrade attended; word went down cells to stay away. Nor did anybody hang around when three squads of Peace Dragoons showed up—this involves Heisenberg principle as applied to Scarlet Pimpernels. Editor of *Pravda* spent bad hour explaining that he did *not* accept ads in person and this one was ordered over counter and paid for in cash. He was told not to take ads from Adam Selene. This was countermanded and he was told to take *anything* from Adam Selene but notify Alvarez *at once*.

New catapult was tested with a load dropped into south Indian

Ocean at 35° E., 60° S., a spot used only by fish. Mike was joyed over his marksmanship since he had been able to sneak only two looks when guidance & tracking radars were not in use and had relied on just one nudge to bring it to bull's-eye. Earthside news reported giant meteor in sub-Antarctic picked up by Capetown Spacetrack with projected impact that matched Mike's attempt perfectly—Mike called me to boast while taking down evening's Reuters transmission. "I told you it was dead on," he gloated. "I watched it. Oh, what a *lovely* splash!" Later reports on shock wave from seismic labs and on tsunamis from oceanographic stations were consistent.

Was only canister we had ready (trouble buying steel) or Mike might have demanded to try his new toy again.

Liberty Caps started appearing on Stilyagi and their girls; Simon Jester began wearing one between his horns. Bon Marché gave them away as premiums. Alvarez had painful talk with Warden in which Mort demanded to know if his fink boss felt that something should be done every time kids took up fad? Had Alvarez gone out of his mind?

I ran across Slim Lemke on Carver Causeway early May; he was wearing a Liberty Cap. He seemed pleased to see me and I thanked him for prompt payment (he had come in three days after Stu's trial and paid Sidris thirty Hong Kong, for gang) and bought him a cooler. While we were seated I asked why young people were wearing red hats? Why a hat? Hats were an earthworm custom, nyet?

He hesitated, then said was sort of a lodge, like Elks. I changed subject. Learned that his full name was Moses Lemke Stone; member of Stone Gang. This pleased me, we were relatives. But surprised me. However, even best families such as Stones sometimes can't always find marriages for all sons; I had been lucky or might have been roving corridors at his age, too. Told him about our connection on my mother's side.

He warmed up and shortly said, "Cousin Manuel, ever think about how we ought to elect our own Warden?"

I said No, I hadn't; Authority appointed him and I supposed they always would. He asked why we had to have an Authority? I asked who had been putting ideas in head? He insisted nobody had, just thinking, was all—didn't he have a right to think?

When I got home was tempted to check with Mike, find out lad's Party name if any. But wouldn't have been proper security, nor fair to Slim.

On 3 May '76 seventy-one males named Simon were rounded up and questioned, then released. No newspaper carried story. But everybody heard it; we were clear down in "J's" and twelve thousand people can spread a story faster than I would have guessed. We emphasized that one of these dangerous males was only four years old, which was not true but very effective.

Stu LaJoie stayed with us during February and March and did not return to Terra until early April; he changed his ticket to next ship and then to next. When I pointed out that he was riding close to invisible line where irreversible physiological changes could set in, he grinned and told me not to worry. But made arrangements to use centrifuge.

Stu did not want to leave even by April. Was kissed good-bye with tears by all my wives and Wyoh, and he assured each one he was coming back. But left as he had work to do; by then he was a Party member.

I did not take part in decision to recruit Stu; I felt prejudiced. Wyoh and Prof and Mike were unanimous in risking it; I happily accepted their judgment.

We all helped to sell Stu LaJoie—self, Prof, Mike, Wyoh, Mum, even Sidris and Lenore and Ludmilla and our kids and Hans and Ali and Frank, as Davis home life was what grabbed him first. Did not hurt that Lenore was prettiest girl in L-City—which is no disparagement of Milla, Wyoh, Anna, and Sidris. Nor did it hurt that Stu could charm a baby away from breast. Mom fussed over him, Hans showed him hydroponic farming and Stu got dirty and sweaty and sloshed around in tunnels with our boys—helped harvest our Chinee fishponds—got stung by our bees—learned to handle a p-suit and went up with me to make adjustments on solar battery—helped Anna butcher a hog and learned about tanning leather—sat with Grandpaw and was respectful to his naïve notions about Terra—washed dishes with Milla, something no male in our family ever did—rolled on floor with babies and puppies—learned to grind flour and swapped recipes with Mum.

I introduced him to Prof and that started political side of feeling him out. Nothing had been admitted—we could back away—when Prof introduced him to "Adam Selene" who could visit only by phone as he was "in Hong Kong at present." By time Stu was committed to Cause, we dropped pretense and let him know that Adam was chairman whom he would not meet in person for security reasons.

But Wyoh did most and was on her judgment that Prof turned cards up and let Stu know that we were building a revolution. Was no surprise; Stu had made up mind and was waiting for us to trust him.

They say a face once launched a thousand ships. I do not know that Wyoh used anything but argument on Stu. I never tried to find out. But Wyoh had more to do with committing *me* than all Prof's theory or Mike's figures. If Wyoh used even stronger methods on Stu, she was not first heroine in history to do so for her country.

Stu went Earthside with a special codebook. I'm no code and cipher expert except that a computerman learns principles during study of information theory. A cipher is a mathematical pattern under which one letter substitutes for another, simplest being one in which alphabet is merely scrambled.

A cipher can be incredibly subtle, especially with help of a computer. But ciphers all have weakness that they are patterns. If one computer can think them up, another computer can break them.

Codes do not have same weakness. Let's say that codebook has letter group GLOPS. Does this mean "Aunt Minnie will be home Thursday" or does it mean "3.14157 . . ."?

Meaning is whatever you assign and no computer can analyze it simply from letter group. Give a computer enough groups and a rational theory involving meanings or subjects for meanings, and it will eventually worry it out because meanings themselves will show patterns. But is a problem of different kind on more difficult level.

Code we selected was commonest commercial codebook, used both on Terra and in Luna for commercial dispatches. But we worked it over. Prof and Mike spent hours discussing what information Party might wish to send to its agent on Terra, or receive from agent, then Mike put his vast information to work and came up with new set of meanings for codebook, ones that could say "Buy Thai rice futures" as easily as "Run for life; they've caught us." Or *anything*, as cipher signals were buried in it to permit anything to be said that had not been anticipated.

Late one night Mike made print-out of new code via *Lunaya Pravda*'s facilities, and night editor turned roll over to another comrade who converted it into a very small roll of film and passed it along in turn, and none ever knew what they handled or why. Wound up in Stu's pouch. Search of off-planet luggage was tight by then and conducted by bad-tempered Dragoons—but Stu was certain he would have no trouble. Perhaps he swallowed it.

Thereafter some of LuNoHo Company's dispatches to Terra reached Stu via his London broker.

Part of purpose was financial. Party needed to spend money Earthside; LuNoHoCo transferred money there (not all stolen, some ventures turned out well); Party needed still more money Earthside, Stu was to speculate, acting on secret knowledge of plan of Revolution—he, Prof, and Mike had spent hours discussing what stocks would go up, what would go down, etc., after Der Tag. This was Prof's pidgin; I am not that sort of gambler.

But money was needed *before* Der Tag to build "climate of opinion." We needed publicity, needed delegates and senators in Federated Nations, needed some nation to recognize us quickly once The Day came, we needed laymen telling other laymen over a beer: "What is there on that pile of rock worth one soldier's life? Let 'em go to hell in their own way, I say!"

Money for publicity, money for bribes, money for dummy organizations and to infiltrate established organizations; money to get true nature of Luna's economy (Stu had gone loaded with figures) brought out as scientific research, then in popular form; money to convince foreign office of at least one major nation that there was advantage in a Free Luna; money to sell idea of Lunar tourism to a major cartel—

Too much money! Stu offered own fortune and Prof did not discourage it— Where treasure is, heart will be. But still too much money and far too much to do. I did not know if Stu could swing a tenth of it; simply kept fingers crossed. At least it gave us a channel to Terra. Prof claimed that communications to enemy were essential to any war if was to be fought and settled sensibly. (Prof was a pacifist. Like his vegetarianism, he did not let it keep him from being "rational." Would have made a terrific theologian.)

As soon as Stu went Earthside, Mike set odds at one in thirteen. I asked him what in hell? "But, Man," he explained patiently, "it increases risk. That it is necessary risk does not change the fact that risk is increased."

I shut up. About that time, early May, a new factor reduced some risks while revealing others. One part of Mike handled Terra-Luna microwave traffic—commercial messages, scientific data, news channels, video, voice radiotelephony, routine Authority traffic—and Warden's top-secret.

Aside from last, Mike could read any of this including commercial codes and ciphers—breaking ciphers was a crossword puzzle to him and nobody mistrusted this machine. Except Warden, and I suspect that his was distrust of all machinery; was sort of person who finds anything more involved than a pair of scissors complex, mysterious, and suspect—Stone Age mind.

Warden used a code that Mike never saw. Also used ciphers and did not work them through Mike; instead he had a moronic little machine in residence office. On top of this he had arrangement with Authority Earthside to switch everything around at preset times. No doubt he felt safe.

Mike broke his cipher patterns and deduced time-change program just to try legs. He did not tackle code until Prof suggested it; it held no interest for him.

But once Prof asked, Mike tackled Warden's top-secret messages. He had to start from scratch; in past Mike had erased Warden's messages once transmission was reported. So slowly, slowly he accumulated data for analysis—painfully slow, for Warden used this method only when he had to. Sometimes a week would pass between such messages. But gradually Mike began to gather meanings for letter groups, each assigned a probability. A code does not crack all at once; possible to know meanings of ninety-nine groups in a message and miss essence because one group is merely GLOPS to you.

However, user has a problem, too; if GLOPS comes through as GLOPT, he's in trouble. Any method of communication needs redundancy, or information can be lost. Was at redundancy that Mike nibbled, with perfect patience of machine.

Mike solved most of Warden's code sooner than he had projected; Warden was sending more traffic than in past and most of it one subject (which helped)—subject being security and subversion.

We had Mort in a twitter; he was yelling for help.

He reported subversive activities still going on despite two phalanges of Peace Dragoons and demanded enough troops to station guards in all key spots inside all warrens.

Authority told him this was preposterous, no more of FN's crack troops could be spared—to be permanently ruined for Earthside duties—and such requests should not be made. If he wanted more guards, he must recruit them from transportees—but such increase in administrative costs must be absorbed in Luna; he would not be allowed more overhead. He was directed to report what steps he had taken to meet new grain quotas set in our such-and-such.

Warden replied that unless extremely moderate requests for trained security personnel—not-repeat-not untrained, unreliable, and unfit convicts—were met, he could no longer assure civil order, much less increased quotas.

Reply asked sneeringly what difference it made if exconsignees chose to riot among themselves in their holes? If it worried him, had he thought of shutting off lights as was used so successfully in 1996 and 2021?

These exchanges caused us to revise our calendar, to speed some phases, slow others. Like a perfect dinner, a revolution has to be "cooked" so that everything comes out even. Stu needed time Earthside. We needed canisters and small steering rockets and associated circuitry for "rock throwing." And steel was a problem—buying it, fabricating it, and above all *moving* it through meander of tunnels to new catapult site. We needed to increase Party at least into "K's"—say 40,000—with lowest echelons picked for fighting spirit rather than talents we had sought earlier. We needed weapons against landings. We needed to move Mike's radars without which he was blind. (Mike could not be moved; bits of him spread all through Luna. But he had a thousand meters of rock over that central part of him at Complex, was surrounded by steel and this armor was cradled in springs; Authority had contemplated that someday somebody might lob H-weapons at their control center.)

All these needed to be done and pot must not boil too soon.

So we cut down on things that worried Warden and tried to speed up everything else. Simon Jester took a holiday. Word went out that Liberty Caps were not stylish—but save them. Warden got no more nervous-making phone calls. We quit inciting incidents with Dragoons—which did not stop them but reduced number.

Despite efforts to quiet Mort's worries a symptom showed up which disquieted us instead. No message (at least we intercepted none) reached Warden agreeing to his demand for more troops—but he started moving people out of Complex. Civil servants who lived there started looking for holes to rent in L-City. Authority started test drills and resonance exploration in a cubic adjacent to L-City which could be converted into a warren.

Could mean that Authority proposed shipping up unusually large draft of prisoners. Could mean that space in Complex was needed for purpose other than quarters. But Mike told us: "Why kid yourselves? The Warden is going to get those troops; that space will be their barracks. Any other explanation I would have heard."

I said, "But Mike, why didn't you hear if it's troops? You have that code of Warden's fairly well whipped."

"Not just 'fairly well,' I've got it whipped. But the last two ships have carried Authority vips and *I* don't know what they talk about away from phones!"

So we tried to plan to cover possibility of having to cope with ten more phalanges, that being Mike's estimate of what cubic being cleared would hold. We could deal with that many—with Mike's help—but it would mean deaths, not bloodless coup d'état Prof had planned.

And we increased efforts to speed up other factors.

When suddenly we found ourselves committed—

THIRTEEN

Her name was Marie Lyons; she was eighteen years old and born in Luna, mother having been exiled via Peace Corps in '56. No record of father. She seems to have been a harmless person. Worked as a stock-control clerk in shipping department, lived in Complex.

Maybe she hated Authority and enjoyed teasing Peace Dragoons. Or perhaps it started as a commercial transaction as cold-blooded as any in a crib behind a slot-machine lock. How can we know? Six Dragoons were in it. Not satisfied with raping her (if rape it was) they abused her other ways and killed her. But they did not dispose of body neatly; another civil service fem found it before was cold. She screamed. Was her last scream.

We heard about it at once; Mike called us three while Alvarez and Peace Dragoon C.O. were digging into matter in Alvarez's office. Appears that Peace Goon boss had no trouble laying hands on guilty; he and Alvarez were questioning them one at a time, and quarreling between grillings. Once we heard Alvarez say: "I told you those goons of yours had to have their own women! I warned you!"

"Stuff it," Dragoon officer answered. "I've told you time and again they won't ship any. The question now is how we hush this up."

"Are you crazy? Warden already knows."

"It's still the question."

"Oh, shut up and send in the next one."

Early in filthy story Wyoh joined me in workshop. Was pale under makeup, said nothing but wanted to sit close and clench my hand.

At last was over and Dragoon officer left Alvarez. Were still quarreling. Alvarez wanted those six executed at once and fact made public (sensible but not nearly enough, for his needs); C.O. was still talking about "hushing it up." Prof said, "Mike, keep an ear there and listen where else you can. Well, Mike? Wyoh? Plans?"

I didn't have any. Wasn't a cold, shrewd revolutionist; just wanted to get my heel into faces that matched those six voices. "I don't know. What do we do, Prof?"

" 'Do'? We're on our tiger; we grab its ears. Mike. Where's Finn Nielsen? Find him."

Mike answered, "He's calling now." He cut Finn in with us; I heard: "—at Tube South. Both guards dead and about six of our people. Just people, I mean, not necessarily comrades. Some wild rumor about Goons going crazy and raping and killing all women at Complex. Adam, I had better talk to Prof."

"I'm here, Finn," Prof answered in a strong, confident voice. "Now we move, we've got to. Switch off and get those laser guns and men who trained with them, any you can round up."

"Da! Okay, Adam?"

"Do as Prof says. Then call back."

"Hold it, Finn!" I cut in. "Mannie here. I want one of those guns."

"You haven't practiced, Mannie."

"If it's a laser, I can use it!"

"Mannie," Prof said forcefully, "shut up. You're wasting time; let Finn go. Adam. Message for Mike. Tell him Plan Alert Four."

Prof's example damped my oscillating. Had forgotten that Finn was not supposed to know Mike was anybody but "Adam Selene"; forgotten everything but raging anger. Mike said, "Finn has switched off, Prof, and I put Alert Four on standby when this broke. No traffic now except routine stuff filed earlier. You don't want it interrupted, do you?"

"No, just follow Alert Four. No Earthside transmission either way that tips any news. If one comes in, hold it and consult." Alert Four was emergency communication doctrine, intended to slap censorship on news to Terra without arousing suspicion. For this Mike was ready to talk in many voices with excuses as to why a direct voice transmission would be delayed—and any taped transmission was no problem.

"Program running," agreed Mike.

"Good. Mannie, calm down, son, and stick to your knitting. Let other people do the fighting; you're needed here, we're going to have to improvise. Wyoh, cut out and get word to Comrade Cecilia to get all Irregulars out of the corridors. Get those children home and keep them home—and have their mothers urging other mothers to do the same thing. We don't know where the fighting will spread. But we don't want children hurt if we can help it."

"Right away, Prof!"

"Wait. As soon as you've told Sidris, get moving on your stilyagi. I want a riot at the Authority's city office—break in, wreck the place, and noise and shouting and destruction—no one hurt if it can be helped. Mike. Alert-Four-Em. Cut off the Complex except for your own lines."

"Prof!" I demanded. "What sense in starting riots here?"

"Mannie, Mannie! This is *The Day*! Mike, has the rape and murder news reached other warrens?"

"Not that I've heard. I'm listening here and there with random jumps. Tube stations are quiet except Luna City. Fighting has just started at Tube Station West. Want to hear it?"

"Not now. Mannie, slide over there and watch it. But stay out of it and stick close to a phone. Mike, start trouble in all warrens. Pass the news down the cells and use Finn's version, not the truth. The Goons are raping and killing all the women in the Complex—I'll give you details or you can invent them. Uh, can you order the guards at tube stations in other warrens back to their barracks? I want riots but there is no point in sending unarmed people against armed men if we can dodge it."

"I'll try."

I hurried to Tube Station West, slowed as I neared it. Corridors were full of angry people. City roared in way I had never heard before and, as I crossed Causeway, could hear shouts and crowd noise from direction of Authority's city office although it seemed to me there had not been time for Wyoh to reach her stilyagi—nor had there been; what Prof had tried to start was under way spontaneously.

Station was mobbed and I had to push through to see what I assumed to be certain, that passport guards were either dead or fled. "Dead" it turned out, along with three Loonies. One was a boy not more than thirteen. He had died with his hands on a Dragoon's throat and his head still sporting a little red cap. I pushed way to a public phone and reported.

"Go back," said Prof, "and read the I.D. of one of those guards. I want name and rank. Have you seen Finn?"

"No."

"He's headed there with three guns. Tell me where the booth you're in is, get that name and come back to it."

One body was gone, dragged away; Bog knows what they wanted with it. Other had been badly battered but I managed to crowd in and snatch dog chain from neck before it, too, was taken somewhere. I elbowed back to phone, found a woman at it. "Lady," I said, "I've *got* to use that phone. Emergency!"

"You're welcome to it! Pesky thing's out of order."

Worked for me; Mike had saved it. Gave Prof guard's name. "Good," he said. "Have you seen Finn? He'll be looking for you at that booth."

"Haven't s— Hold it, just spotted him."

"Okay, hang onto him. Mike, do you have a voice to fit that Dragoon's name?"

"Sorry, Prof. No."

"All right, just make it hoarse and frightened; chances are the C.O. won't know it that well. Or would the trooper call Alvarez?"

"He would call his C.O. Alvarez gives orders through him."

"So call the C.O. Report the attack and call for help and die in the middle of it. Riot sounds behind you and maybe a shout of 'There's the dirty bastard now!' just before you die. Can you swing it?"

"Programmed. No huhu," Mike said cheerfully.

"Run it. Mannie, put Finn on."

Prof's plan was to sucker off-duty guards out of barracks and keep suckering them—with Finn's men posted to pick them off as they got out of capsules. And it worked, right up to point where Mort the Wart lost his nerve and kept remaining few to protect himself while he sent frantic messages Earthside—none of which got through.

I wiggled out of Prof's discipline and took a laser gun when second capsule of Peace Dragoons was due. I burned two Goons, found blood lust gone and let other snipers have rest of squad. Too easy. They would stick heads up out of hatch and that would be that. Half of squad would not come out—until smoked out and then died with rest. By that time I was back at my advance post at phone.

Warden's decision to hole up caused trouble at Complex; Alvarez was killed and so was Goon C.O. and two of original yellow jackets. But a mixed lot of Dragoons and yellows, thirteen, holed up with Mort, or perhaps were already with him; Mike's ability to follow events by listening was spotty. But once it seemed clear that all armed effectives were inside Warden's residence, Prof ordered Mike to start next phase.

Mike turned out all lights in Complex save those in Warden's residence, and reduced oxygen to gasping point—not killing point but low enough to insure that anyone looking for trouble would not be in shape. But in residence, oxygen supply was cut to zero, leaving pure nitrogen, and left that way ten minutes. At end of that time Finn's men, waiting in p-suits at Warden's private tube station, broke latch on airlock and went in, "shoulder to shoulder." Luna was ours.

BOOK TWO

A Rabble in Arms

FOURTEEN

So a wave of patriotism swept over our new nation and unified it.

Isn't that what histories say? Oh, brother!

My dinkum word, preparing a revolution isn't as much huhu as having won it. Here we were, in control too soon, nothing ready and a thousand things to do. Authority in Luna was gone—but Lunar Authority Earthside and Federated Nations behind it were very much alive. Had they landed one troopship, orbited one cruiser, anytime next week or two, could have taken Luna back *cheap*. We were a mob.

New catapult had been tested but canned rock missiles ready to go you could count on fingers of one hand—my left hand. Nor was catapult a weapon that could be used against ships, nor against troops. We had notions for fighting off ships; at moment were just notions. We had a few hundred cheap laser guns stockpiled in Hong Kong Luna—Chinee engineers are smart—but few men trained to use them.

Moreover, Authority had useful functions. Bought ice and grain, sold air and water and power, held ownership or control at a dozen key points. No matter what was done in future, wheels had to turn. Perhaps wrecking city offices of Authority had been hasty (I thought so) as records were destroyed. However, Prof maintained that Loonies, all Loonies, needed a symbol to hate and destroy and those offices were least valuable and most public.

But Mike controlled communications and that meant control of most everything. Prof had started with control of news to and from Earthside, leaving to Mike censorship and faking of news until we could get around to what to tell Terra, and had added subphase "M" which cut off Complex from rest of Luna, and with it Richardson Observatory and associated laboratories—Pierce Radioscope, Selenophysical Station, and so forth. There was a problem as Terran scientists were always coming and going and staying as long as six months, stretching time by centrifuge. Most Terrans in Luna, save for a handful of tourists—thirty-four—were scientists. Something had to be done about these Terrans, but meanwhile keeping them from talking to Terra was enough.

For time being, Complex was cut off by phone and Mike did not permit capsules to stop at any station in Complex even after travel was resumed, which it was as soon as Finn Nielsen and squad were through with dirty work.

Turned out Warden was not dead, nor had we planned to kill him; Prof figured that a live warden could always be made dead, whereas a dead one could not be made live if we needed him. So plan was to half kill him, make sure he and his guards could put up no fight, then break in fast while Mike restored oxygen.

With fans turning at top speed, Mike computed it would take four minutes and a bit to reduce oxygen to effective zero—so, five minutes of increasing hypoxia, five minutes of anoxia, then force lower lock while Mike shot in pure oxygen to restore balance. This should not kill anyone—but would knock out a person as thoroughly as anesthesia. Hazard to attackers would come from some or all of those inside having p-suits. But even that might not matter; hypoxia is sneaky, you can pass out without realizing you are short on oxygen. Is new chum's favorite fatal mistake.

So Warden lived through it and three of his women. But Warden, though he lived, was no use; brain had been oxygen-starved too long, a vegetable. No guard recovered, even though younger than he; would appear anoxia broke necks.

In rest of Complex nobody was hurt. Once lights were on and oxygen restored they were okay, including six rapist-murderers under lock in barracks. Finn decided that shooting was too good for them, so he went judge and used his squad as jury.

They were stripped, hamstrung at ankles and wrists, turned over to women in Complex. Makes me sick to think about what happened next but don't suppose they lived through as long an ordeal as Marie Lyons endured. Women are amazing creatures—sweet, soft, gentle, and far more savage than we are.

Let me mention those fink spies out of order. Wyoh had been fiercely ready to eliminate them but when we got around to them she had lost stomach. I expected Prof to agree. But he shook head. "No, dear Wyoh, much as I deplore violence, there are only two things to do with an enemy: Kill him. Or make a friend of him. Anything in between piles up trouble for the future. A man who finks on his friends once will do it again and we have a long period ahead in which a fink can be dangerous; they must go. And publicly, to cause others to be thoughtful."

Wyoh said, "Professor, you once said that if you condemned a man, you would eliminate him personally. Is that what you are going to do?"

"Yes, dear lady, and no. Their blood shall be on my hands; I accept responsibility. But I have in mind a way more likely to discourage other finks."

So Adam Selene announced that these persons had been employed by Juan Alvarez, late Security Chief for former Authority, as undercover spies—and gave names and addresses. Adam did not suggest that anything be done.

One man remained on dodge for seven months by changing

warrens and name. Then early in '77 his body was found outside Novylen's lock. But most of them lasted no more than hours.

During first hours after coup d'état we were faced with a problem we had never managed to plan—Adam Selene himself. *Who* is Adam Selene? Where is he? This is his revolution; he handled every detail, every comrade knows his voice. We're out in open now . . . so *where is Adam?*

We batted it around much of that night, in room L of Raffles—argued it between decisions on a hundred things that came up and people wanted to know what to do, while "Adam" through other voices handled other decisions that did not require talk, composed phony news to send Earthside, kept Complex isolated, many things. (Is no possible doubt: without Mike we could not have taken Luna nor held it.)

My notion was that Prof should become "Adam." Prof was always our planner and theoretician; everybody knew him; some key comrades knew that he was "Comrade Bill" and all others knew and respected Professor Bernardo de la Paz— My word, he had taught half of leading citizens in Luna City, many from other warrens, was known to every vip in Luna.

"No," said Prof.

"Why not?" asked Wyoh. "Prof, you're opted. Tell him, Mike."

"Comment reserved," said Mike. "I want to hear what Prof has to say."

"I say you've analyzed it, Mike," Prof answered. "Wyoh dearest comrade, I would not refuse were it possible. But there is *no* way to make my voice match that of Adam—and every comrade knows Adam by his *voice;* Mike made it memorable for that very purpose."

We then considered whether Prof could be slipped in anyhow, showing him only on video and letting Mike reshape whatever Prof said into voice expected from Adam.

Was turned down. Too many people knew Prof, had heard him speak; his voice and way of speaking could not be reconciled with Adam. Then they considered same possibility for me—my voice and Mike's were baritone and not too many people knew what I sounded like over phone and none over video.

I tromped on it. People were going to be surprised enough to find me one of our Chairman's lieutenants; they would never believe I was number one.

I said, "Let's combine deals. Adam has been a mystery all along; keep him that way. He'll be seen only over video—in a mask. Prof, you supply body; Mike, you supply voice."

Prof shook head. "I can think of no surer way to destroy confidence at our most critical period than by having a leader who wears a mask. No, Mannie."

We talked about finding an actor to play it. Were no professional actors in Luna then but were good amateurs in Luna Civic Players and in Novy Bolshoi Teatr Associates.

"No," said Prof, "aside from finding an actor of requisite character—one who would not decide to be Napoleon—we can't wait. Adam must start handling things not later than tomorrow morning."

"In that case," I said, "you've answered it. Have to use Mike and never put him on video. Radio only. Have to figure excuse but Adam must never be seen."

"I'm forced to agree," said Prof.

"Man my oldest friend," said Mike, "why do you say that I can't be seen?"

"Haven't you listened?" I said. "Mike, we have to show a face and body on video. You have a body—but it's several tons of metal. A face you don't have—lucky you, don't have to shave."

"But what's to keep me from showing a face, Man? I'm showing a voice this instant. But there's no sound behind it. I can show a face the same way."

Was so taken aback I didn't answer. I stared at video screen, installed when we leased that room. A pulse is a pulse is a pulse. Electrons chasing each other. To Mike, whole world was variable series of electrical pulses, sent or received or chasing around his innards.

I said, "No, Mike."

"Why not, Man?"

"Because you *can't!* Voice you handle beautifully. Involves only a few thousand decisions a second, a slow crawl to you. But to build up video picture would require, uh, say ten million decisions every second. Mike, you're so fast I can't even think about it. But you aren't *that* fast."

Mike said softly, "Want to bet, Man?"

Wyoh said indignantly, "Of course Mike can if he says he can! Mannie, you shouldn't talk that way." (Wyoh thinks an electron is something about size and shape of a small pea.)

"Mike," I said slowly, "I won't put money on it. Okay, want to try? Shall I switch on video?"

"I can switch it on," he answered.

"Sure you'll get right one? Wouldn't do to have this show somewhere else."

He answered testily, "I'm not stupid. Now let me be, Man—for I admit this is going to take just about all I've got."

We waited in silence. Then screen showed neutral gray with a hint of scan lines. Went black again, then a faint light filled middle and congealed into cloudy areas light and dark, ellipsoid. Not a face, but suggestion of face that one sees in cloud patterns covering Terra.

It cleared a little and reminded me of pictures alleged to be ectoplasm. A ghost of a face.

Suddenly firmed and we *saw* "Adam Selene."

Was a still picture of a mature man. No background, just a face as if trimmed out of a print. Yet was, to me, "Adam Selene." Could not be anybody else.

Then he smiled, moving lips and jaw and touching tongue to lips, a quick gesture—and I was frightened.

"How do I look?" he asked.

"Adam," said Wyoh, "your hair isn't that curly. And it should go back on each side above your forehead. You look as if you were wearing a wig, dear."

Mike corrected it. "Is that better?"

"Not quite so much. And don't you have dimples? I was sure I could hear dimples when you chuckle. Like Prof's."

Mike-Adam smiled again; this time he had dimples. "How should I be dressed, Wyoh?"

"Are you at your office?"

"I'm still at office. Have to be, tonight." Background turned gray, then came into focus and color. A wall calendar behind him gave date, Tuesday 19 May 2076; a clock showed correct time. Near his elbow was a carton of coffee. On desk was a solid picture, a family group, two men, a woman, four children. Was background noise, muted roar of Old Dome Plaza louder than usual; I heard shouts and in distance some singing: Simon's version of "Marseillaise."

Off screen Ginwallah's voice said, "Gospodin?"

Adam turned toward it. "I'm busy, Albert," he said patiently. "No calls from anyone but cell B. You handle everything else." He looked back at us. "Well, Wyoh? Suggestions? Prof? Man my doubting friend? Will I pass?"

I rubbed eyes. "Mike, can you cook?"

"Certainly. But I don't; I'm married."

"Adam," said Wyoh, "how can you look so neat after the day we've had?"

"I don't let little things worry me." He looked at Prof. "Professor, if the picture is okay, let's discuss what I'll say tomorrow. I was thinking of pre-empting the eight hundred newscast, have it announced all night, and pass the word down the cells."

We talked rest of night. I sent up for coffee twice and Mike-Adam had his carton renewed. When I ordered sandwiches, he asked Ginwallah to sent out for some. I caught a glimpse of Albert Ginwallah in profile, a typical babu, polite and faintly scornful. Hadn't known what he looked like. Mike ate while we ate, sometimes mumbling around a mouthful of food.

When I asked (professional interest) Mike told me that, after he had picture built up, he had programmed most of it for automatic and gave his attention just to facial expressions. But soon I forgot it was fake. Mike-Adam was talking with us by video, was all, much more convenient than by phone.

By oh-three-hundred we had policy settled, then Mike rehearsed speech. Prof found points he wanted to add; Mike made revisions, then we decided to get some rest, even Mike-Adam was yawning—although in fact Mike held fort all through night, guarding transmissions to Terra, keeping Complex walled off, listening at many phones. Prof and I shared big bed, Wyoh stretched out on couch, I whistled lights out. For once we slept without weights.

While we had breakfast, Adam Selene addressed Free Luna.

He was gentle, strong, warm, and persuasive. "Citizens of Free Luna, friends, comrades—to those of you who do not know me let me introduce myself. I am Adam Selene. Chairman of the Emergency Committee of Comrades for Free Luna . . . now *of* Free Luna, we are free at last. The so-called 'Authority' which has long usurped power in this our home has been overthrown. I find myself temporary head of such government as we have—the Emergency Committee.

"Shortly, as quickly as can be arranged, you will opt your own government." Adam smiled and made a gesture inviting help. "In the meantime, with your help, I shall do my best. We will make mistakes—be tolerant. Comrades, if you have not revealed yourselves to friends and neighbors, it is time you did so. Citizens, requests may reach you through your comrade neighbors. I hope you will comply willingly; it will speed the day when I can bow out and life can get back to normal—a *new* normal, free of the Authority, free of guards, free of troops stationed on us, free of passports and searches and arbitrary arrests.

"There has to be a transition. To all of you—please go back to work, resume normal lives. To those who worked for the Authority, the need is the same. Go back to work. Wages will go on, your jobs stay the same, until we can decide what is needed, what happily no longer is needed now that we are free, and what must be kept but modified. You new citizens, transportees sweating out sentences pronounced on you Earthside—you are free, your sentences are finished! But in the meantime I hope that you will go on working. You are not required to—the days of coercion are gone—but you are urged to. You are of course free to leave the Complex, free to go anywhere . . . and capsule service to and from the Complex will resume at once. But before you use your new freedom to rush into town, let me remind you: 'There is no such thing as a free lunch.' You are better off for the time being where you are; the food may not be fancy but will continue hot and on time.

"To take on temporarily those necessary functions of the defunct Authority I have asked the General Manager of LuNoHo Company to serve. This company will provide temporary supervision and will start analyzing how to do away with the tyrannical parts of the Authority and how to transfer the useful parts to private hands. So please help them.

"To you citizens of Terran nations among us, scientists and travelers and others, greetings! You are witnessing a rare event, the birth of a nation. Birth means blood and pain; there has been some. We hope it is over. You will not be inconvenienced unnecessarily and your passage home will be arranged as soon as possible. Conversely, you are welcome to stay, still more welcome to become citizens. But for the present I urge you to stay out of the corridors, avoid incidents that might lead to unnecessary blood, unnecessary pain. Be patient with us and I urge my fellow citizens to be patient with you. Scientists from Terra, at the Observatory and elsewhere, go on with your work and ignore us. Then you won't even notice that we are going through the pangs of creating a new nation. One thing—I am sorry to say that we are temporarily interfering with your right to communicate with Earthside. This we do from necessity; censorship will be lifted as quickly as possible—we hate it as much as you do."

Adam added one more request: "Don't try to see me, comrades, and phone me only if you must; all others, write if you need to, your letters will receive prompt attention. But I am not twins, I got no sleep last night and can't expect much tonight. I can't address meetings, can't shake hands, can't meet delegations; I must stick to this desk and work—so that I can get rid of this job and turn it over to your choice." He grinned at them. "Expect me to be as hard to see as Simon Jester!"

It was a fifteen-minute cast but that was essence: Go back to work, be patient, give us time.

Those scientists gave us almost no time—I should have guessed; was my sort of pidgin.

All communication Earthside channeled through Mike. But those brain boys had enough electronic equipment to stock a warehouse; once they decided to, it took them only hours to breadboard a rig that could reach Terra.

Only thing that saved us was a fellow traveler who thought Luna should be free. He tried to phone Adam Selene, wound up talking to one of a squad of women we had co-opted from C and D level—a system thrown together in self-defense as, despite Mike's request, half of Luna tried to phone Adam Selene after that videocast, everything from requests and demands to busybodies who wanted to tell Adam how to do his job.

After about a hundred calls got routed to me through too much zeal by a comrade in phone company, we set up this buffer squad. Happily, comrade lady who took this call recognized that soothe-'em-down doctrine did not apply; she phoned me.

Minutes later myself and Finn Nielsen plus some eager guns headed by capsule for laboratory area. Our informant was scared to give name but had told me where to find transmitter. We caught them transmitting, and only fast action on Finn's part kept them breathing; his boys were itchy. But we did not want to "make an example"; Finn and I had settled that on way out. Is hard to frighten scientists, their minds don't work that way. Have to get at them from other angles.

I kicked that transmitter to pieces and ordered Director to have everyone assemble in mess hall and required roll call—where a phone could hear. Then I talked to Mike, got names from him, and said to Director: "Doctor, you told me they were all here. We're missing so-and-so"—seven names. "*Get them here!*"

Missing Terrans had been notified, had refused to stop what they were doing—typical scientists.

Then I talked, Loonies on one side of room, Terrans on other. To Terrans I said; "We tried to treat you as guests. But three of you tried and perhaps succeeded in sending message Earthside."

I turned to Director. "Doctor, I could search—warren, surface structures, all labs, every space—and destroy everything that might be used for transmitter. I'm electron pusher by trade; I know what wide variety of components can be converted into transmitters. Suppose I destroy everything that might be useful for that and, being stupid, take no chance and smash anything I don't understand. What result?"

Would have thought I was about to kill his baby! He turned gray. "That would stop every research . . . destroy priceless data . . .

waste, oh, I don't know how much! Call it a half billion dollars!"

"So I thought. Could take all that gear instead of smashing and let you go on best you can."

"That would be almost as bad. You must understand, Gospodin, that when an experiment is interrupted—"

"I know. Easier than moving anything—and maybe missing some—is to take you all to Complex and quarter you there. We have what used to be Dragoon barracks. But that too would ruin experiments. Besides— Where you from, Doctor?"

"Princeton, New Jersey."

"So? You've been here five months and no doubt exercising and wearing weights. Doctor, if we did that, you might never see Princeton again. If we move you, we'll keep you locked up. You'll get soft. If emergency goes on very long, you'll be a Loonie like it or not. And all your brainy help with you."

A cocky chum stepped forward—one who had to be sent for twice. "You can't do this! It's against the law!"

"What law, Gospodin? Some law back in your hometown?" I turned. "Finn, show him law."

Finn stepped forward and placed emission bell of gun at man's belly button. Thumb started to press down—safety-switched, I could see. I said, "Don't kill him, Finn!"—then went on: "I will eliminate this man if that's what it takes to convince you. So watch each other! One more offense will kill *all* your chances of seeing home again—as well as ruining researches. Doctor, I warn *you* to find ways to keep check on your staff."

I turned to Loonies. "Tovarishchee, keep them honest. Work up own guard system. Don't take nonsense; every earthworm is on probation. If you have to eliminate some, don't hesitate." I turned to Director. "Doctor, any Loonie can go anywhere any time—even your bedroom. Your assistants are now your bosses so far as security is concerned; if a Loonie decides to follow you or anybody into a W.C., don't argue; he might be jumpy."

I turned to Loonies. "Security first! You each work for some earthworm—*watch him!* Split it among you and don't miss anything. Watch 'em so close they can't build mouse trap, much less transmitter. If interferes with work for them, don't worry; wages will go on."

Could see grins. Lab assistant was best job a Loonie could find those days—but they worked under earthworms who looked down on us, even ones who pretended and were oh so gracious.

I let it go at that. When I had been phoned, I had intended to eliminate offenders. But Prof and Mike set me straight: Plan did not permit violence against Terrans that could be avoided.

We set up "ears," wideband sensitive receivers, around lab area, since even most directional rig spills a little in neighborhood. And Mike listened on all phones in area. After that we chewed nails and hoped.

Presently we relaxed as news up from Earthside showed nothing, they seemed to accept censored transmissions without suspicion, and private and commercial traffic and Authority's transmissions all seemed routine. Meanwhile we worked, trying in days what should take months.

We received one break in timing; no passenger ship was on Luna and none was due until 7 July. We could have coped—suckered a ship's officers to "dine with Warden" or something, then mounted guard on its senders or dismantled them. Could not have lifted without our help; in those days one drain on ice was providing water for reaction mass. Was not much drain compared with grain shipments; one manned ship a month was heavy traffic then, while grain lifted every day. What it did mean was that an incoming ship was not an insuperable hazard. Nevertheless was lucky break; we were trying so hard to make everything look normal until we could defend ourselves.

Grain shipments went on as before; one was catapulted almost as Finn's men were breaking into Warden's residence. And next went out on time, and all others.

Neither oversight nor faking for interim; Prof knew what he was doing. Grain shipments were a big operation (for a little country like Luna) and couldn't be changed in one semi-lunar; bread-and-beer of too many people was involved. If our Committee had ordered embargo and quit buying grain, we would have been chucked out and a new committee with other ideas would have taken over.

Prof said that an educational period was necessary. Meanwhile grain barges catapulted as usual; LuNoHoCo kept books and issued receipts, using civil service personnel. Dispatches went out in Warden's name and Mike talked to Authority Earthside, using Warden's voice. Deputy Administrator proved reasonable, once he understood it upped his life expectancy. Chief Engineer stayed on job, too—McIntyre was a real Loonie, given chance, rather than fink by nature. Other department heads and minor stooges were no problem; life went on as before and we were too busy to unwind Authority system and put useful parts up for sale.

Over a dozen people turned up claiming to be Simon Jester; Simon wrote a rude verse disclaiming them and had picture on front page of *Lunatic*, *Pravda*, and *Gong*. Wyoh let herself go blond and made trip to see Greg at new catapult site, then a longer trip, ten days, to old home in Hong Kong Luna, taking Anna who wanted to see it. Wyoh needed a vacation and Prof urged her to take it, pointing out that she was in touch by phone and that closer Party contact was needed in Hong Kong. I took over her stilyagi with Slim and Hazel as my lieutenants—bright, sharp kids I could trust. Slim was awed to discover that I was "Comrade Bork" and saw "Adam Selene" every day; his Party name started with "G." Made a good team for other reason, too. Hazel suddenly started showing cushiony curves and not all from Mimi's superb table; she had reached that point in her orbit. Slim was ready to change her name to "Stone" any time she was willing to opt. In meantime he was anxious to do Party work he could share with our fierce little redhead.

Not everybody was willing. Many comrades turned out to be talk-talk soldiers. Still more thought war was over once we had eliminated Peace Goons and captured Warden. Others were indignant to learn how far down they were in Party structure; they wanted to elect a new structure, themselves at top. Adam received endless calls proposing this or something like it—would listen, agree, assure them that their services must not be wasted by waiting for election—and refer them to Prof or me. Can't recall any of these ambitious people who amounted to anything when I tried to put them to work.

Was endless work and *nobody* wanted to do it. Well, a few. Some best volunteers were people Party had never located. But in general, Loonies in and out of Party had no interest in "patriotic" work unless well paid. One chum who claimed to be a Party member (was not) spragged me in Raffles where we set up headquarters and wanted me to contract for fifty thousand buttons to be worn by pre-coup "Veterans of Revolution"—a "small" profit for him (I estimate 400 percent markup), easy dollars for me, a fine thing for everybody.

When I brushed him off, he threatened to denounce me to Adam Selene—"A very good friend of mine, I'll have you know!"—for sabotage.

That was "help" we got. What we needed was something else. Needed steel at new catapult and plenty—Prof asked if really necessary to put steel around rock missiles; I had to point out that an induction field won't grab bare rock. We needed to relocate Mike's ballistic radars at old site and install doppler radar at new site—both jobs because we could expect attacks from space at old site.

We called for volunteers, got only two who could be used—and needed several hundred mechanics who did not mind hard work in p-suits. So we hired, paying what we had to—LuNoHoCo went in hock to Bank of Hong Kong Luna; was no time to steal that much and most funds had been transferred Earthside to Stu. A dinkum comrade, Foo Moses Morris, co-signed much paper to keep us going—and wound up broke and started over with a little tailoring shop in Kongville. That was later.

Authority Scrip dropped from 3-to-1 to 17-to-1 after coup and civil service people screamed, as Mike was still paying in Authority checks. We said they could stay on or resign; then those we needed, we rehired with Hong Kong dollars. But created a large group not on our side from then on; they longed for good old days and were ready to stab new regime.

Grain farmers and brokers were unhappy because payment at catapult head continued to be Authority scrip at same old fixed prices. "We won't take it!" they cried—and LuNoHoCo man would shrug and tell them they didn't have to but this grain still went to Authority Earthside (it did) and Authority scrip was all they would get. So take cheque, or load your grain back into rolligons and get it out of here.

Most took it. All grumbled and some threatened to get out of grain and start growing vegetables or fibers or something that brought Hong Kong dollars—and Prof smiled.

We needed every drillman in Luna, especially ice miners who owned heavy-duty laser drills. As soldiers. We needed them so badly that, despite being shy one wing and rusty, I considered joining up, even though takes muscle to wrestle a big drill, and prosthetic just isn't muscle. Prof told me not to be a fool.

Dodge we had in mind would not work well Earthside; a laser beam carrying heavy power works best in vacuum—but there it works just dandy for whatever range its collimation is good for. These big drills, which had carved through rock seeking pockets of ice, were now being mounted as "artillery" to repel space attacks. Both ships and missiles have electronic nervous systems and does electronic gear no good to blast it with umpteen joules placed in a tight beam. If target is pressured (as manned ships are and most missiles), all it takes is to burn a hole, depressure it. If not pressured, a heavy laser beam can still kill it—burn eyes, louse guidance, spoil anything depending on electronics as most everything does.

An H-bomb with circuitry ruined is not a bomb, is just big tub of lithium deuteride that can't do anything but crash. A ship with eyes gone is a derelict, not a warship.

Sounds easy, is *not*. Those laser drills were never meant for targets a thousand kilometers away, or even one, and was no quick way to rig their cradles for accuracy. Gunner had to have guts to hold fire until last few seconds—on a target heading at him maybe two kilometers per second.

But was best we had, so we organized First and Second Volunteer Defense Gunners of Free Luna—two regiments so that First could snub lowly Second and Second could be jealous of First. First got older men, Second got young and eager.

Having called them "volunteers," we hired in Hong Kong dollars—and was no accident that ice was being paid for in controlled market in wastepaper Authority scrip.

On top of all, we were talking up a war scare. Adam Selene

talked over video, reminding that Authority was certain to try to regain its tyranny and we had only days to prepare; papers quoted him and published stories of their own—we had made special effort to recruit newsmen before coup. People were urged to keep p-suits always near and to test pressure alarms in homes. A volunteer Civil Defense Corps was organized in each warren.

What with moonquakes always with us, each warren's pressure co-op always had sealing crews ready at any hour; even with silicone stay-soft and fiberglass any warren leaks. In Davis Tunnels our boys did maintenance on seal every day. But now we recruited hundreds of emergency sealing crews, mostly stilyagi, drilled them with fake emergencies, had them stay in p-suits with helmets open when on duty.

They did beautifully. But idiots made fun of them—"play soldiers," "Adam's little apples," other names. A team was going through a drill, showing they could throw a temporary lock around one that had been damaged, and one of these pinheads stood by and rode them loudly.

Civil Defense team went ahead, completed temporary lock, tested it with helmets closed; it held—came out, grabbed this joker, took him through into temporary lock and on out into zero pressure, dumped him.

Belittlers kept opinions to selves after that. Prof thought we ought to send out a gentle warning not to eliminate so peremptorily. I opposed it and got my way; could see no better way to improve breed. Certain types of loudmouthism should be a capital offense among decent people.

But our biggest headaches were self-anointed statesmen.

Did I say that Loonies are "non-political"? They are, when comes to doing anything. But doubt if was ever a time two Loonies over a liter of beer did not swap loud opinions about how things ought to be run.

As mentioned, these self-appointed political scientists tried to grab Adam Selene's ear. But Prof had a place for them; each was invited to take part in "Ad-Hoc Congress for Organization of Free Luna"—which met in Community Hall in Luna City, then resolved to stay in session until work was done, a week in L-City, a week in Novylen, then Hong Kong, and start over. All sessions were in video. Prof presided over first and Adam Selene addressed them by video and encouraged them to do a thorough job—"History is watching you."

I listened to some sessions, then cornered Prof and asked what in Bog's name he was up to? "Thought you didn't want *any* government. Have you heard those nuts since you turned them loose?"

He smiled most dimply smile. "What's troubling you, Manuel?"

Many things were troubling me. With me breaking heart trying to round up heavy drills and men who could treat them as guns these idlers had spent an entire afternoon discussing immigration. Some wanted to stop it entirely. Some wanted to tax it, high enough to finance government (when ninety-nine out of a hundred Loonies had had to be dragged to The Rock!); some wanted to make it selective by "ethnic ratios." (Wondered how they would count *me?*) Some wanted to limit it to females until we were 50-50. That had produced a Scandinavian shout: "Ja, cobber! Tell 'em send us hoors! Tousands and tousands of hoors! I marry 'em, I betcha!"

Was most sensible remark all afternoon.

Another time they argued "time." Sure, Greenwich time bears no relation to lunar. But why should it when we live underground? Show me a Loonie who can sleep two weeks and work two weeks; lunars don't fit our metabolism. What was urged was to make a lunar exactly equal to twenty-eight days (instead of 29 days, 12 hours, 44 minutes, 2.78 seconds) and do this by making days longer—and hours, minutes, and seconds, thus making each semi-lunar exactly two weeks.

Sure, lunar is necessary for many purposes. Controls when we go up on surface, why we go, and how long we stay. But, aside from throwing us out of gear with our only neighbor, had that wordy vacuum skull thought what this would do to every critical figure in science and engineering? As an electronics man I shuddered. Throw away every book, table, instrument, and start over? I know that some of my ancestors did that in switching from old English units to MKS—but they did it to make things *easier*. Fourteen inches to a foot and some odd number of feet to a mile. Ounces and pounds. Oh, Bog!

Made sense to change *that*—but why go out of your way to *create* confusion?

Somebody wanted a committee to determine exactly what Loonie language is, then fine everybody who talked Earthside English or other language. Oh, my people!

I read tax proposals in *Lunatic*—four sorts of "Single-Taxers"—a cubic tax that would penalize a man if he extended tunnels, a head tax (everybody pay same), income tax (like to see anyone figure income of Davis Family or try to get information out of Mum!), and an "air tax" which was not fees we paid then but something else.

Hadn't realized "Free Luna" was going to have taxes. Hadn't had any before and got along. You paid for what you got. Tanstaafl. How else?

Another time some pompous choom proposed that bad breath and body odors be made an elimination offense. Could almost sympathize, having been stuck on occasion in a capsule with such stinks. But doesn't happen often and tends to be self-correcting; chronic offenders, or unfortunates who can't correct, aren't likely to reproduce, seeing how choosy women are.

One female (most were men, but women made up for it in silliness) had a long list she wanted made permanent laws—about private matters. No more plural marriage of any sort. No divorces. No "fornication"—had to look that one up. No drinks stronger than 4% beer. Church services only on Saturdays and all else to stop that day. (Air and temperature and pressure engineering, lady? Phones and capsules?) A long list of drugs to be prohibited and a shorter list dispensed only by licensed physicians. (What is a "licensed physician"? Healer I go to has a sign reading "practical doctor"—makes book on side, which is why I go to him. Look, lady, *aren't* any medical schools in Luna!) (Then, I mean.) She even wanted to make *gambling* illegal. If a Loonie couldn't roll double or nothing, he would go to a shop that would, even if dice were loaded.

Thing that got me was not her list of things she hated, since she was obviously crazy as a Cyborg, but fact that always somebody agreed with her prohibitions. Must be a yearning deep in human heart to stop other people from doing as they please. Rules, laws—always for *other* fellow. A murky part of us, something we had before we came down out of trees, and failed to shuck when we stood up. Because *not one* of those people said: "Please pass this so that I won't be able to do something I know I should stop." Nyet, tovarishchee, was *always* something they hated to see neighbors doing. Stop them "for their own good"—not because speaker claimed to be harmed by it.

Listening to that session I was almost sorry we got rid of Mort the Wart. He stayed holed up with his women and didn't tell us how to run private lives.

But Prof didn't get excited; he went on smiling. "Manuel, do you really think that mob of retarded children can pass any laws?"

"You told them to. Urged them to."

"My dear Manuel, I was simply putting all my nuts in one basket. I know those nuts; I've listened to them for years. I was very careful in selecting their committees; they all have built-in confusion, they will quarrel. The chairman I forced on them while letting them elect him is a ditherer who could not unravel a piece of string—thinks every subject needs 'more study.' I almost needn't have bothered; more than six people cannot agree on anything, three is better—and one is perfect for a job that one can do. This is why parliamentary bodies all through history, when they accomplished anything, owed it to a few strong men who dominated the rest. Never fear, son, this Ad-Hoc Congress will do nothing . . . or if they pass something through sheer fatigue, it will be so loaded with contradictions that it will have to be thrown out. In the meantime they are out of our hair. Besides, there *is* something we need them for, later."

"Thought you said they could do nothing."

"They won't do this. One man will write it—a dead man—and late at night when they are very tired, they'll pass it by acclamation."

"Who's this dead man? You don't mean Mike?"

"No, no! Mike is far more alive than those yammerheads. The dead man is Thomas Jefferson—first of the rational anarchists, my boy, and one who once almost managed to slip over his non-system through the most beautiful rhetoric ever written. But they caught him at it, which I hope to avoid. I cannot improve on his phrasing; I shall merely adapt it to Luna and the twenty-first century."

"Heard of him. Freed slaves, nyet?"

"One might say he tried but failed. Never mind. How are the defenses progressing? I don't see how we can keep up the pretense past the arrival date of this next ship."

"Can't be ready then."

"Mike says we must be."

We weren't but ship never arrived. Those scientists outsmarted me and Loonies I had told to watch them. Was a rig at focal point of biggest reflector and Loonie assistants believed doubletalk about astronomical purpose—a new wrinkle in radiotelescopes.

I suppose it was. Was ultramicrowave and stuff was bounced at reflector by a wave guide and thus left scope lined up nicely by mirror. Remarkably like early radar. And metal latticework and foil heat shield of barrel stopped stray radiation, thus "ears" I had staked out heard nothing.

They put message across, their version and in detail. First we heard was demand from Authority to Warden to deny this hoax, find hoaxer, put stop to it.

So instead we gave them a Declaration of Independence.

"In Congress assembled, July Fourth, Twenty-Seventy-Six—"

Was *beautiful*.

FIFTEEN

Signing of Declaration of Independence went as Prof said it would. He sprang it on them at end of long day, announced a special session after dinner at which Adam Selene would speak. Adam read aloud, discussing each sentence, then read it without stopping, making music of sonorous phrases. People wept. Wyoh, seated by me, was one, and I felt like it even though had read it earlier.

Then Adam looked at them and said, "The future is waiting. Mark well what you do," and turned meeting over to Prof rather than usual chairman.

Was twenty-two hundred and fight began. Sure, they were in favor of it; news all day had been jammed with what bad boys we were, how we were to be punished, taught a lesson, so forth. Not necessary to spice it up; stuff up from Earthside was nasty—Mike merely left out on-other-hand opinions. If ever was a day when Luna felt unified it was probably second of July 2076.

So they were going to pass it; Prof knew that before he offered it.

But not as written—"Honorable Chairman, in second paragraph, that word 'unalienable,' is no such word; should be '*in*-alienable'—and anyhow wouldn't it be more dignified to say 'sacred rights' rather than 'inalienable rights'? I'd like to hear discussion on this."

That choom was almost sensible, merely a literary critic, which is harmless, like dead yeast left in beer. But—Well, take that woman who hated everything. She was there with list; read it aloud and moved to have it incorporated into Declaration "so that the peoples of Terra will know that we are civilized and fit to take our places in the councils of mankind!"

Prof not only let her get away with it; he encouraged her, letting her talk when other people wanted to—then blandly put her proposal to a vote when hadn't even been seconded. (Congress operated by rules they had wrangled over for days. Prof was familiar with rules but followed them only as suited him.) She was voted down in a shout, and left.

Then somebody stood up and said of course that long list didn't belong in Declaration—but shouldn't we have general principles? Maybe a statement that Luna Free State guaranteed freedom, equality, and security to all? Nothing elaborate, just those fundamental principles that everybody knew was proper purpose of government.

True enough and let's pass it—but must read "Freedom, equality, *peace*, and security"—right, Comrade? They wrangled over whether "freedom" included "free air," or was that part of "security"? Why not be on safe side and list "free air" by name? Move to amend to make it "free air *and* water"—because you didn't have "freedom" or "security" unless you had both air and water.

Air, water, and *food*.

Air, water, food, and *cubic*.

Air, water, food, cubic, and *heat*.

No, make "heat" read "power" and you had it all covered. Everything.

Cobber, have you lost your mind? That's far from everything and what you've left out is an affront to all womankind— Step outside and say that! Let me finish. We've got to tell them right from deal that we will permit no more ships to land unless they carry at least as many women as men. *At least*, I said—and I for one won't chop it unless it sets immigration issue straight.

Prof never lost dimples.

Began to see why Prof had slept all day and was not wearing weights. Me, I was tired, having spent all day in p-suit out beyond catapult head cutting in last of relocated ballistic radars. And everybody was tired; by midnight crowd began to thin, convinced that nothing would be accomplished that night and bored by any yammer not their own.

Was later than midnight when someone asked why this Declaration was dated fourth when today was second? Prof said mildly that it was July third now—and it seemed unlikely that our Declaration could be announced earlier than fourth . . . and that July fourth carried historical symbolism that might help.

Several people walked out at announcement that probably nothing would be settled until fourth of July. But I began to notice something: Hall was filling as fast as was emptying. Finn Nielsen slid into a seat that had just been vacated. Comrade Clayton from Hong Kong showed up, pressed my shoulder, smiled at Wyoh, found a seat. My youngest lieutenants, Slim and Hazel, I spotted down front—and was thinking I must alibi Hazel by telling Mum I had kept her out on Party business—when was amused to see Mum herself next to them. And Sidris. And Greg, who was supposed to be at new catapult.

Looked around and picked out a dozen more—night editor of *Lunaya Pravda*, General Manager of LuNoHoCo, others, and each one a working comrade. Began to see that Prof had stacked deck. That Congress never had a fixed membership; these dinkum comrades had as much right to show up as those who had been talking a month. Now they sat—and voted down amendments.

About three hundred, when I was wondering how much more I

could take, someone brought a note to Prof. He read it, banged gavel and said, "Adam Selene begs your indulgence. Do I hear unanimous consent?"

So screen back of rostrum lighted up again and Adam told them that he had been following debate and was warmed by many thoughtful and constructive criticisms. But could he make a suggestion? Why not admit that any piece of writing was imperfect? If this declaration was *in general* what they wanted, why not postpone perfection for another day and pass this as it stands? "Honorable Chairman, I so move."

They passed it with a yell. Prof said, "Do I hear objection?" and waited with gavel raised. A man who had been talking when Adam had asked to be heard said, "Well . . . I *still* say that's a dangling participle, but okay, leave it in."

Prof banged gavel. "So ordered!"

Then we filed up and put our chops on a big scroll that had been "sent over from Adam's office"—and I noticed Adam's chop on it. I signed right under Hazel—child now could write although was still short on book learning. Her chop was shaky but she wrote it large and proud. Comrade Clayton signed his Party name, real name in letters, and Japanese chop, three little pictures one above other. Two comrades chopped with X's and had them witnessed. All Party leaders were there that night (morning), all chopped it, and not more than a dozen yammerers stuck. But those who did, put their chops down for history to read. And thereby committed "their lives, their fortunes, and their sacred honors."

While queue was moving slowly past and people were talking, Prof banged for attention. "I ask for volunteers for a dangerous mission. This Declaration will go on the news channels—but must be presented in person to the Federated Nations, on Terra."

That put stop to noise. Prof was looking at me. I swallowed and said, "I volunteer." Wyoh echoed, "So do I!"—and little Hazel Meade said, "Me, too!"

In moments were a dozen, from Finn Nielson to Gospodin Dangling-Participle (turned out to be good cobber aside from his fetish). Prof took names, murmured something about getting in touch as transportation became available.

I got Prof aside and said, "Look, Prof, you too tired to track? You know ship for seventh was canceled; now they're talking about slapping embargo on us. Next ship they lift for Luna will be a warship. How you planning to travel? As prisoner?"

"Oh, we won't use their ships."

"So? Going to build one? Any idea how long that takes? If could build one at all. Which I doubt."

"Manuel, Mike says it's necessary—and has it all worked out."

I did know Mike said was necessary; he had rerun problem soon as we learned that bright laddies at Richardson had snuck one home—he now gave us only one chance in fifty-three . . . with imperative need for Prof to go Earthside. But I'm not one to worry about impossibilities; I had spent day working to make that one chance in fifty-three turn up.

"Mike will provide the ship," Prof went on. "He has completed its design and it is being worked on."

"He has? It is? Since when is Mike engineer?"

"Isn't he?" asked Prof.

I started to answer, shut up. Mike had no degrees. Simply knew more engineering than any man alive. Or about Shakespeare's plays, or riddles, or history, name it. "Tell me more."

"Manuel, we'll go to Terra as a load of grain."

"*What?* Who's 'we'?"

"You and myself. The other volunteers are merely decorative."

I said, "Look, Prof. I've stuck. Worked hard when whole thing seemed silly. Worn these weights—got 'em on now—on chance I might have to go to that dreadful place. But contracted to go in a *ship*, with at least a Cyborg pilot to help me get down safely. Did *not* agree to go as meteorite."

He said, "Very well, Manuel. I believe in free choice, always. Your alternate will go."

"My— *Who?*"

"Comrade Wyoming. So far as I know she is the only other person in training for the ship . . . other than a few Terrans."

So I went. But talked to Mike first. He said patiently, "Man my first friend, there isn't a thing to worry about. You are scheduled load KM187 series '76 and you'll arrive in Bombay with no trouble. But to be sure—to reassure *you*—I selected that barge because it will be taken out of parking orbit and landed when India is faced toward me . . . and I've added an override so that I can take you away from ground control if I don't like the way they handle you. Trust me, Man, it has all been thought through. Even the decision to continue shipments when security was broken was part of this plan."

"Might have told me."

"There was no need to worry you. Professor had to know and I've kept in touch with him. But you are going simply to take care of him and back him up—do his job if he dies, a factor on which I can give you no reassurance."

I sighed. "Okay. But, Mike, surely you don't think you can pilot a barge into a soft landing at this distance? Speed of light alone would trip you."

"Man, don't you think I understand ballistics? For the orbital position then, from query through reply and then to command-received is under four seconds . . . and you can rely on me not to waste microseconds. Your maximum parking-orbit travel in four seconds is only thirty-two kilometers, diminishing asymptomatically to zero at landing. My reflex time will be effectively less than that of a pilot in a manual landing because I don't waste time grasping a situation and deciding on correct action. So my maximum is four seconds. But my *effective* reflex time is much less, as I project and predict constantly, see ahead, program it out—in effect, I'll stay four seconds ahead of you in your trajectory and respond instantly."

"That steel can doesn't even have an altimeter!"

"It does now. Man, *please* believe me; I've thought of *everything*. The only reason I've ordered this extra equipment is to reassure you. Poona ground control hasn't made a bobble in the last five thousand loads. For a computer it's fairly bright."

"Okay. Uh, Mike, how hard do they splash those bleeding barges? What gee?"

"Not high, Man. Ten gravities at injection, then that programs down to a steady, soft four gees . . . then you'll be nudged again between six and five gees just before splash. The splash itself is gentle, equal to a fall of fifty meters and you enter ogive first with no sudden shock, less than three gees. Then you surface and splash again, lightly, and simply float at one gee. Man, those barge shells are built as lightly as possible for economy's sake. We can't afford to toss them around or they would split their seams."

"How sweet. Mike, what would 'six to five gees' do to you? Split your seams?"

"I conjecture that I was subjected to about six gravities when they shipped me up here. Six gravities in my present condition would shear many of my essential connections. However, I'm more interested in the extremely high, transient accelerations I am going to experience from shock waves when Terra starts bombing us. Data are insufficient for prediction . . . but I may lose control of my outlying functions, Man. This could be a major factor in any tactical situation."

"Mike, you really think they are going to bomb us?"

"Count on it, Man. That is why this trip is so important."

Left it at that and went out to see this coffin. Should have stayed home.

Ever looked at one of those silly barges? Just a steel cylinder with retro and guidance rockets and radar transponder. Resembles a spaceship way a pair of pliers resembles my number-three arm. They had this one cut open and were outfitting our "living quarters."

No galley. No W.C. No nothing. Why bother? We were going to be in it only fifty hours. Start empty so that you won't need a honey sack in your suit. Dispense with lounge and bar; you'll never be out of your suit, you'll be drugged and not caring.

At least Prof would be drugged almost whole time; I had to be alert at landing to try to get us out of this death trap if something went wrong and nobody came along with a tin opener. They were building a shaped cradle in which backs of our p-suits would fit; we would be strapped into these holes. And stay there, clear to Terra. They seemed more concerned about making total mass equal to displaced wheat and same center of gravity and all moment arms adding up correctly than they did about our comfort; engineer in charge told me that even padding to be added inside our p-suits was figured in.

Was glad to learn we were going to have padding; those holes did not look soft.

Returned home in thoughtful condition.

Wyoh was not at dinner, unusual; Greg was, more unusual. Nobody said anything about my being scheduled to imitate a falling rock next day although all knew. But did not realize anything special was on until all next generation left table without being told. Then knew why Greg had not gone back to Mare Undarum site after Congress adjourned that morning; somebody had asked for a Family-talk.

Mum looked around and said, "We're all here. Ali, shut that door; that's a dear. Grandpaw, will you start us?"

Our senior husband stopped nodding over coffee and firmed up. He looked down table and said strongly, "I see that we are all here. I see that children have been put to bed. I see that there is no stranger, no guest. I say that we are met in accordance with customs created by Black Jack Davis our First Husband and Tillie our First Wife. If there is any matter that concerns safety and happiness of our marriage, haul it out in the light *now*. Don't let it fester. This is our custom."

Grandpaw turned to Mum and said softly, "Take it, Mimi," and slumped back into gentle apathy. But for a minute he had been strong, handsome, virile, dynamic man of days of my opting . . . and I thought with sudden tears how lucky I had been!

Then didn't know whether I felt lucky or not. Only excuse I could see for a Family talk-talk was fact that I was due to be shipped Earthside next day, labeled as grain. Could Mum be thinking of trying to set Family against it? Nobody *had* to abide by results of a talk-talk. But one always did. That was strength of our marriage: When came down to issues, we stood together.

Mimi was saying, "Does anyone have anything that needs to be discussed? Speak up, dears."

Greg said, "I have."

"We'll listen to Greg."

Greg is a good speaker. Can stand up in front of a congregation and speak with confidence about matters I don't feel confident about even when alone. But that night he seemed anything but sure of himself. "Well, uh, we've always tried to keep this marriage in balance, some old, some young, a regular alternation, well spaced, just as it was handed down to us. But we've varied sometimes—for good reason." He looked at Ludmilla. "And adjusted it later." He looked again at far end of table, at Frank and Ali, on each side of Ludmilla.

"Over years, as you can see from records, average age of husbands has been about forty, wives about thirty-five—and that age spread was just what our marriage started with, nearly a hundred years gone by, for Tillie was fifteen when she opted Black Jack and he had just turned twenty. Right now I find that average age of husbands is almost exactly forty, while average—"

Mum said firmly, "Never mind arithmetic, Greg dear. Simply state it."

I was trying to think who Greg could possibly mean. True, I had been much away during past year, and if did get home, was often after everybody was asleep. But he was clearly talking about marriage and nobody ever proposes another wedding in our marriage without first giving everybody a long careful chance to look prospect over. You just didn't *do* it any other way!

So I'm stupid. Greg stuttered and said, "I propose Wyoming Knott!"

I *said* I was stupid. I understand machinery and machinery understands me. But didn't claim to know anything about people. When I get to be senior husband, if live that long, am going to do exactly what Grandpaw does with Mum: Let Sidris run it. Just same— Well, look, Wyoh joined Greg's church. I like Greg, *love* Greg. And admire him. But you could never feed theology of his church through a computer and get anything but null. Wyoh surely knew this, since she encountered it in adult years—truthfully, I had suspected that Wyoh's conversion was proof that she would do *anything* for our Cause.

But Wyoh had recruited Greg even earlier. And had made most of trips out to new site, easier for her to get away than me or Prof. Oh, well. Was taken by surprise. Should not have been.

Mimi said, "Greg, do you have reason to think that Wyoming would accept an opting from us?"

"Yes."

"Very well. We all know Wyoming; I'm sure we've formed our opinions of her. I see no reason to discuss it . . . unless someone has something to say? Speak up."

Was no surprise to Mum. But wouldn't be. Nor to anyone else, either, since Mum never let a talk-talk take place until she was sure of outcome.

But wondered why Mum was sure of my opinion, so certain that she had not felt me out ahead of time? And sat there in a soggy quandary, knowing I should speak up, knowing I knew something terribly pertinent which nobody else knew or matter would never have gone this far. Something that didn't matter to me but would matter to Mum and all our women.

Sat there, miserable coward, and said nothing.

Mum said, "Very well. Let's call the roll. Ludmilla?"

"Me? Why, I love Wyoh, everybody knows that. Sure!"

"Lenore dear?"

"Well, I may try to talk her into going back to being a brownie again; I think we set each other off. But that's her only fault, being blonder than I am. Da!"

"Sidris?"

"Thumbs up. Wyoh is our kind of people."

"Anna?"

"I've something to say before I express my opinion, Mimi."

"I don't think it's necessary, dear."

"Nevertheless I'm going to haul it out in the open, just as Tillie always did according to our traditions. In this marriage every wife has carried her load, given children to the family. It may come as a surprise to some of you to learn that Wyoh has had eight children—"

Certainly surprised Ali; his head jerked and jaw dropped. I stared at plate. Oh, Wyoh, Wyoh! How could I let this happen? Was going to *have* to speak up.

And realized Anna was still speaking: "—so now she can have children of her own; the operation was successful. But she worries about possibility of another defective baby, unlikely as that is according to the head of the clinic in Hong Kong. So we'll just have to love her enough to make her quit fretting."

"We will love her," Mum said serenely. "We do love her. Anna, are you ready to express opinion?"

"Hardly necessary, is it? I went to Hong Kong with her, held her hand while her tubes were restored. I opt Wyoh."

"In this family," Mum went on, "we have always felt that our husbands should be allowed a veto. Odd of us perhaps, but Tillie started it and it has always worked well. Well, Grandpaw?"

"Eh? What were you saying, my dear?"

"We are opting Wyoming, Gospodin Grandpaw. Do you give consent?"

"What? Why, of course, of course! Very nice little girl. Say, whatever became of that pretty little Afro, name something like that? She get mad at us?"

"Greg?"

"I proposed it."

"Manuel? Do you forbid this?"

"Me? Why, you know me, Mum."

"I do. I sometimes wonder if *you* know you. Hans?"

"What would happen if I said No?"

"You'd lose some teeth, that's what," Lenore said promptly. "Hans votes Yes."

"Stop it, darlings," Mum said with soft reproof. "Opting is a serious matter. Hans, speak up."

"Da. Yes. Ja. Oui. Sí. High time we had a pretty blonde in this—*Ouch!*"

"Stop it, Lenore. Frank?"

"Yes, Mum."

"Ali dear? Is it unanimous?"

Lad blushed bright pink and couldn't talk. Nodded vigorously.

Instead of appointing a husband and a wife to seek out selectee and propose opting for us, Mum sent Ludmilla and Anna to fetch Wyoh at once—and turned out she was only as far away as Bon Ton. Nor was that only irregularity; instead of setting a date and arranging a wedding party, our children were called in, and twenty minutes later Greg had his Book open and we did be taking vows—

and I finally got it through my confused head that was being done with breakneck speed because of my date to break my neck next day.

Not that it could matter save as symbol of my family's love for me, since a bride spent her first night with her senior husband, and second night and third I was going to spend out in space. But *did* matter anyhow and when women started to cry during ceremony, I found self dripping tears right with them.

Then I went to bed, alone in workshop, once Wyoh had kissed us and left on Grandpaw's arm. Was terribly tired and last two days had been hard. Thought about exercises and decided was too late to matter; thought about calling Mike and asking him for news from Terra. Went to bed.

Don't know how long had been asleep when realized was no longer asleep and somebody was in room. "Manuel?" came soft whisper in dark.

"Huh? Wyoh, you aren't supposed to be here, dear."

"I am indeed supposed to be here, my husband. Mum knows I'm here, so does Greg. And Grandpaw went right to sleep."

"Oh. What time is?"

"About four hundred. Please, dear, may I come to bed?"

"What? Oh, certainly." Something I should remember. Oh, yes. "Mike!"

"Yes, Man?" he answered.

"Switch off. Don't listen. If you want me, call me on Family phone."

"So Wyoh told me, Man. Congratulations!"

Then her head was pillowed on my stump and I put right arm around her. "What are you crying about, Wyoh?"

"I'm not crying! I'm just frightened silly that you won't come back!"

SIXTEEN

Woke up scared silly in pitch darkness. "Manuel!" Didn't know which end was up. "Manuel!" it called again. "*Wake up!*"

That brought me out some; was signal intended to trigger me. Recalled being stretched on a table in infirmary at Complex, staring up at a light and listening to a voice while a drug dripped into my veins. But was a hundred years ago, endless time of nightmares, unendurable pressure, pain.

Knew now what no-end-is-up feeling was; had experienced before. Free fall. Was in space.

What had gone wrong? Had Mike dropped a decimal point? Or had he given in to childish nature and played a joke, not realizing would kill? Then why, after all years of pain, was I alive? Or was I?

Was this normal way for ghost to feel, just lonely, lost, nowhere?

"Wake up, Manuel! Wake up, Manuel!"

"Oh, shut up!" I snarled. "Button your filthy king-and-ace!" Recording went on; I paid no attention. Where was that reeking light switch? No, doesn't take a century of pain to accelerate to Luna's escape speed at three gravities, merely feels so. Eighty-two seconds—but is one time when human nervous system feels every microsecond. Three gees at eighteen grim times as much as a Loonie ought to weigh.

Then discovered those vacuum skulls had not put arm back on. For some silly reason they had taken it off when they stripped me to prepare me and I was loaded with enough don't-worry and let's-sleep pills not to protest. No huhu had they put it on again. But that drecklich switch was on my left and sleeve of p-suit was empty.

Spent next ten years getting unstrapped with one hand, then a twenty-year sentence floating around in dark before managed to find my cradle again, figure out which was head end, and from that hint locate switch by touch. That compartment was not over two meters in any dimension. This turns out to be larger than Old Dome in free fall and total darkness. Found it. We had light.

(And don't ask why that coffin did not have at least three lighting systems all working all time. Habit, probably. A lighting system implies a switch to control it, nyet? Thing was built in two days; should be thankful switch worked.)

Once I had light, cubic shrank to true claustrophobic dimensions and ten percent smaller, and I took a look at Prof.

Dead, apparently. Well, he had every excuse. Envied him but was now supposed to check his pulse and breathing and suchlike in case he had been unlucky and still had such troubles. And was again hampered and not just by being one-armed. Grain load had been dried and depressured as usual before loading but that cell was supposed to be pressured—oh, nothing fancy, just a tank with air in it. Our p-suits were supposed to handle needs such as life's breath for those two days. But even best p-suit is more comfortable in pressure than in vacuum and, anyhow, I was supposed to be able to get at my patient.

Could not. Didn't need to open helmet to know this steel can had not stayed gas tight, knew at once, naturally, from way p-suit felt. Oh, drugs I had for Prof, heart stimulants and so forth, were in field ampules; could jab them through his suit. But how to check heart and breathing? His suit was cheapest sort, sold for Loonie who rarely leaves warren; had no readouts.

His mouth hung open and eyes stared. A deader, I decided. No need to ex Prof beyond that old limen; had eliminated himself. Tried to see pulse on throat; his helmet was in way.

They had provided a program clock which was mighty kind of them. Showed I had been out forty-four-plus hours, all to plan, and in three hours we should receive horrible booting to place us in parking orbit around Terra. Then, after two circums, call it three more hours, we should start injection into landing program—if Poona Ground Control didn't change its feeble mind and leave us in orbit. Reminded self that was unlikely; grain is not left in vacuum longer than necessary. Has tendency to become puffed wheat or popped corn, which not only lowers value but can split those thin canisters like a melon. Wouldn't that be sweet? Why had they packed us in with grain? Why not just a load of rock that doesn't mind vacuum?

Had time to think about that and to become very thirsty. Took nipple for half a mouthful, no more, because certainly did not want to take six gees with a full bladder. (Need not have worried; was equipped with catheter. But did not know.)

When time got short I decided couldn't hurt Prof to give him a jolt of drug that was supposed to take him through heavy acceleration; then, after in parking orbit, give him heart stimulant—since didn't seem as if anything could hurt him.

Gave him first drug, then spent rest of minutes struggling back into straps, one-handed. Was sorry I didn't know name of my helpful friend; could have cursed him better.

Ten gees gets you into parking orbit around Terra in a mere 3.26×10^7 microseconds; merely seems longer, ten gravities being sixty times what a fragile sack of protoplasm should be asked to endure. Call it thirty-three seconds. My truthful word, I suspect my ancestress in Salem spent a worse half minute day they made her dance.

Gave Prof heart stimulant, then spent three hours trying to decide whether to drug self as well as Prof for landing sequence. Decided against. All drug had done for me at catapulting had been to swap a minute and a half of misery and two days of boredom for a century of terrible dreams—and besides, if those last minutes were going to be my very last, I decided to experience them. Bad as they would be, they were my very own and I would not give them up.

They were bad. Six gees did not feel better than ten; felt worse. Four gees no relief. Then we were kicked harder. Then suddenly, just for seconds, in free fall again. Then came splash which was *not* "gentle" and which we took on straps, not pads, as we went in head-first. Also, don't think Mike realized that, after diving in hard, we would then surface and splash hard again before we damped down into floating. Earthworms call it "floating" but is nothing like floating in free fall; you do it at one gee, six times what is decent, and odd side motions tacked on. *Very* odd motions—Mike had assured us that solar weather was good, no radiation danger inside that Iron Maiden. But he had not been so interested in Earthside Indian Ocean weather; prediction was acceptable for landing barges and suppose he felt that was good enough—and I would have thought so, too.

Stomach was supposed to be empty. But I filled helmet with sourest, nastiest fluid you would ever go a long way to avoid. Then we turned completely over and I got it in hair and eyes and some in nose. This is thing earthworms call "seasickness" and is one of many horrors they take for granted.

Won't go into long period during which we were towed into port. Let it stand that, in addition to seasickness, my air bottles were playing out. They were rated for twelve hours, plenty for a fifty-hour orbit most of which I was unconscious and none involving heavy exercise, but not quite enough with some hours of towing added. By time barge finally held still I was almost too dopy to care about trying to break out.

Except for one fact— We were picked up, I think, and tumbled a bit, then brought to rest with me upside down. This is a no-good position at best under one gravity; simply impossible when supposed to a) unstrap self, b) get out of suit-shaped cavity, c) get loose a sledgehammer fastened with butterfly nuts to bulkhead, d) smash same against breakaways guarding escape hatch, e) batter way out, and f) finally, drag an old man in a p-suit out after you.

Didn't finish step a); passed out head downwards.

Lucky this was emergency-last-resort routine. Stu LaJoie had been notified before we left; news services had been warned shortly before we landed. I woke up with people leaning over me, passed out again, woke up second time in hospital bed, flat on back with heavy feeling in chest—was heavy and weak all over—but not ill, just tired, bruised, hungry, thirsty, languid. Was a transparent plastic tent over bed which accounted for fact I was having no trouble breathing.

At once was closed in on from both sides, a tiny Hindu nurse with big eyes on one side, Stuart LaJoie on other. He grinned at me. "Hi, cobber! How do you feel?"

"Uh . . . I'm right. But oh *bloody!* What a way to travel!"

"Prof says it's the only way. What a tough old boy he is."

"Hold it. *Prof* said? Prof is dead."

"Not at all. Not in good shape—we've got him in a pneumatic bed with a round-the-clock watch and more instruments wired into him than you would believe. But he's alive and will be able to do his job. But, truly, he didn't mind the trip; he never knew about it, so he says. Went to sleep in one hospital, woke up in another. I thought he was wrong when he refused to let me wangle it to send a ship but he was not—the publicity has been *tremendous!*"

I said slowly, "You say Prof 'refused' to let you send a ship?"

"I should say 'Chairman Selene' refused. Didn't you see the dispatches, Mannie?"

"No." Too late to fight over it. "But last few days have been busy."

"A dinkum word! Here, too—don't recall when last I dossed."

"You sound like a Loonie."

"I *am* a Loonie, Mannie, don't ever doubt it. But the sister is looking daggers at me." Stu picked her up, turned her around. I decided he wasn't all Loonie yet. But nurse didn't resent. "Go play somewhere else, dear, and I'll give your patient back to you—still warm—in a few minutes." He shut a door on her and came back to bed. "But Adam was right; this way was not only wonderful publicity but safer."

"Publicity, I suppose. But 'safer'? Let's not talk about!"

"Safer, my old. You weren't shot at. Yet they had two hours in which they knew right where you were, a big fat target. They couldn't make up their minds what to do; they haven't formed a policy yet. They didn't even dare not bring you down on schedule; the news was full of it, I had stories slanted and waiting. Now they don't dare touch you, you're popular heroes. Whereas if I had waited to charter a ship and fetch you . . . Well, I don't know. We probably would have been ordered into parking orbit; then you two—and myself, perhaps—would have been taken off under arrest. No skipper is going to risk missiles no matter how much he's paid. The proof of the pudding, cobber. But let me brief you. You're both citizens of The People's Directorate of Chad, best I could do on short notice. Also, Chad has recognized Luna. I had to buy one prime minister, two generals, some tribal chiefs and a minister of finance—cheap for such a hurry-up job. I haven't been able to get you diplomatic immunity but I hope to, before you leave hospital. At present they haven't even dared arrest you; they can't figure out what you've done. They have guards outside but simply for your 'protection'—and a good thing, or you would have reporters nine deep shoving microphones into your face."

"Just what have we done?—that they know about, I mean. Illegal immigration?"

"Not even that, Mannie. You never were a consignee and you have derivative PanAfrican citizenship through one of your grandfathers, no huhu. In Professor de la Paz's case we dug up proof that he had been granted naturalized Chad citizenship forty years back, waited for the ink to dry, and used it. You're not even illegally entered here in India. Not only did they bring you down themselves, knowing that you were in that barge, but also a control officer very kindly and fairly cheaply stamped your virgin passports. In addition to that, Prof's exile has no legal existence as the government that proscribed him no longer exists and a competent court has taken notice—that was more expensive."

Nurse came back in, indignant as a mother cat. "Lord Stuart . . . you *must* let my patient rest!"

"At once, ma chère."

"You're 'Lord Stuart'?"

"Should be 'Comte.' Or I can lay a dubious claim to being the Macgregor. The blue-blood bit helps; these people haven't been happy since they took their royalty away from them."

As he left he patted her rump. Instead of screaming, she wiggled it. Was smiling as she came over to me. Stu was going to have to watch that stuff when he went back to Luna. If did.

She asked how I felt. Told her I was right, just hungry. "Sister, did you see some prosthetic arms in our luggage?"

She had and I felt better with number-six in place. Had selected it and number-two and social arm as enough for trip. Number-two was presumably still in Complex; I hoped somebody was taking care of it. But number-six is most all-around useful arm; with it and social one I'd be okay.

Two days later we left for Agra to present credentials to Federated Nations. I was in bad shape and not just high gee; could do well enough in a wheel chair and could even walk a little although did not in public. What I had was a sore throat that missed pneumonia only through drugs, traveler's trots, skin disease on hands and spreading to feet—just like my other trips to that disease-ridden hole, Terra. We Loonies don't know how lucky we are, living in a place that has tightest of quarantines, almost no vermin and what we have controlled by vacuum anytime necessary. Or unlucky, since we have almost no immunities if turns out we need them. Still, wouldn't swap; never heard word "venereal" until first went Earthside and had thought "common cold" was state of ice miner's feet.

And wasn't cheerful for other reason. Stu had fetched us a message from Adam Selene; buried in it, concealed even from Stu, was news that chances had dropped to worse than one in a hundred. Wondered what point in risking crazy trip if made odds worse? Did Mike really *know* what chances were? Couldn't see any way he could compute them no matter how many facts he had.

But Prof didn't seem worried. He talked to platoons of reporters, smiled at endless pictures, gave out statements, telling world he placed great confidence in Federated nations and was sure our just claims would be recognized and that he wanted to thank "Friends of Free Luna" for wonderful help in bringing true story of our small but sturdy nation before good people of Terra—F. of F.L. being Stu, a professional public opinion firm, several thousand chronic petition signers, and a great stack of Hong Kong dollars.

I had picture taken, too, and tried to smile, but dodged questions by pointing to throat and croaking.

In Agra we were lodged in a lavish suite in hotel that had once been palace of a maharajah (and still belonged to him, even though India is supposed to be socialist) and interviews and picture-taking went on—hardly dared get out of wheel chair even to visit W.C. as was under orders from Prof *never* to be photographed vertically. He was always either in bed or in a stretcher—bed baths, bedpans, everything—not only because safer, considering age, and easier for any Loonie, but also for pictures. His dimples and wonderful, gentle, persuasive personality were displayed in hundreds of millions of video screens, endless news pictures.

But his personality did not get us anywhere in Agra. Prof was carried to office of President of Grand Assembly, me being pushed alongside, and there he attempted to present his credentials as Ambassador to F.N. and prospective Senator for Luna—was referred to Secretary General and at his offices we were granted ten minutes with assistant secretary who sucked teeth and said he could accept our credentials "without prejudice and without implied commitment." They were referred to Credentials Committee—who sat on them.

I got fidgety. Prof read Keats. Grain barges continued to arrive at Bombay.

In a way was not sorry about latter. When we flew from Bombay to Agra we got up before dawn and were taken out to field as city was waking. Every Loonie has his hole, whether luxury of a long-established home like Davis Tunnels or rock still raw from drill; cubic is no problem and can't be for centuries.

Bombay was bee-swarms of people. Are over million (was told) who have no home but some piece of pavement. A family might claim right (and hand down by will, generation after generation) to sleep on a piece two meters long and one wide at a described location in front of a shop. Entire family sleeps on that space, meaning mother, father, kids, maybe a grandmother. Would not have believed if had not seen. At dawn in Bombay roadways, side pavements, even bridges are covered with tight carpet of human bodies. What do they do? Where do they work? How do they *eat?* (Did not look as if they did. Could count ribs.)

If I hadn't believed simple arithmetic that you can't ship stuff downhill forever without shipping replacement back, would have tossed in cards. But . . . tanstaafl. "There ain't no such thing as a free lunch," in Bombay or in Luna.

At last we were given appointment with an "Investigating Committee." Not what Prof had asked for. He had requested public hearing before Senate, complete with video cameras. Only camera at this session was its "in-camera" nature; was closed. Not *too* closed, I had little recorder. But no video. And took Prof two minutes to discover that committee was actually vips of Lunar Authority or their tame dogs.

Nevertheless was chance to talk and Prof treated them as if they had power to recognize Luna's independence and willingness to do so. While they treated us as a cross between naughty children and criminals up for sentencing.

Prof was allowed to make opening statement. With decorations trimmed away was assertion that Luna was de-facto a sovereign state, with an unopposed government in being, a civil condition of peace and order, a provisional president and cabinet carrying on necessary functions but anxious to return to private life as soon as Congress completed writing a constitution—and that we were here to ask that these facts be recognized de-jure and that Luna be allowed to take her rightful place in councils of mankind as a member of Federated Nations.

What Prof told them bore a speaking acquaintance with truth and they were not where they could spot discrepancies. Our "provisional president" was a computer, and "cabinet" was Wyoh, Finn, Comrade Clayton, and Terence Sheehan, editor of *Pravda,* plus Wolfgang Korsakov, board chairman of LuNoHoCo and a director of Bank of Hong Kong in Luna. But Wyoh was only person now in Luna who knew that "Adam Selene" was false face for a computer. She had been terribly nervous at being left to hold fort alone.

As it was, Adam's "oddity" in never being seen save over video was always an embarrassment. We had done our best to turn it into a "security necessity" by opening offices for him in cubic of Authority's Luna City office and then exploding a small bomb. After this "assassination attempt" comrades who had been most fretful about Adam's failure to stir around became loudest in demands that Adam must not take *any* chances—this being helped by editorials.

But I wondered while Prof was talking what these pompous chooms would think if they knew that our "president" was a collection of hardware owned by Authority?

But they just sat staring with chill disapproval, unmoved by Prof's rhetoric—probably best performance of his life considering he delivered it flat on back, speaking into a microphone without notes, and hardly able to see his audience.

Then they started in on us. Gentleman member from Argentina—never given their names; we weren't socially acceptable—this Argentino objected to phrase "former Warden" in Prof's speech; that designation had been obsolete half a century; he insisted that it be struck out and proper title inserted: "Protector of the Lunar Colonies by Appointment of the Lunar Authority." Any other wording offended dignity of Lunar Authority.

Prof asked to comment; "Honorable Chairman" permitted it. Prof said mildly that he accepted change since Authority was free to designate its servants in any fashion it pleased and was no intention to offend dignity of any agency of Federated Nations . . . but in view of functions of this office—former functions of this former office—citizens of Luna Free State would probably go on thinking of it by traditional name.

That made about six of them try to talk at once. Somebody objected to use of word "Luna" and still more to "Luna Free State"—it was "the Moon," Earth's Moon, a satellite of Earth and property of Federated Nations, just as Antarctica was—and these proceedings were a farce.

Was inclined to agree with last point. Chairman asked gentleman member from North America to please be in order and to address his remarks through Chair. Did Chair understand from witness's last remark that this alleged de-facto regime intended to interfere with consignee system?

Prof fielded that and tossed it back. "Honorable Chairman, I myself was a consignee, now Luna is my beloved home. My colleague, the Honorable the Undersecretary for Foreign Affairs Colonel O'Kelly Davis"—myself!—"is Luna born, and proud of his descent from four transported grandparents. Luna has grown strong on your outcasts. Give us your poor, your wretched; we welcome them. Luna has room for them, nearly forty million square kilometers, an area greater than all Africa—and almost totally empty. More than that, since by our method of living we occupy not 'area' but 'cubic' the mind cannot imagine the day when Luna would refuse another shipload of weary homeless."

Chairman said, "The witness is admonished to refrain from making speeches. The Chair takes it that your oratory means that the group you represent agrees to accept prisoners as before."

"No, sir."

"What? Explain yourself."

"Once an immigrant sets foot on Luna today he is a free man, no matter what his previous condition, free to go where he listeth."

"So? Then what's to keep a consignee from walking across the field, climbing into another ship, and returning here? I admit that I am puzzled at your apparent willingness to accept them . . . but *we* do not want them. It is our humane way of getting rid of incorrigibles who would otherwise have to be executed."

(Could have told him several things that would stop what he pictured; he had obviously never been to Luna. As for "incorrigibles," if really are, Luna eliminates such faster than Terra ever did. Back when I was very young, they sent us a gangster lord, from Los Angeles I believe; he arrived with squad of stooges, his bodyguards, and was cockily ready to take over Luna, as was rumored to have taken over a prison somewhere Earthside.

(None lasted two weeks. Gangster boss didn't make it to barracks; hadn't listened when told how to wear a p-suit.)

"There is nothing to keep him from going home so far as we are concerned, sir," Prof answered, "although your police here on Terra might cause him to think. But I've never heard of a consignee arriving with funds enough to buy a ticket home. Is this truly an issue? The ships are yours; Luna has no ships—and let me add that we are sorry that the ship scheduled for Luna this month was canceled.

I am not complaining that it forced on my colleague and myself"—Prof stopped to smile—"a most informal method of travel. I simply hope that this does not represent policy. Luna has no quarrel with you; your ships are welcome, your trade is welcome, we are at peace and wish to stay so. Please note that all scheduled grain shipments have come through on time."

(Prof did always have gift for changing subject.)

They fiddled with minor matters then. Nosy from North America wanted to know what had really happened to "the Ward—" He stopped himself. "The Protector. Senator Hobart." Prof answered that he had suffered a stroke (a "coup" is a "stroke") and was no longer able to carry out his duties—but was in good health otherwise and receiving constant medical care. Prof added thoughtfully that he suspected that the old gentleman had been failing for some time, in view of his indiscretions this past year . . . especially his many invasions of rights of free citizens, including ones who were not and never had been consignees.

Story was not hard to swallow. When those busy scientists managed to break news of our coup, they had reported Warden as dead . . . whereas Mike had kept him alive and on job by impersonating him. When Authority Earthside demanded a report from Warden on this wild rumor, Mike had consulted Prof, then had accepted call and given a convincing imitation of senility, managing to deny, confirm, and confuse every detail. Our announcements followed, and thereafter Warden was no longer available even in his computer alter ego. Three days later we declared independence.

This North American wanted to know what reason they had to believe that one word of this was true? Prof smiled most saintly smile and made effort to spread thin hands before letting them fall to coverlet. "The gentleman member from North America is urged to go to Luna, visit Senator Hobart's sickbed, and see for himself. Indeed all Terran citizens are invited to visit Luna at any time, see anything. We wish to be friends, we are at peace, we have nothing to hide. My only regret is that my country is unable to furnish transportation; for that we must turn to you."

Chinee member looked at Prof thoughtfully. He had not said a word but missed nothing.

Chairman recessed hearing until fifteen hundred. They gave us a retiring room and sent in lunch. I wanted to talk but Prof shook head, glanced around room, tapped ear. So I shut up. Prof napped then and I leveled out my wheel chair and joined him; on Terra we both slept all we could. Helped. Not enough.

They didn't wheel us back in until sixteen hundred; committee was already sitting. Chairman then broke own rule against speeches and made a long one more-in-sorrow-than-anger.

Started by reminding us that Luna Authority was a nonpolitical trusteeship charged with solemn duty of insuring that Earth's satellite the Moon—Luna, as some called it—was never used for military purposes. He told us that Authority had guarded this sacred trust more than a century, while governments fell and new governments rose, alliances shifted and shifted again—indeed, Authority was older than Federated Nations, deriving original charter from an older international body, and so well had it kept that trust that it had lasted through wars and turmoils and realignments.

(This is news? But you see what he was building towards.)

"The Lunar Authority cannot surrender its trust," he told us solemnly. "However, there appears to be no insuperable obstacle to the Lunar colonists, if they show political maturity, enjoying a degree of autonomy. This can be taken under advisement. Much depends on your behavior. The behavior, I should say, of all you colonists. There have been riots and destruction of property; this must not be."

I waited for him to mention ninety dead Goons; he never did. I will never make a statesman; I don't have high-level approach.

"Destroyed property must be paid for," he went on. "Commitments must be met. If this body you call a Congress can guarantee such things, it appears to this committee that this so-called Congress could in time be considered an agency of the Authority for many internal matters. Indeed it is conceivable that a stable local government might, in time, assume many duties now falling on the Protector and even be allowed a delegate, non-voting, in the Grand Assembly. But such recognition would have to be earned.

"But one thing must be made clear. Earth's major satellite, the Moon, is by nature's law forever the joint property of all the peoples of Earth. It does *not* belong to that handful who by accident of history happen to live there. The sacred trust laid upon the Lunar Authority is and forever must be the supreme law of Earth's Moon."

("—accident of history," huh? I expected Prof to shove it down his throat. I thought he would say—No, never did know what Prof would say. Here's what he did say):

Prof waited through several seconds of silence, then said, "Honorable Chairman, *who is to be exiled this time?*"

"What did you say?"

"Have you decided which one of you is to go into exile? Your Deputy Warden won't take the job"—this was true; he preferred to stay alive. "He is functioning now only because we have asked him to. If you persist in believing that we are not independent, then you must be planning to send up a new warden."

"Protector!"

"Warden. Let us not mince words. Though if we knew who he is to be, we might be happy to call him 'Ambassador.' We might be able to work with him, it might not be necessary to send with him armed hoodlums . . . to rape and murder our women!"

"Order! *Order!* The witness will come to order!"

"It is not I who was not in order, Honorable Chairman. Rape it was and murder most foul. But that is history and now we must look to the future. Whom are you going to exile?"

Prof struggled to raise self on elbow and I was suddenly alert; was a cue. "For you all know, sir, that it is a one-way trip. I was born here. You can see what effort it is for me to return even temporarily to the planet which has disinherited me. We are outcasts of Earth who—"

He collapsed. Was up out of my chair—and collapsed myself, trying to reach him.

Was not all play-acting even though I answered a cue. Is terrible strain on heart to get up suddenly on Terra; thick field grabbed and smashed me to floor.

SEVENTEEN

Neither of us was hurt and it made juicy news breaks, for I put recording in Stu's hands and he turned it over to his hired men. Nor were all headlines against us; Stu had recording cut and edited and slanted. AUTHORITY TO PLAY ODD MAN OUT?—LUNAR AMBASSADOR COLLAPSES UNDER GRILLING: "OUTCASTS!" HE CRIES—PROF PAZ POINTS FINGER OF SHAME: STORY PAGE 8.

Not all were good; nearest to a favorable story in India was editorial in New India *Times* inquiring whether Authority was risking bread of masses in failing to come to terms with Lunar insurgents. Was suggested that concessions could be made if would insure increased grain deliveries. Was filled with inflated statistics;

Luna did *not* feed "a hundred million Hindus"—unless you choose to think of our grain as making difference between malnutrition and starvation.

On other hand biggest New York paper opined that Authority had made mistake in treating with us at all, since only thing convicts understood was taste of lash—troops should land, set us in order, hang guilty, leave forces to keep order.

Was a quick mutiny, quickly subdued, in Peace Dragoons regiment from which our late oppressors had come, one started by rumor that they were to be shipped to Moon. Mutiny not hushed up perfectly; Stu hired good men.

Next morning a message reached us inquiring if Professor de la Paz was well enough to resume discussions? We went, and committee supplied doctor and nurse to watch over Prof. But this time we were searched—and a recorder removed from my pouch.

I surrendered it without much fuss; was Japanese job supplied by Stu—to be surrendered. Number-six arm has recess intended for a power pack but near enough size of my mini-recorder. Didn't need power that day—and most people, even hardened police officers, dislike to touch a prosthetic.

Everything discussed day before was ignored . . . except that chairman started session by scolding us for "breaking security of a closed meeting."

Prof replied that it had not been closed so far as we were concerned and that we would welcome newsmen, video cameras, a gallery, anyone, as Luna Free State had nothing to hide.

Chairman replied stiffly that so-called Free State did not control these hearings; these sessions were *closed*, not to be discussed outside this room, and that it was so ordered.

Prof looked at me. "Will you help me, Colonel?" I touched controls of chair, scooted around, was shoving his stretcher wagon with my chair toward door before chairman realized bluff had been called. Prof allowed himself to be persuaded to stay without promising anything. Hard to coerce a man who faints if he gets overexcited.

Chairman said that there had been many irrelevancies yesterday and matters discussed best left undiscussed—and that he would permit no digressions today. He looked at Argentino, then at North American.

He went on: "Sovereignty is an abstract concept, one that has been redefined many times as mankind has learned to live in peace. We need not discuss it. The real question, Professor—or even Ambassador de-facto, if you like; we shan't quibble—the real question is this: Are you prepared to guarantee that the Lunar Colonies will keep their commitments?"

"What commitments, sir?"

"All commitments, but I have in mind specifically your commitments concerning grain shipments."

"I know of no such commitments, sir," Prof answered with bland innocence.

Chairman's hand tightened on gavel. But he answered quietly, "Come, sir, there is no need to spar over words. I refer to the quota of grain shipments—and to the increased quota, a matter of thirteen percent, for this new fiscal year. Do we have your assurance that you will honor those commitments? This is a minimum basis for discussion, else these talks can go no further."

"Then I am sorry to say, sir, that it would appear that our talks must cease."

"You're not being serious."

"Quite serious, sir. The sovereignty of Free Luna is not the abstract matter you seem to feel it is. These commitments you speak of were the Authority contracting with itself. My country is not bound by such. Any commitments from the sovereign nation I have the honor to represent are still to be negotiated."

"Rabble!" growled North American. "I told you you were being too soft on them. Jailbirds. Thieves and whores. They don't understand decent treatment."

"Order!"

"Just remember, I told you. If I had them in Colorado, we would teach them a thing or two; we know how to handle their sort."

"The gentleman member will please be in order."

"I'm afraid," said Hindu member—Parsee in fact, but committeeman from India—"I'm afraid I must agree in essence with the gentleman member from the North American Directorate. India cannot accept the concept that the grain commitments are mere scraps of paper. Decent people do not play politics with hunger."

"And besides," the Argentino put in, "they breed like animals. Pigs!"

(Prof made me take a tranquilizing drug before that session. Had insisted on seeing me take it.)

Prof said quietly, "Honorable Chairman, may I have consent to amplify my meaning before we conclude, perhaps too hastily, that these talks must be abandoned?"

"Proceed."

"Unanimous consent? Free of interruption?"

Chairman looked around. "Consent is unanimous," he stated, "and the gentlemen members are placed on notice that I will invoke special rule fourteen at the next outburst. The sergeant-at-arms is directed to note this and act. The witness will proceed."

"I will be brief, Honorable Chairman." Prof said something in Spanish; all I caught was "Señor." Argentino turned dark but did not answer. Prof went on, "I must first answer the gentleman member from North America on a matter of personal privilege since he has impugned my fellow countrymen. I for one have seen the inside of more than one jail; I accept the title—nay, I glory in the title of 'jailbird.' We citizens of Luna are jailbirds and descendants of jailbirds. But Luna herself is a stern schoolmistress; those who have lived through her harsh lessons have no cause to feel ashamed. In Luna City a man may leave purse unguarded or home unlocked and feel no fear . . . I wonder if this is true in Denver? As may be, I have no wish to visit Colorado to learn a thing or two; I am satisfied with what Mother Luna has taught me. And rabble we may be, but we are now a rabble in arms."

"To the gentleman member from India let me say that we do not 'play politics with hunger.' What we ask is an open discussion of facts of nature unbound by political assumptions false to fact. If we can hold this discussion, I can promise to show a way in which Luna can continue grain shipments and expand them enormously . . . to the great benefit of India."

Both Chinee and Indian looked alert. Indian started to speak, checked himself, then said, "Honorable Chairman, will the Chair ask the witness to explain what he means?"

"The witness is invited to amplify."

"Honorable Chairman, gentlemen members, there is indeed a way for Luna to expand by tenfold or even a hundred her shipments to our hungry millions. The fact that grain barges continued to arrive on schedule during our time of trouble and are still arriving today is proof that our intentions are friendly. But you do not get milk by beating the cow. Discussions of how to augment our shipments must be based on the facts of nature, not on the false assumption that we are slaves, bound by a work quota we never made. So which shall it be? Will you persist in believing that we are slaves, indentured to an Authority other than ourselves? Or will you acknowledge that we are free, negotiate with us, and learn how we can help you?"

Chairman said, "In other words you ask us to buy a pig in a poke. You demand that we legalize your outlaw status . . . *then* you will talk about fantastic claims that you can increase grain shipments ten- or a hundredfold. What you claim is impossible; I am expert in Lunar economics. And what you ask is impossible; it takes the Grand Assembly to admit a new nation."

"Then place it before the Grand Assembly. Once seated as sovereign equals, we will discuss how to increase shipments and negotiate terms. Honorable Chairman, *we* grow the grain, we *own* it. We can grow far more. But not as slaves. Luna's sovereign freedom must first be recognized."

"Impossible and you know it. The Lunar Authority cannot abdicate its sacred responsibility."

Prof sighed. "It appears to be an impasse. I can only suggest that these hearings be recessed while we all take thought. Today our barges are arriving . . . but the moment that I am forced to notify my government that I have failed . . . they . . . will . . . *stop!*"

Prof's head sank back on pillow as if it had been too much for him—as may have been. I was doing well enough but was young and had had practice in how to visit Terra and stay alive. A Loonie his age should not risk it. After minor foofooraw which Prof ignored they loaded us into a lorry and scooted us back to hotel. Once under way I said, "Prof, what was it you said to Señor Jellybelly that raised blood pressure?"

He chuckled. "Comrade Stuart's investigations of these gentlemen turn up remarkable facts. I asked who owned a certain brothel off Calle Florida in B.A. these days and did it now have a star redhead?"

"Why? You used to patronize it?" Tried to imagine Prof in such!

"Never. It has been forty years since I was last in Buenos Aires. *He* owns that establishment, Manuel, through a dummy, and his wife, a beauty with Titian hair, once worked in it."

Was sorry had asked. "Wasn't that a foul blow? And undiplomatic?"

But Prof closed eyes and did not answer.

He was recovered enough to spend an hour at a reception for newsmen that night, with white hair framed against a purple pillow and thin body decked out in embroidered pajamas. Looked like vip corpse at an important funeral, except for eyes and dimples. I looked mighty vip too, in black and gold uniform which Stu claimed was Lunar diplomatic uniform of my rank. Could have been, if Luna had had such things—did not or I would have known. I prefer a p-suit; collar was tight. Nor did I ever find out what decorations on it meant. A reporter asked me about one, based on Luna at crescent as seen from Terra; told him it was a prize for spelling. Stu was in earshot and said, "The Colonel is modest. That decoration is of the same rank as the Victoria Cross and in his case was awarded for an act of gallantry on the glorious, tragic day of—"

He led him away, still talking. Stu could lie standing up almost as well as Prof. Me, I have to think out a lie ahead of time.

India newspapers and casts were rough that night; "threat" to stop grain shipments made them froth. Gentlest proposal was to clean out Luna, exterminate us "criminal troglodytes" and replace us with "honest Hindu peasants" who understood sacredness of life and would ship grain and more grain.

Prof picked that night to talk and give handouts about Luna's inability to continue shipments, and why—and Stu's organization spread release throughout Terra. Some reporters took time to dig out sense of figures and tackled Prof on glaring discrepancy:

"Professor de la Paz, here you say that grain shipments will dwindle away through failure of natural resources and that by 2082 Luna won't even be able to feed its own people. Yet earlier today you told the Lunar Authority that you could increase shipments a dozen times or more."

Prof said sweetly, "That committee is the Lunar Authority?"

"Well . . . it's an open secret."

"So it is, sir, but they have maintained the fiction of being an impartial investigating committee of the Grand Assembly. Don't you think they should disqualify themselves? So that we could receive a fair hearing?"

"Uh . . . it's not my place to say, Professor. Let's get back to my question. How do you reconcile the two?"

"I'm interested in why it's not your place to say, sir. Isn't it the concern of every citizen of Terra to help avoid a situation which will produce war between Terra and her neighbor?"

" '*War*'? What in the world makes you speak of 'war,' Professor?"

"Where else can it end, sir? If the Lunar Authority persists in its intransigence? We *cannot* accede to their demands; those figures show why. If they will not see this, then they will attempt to subdue us by force . . . and we will fight back. Like cornered rats—for cornered we are, unable to retreat, unable to surrender. *We* do not choose war; we wish to live in peace with our neighbor planet—in peace and peacefully trade. But the choice is not ours. We are small, you are gigantic. I predict that the next move will be for the Lunar Authority to attempt to subdue Luna by force. This 'peacekeeping' agency will start the first interplanetary war."

Journalist frowned. "Aren't you overstating it? Let's assume that the Authority—or the Grand Assembly, as the Authority hasn't any warships of its own—let's suppose the nations of Earth decide to displace your, uh, 'government.' You might fight, on Luna—I suppose you would. But that hardly constitutes interplanetary war. As you pointed out, Luna has no ships. To put it bluntly, you can't reach us."

I had chair close by Prof's stretcher, listening. He turned to me. "Tell them, Colonel."

I parroted it. Prof and Mike had worked out stock situations; I had memorized and was ready with answers. I said, "Do you gentlemen remember the *Pathfinder?* How she came plunging in, out of control?"

They remembered. Nobody forgets greatest disaster of early days of space flight when unlucky *Pathfinder* hit a Belgian village.

"We have no ships," I went on, "but would be possible to *throw* those bargeloads of grain . . . instead of delivering them into parking orbit."

Next day this evoked a headline: LOONIES THREATEN TO THROW RICE. At moment it produced awkward silence.

Finally journalist said, "Nevertheless I would like to know how you reconcile your two statements—no more grain after 2082 . . . and ten or a hundred times as much."

"There is no conflict," Prof answered. "They are based on different sets of circumstances. The figures you have been looking at show the present circumstances . . . and the disaster they will produce in only a few years through drainage of Luna's natural resources—disaster which these Authority bureaucrats—or should I say 'authoritarian bureaucrats?'—would avert by telling us to stand in the corner like naughty children!"

Prof paused for labored breathing, went on: "The circumstances under which we can continue, or greatly increase, our grain shipments are the obvious corollary of the first. As an old teacher I can hardly refrain from classroom habits; the corollary should be left as an exercise for the student. Will someone attempt it?"

Was uncomfortable silence, then a little man with strange accent said slowly, "It sound to me as if you talk about way to replenish natural resource."

"Capital! Excellent!" Prof flashed dimples. "You, sir, will have a gold star on your term report! To make grain requires water and plant foods—phosphates, other things, ask the experts. Send these things to us; we'll send them back as wholesome grain. Put down a hose in the limitless Indian Ocean. Line up those millions of cattle here in India; collect their end product and ship it to us. Collect your own night soil—don't bother to sterilize it; we've learned to do such things cheaply and easily. Send us briny sea water, rotten fish, dead animals, city sewage, cow manure, offal of any sort—and we will send it back, tonne for tonne as golden grain. Send ten times as much, we'll send back ten times as much grain. Send us your poor, your dispossessed, send them by thousands and hundreds of thousands; we'll teach them swift, efficient Lunar methods of tunnel farming and ship you back unbelievable tonnage. Gentlemen, Luna is one enormous fallow farm, four thousand million hectares, waiting to be plowed!"

That startled them. Then someone said slowly, "But what do you get out of it? Luna, I mean."

Prof shrugged. "Money. In the form of trade goods. There are many things you make cheaply which are dear in Luna. Drugs. Tools. Book films. Gauds for our lovely ladies. Buy our grain and you can sell to us at a happy profit."

A Hindu journalist looked thoughtful, started to write. Next to him was a European type who seemed unimpressed. He said, "Professor, have you any idea of the *cost* of shipping that much tonnage to the Moon?"

Prof waved it aside. "A technicality. Sir, there was a time when it was not simply expensive to ship goods across oceans but impossible. Then it was expensive, difficult, dangerous. Today you sell goods half around your planet almost as cheaply as next door; long-distance shipping is the least important factor in cost. Gentlemen, I am not an engineer. But I have learned this about engineers. When something *must* be done, engineers can find a way that is economically feasible. If you *want* the grain that we can grow, turn your engineers loose." Prof gasped and labored, signaled for help and nurses wheeled him away.

I declined to be questioned on it, telling them that they must talk to Prof when he was well enough to see them. So they pecked at me on other lines. One man demanded to know why, since we paid no taxes, we colonists thought we had a right to run things our own way? After all, those colonies had been established by Federated Nations—by some of them. It had been terribly expensive, Earth had paid all bills—and now you colonists enjoy benefits and pay not one dime of taxes. Was that fair?

I wanted to tell him to blow it. But Prof had again made me take a tranquillizer and had required me to swot that endless list of answers to trick questions. "Let's take that one at a time," I said. "First, what is it you want us to pay taxes *for?* Tell me what I get and perhaps I'll buy it. No, put it this way. Do *you* pay taxes?"

"Certainly I do! And so should you."

"And what do you get for your taxes?"

"Huh? Taxes pay for government."

I said, "Excuse me, I'm ignorant. I've lived my whole life in Luna, I don't know much about your government. Can you feed it to me in small pieces? What do you get for your money?"

They all got interested and anything this aggressive little choom missed, others supplied. I kept a list. When they stopped, I read it back:

"Free hospitals—aren't any in Luna. Medical insurance—we have that but apparently not what you mean by it. If a person wants insurance, he goes to a bookie and works out a bet. You can hedge anything, for a price. I don't hedge my health, I'm healthy. Or was till I came here. We have a public library, one Carnegie Foundation started with a few book films. It gets along by charging fees. Public roads. I suppose that would be our tubes. But they are no more free than air is free. Sorry, you have free air here, don't you? I mean our tubes were built by companies who put up money and are downright nasty about expecting it back and then some. Public schools. There are schools in all warrens and I never heard of them turning away pupils, so I guess they are 'public.' But they pay well, too, because anyone in Luna who knows something useful and is willing to teach it, charges all the traffic will bear."

I went on: "Let's see what else— Social security. I'm not sure what that is but, whatever it is, we don't have it. Pensions. You can buy a pension. Most people don't; most families are large and old people, say a hundred and up, either fiddle along at something they like, or sit and watch video. Or sleep. They sleep a lot, after say a hundred and twenty."

"Sir, excuse me. Do people *really* live as long on the Moon as they say?"

I looked surprised but wasn't; this was a "stimulated question" for which an answer had been taped. "Nobody knows how long a person will live in Luna; we haven't been there long enough. Our oldest citizens were born Earthside, it's no test. So far, no one born in Luna died of old age, but that's still no test; they haven't had time to grow old yet, less than a century. But— Well, take me, madam; how old would you say I am? I'm authentic Loonie, third generation."

"Uh, truthfully, Colonel Davis, I was surprised at your

youthfulness—for this mission, I mean. You appear to be about twenty-two. Are you older? Not much, I fancy."

"Madam, I regret that your local gravitation makes it impossible for me to bow. Thank you. I've been married longer than that."

"What? Oh, you're jesting!"

"Madam, I would never venture to guess a lady's age but, if you will emigrate to Luna, you will keep your present youthful loveliness much longer and add at least twenty years to your life." I looked at list. "I'll lump the rest of this together by saying we don't have any of it in Luna, so I can't see any reason to pay taxes for it. On that other point, sir, surely you know that the initial cost of the colonies has long since been repaid several times over through grain shipments alone? We are being bled white of our most essential resources . . . and not even being paid an open-market price. That's why the Lunar Authority is being stubborn; they intend to go on bleeding us. The idea that Luna has been an expense to Terra and the investment must be recovered is a lie invented by the Authority to excuse their treating us as slaves. The truth is that Luna has not cost Terra one dime this century—and the original investment has long since been paid back."

He tried to rally. "Oh, surely you're not claiming that the Lunar colonies have paid all the billions of dollars it took to develop space flight?"

"I could present a good case. However there is no excuse to charge that against *us*. *You* have space flight, you people of Terra. *We* do *not*. Luna has not one ship. So why should we pay for what we never received? It's like the rest of this list. We don't get it, why should we pay for it?"

Had been stalling, waiting for a claim that Prof had told me I was sure to hear . . . and got it at last.

"Just a moment, please!" came a confident voice. "You ignored the two most important items on that list. Police protection and armed forces. You boasted that you were willing to pay for what you get . . . so how about paying almost a century of back taxes for those two? It should be quite a bill, quite a bill!" He smiled smugly.

Wanted to thank him!—thought Prof was going to chide me for failing to yank it out. People looked at each other and nodded, pleased I had been scored on. Did best to look innocent. "Please? Don't understand. Luna has neither police nor armed forces."

"You know what I mean. You enjoy the protection of the Peace Forces of the Federated Nations. And you do have police. Paid for by the Lunar Authority! I know, to my certain knowledge, that two phalanges were sent to the Moon less than a year ago to serve as policemen."

"Oh." I sighed. "Can you tell me how F.N. peace forces protect Luna? I did not know that any of your nations wanted to attack us. We are far away and have nothing anyone envies. Or did you mean we should pay them to leave us alone? If so, there is an old saying that once you pay Danegeld, you never get rid of the Dane. Sir, we will *fight* F.N. armed forces if we must . . . we shall never *pay* them.

"Now about those so-called 'policemen.' They were not sent to protect *us*. Our Declaration of Independence told the true story about those hoodlums—did your newspapers print it?" (Some had, some hadn't—depended on country.) "They went mad and started raping and murdering! And now they are *dead!* So don't send us any more troops!"

Was suddenly "tired" and had to leave. Really was tired; not much of an actor and making that talk-talk come out way Prof thought it should was strain.

EIGHTEEN

Was not told till later that I had received an assist in that interview; lead about "police" and "armed forces" had been fed by a stooge; Stu LaJoie took no chances. But by time I knew, I had had experience in handling interviews; we had them endlessly.

Despite being tired was not through that night. In addition to press some Agra diplomatic corps had risked showing up—few and none officially, even from Chad. But we were curiosities and they wanted to look at us.

Only one was important, a Chinee. Was startled to see him; he was Chinee member of committee. I met him, simply as "Dr. Chan" and we pretended to be meeting first time.

He was that Dr. Chan who was then Senator from Great China

and also Great China's long-time number-one boy in Lunar Authority—and, much later, Vice-Chairman and Premier, shortly before his assassination.

After getting out point I was supposed to make, with bonus through others that could have waited, I guided chair to bedroom and was at once summoned to Prof's. "Manuel, I'm sure you noticed our distinguished visitor from the Middle Kingdom."

"Old Chinee from committee?"

"Try to curb the Loonie talk, son. Please don't use it at all here, even with me. Yes. He wants to know what we meant by 'tenfold or a hundredfold.' So tell him."

"Straight? Or swindle?"

"The straight. This man is no fool. Can you handle the technical details?"

"Done my homework. Unless he's expert in ballistics."

"He's not. But don't pretend to know anything you don't know. And don't assume that he's friendly. But he could be enormously helpful if he concludes that our interests and his coincide. But don't try to persuade him. He's in my study. Good luck. And remember—speak standard English."

Dr. Chan stood up as I came in; I apologized for not standing. He said that he understood difficulties that a gentleman from Luna labored under here and for me not to exert myself—shook hands with himself and sat down.

I'll skip some formalities. Did we or did we not have some specific solution when we claimed there was a cheap way to ship massive tonnage to Luna?

Told him was a method, expensive in investment but cheap in running expenses. "It's the one we use on Luna, sir. A catapult, an escape-speed induction catapult."

His expression changed not at all. "Colonel, are you aware that such has been proposed many times and always rejected for what seemed good reasons? Something to do with air pressure."

"Yes, Doctor. But we believe, based on extensive analyses by computer and on our experience with catapulting, that today the problem can be solved. Two of our larger firms, the LuNoHo Company and the Bank of Hong Kong in Luna, are ready to head a syndicate to do it as a private venture. They would need help here on Earth and might share voting stock—though they would prefer to sell bonds and retain control. Primarily what they need is a concession from some government, a permanent easement on which to build the catapult. Probably India."

(Above was set speech. LuNoHoCo was bankrupt if anybody examined books, and Hong Kong Bank was strained; was acting as central bank for country undergoing upheaval. Purpose was to get in last word. "India." Prof had coached me that this word *must* come *last*.)

Dr. Chan answered, "Never mind financial aspects. Anything which is physically possible can always be made financially possible; money is a bugaboo of small minds. Why do you select India?"

"Well, sir, India now consumes, I believe, over ninety percent of our grain shipments—"

"Ninety-three point one percent."

"Yes, sir. India is deeply interested in our grain, so it seemed likely that she would cooperate. She could grant us land, make labor and materials available, and so forth. But I mentioned India because she holds a wide choice of possible sites, very high mountains not too far from Terra's equator. The latter is not essential, just helpful. But the site *must* be a high mountain. It's that air pressure you spoke of, or air density. The catapult head should be at as high altitude as feasible but the ejection end, where the load travels over eleven kilometers per second, *must* be in air so thin that it approaches vacuum. Which calls for a very high mountain. Take the peak Nanda Devi, around four hundred kilometers from here. It has a railhead sixty kilometers from it and a road almost to its base. It is eight thousand meters high. I don't know that Nanda Devi is ideal. It is simply a possible site with good logistics; the ideal site would have to be selected by Terran engineers."

"A higher mountain would be better?"

"Oh, yes, sir!" I assured him. "A higher mountain would be preferred over one nearer the equator. The catapult can be designed to make up for loss in free ride from Earth's rotation. The difficult thing is to avoid so far as possible this pesky thick atmosphere. Excuse me, Doctor; I did not mean to criticize your planet."

"There are higher mountains. Colonel, tell me about this proposed catapult."

I started to. "The length of an escape-speed catapult is determined by the acceleration. We think—or the computer calculates—that an acceleration of twenty gravities is about optimum. For Earth's escape speed this requires a catapult three hundred twenty-three kilometers in length. Therefore—"

"Stop, please! Colonel, are you seriously proposing to bore a hole over three hundred kilometers deep?"

"Oh, no! Construction has to be aboveground to permit shock waves to expand. The stator would stretch nearly horizontally, rising perhaps four kilometers in three hundred and in a straight line—almost straight, as Coriolis acceleration and other minor variables make it a gentle curve. The Lunar catapult is straight so far as the eye can see and so nearly horizontal that the barges just miss some peaks beyond it."

"Oh. I thought that you were overestimating the capacity of present-day engineering. We drill deeply today. Not that deeply. Go on."

"Doctor, it may be that common misconception which caused you to check me is why such a catapult has not been constructed before this. I've seen those earlier studies. Most assumed that a catapult would be vertical, or that it would have to tilt up at the end to toss the spacecraft into the sky—and neither is feasible nor necessary. I suppose the assumption arose from the fact that your spaceships *do* boost straight up, or nearly."

I went on: "But they do that to get above atmosphere, not to get into orbit. Escape speed is not a vector quantity; it is scalar. A load bursting from a catapult at escape speed will not return to Earth no matter what its direction. Uh . . . two corrections: it must not be headed toward the Earth itself but at some part of the sky hemisphere, and it must have enough added velocity to punch through whatever atmosphere it still traverses. If it is headed in the right direction it will wind up at Luna."

"Ah, yes. Then this catapult could be used but once each lunar month?"

"No, sir. On the basis on which you were thinking it would be once every day, picking the time to fit where Luna will be in her orbit. But in fact—or so the computer says; I'm not an astronautics expert—in fact this catapult could be used almost any time, simply by varying ejection speed, and the orbits could still wind up at Luna."

"I don't visualize that."

"Neither do I, Doctor, but— Excuse me but isn't there an exceptionally fine computer at Peiping University?"

"And if there is?" (Did I detect an increase in bland inscrutability? A Cyborg-computer— Pickled brains? Or live ones, aware? Horrible, either way.)

"Why not ask a topnotch computer for all possible ejection times for such a catapult as I have described? Some orbits go far outside Luna's orbit before returning to where they can be captured by Luna, taking a fantastically long time. Others hook around Terra and then go quite directly. Some are as simple as the ones we use from Luna. There are periods each day when short orbits may be selected. But a load is in the catapult less than one minute; the limitation is how fast the loads can be made ready. It is even possible to have more than one load going up the catapult at a time if the power is sufficient and computer control is versatile. The only thing that worries me is— These high mountains, they are covered with snow?"

"Usually," he answered. "Ice and snow and bare rock."

"Well, sir, being born in Luna, I don't know anything about snow. The stator would not only have to be rigid under the heavy gravity of this planet but would have to withstand dynamic thrusts at twenty gravities. I don't suppose it could be anchored to ice or snow. Or could it be?"

"I'm not an engineer, Colonel, but it seems unlikely. Snow and ice would have to be removed. And kept clear. Weather would be a problem, too."

"Weather I know nothing about, Doctor, and all I know about ice is that it has a heat of crystallization of three hundred thirty-five million joules per tonne. I have no idea how many tonnes would have to be melted to clear the site, or how much energy would be required to keep it clear, but it seems to me that it might take as large a reactor to keep it free of ice as to power the catapult."

"We can build reactors, we can melt ice. Or engineers can be sent north for re-education until they *do* understand ice." Dr. Chan smiled and I shivered. "However, the engineering of ice and snow was solved in Antarctica years ago; don't worry about it. A clear, solid-rock site about three hundred fifty kilometers long at a high altitude— Anything else I should know?"

"Not much, sir. Melted ice could be collected near the catapult head and thus be the most massy part of what will be shipped to Luna—quite a saving. Also the steel canisters would be re-used to ship grain to Earth, thus stopping another drain that Luna can't take. No reason why a canister should not make the trip hundreds of times. At Luna it would be much the way barges are now landed off Bombay, solid-charge retrorockets programmed by ground control—except that it would be much cheaper, two and a half kilometer-seconds change of motion versus eleven-plus, a squared factor of about twenty—but actually even more favorable, as retros are parasitic weight and the payload improves accordingly. There is even a way to improve that."

"How?"

"Doctor, this is outside my specialty. But everybody knows that your best ships use hydrogen as reaction mass heated by a fusion reactor. But hydrogen is expensive in Luna and any mass could be reaction mass; it just would not be as efficient. Can you visualize an enormous, brute-force space tug designed to fit Lunar conditions? It would use raw rock, vaporized, as reaction mass and would be designed to go up into parking orbit, pick up those shipments from Terra, bring them down to Luna's surface. It would be ugly, all the fancies stripped away—might not be manned even by a Cyborg. It can be piloted from the ground, by computer."

"Yes, I suppose such a ship could be designed. But let's not complicate things. Have you covered the essentials about this catapult?"

"I believe so, Doctor. The site is the crucial thing. Take that peak Nanda Devi. By the maps I have seen it appears to have a long, very high ridge sloping to the west for about the length of our catapult. If that is true, it would be ideal—less to cut away, less to bridge. I don't mean that it is *the* ideal site but that is the sort to look for: a very high peak with a long, long ridge west of it."

"I understand." Dr. Chan left abruptly.

Next few weeks I repeated that in a dozen countries, always in private and with implication that it was secret. All that changed was name of mountain. In Ecuador I pointed out that Chimborazo was almost on equator—ideal! But in Argentina I emphasized that their Aconcagua was highest peak in Western Hemisphere. In Bolivia I noted that Altoplano was as high as Tibetan Plateau (almost true), much nearer equator, and offered a wide choice of sites for easy construction leading up to peaks comparable to any on Terra.

I talked to a North American who was a political opponent of that choom who had called us "rabble." I pointed out that, while Mount McKinley was comparable to anything in Asia or South America, there was much to be said for Mauna Loa—extreme ease of construction. Doubling gees to make it short enough to fit, and Hawaii would be Spaceport of World . . . *whole* world, for we talked about day when Mars would be exploited and freight for three (possibly four) planets would channel through their "Big Island."

Never mentioned Mauna Loa's volcanic nature; instead I noted that location permitted an aborted load to splash harmlessly in Pacific Ocean.

In Sovunion was only one peak discussed—Lenin, over seven thousand meters (and rather too close to their big neighbor).

Kilimanjaro, Popocatepetl, Logan, El Libertado—my favorite peak changed by country; all that we required was that it be "highest mountain" in hearts of locals. I found something good to say about modest mountains of Chad when we were entertained there and rationalized so well I almost believed it.

Other times, with help of leading questions from Stu LaJoie's stooges, I talked about chemical engineering (of which I know nothing but had memorized facts) on surface of Luna, where endless free vacuum and sunpower and limitless raw materials and predictable conditions permitted ways of processing expensive or impossible Earthside—when day arrived that cheap shipping both ways made it profitable to exploit Luna's virgin resources. Was always a suggestion that entrenched bureaucracy of Lunar Authority had failed to see great potential of Luna (true), plus answer to a question always asked, which answer asserted that Luna could accept any number of colonists.

This also was true, although never mentioned that Luna (yes, and sometimes Luna's Loonies) killed about half of new chums. But people we talked to rarely thought of emigrating themselves; they thought of forcing or persuading others to emigrate to relieve crowding—and to reduce their own taxes. Kept mouth shut about fact that half-fed swarms we saw everywhere did breed faster than even catapulting could offset.

We could not house, feed, and train even a million new chums each year—and a million wasn't a drop on Terra; more babies than that were conceived every night. We could accept far more than would emigrate voluntarily but if they used forced emigration and flooded us . . . Luna has only one way to deal with a new chum: Either he makes not one fatal mistake, in personal behavior or in coping with environment that will bite without warning . . . or he winds up as fertilizer in a tunnel farm.

All that immigration in huge numbers could mean would be that a larger percentage of immigrants would die—too few of us to help them past natural hazards.

However, Prof did most talking about "Luna's great future." I talked about catapults.

During weeks we waited for committee to recall us, we covered much ground. Stu's men had things set up and only question was how much we could take. Would guess that every week on Terra chopped a year off our lives, maybe more for Prof. But he never complained and was always ready to be charming at one more reception.

We spent extra time in North America. Date of our Declaration of Independence, exactly three hundred years after that of North American British colonies, turned out to be wizard propaganda and Stu's manipulators made most of it. North Americans are sentimental about their "United States" even though it ceased to mean anything once their continent had been rationalized by F.N. They elect a president every eight years, why, could not say—why do

British still have Queen?—and boast of being "sovereign." "Sovereign," like "love," means anything you want it to mean; it's a word in dictionary between "sober" and "sozzled."

"Sovereignty" meant much in North America and "Fourth of July" was a magic date; Fourth-of-July League handled our appearances and Stu told us that it had not cost much to get it moving and nothing to keep going; League even raised money used elsewhere—North Americans enjoy giving no matter who gets it.

Farther south Stu used another date; his people planted idea that coup d'état had been 5 May instead of two weeks later. We were greeted with "Cinco de Mayo! Libertad! Cinco de Mayo!" I thought they were saying, "Thank you"— Prof did all talking.

But in 4th-of-July country I did better. Stu had me quit wearing a left arm in public, sleeves of my costumes were sewed up so that stump could not be missed, and word was passed that I had lost it "fighting for freedom." Whenever I was asked about it, all I did was smile and say, "See what comes of biting nails?"—then change subject.

I never liked North America, even first trip. It is not most crowded part of Terra, has a mere billion people. In Bombay they sprawl on pavements; in Great New York they pack them vertically—not sure anyone sleeps. Was glad to be in invalid's chair.

Is mixed-up place another way; they care about skin color—by making point of how they *don't* care. First trip I was always too light or too dark, and somehow blamed either way, or was always being expected to take stand on things I have no opinions on. Bog knows *I* don't know what genes I have. One grandmother came from a part of Asia where invaders passed through as regularly as locusts, raping as they went—why not ask *her?*

Learned to handle it by my second makee-learnee but it left a sour taste. Think I prefer a place as openly racist as India, where if you aren't Hindu, you're nobody—except that Parsees look down on Hindus and vice versa. However I never really had to cope with North America's reverse-racism when being "Colonel O'Kelly Davis, Hero of Lunar Freedom."

We had swarms of bleeding hearts around us, anxious to help. I let them do two things for me, things I had never had time, money, or energy for as a student: I saw Yankees play and visited Salem.

Should have kept my illusions. Baseball is better over video, you can really see it and aren't pushed in by two hundred thousand other people. Besides, somebody should have shot that outfield. I spent most of that game dreading moment when they would have to get my chair out through crowd—that and assuring host that I was having a wonderful time.

Salem was just a place, no worse (and no better) than rest of Boston. After seeing it I suspected they had hanged wrong witches. But day wasn't wasted; I was filmed laying a wreath on a place where a bridge had been in another part of Boston, Concord, and made a memorized speech—bridge is still there, actually; you can see it, down through glass. Not much of a bridge.

Prof enjoyed it all, rough as it was on him; Prof had great capacity for enjoying. He always had something new to tell about great future of Luna. In New York he gave managing director of a hotel chain, one with rabbit trade mark, a sketch of what could be done with resorts in Luna—once excursion rates were within reach of more people—visits too short to hurt anyone, escort service included, exotic side trips, gambling—no taxes.

Last point grabbed attention, so Prof expanded it into "longer old age" theme—a chain of retirement hostels where an earthworm could live on Terran old-age pension and go on living, twenty, thirty, forty years longer than on Terra. As an exile—but which was better? A live old age in Luna? Or a funeral crypt on Terra? His descendants could pay visits and fill those resort hotels. Prof embellished with pictures of "nightclubs" with acts impossible in Terra's horrible gravity, sports to fit our decent level of gravitation—even talked about swimming pools and ice skating and possibility of *flying!* (Thought he had tripped his safeties.) He finished by hinting that Swiss cartel had tied it up.

Next day he was telling foreign-divisions manager of Chase International Panagra that a Luna City branch should be staffed with paraplegics, paralytics, heart cases, amputees, others who found high gravity a handicap. Manager was a fat man who wheezed, he may have been thinking of it personally—but his ears pricked up at "no taxes."

We didn't have it all our own way. News was often against us and were always hecklers. Whenever I had to take them on without Prof's help I was likely to get tripped. One man tackled me on Prof's statement to committee that we "owned" grain grown in Luna; he seemed to take it for granted that we did not. Told him I did not understand question.

He answered, "Isn't it true, Colonel, that your provisional government has asked for membership in Federated Nations?"

Should have answered, "No comment." But fell for it and agreed. "Very well," he said, "the impediment seems to be the counterclaim that the Moon belongs to the Federated Nations—as it always has—under supervision of the Lunar Authority. Either way, by your own admission, that grain belongs to the Federated Nations, in trust."

I asked how he reached that conclusion? He answered, "Colonel, you style yourself 'Undersecretary of Foreign Affairs.' Surely you are familiar with the charter of the Federated Nations."

I had skimmed it. "Reasonably familiar," I said—cautiously, I thought.

"Then you know the First Freedom guaranteed by the Charter and its current application through F & A Control Board Administrative Order Number eleven-seventy-six dated three March of this year. You concede therefore that all grain grown on the Moon in excess of the local ration is ab initio and beyond contest the property of all, title held in trust by the Federated Nations through its agencies for distribution as needed." He was writing as he talked. "Have you anything to add to that concession?"

I said, "What in Bog's name you talking about?" Then, "Come back! Haven't conceded anything!"

So *Great New York Times* printed:

LUNAR "UNDERSECRETARY" SAYS: "FOOD BELONGS TO HUNGRY"

New York Today—O'Kelly Davis, soi-disant "Colonel of the Armed Forces of Free Luna" here on a junket to stir up support for the insurgents in the F.N. Lunar colonies, said in a voluntary statement to this paper that the "Freedom from

Hunger" clause in the Grand Charter applied to the Lunar grain shipments—

I asked Prof how should have handled? "Always answer an unfriendly question with another question," he told me. "Never ask him to clarify; he'll put words in your mouth. This reporter— Was he skinny? Ribs showing?"

"No. Heavyset."

"Not living on eighteen hundred calories a day, I take it, which is the subject of that order he cited. Had you known you could have asked him how long he had conformed to the ration and why he quit? Or asked him what he had for breakfast—and then looked unbelieving no matter what he answered. Or, when you don't know what a man is getting at, let your counter-question shift the subject to something you *do* want to talk about. Then, no matter what he answers, make your point and call on someone else. Logic does not enter into it—just tactics."

"Prof, *nobody* here is living on eighteen hundred calories a day. Bombay, maybe. Not here."

"Less than that in Bombay. Manuel, that 'equal ration' is a fiction. Half the food on this planet is in the black market, or is not reckoned through one ruling or another. Or they keep two sets of books, and figures submitted to the F.N. having nothing to do with the economy. Do you think that grain from Thailand and Burma and Australia is correctly reported to the Control Board by Great China? I'm sure that the India representative on that food board doesn't. But India keeps quiet because she gets the lion's share from Luna . . . and then 'plays politics with hunger'—a phrase you may remember—by using our grain to control her elections. Kerala had a planned famine last year. Did you see it in the news?"

"No."

"Because it wasn't in the news. A managed democracy is a wonderful thing, Manuel, for the managers . . . and its greatest strength is a 'free press' when 'free' is defined as 'responsible' and the managers define what is 'irresponsible.' Do you know what Luna needs most?"

"More ice."

"A new system that does *not* bottleneck through one channel. Our friend Mike is our greatest danger."

"*Huh?* Don't you trust Mike?"

"Manuel, on some subjects I don't trust even myself. Limiting the freedom of news 'just a little bit' is in the same category with the classic example 'a little bit pregnant.' We are not yet free nor will we be as long as anyone—even our ally Mike—controls our news. Someday I hope to own a newspaper independent of any source or channel. I would happily set print by hand, like Benjamin Franklin."

I gave up. "Prof, suppose these talks fail and grain shipments stop. What happens?"

"People back home will be vexed with us . . . and many here on Terra would die. Have you read Malthus?"

"Don't think so."

"Many would die. Then a new stability would be reached with somewhat more people—more efficient people and better fed. This planet isn't crowded; it is just mismanaged . . . and the unkindest thing you can do for a hungry man is to give him food. 'Give.' Read Malthus. It is never safe to laugh at Dr. Malthus; he always has the last laugh. A depressing man, I'm glad he's dead. But don't read him until this is over; too many facts hamper a diplomat, especially an honest one."

"I'm not especially honest."

"But you have no talent for dishonesty, so your refuge must be ignorance and stubbornness. You have the latter; try to preserve the former. For the nonce. Lad, Uncle Bernardo is terribly tired."

I said, "Sorry," and wheeled out of his room. Prof was hitting too hard a pace. I would have been willing to quit if would insure his getting into a ship and out of that gravity. But traffic stayed one way—grain barges, naught else.

But Prof had fun. As I left and waved lights out, noticed again a toy he had bought, one that delighted him like a kid on Christmas—a brass cannon.

A real one from sailing ship days. Was small, barrel about half a meter long and massing, with wooden carriage, only kilos fifteen. A "signal gun" its papers said. Reeked of ancient history, pirates, men "walking plank." A pretty thing but I asked Prof *why?* If we ever managed to leave, price to lift that mass to Luna would hurt—I was resigned to abandoning a p-suit with years more wear in it—abandon everything but two left arms and a pair of shorts. If pressed, might give up social arm. If very pressed, would skip shorts.

He reached out and stroked shiny barrel. "Manuel, once there was a man who held a political make-work job like so many here in this Directorate, shining brass cannon around a courthouse."

"Why would courthouse have cannon?"

"Never mind. He did this for years. It fed him and let him save a bit, but he was not getting ahead in the world. So one day he quit his job, drew out his savings, bought a brass cannon—and went into business for himself."

"Sounds like idiot."

"No doubt. And so were we, when we tossed out the Warden. Manuel, you'll outlive me. When Luna adopts a flag, I would like it to be a cannon *or*, on field *sable*, crossed by bar sinister *gules* of our proudly ignoble lineage. Do you think it could be managed?"

"Suppose so, if you'll sketch. But why a flag? Not a flagpole in all Luna."

"It can fly in our hearts . . . a symbol for all fools so ridiculously impractical as to think they can fight city hall. Will you remember, Manuel?"

"Sure. That is, will remind you when time comes." Didn't like such talk. He had started using oxygen tent in private—and would *not* use in public.

Guess I'm "ignorant" and "stubborn"—was both in place called Lexington, Kentucky, in Central Managerial Area. One thing no doctrine about, no memorized answers, was life in Luna. Prof said to tell truth and emphasize warm, friendly things, especially anything different. "Remember, Manuel, the thousands of Terrans who have made short visits Luna are only a tiny fraction of one percent. To most people we will be as weirdly interesting as strange animals in a zoo. Do you remember that turtle on exhibition in Old Dome? That's us."

Certainly did; they wore that insect out, staring at. So when this male-female team started quizzing about family life in Luna, was happy to answer. I prettied it only by what I left out—things that aren't family life but poor substitutes in a community overloaded with males, Luna City is homes and families mainly, dull by Terra standards—but I like it. And other warrens much same, people who work and raise kids and gossip and find most of their fun around dinner table. Not much to tell, so I discussed anything they found interesting. Every Luna custom comes from Terra since that's where we all came from, but Terra is such a *big* place that a custom from Micronesia, say, may be strange in North America.

This woman—can't call her lady—wanted to know about various sorts of marriage. First, was it true that one could get married without a license "on" Luna?

I asked what a marriage license was?

Her companion said, "Skip it, Mildred. Pioneer societies never have marriage licenses."

"But don't you keep records?" she persisted.

"Certainly," I agreed. "My family keeps a family book that goes back almost to first landing at Johnson City—every marriage, birth, death, every event of importance not only in direct line but all branches so far as we can keep track. And besides, is a man, a schoolteacher, going around copying old family records all over our warren, writing a history of Luna City. Hobby."

"But don't you have *official* records? Here in Kaintucky we have records that go back hundreds of years."

"Madam, we haven't lived there that long."

"Yes, but— Well, Luna City must have a city clerk. Perhaps you call him 'county recorder.' The official who keeps track of such things. Deeds and so forth."

I said. "Don't think so, madam. Some bookies do notary work, witnessing chops on contracts, keeping records of them. Is for people who don't read and write and can't keep own records. But never heard of one asked to keep record of marriage. Not saying couldn't happen. But haven't heard."

"How delightfully informal! Then this other rumor, about how simple it is to get a divorce on the Moon. I daresay that's true, too?"

"No, madam, wouldn't say divorce is simple. Too much to untangle. Mmm . . . take a simple example, one lady and say she has two husbands—"

"*Two?*"

"Might have more, might have just one. Or might be complex marriage. But let's take one lady and two men as typical. She decides to divorce one. Say it's friendly, with other husband agreeing and one she is getting rid of not making fuss. Not that it would do him any good. Okay, she divorces him; he leaves. Still leaves endless things. Men might be business partners, co-husbands often are. Divorce may break up partnership. Money matters to settle. This three may own cubic together, and while will be in her name, ex-husband probably has cash coming or rent. And almost always are children to consider, support and so forth. Many things. No, madam, divorce is never simple. Can divorce him in ten seconds but may take ten years to straighten out loose ends. Isn't it much that way here?"

"Uh . . . just fuhget ah evah asked the question, Cunn'l; it may be simpluh hyuh." (She did talk that way but was understandable once I got program. Won't spell it again.) "But if that is a *simple* marriage, what is a 'complex' one?"

Found self explaining polyandries, clans, groups, lines, and less common patterns considered vulgar by conservative people such as my own family—deal my mother set up, say, after she ticked off my old man, though didn't describe that one; Mother was always too extreme.

Woman said, "You have me confused. What is the difference between a line and a clan?"

"Are quite different. Take own case. I have honor to be member of one of oldest line marriages in Luna—and, in my prejudiced opinion, best. You asked about divorce. Our family has never had one and would bet long odds never will. A line marriage increases in stability year after year, gains practice in art of getting along together, until notion of anybody leaving is unthinkable. Besides, takes unanimous decision of all wives to divorce a husband—could never happen. Senior wife would never let it get that far."

Went on describing advantages—financial security, fine home life it gives children, fact that death of a spouse, while tragic, could never be tragedy it was in a temporary family, especially for children—children simply could *not* be orphaned. Suppose I waxed too enthusiastic—but my family *is* most important thing in my life.

Without them I'm just one-armed mechanic who could be eliminated without causing a draft.

"Here's why is stable," I said. "Take my youngest wife, sixteen. Likely be in her eighties before is senior wife. Doesn't mean all wives senior to her will die by then; unlikely in Luna, females seem to be immortal. But may all opt out of family management by then; by our family traditions they usually do, without younger wives putting pressure on them. So Ludmilla—"

"Ludmilla?"

"Russki name. From fairy tale. Milla will have over fifty years of good example before has to carry burden. She's sensible to start with, not likely to make mistakes and if did, has other wives to steady her. Self-correcting, like a machine with proper negative feedback. A good line marriage is immortal; expect mine to outlast me at least a thousand years—and is why shan't mind dying when time comes; best part of me will go on living."

Prof was being wheeled out; he had them stop stretcher cart and listened. I turned to him. "Professor," I said, "you know my family. Would mind telling this lady why it's a happy family? If you think so."

"It is," agreed Prof. "However, I would rather make a more general remark. Dear madam, I gather that you find our Lunar marriage customs somewhat exotic."

"Oh, I wouldn't go that far!" she said hastily. "Just somewhat *unusual*."

"They arise, as marriage customs always do, from economic necessities of the circumstances—and our circumstances are very different from those here on Earth. Take the line type of marriage which my colleague has been praising . . . and justifiably, I assure you, despite his personal bias—I am a bachelor and have no bias. Line marriage is the strongest possible device for conserving capital and insuring the welfare of children—the two basic societal functions for marriage everywhere—in an environment in which there is *no* security, neither for capital nor for children, other than that devised by individuals. Somehow human beings always cope with their environments. Line marriage is a remarkably successful invention to that end. All other Lunar forms of marriage serve that same purpose, though not as well."

He said goodnight and left. I had with me—always!—a picture of my family, newest one, our wedding with Wyoming. Brides are at their prettiest and Wyoh was radiant—and rest of us looked handsome and happy, with Grandpaw tall and proud and not showing failing faculties.

But was disappointed; they looked at it oddly. But man—Mathews, name was—said, "Can you spare this picture, Colonel?"

Winced. "Only copy I have. And a long way from home."

"For a moment, I mean. Let me have it photographed. Right here, it need never leave your hands."

"Oh. Oh, certainly!" Not a good picture of me but is face I have, and did Wyoh justice and they just don't come prettier than Lenore.

So he photographed it and next morning they did come right into our hotel suite and woke me before time and did arrest me and take me away wheel chair and all and did lock me in a cell with *bars!* For bigamy. For polygamy. For open immorality and publicly inciting others to same.

Was glad Mum couldn't see.

NINETEEN

Took Stu all day to get case transferred to an F.N. court and dismissed. His lawyers asked to have it tossed out on "diplomatic immunity" but F.N. judges did not fall into trap, merely noted that alleged offenses had taken place outside jurisdiction of lower court, except alleged "inciting" concerning which they found insufficient evidence. Aren't any F.N. laws covering marriage; can't be—just a rule about each nation required to give "full faith and credence" to marriage customs of other member nations.

Out of those eleven billion people perhaps seven billion lived where polygamy is legal, and Stu's opinion manipulators played up "persecution"; it gained us sympathy from people who otherwise would never have heard of us—even gained it in North America and other places where polygamy is not legal, from people who believe in "live and let live." All good, because always problem was to be noticed. To most of those beeswarm billions Luna was nothing; our rebellion hadn't been noticed.

Stu's operators had gone to much thought to plan setup to get me arrested. Was not told until weeks later after time to cool off and see benefits. Took a stupid judge, a dishonest sheriff, and barbaric local prejudice which I triggered with that sweet picture, for Stu admitted later that range of color in Davis family was what got judge angry enough to be foolish even beyond native talent for nonsense.

My one consolation, that Mum could not see my disgrace, turned out mistaken; pictures, taken through bars and showing grim face, were in every Luna paper, and write-ups used nastiest Earthside stories, not larger number that deplored injustice. But should have had more faith in Mimi; she wasn't ashamed, simply wanted to go Earthside and rip some people to pieces.

While helped Earthside, greatest good was in Luna. Loonies became more unified over this silly huhu than had ever been before. They took it personally and "Adam Selene" and "Simon Jester" pushed it. Loonies are easygoing except on one subject, women. Every lady felt insulted by Terran news stories—so male Loonies who had ignored politics suddenly discovered I was their boy.

Spin-off—old lags feel superior to those not transported. Later found self greeted by ex-cons with: "Hi, jailbird!" A lodge greeting—I was accepted.

But saw nothing good about it then! Pushed around, treated like cattle, fingerprinted, photographed, given food we wouldn't offer hogs, exposed to endless indignity, and only that heavy field kept me from trying to kill somebody—had I been wearing number-six arm when grabbed, might have tried.

But steadied down once I was freed. Hour later we were on way to Agra; had at last been summoned by committee. Felt good to be back in suite in maharajah's palace but eleven-hour zone change in less than three did not permit rest; we went to hearing bleary-eyed and held together by drugs.

"Hearing" was one-sided; we listened while chairman talked. Talked an hour; I'll summarize:

Our preposterous claims were rejected. Lunar Authority's sacred trust could not be abandoned. Disorders on Earth's Moon could not be tolerated. Moreover, recent disorders showed that Authority had been too lenient. Omission was now to be corrected by an activist program, a five-year plan in which all phases of life in Authority's trusteeship would be overhauled. A code of laws was being drafted; civil and criminal courts would be instituted for benefit of "client-employees"—which meant *all* persons in trust area, not just consignees with uncompleted sentences. Public schools would be established, plus indoctrinal adult schools for client-employees in need of same. An economic, engineering, and agricultural planning board would be created to provide fullest and most efficient use of Moon's resources and labor of client-employees. An interim goal of quadrupling grain shipments in five years had been adopted as a figure easily obtainable once scientific planning of resources and labor was in effect. First phase would be to withdraw client-employees from occupations found not to be productive and put them to drilling a vast new system of farm tunnels in order that hydroponics would commence in them not later than March 2078. These new giant farms would be operated by Lunar Authority, scientifically, and not left to whims of private owners. It was contemplated that this system would, by end of five-year plan, produce entire new grain quota; in meantime client-employees producing grain privately would be allowed to continue. But they would be absorbed into new system as their less efficient methods were no longer needed.

Chairman looked up from papers. "In short, the Lunar colonies are going to be civilized and brought into managerial coordination with the rest of civilization. Distasteful as this task has been, I feel—speaking as a citizen rather than as chairman of this committee—I feel that we owe you thanks for bringing to our attention a situation so badly in need of correction."

Was ready to burn his ears off. "Client-employees!" What a fancy way to say "slaves"! But Prof said tranquilly, "I find the proposed plans most interesting. Is one permitted to ask questions? Purely for information?"

"For information, yes."

North American member leaned forward. "But don't assume

that we are going to take any backtalk from you cavemen! So mind your manners. You aren't in the clear on this, you know."

"Order," chairman said. "Proceed, Professor."

"This term 'client-employee' I find intriguing. Can it be stipulated that the majority of inhabitants of Earth's major satellite are not undischarged consignees but free individuals?"

"Certainly," chairman agreed blandly. "All legal aspects of the new policy have been studied. With minor exceptions some ninety-one percent of the colonists have citizenship, original or derived, in various member nations of the Federated Nations. Those who wish to return to their home countries have a right to do so. You will be pleased to learn that the Authority is considering a plan under which loans for transportation can be arranged . . . probably under supervision of International Red Cross and Crescent. I might add that I myself am heartily backing this plan—as it renders nonsensical any talk about 'slave labor.' " He smiled smugly.

"I see," agreed Prof. "Most humane. Has the committee—or the Authority—pondered the fact that most—effectively all, I should say—considered the fact that inhabitants of Luna are physically unable to live on this planet? That they have undergone involuntary permanent exile through irreversible physiological changes and can never again live in comfort and health in a gravitational field six times greater than that to which their bodies have become adjusted?"

Scoundrel pursed lips as if considering totally new idea. "Speaking again for myself, I would not be prepared to stipulate that what you say is necessarily true. It might be true of some, might not be of others; people vary widely. Your presence here proves that it is not impossible for a Lunar inhabitant to return to Earth. In any case we have no intention of *forcing* anyone to return. We hope that they will choose to stay and we hope to encourage others to emigrate to the Moon. But these are individual choices, under the freedoms guaranteed by the Great Charter. But as to this alleged physiological phenomenon—it is not a legal matter. If anyone deems it prudent, or thinks he would be happier, to stay on the Moon, that's his privilege."

"I see, sir. We are free. Free to remain in Luna and work, at tasks and for wages set by you . . . or free to return to Earth to die."

Chairman shrugged. "You assume that we are villains—we're not. Why, if I were a young man I would emigrate to the Moon myself. Great opportunities! In any case I am not troubled by your distortions—history will justify us."

Was surprised at Prof; he was not fighting. Worried about him—weeks of strain and a bad night on top. All he said was, "Honorable Chairman, I assume that shipping to Luna will soon be resumed. Can passage be arranged for my colleague and myself in the first ship? For I must admit, sir, that this gravitational weakness of which I spoke is, in our cases, very real. Our mission is completed; we need to go home."

(Not a word about grain barges. Nor about "throwing rocks," nor even futility of beating a cow. Prof just sounded tired.)

Chairman leaned forward and spoke with grim satisfaction. "Professor, that presents difficulties. To put it bluntly, you appear to be guilty of treason against the Great Charter, indeed against all humanity . . . and an indictment is being considered. I doubt if anything more than a suspended sentence would be invoked against a man of your age and physical condition, however. Do you think it would be prudent of us to give you passage back to the place where you committed these acts—there to stir up more mischief?"

Prof sighed. "I understand your point. Then, sir, may I be excused? I am weary."

"Certainly. Hold yourself at the disposal of this committee. The hearing stands adjourned. Colonel Davis—"

"Sir?" I was directing wheel chair around, to get Prof out at once; our attendants had been sent outside.

"A word with you, please. In my office."

"Uh—" Looked at Prof; eyes were closed and seemed unconscious. But he moved one finger, motioning me to him. "Honorable Chairman, I'm more nurse than diplomat; have to look after him. He's an old man, he's ill."

"The attendants will take care of him."

"Well . . ." Got as close to Prof as I could from chair, leaned over him. "Prof, are you right?"

He barely whispered. "See what he wants. Agree with him. But stall."

Moments later was alone with chairman, soundproof door

locked—meant nothing; room could have a dozen ears, plus one in my left arm.

He said, "A drink? Coffee?"

I answered, "No, thank you, sir. Have to watch my diet here."

"I suppose so. Are you really limited to that chair? You look healthy."

I said, "I could, if had to, get up and walk across room. Might faint. Or worse. Prefer not to risk. Weigh six times what I should. Heart's not used to it."

"I suppose so. Colonel, I hear you had some silly trouble in North America. I'm sorry, I truly am. Barbaric place. Always hate to have to go there. I suppose you're wondering why I wanted to see you."

"No, sir, assume you'll tell when suits you. Instead was wondering why you still call me 'Colonel.' "

He gave a barking laugh. "Habit, I suppose. A lifetime of protocol. Yet it might be well for you to continue with that title. Tell me, what do you think of our five-year plan?"

Thought it stunk. "Seems to have been carefully thought out."

"Much thought went into it. Colonel, you seem to be a sensible man— I know you are, I know not only your background but practically every word you've spoken, almost your thoughts, ever since you set foot on Earth. You were born on the Moon. Do you regard yourself as a patriot? Of the Moon?"

"Suppose so. Though tend to think of what we did just as something that had to be done."

"Between ourselves—yes. That old fool Hobart. Colonel, that *is* a good plan . . . but lacks an executive. If you are *really* a patriot or let's say a practical man with your country's best interests at heart, you might be the man to carry it out." He held up hand. "Don't be hasty! I'm not asking you to sell out, turn traitor, or any nonsense like that. This is your chance to be a *real* patriot—not some phony hero who gets himself killed in a lost cause. Put it this way. Do you think it is possible for the Lunar colonies to hold out against all the force that the Federated Nations of Earth can bring to bear? You're not really a military man, I know—and I'm glad you're not—but you *are* a technical man, and I know that, too. In your honest estimation, how many ships and bombs do you think it would take to destroy the Lunar colonies?"

I answered, "One ship, six bombs."

"Correct! My God, it's good to talk to a sensible man. Two of them would have to be awf'ly big, perhaps specially built. A few people would stay alive, for a while, in smaller warren beyond the blast areas. But one ship would do it, in ten minutes."

I said, "Conceded, sir, but Professor de la Paz pointed out that you don't get milk by beating a cow. And certainly can't by shooting it."

"Why do you think we've held back, done nothing, for over a month? That idiot colleague of mine—I won't name him—spoke of 'backtalk.' Backtalk doesn't fret me; it's just talk and I'm interested in results. No, my dear Colonel, we won't shoot the cow . . . but we would, if forced to, let the cow know that it *could* be shot. H-missiles are expensive toys but we could afford to expend some as warning shots, wasted on bare rock to let the cow know what could happen. But that is more force than one likes to use—it might frighten the cow and sour its milk." He gave another barking laugh. "Better to persuade old bossy to give down willingly."

I waited. "Don't you want to know how?" he asked.

"How?" I agreed.

"Through you. Don't say a word and let me explain—"

He took me up on that high mountain and offered me kingdoms of Earth. Or of Luna. Take job of "Protector Pro Tem" with understanding was mine permanently if I could deliver. Convince Loonies they could not win. Convince them that this new setup was to their advantage—emphasize benefits, free schools, free hospitals, free this and that—details later but an everywhere government just like on Terra. Taxes starting low and handled painlessly by automatic checkoff and through kickback revenues from grain shipments. But, most important, this time Authority would not send a boy to do a man's job—two regiments of police at once.

"Those damned Peace Dragoons were a mistake," he said, "one we won't make again. Between ourselves, the reason it has taken us a month to work this out is that we had to convince the Peace Control Commission that a handful of men cannot police three million people spread through six largish warrens and fifty and more small ones. So you'll start with enough police—not combat troops but military police used to quelling civilians with a minimum of fuss. Besides that, this time they'll have female auxiliaries, the standard ten percent—no more rape complaints. Well, sir? Think you can swing it? Knowing it's best in the long run for your own people?"

I said I ought to study it in detail, particularly plans and quotas for five-year plan, rather than make snap decision.

"Certainly, certainly!" he agreed. "I'll give you a copy of the white paper we've made up; take it home, study it, sleep on it. Tomorrow we'll talk again. Just give me your word as a gentleman to keep it under your hair. No secret, really . . . but these things are best settled before they are publicized. Speaking of publicity, you'll need help—and you'll get it. We'll go to the expense of sending up topnotch men, pay them what it's worth, have them centrifuge the way those scientists do—you know. *This* time we're doing it right. That fool Hobart—he's actually dead, isn't he?"

"No, sir. Senile, however."

"Should have killed him. Here's your copy of the plan."

"Sir? Speaking of old men—Professor de la Paz can't stay here. Wouldn't live six months."

"That's best, isn't it?"

I tried to answer levelly, "You don't understand. He is greatly loved and respected. Best thing would be for me to convince him that you mean business with those H-missiles—and that it is his patriotic duty to salvage what we can. But, either way, if I return without him . . . well, not only could not swing it; wouldn't live long enough to try."

"Hmm— Sleep on it. We'll talk tomorrow. Say fourteen o'clock."

I left and as soon as was loaded into lorry gave way to shakes. Just don't have high-level approach.

Stu was waiting with Prof. "Well?" said Prof.

I glanced around, tapped ear. We huddled, heads over Prof's head and two blankets over us all. Stretcher wagon was clean and so was my chair; I checked them each morning. But for room itself seemed safer to whisper under blankets.

Started in. Prof stopped me. "Discuss his ancestry and habits later. The facts."

"He offered me job of Warden."

"I trust you accepted."

"Ninety percent. I'm to study this garbage and give answer tomorrow. Stu, how fast can we execute Plan Scoot?"

"Started. We were waiting for you to return. If they let you return."

Next fifty minutes were busy. Stu produced a gaunt Hindu in a dhoti; in thirty minutes he was a twin of Prof, and Stu lifted Prof off wagon onto a divan. Duplicating me was easier. Our doubles were wheeled into suite's living room just at dusk and dinner was brought in. Several people came and went—among them elderly Hindu woman in sari, on arm of Stuart LaJoie. A plump babu followed them.

Getting Prof up steps to roof was worst; he had never worn powered walkers, had no chance to practice, and had been flat on back for more than a month.

But Stu's arm kept him steady; I gritted teeth and climbed those thirteen terrible steps by myself. By time I reached roof, heart was ready to burst. Was put to it not to black out. A silent little flitter craft came out of gloom right on schedule and ten minutes later we were in chartered ship we had used past month—two minutes after that we jetted for Australia. Don't know what it cost to prepare this dance and keep it ready against need, but was no hitch.

Stretched out by Prof and caught breath, then said, "How you feel, Prof?"

"Okay. A bit tired. Frustrated."

"Ja da. Frustrated."

"Over not seeing the Taj Mahal, I mean. I never had opportunity as a young man—and here I've been within a kilometer of it twice, once for several days, now for another day . . . and still I haven't seen it and never shall."

"Just a tomb."

"And Helen of Troy was just a woman. Sleep, lad."

We landed in Chinee half of Australia, place called Darwin, and were carried straight into a ship, placed in acceleration couches and dosed. Prof was already out and I was beginning to feel dopy when Stu came in, grinned, and strapped down by us. I looked at him. "You, too? Who's minding shop?"

"The same people who've been doing the real work all along. It's a good setup and doesn't need me any longer. Mannie old cobber, I did not want to be marooned a long way from home. Luna, I mean, in case you have doubts. This looks like the last train from Shanghai."

"What's Shanghai got to do with?"

"Forget I mentioned it. Mannie, I'm flat broke, concave. I owe money in all directions—debts that will be paid only if certain stocks move the way Adam Selene convinced me they would move, shortly after this point in history. And I'm wanted, or will be, for offenses against the public peace and dignity. Put it this way: I'm saving them the trouble of transporting me. Do you think I can learn to be a drillman at my age?"

Was feeling foggy, drug taking hold. "Stu, in Luna y'aren't old . . . barely started . . . 'nyway . . . eat our table f'ever! Mimi *likes* you."

"Thanks, cobber, I might. Warning light! Deep breath!"

Suddenly was kicked by ten gee.

TWENTY

Our craft was ground-to-orbit ferry type used for manned satellites, for supplying F.N. ships in patrol orbit, and for passengers to and from pleasure-and-gambling satellites. She was carrying three passengers instead of forty, no cargo except three p-suits and a brass cannon (yes, silly toy was along; p-suits and Prof's bang-bang were in Australia a week before we were) and good ship *Lark* had been stripped—total crew was skipper and a Cyborg pilot.

She was heavily overfueled.

We made (was told) normal approach on *Elysium* satellite . . . then suddenly scooted from orbital speed to escape speed, a change even more violent than liftoff.

This was scanned by F.N. Skytrack; we were commanded to

stop and explain. I got this secondhand from Stu, self still recovering and enjoying luxury of no-gee with one strap to anchor. Prof was still out.

"So they want to know who we are and what we think we are doing," Stu told me. "We told them that we were Chinese registry sky wagon Opening Lotus bound on an errand of mercy, to wit, rescuing those scientists marooned on the Moon, and gave our identification—as Opening Lotus."

"How about transponder?"

"Mannie, if I got what I paid for, our transponder identified us as the Lark up to ten minutes ago . . . and now has I.D.'d us as the Lotus. Soon we will know. Just one ship is in position to get a missile off and it must blast us in"—he stopped to look—"another twenty-seven minutes according to the wired-up gentleman booting this bucket, or its chances of getting us are poor to zero. So if it worries you—if you have prayers to say or messages to send or whatever it is one does at such times—now is the time."

"Think we ought to rouse Prof?"

"Let him sleep. Can you think of a better way to make the jump than from peaceful sleep instantaneously into a cloud of radiant gas? Unless you know that he has religious necessities to attend to? He never struck me as a religious man, orthodoctrinally speaking."

"He's not. But if you have such duties, don't let me keep you."

"Thank you, I took care of what seemed necessary before we left ground. How about yourself, Mannie? I'm not much of a padre but I'll do my best, if I can help. Any sins on your mind, old cobber? If you need to confess, I know quite a little about sin."

Told him my needs did not run that way. Then did recall sins, some I cherished, and gave him a version more or less true. That reminded him of some of his own, which reminded me— Zero time came and went before we ran out of sins. Stu LaJoie is a good person to spend last minutes with, even if don't turn out to be last.

We had two days with naught to do but undergo drastic routines to keep us from carrying umpteen plagues to Luna. But didn't mind shaking from induced chills and burning with fever; free fall was such a relief and was so happy to be going home.

Or almost happy— Prof asked what was troubling me. "Nothing," I said. "Can't wait to be home. But— Truth is, ashamed to show face after we've failed. Prof, what did we do wrong?"

"Failed, my boy?"

"Don't see what else can call it. Asked to be recognized. Not what we got."

"Manuel, I owe you an apology. You will recall Adam Selene's projection of our chances just before we left home." Stu was not in earshot but "Mike" was word we never used; was always "Adam Selene" for security.

"Certainly do! One in fifty-three. Then when we reached Earthside dropped to reeking one in hundred. What you guess it is now? One in thousand?"

"I've had new projections every few days . . . which is why I owe you an apology. The last, received just before we left, included the then-untested assumption that we would escape, get clear of Terra and home safely. Or that at least one of us three would make it, which is why Comrade Stu was summoned home, he having a Terran's tolerance of high acceleration. Eight projections, in fact, ranging from three of us dead, through various combinations up to three surviving. Would you care to stake a few dollars on what that last projection is, setting a bracket and naming your own odds? I'll give a hint. You are far too pessimistic."

"Uh . . . no, damn it! Just tell."

"The odds against us are now only seventeen to one . . . and they've been shortening all month. Which I couldn't tell you."

Was amazed, delighted, overjoyed—hurt. "What you mean, couldn't tell me? Look, Prof, if not trusted, deal me out and put Stu in executive cell."

"Please, son. That's where he will go if anything happens to any of us—you, me, or dear Wyoming. I could not tell you Earthside—and *can* tell you now—not because you aren't trusted but because you are no actor. You could carry out your role more effectively if you believed that our purpose was to achieve recognition of independence."

"Now he tells!"

"Manuel, Manuel, we had to fight hard every instant—and lose."

"So? Am big enough boy to be told?"

"Please, Manuel. Keeping you temporarily in the dark greatly enhanced our chances; you can check this with Adam. May I add that Stuart accepted his summons to Luna blithely without asking why? Comrade, that committee was too small, its chairman too intelligent; there was always the hazard that they might offer an acceptable compromise—that first day there was grave danger of it. Had we been able to force our case before the Grand Assembly there would have been no danger of intelligent action. But we were balked. The best I could do was to antagonize the committee, even stooping to personal insult to make certain of at least one holdout against common sense."

"Guess I never will understand high-level approach."

"Possibly not. But your talents and mine complement each other. Manuel, you wish to see Luna free."

"You know I do."

"You also know that Terra can defeat us."

"Sure. No projection ever gave anything close to even money. So don't see why you set out to antagonize—"

"Please. Since they *can* inflict their will on us, our only chance lies in weakening their will. That was why we *had* to go to Terra. To be divisive. To create many opinions. The shrewdest of the great generals in China's history once said that perfection in war lay in so sapping the opponent's will that he surrenders without fighting. In that maxim lies both our ultimate purpose and our most pressing danger. Suppose, as seemed possible that first day, we had been offered an inviting compromise. A governor in place of a warden, possibly from our own number. Local autonomy. A delegate in the Grand Assembly. A higher price for grain at the catapult head, plus a bonus for increased shipments. A disavowal of Hobart's policies combined with an expression of regret over the rape and the killings with handsome cash settlements to the victims' survivors. Would it have been accepted? Back home?"

"They did not offer that."

"The chairman was ready to offer something like it that first afternoon and at that time he had his committee in hand. He offered us an asking price close enough to permit such a dicker. Assume that we reached in substance what I outlined. Would it have been acceptable at home?"

"Uh . . . maybe."

"More than a 'maybe' by the bleak projection made just before we left home; it was the thing to be avoided at any cost—a settlement which would quiet things down, destroy our will to resist, without changing any essential in the longer-range prediction of disaster. So I switched the subject and squelched possibility by being difficult about irrelevancies and politely offensive. Manuel, you and I know—and Adam knows—that there must be an end to food shipments; nothing less will save Luna from disaster. But can you imagine a wheat farmer fighting to end those shipments?"

"No. Wonder if can pick up news from home on how they're taking stoppage?"

"There won't be any. Here is how Adam has timed it, Manuel: No announcement is to be made on either planet until after we get home. We are still buying wheat. Barges are still arriving at Bombay."

"You told them shipments would stop at once."

"That was a threat, not a moral commitment. A few more loads won't matter and we need time. We don't have everyone on our side; we have only a minority. There is a majority who don't care either way but can be swayed—temporarily. We have another minority against us . . . especially grain farmers whose interest is never politics but the price of wheat. They are grumbling but accepting Scrip, hoping it will be worth face value later. But the instant we announce that shipments have stopped they will be actively against us. Adam plans to have the majority committed to us at the time the announcement is made."

"How long? One year? Two?"

"Two days, three days, perhaps four. Carefully edited excerpts from that five-year plan, excerpts from the recordings you've made—especially that yellow-dog offer—exploitation of your arrest in Kentucky—"

"Hey! I'd rather forget that."

Prof smiled and cocked an eyebrow. "Uh—" I said uncomfortably. "Okay. If will help."

"It will help more than any statistics about natural resources."

Wired-up ex-human piloting us went in as one maneuver without bothering to orbit and gave us even heavier beating; ship was light and lively. But change in motion is under two-and-a-half kilometers; was over in nineteen seconds and we were down at Johnson City. I took it right, just a terrible constriction in chest and a feeling as if giant were squeezing heart, then was over and I was gasping back to normal and glad to be proper weight. But did almost kill poor old Prof.

Mike told me later that pilot refused to surrender control; Mike would have brought ship down in a low-gee, no-breakum-egg, knowing Prof was aboard. But perhaps that Cyborg knew what he was doing; a low-gee landing wastes mass and *Lotus-Lark* grounded almost dry.

None of which we cared about, as looked as if that Garrison landing had wasted Prof. Stu saw it while I was still gasping, then we were both at him—heart stimulant, manual respiration, massage. At last he fluttered eyelids, looked at us, smiled. "*Home,*" he whispered.

We made him rest twenty minutes before we let him suit up to leave ship; had been as near dead as can be and not hear angels. Skipper was filling tanks, anxious to get rid of us and take on passengers—that Dutchman never spoke to us whole trip; think he regretted letting money talk him into a trip that could ruin or kill him.

By then Wyoh was inside ship, p-suited to come meet us. Don't think Stu had ever seen her in a p-suit and certain he had never seen her as a blonde; did not recognize. I was hugging her in spite of p-suit; he was standing by, waiting to be introduced. Then strange "man" in p-suit hugged him—he was surprised.

Heard Wyoh's muffled voice: "Oh heavens! Mannie, my helmet."

I unclamped it, lifted off. She shook curls and grinned. "Stu, aren't you glad to see me? Don't you *know* me?"

A grin spread over his face, slowly as dawn across maria. "Zdra'stvooeet'ye, Gospazha! I am most happy to see you."

" 'Gospazha' indeed! I'm Wyoh to you, dear, always. Didn't Mannie tell you I'd gone back to blonde?"

"Yes, he did. But knowing it and seeing are not the same."

"You'll get used to it." She stopped to bend over Prof, kiss him, giggle at him, then straightened up and gave me a no-helmet welcome-home that left us both with tears despite pesky suit. Then turned again to Stu, started to kiss him.

He held back a little. She stopped. "Stu, am I going to have to put on brown makeup to welcome you?" Stu glanced at me, then kissed her. Wyoh put in as much time and thought as she had to welcoming me.

Was later I figured out his odd behavior. Stu, despite commitment, was still not a Loonie—and in meantime Wyoh had married. What's that got to do with it? Well, Earthside it makes a difference, and Stu did not know deep down in bones that a Loonie lady is own mistress. Poor chum thought *I* might take offense!

We got Prof into suit, ourselves same, and left, me with cannon under arm. Once underground and locked through, we unsuited—and I was flattered to see that Wyoh was wearing crushed under p-suit that red dress I bought her ages ago. She brushed it and skirt flared out.

Immigration room was empty save for about forty men lined up along wall like new transportees; were wearing p-suits and carrying helmets—Terrans going home, stranded tourists and some scientists. Their p-suits would not go, would be unloaded before lift. I looked at them and thought about Cyborg pilot. When *Lark* had been stripped, all but three couches had been removed; these people were going to take acceleration lying on floorplates—if skipper was not careful he was going to have mashed Terrans au blut.

Mentioned to Stu. "Forget it," he said. "Captain Leures has foam pads aboard. He won't let them be hurt, they're his life insurance."

TWENTY-ONE

My family, all thirty-odd from Grandpaw to babies, was waiting beyond next lock on level below and we got cried on and slobbered on and hugged and this time Stu did not hold back. Little Hazel made ceremony of kissing us; she had Liberty Caps, set one on each, then kissed us—and at that signal whole family put on Liberty Caps, and I got sudden tears. Perhaps is what patriotism feels like, choked up and so happy it hurts. Or maybe was just being with my beloveds again.

"Where's Slim?" I asked Hazel. "Wasn't he invited?"

"Couldn't come. He's junior marshal of your reception."

"Reception? This is all we want."

"You'll see."

Did. Good thing family came out to meet us; that and ride to

L-City (filled a capsule) were all I saw of them for some time. Tube Station West was a howling mob, all in Liberty Caps. We three were carried on shoulders all way to Old Dome, surrounded by a stilyagi bodyguard, elbows locked to force through cheering, singing crowds. Boys were wearing red caps and white shirts and their girls wore white jumpers and red shorts color of caps.

At station and again when they put us down in Old Dome I got kissed by fems I have never seen before or since. Remember hoping that measures we had taken in lieu of quarantine were effective—or half of L-City would be down with colds or worse. (Apparently we were clean; was no epidemic. But I remember time—was quite small—when measles got loose and thousands died.)

Worried about Prof, too; reception was too rough for a man good as dead an hour earlier. But he not only enjoyed it, he made a wonderful speech in Old Dome—one short on logic, loaded with ringing phrases. "Love" was in it, and "home" and "Luna" and "comrades and neighbors" and even "shoulder to shoulder" and all sounded good.

They had erected a platform under big news video on south face. Adam Selene greeted us from video screen and now Prof's face and voice were projected from it, much magnified, over his head—did not have to shout. But did have to pause after every sentence; crowd roars drowned out even bull voice from screen—and no doubt pauses helped, as rest. But Prof no longer seemed old, tired, ill; being back inside The Rock seemed to be tonic he needed. And me, too! Was wonderful to be right weight, feel *strong*, breathe pure, replenished air of own city.

No mean city! Impossible to get all of L-City inside Old Dome—but looked as if they tried. I estimated an area ten meters square, tried to count heads, got over two hundred not half through and gave up. *Lunatic* placed crowd at thirty thousand, seems impossible.

Prof's words reached more, nearly three million; video carried scene to those who could not crowd into Old Dome, cable and relay flashed it across lonely maria to all warrens. He grabbed chance to tell of slave future Authority planned for them. Waved that "white paper." "Here is it!" he cried. "Your fetters! Your leg irons! Will you wear them?"

"NO!"

"They say you must. They say they will H-bomb . . . then survivors will surrender and put on these chains. Will you?"

"NO! NEVER!"

"Never," agreed Prof. "They threaten to send troops . . . more and more troops to rape and murder. We shall fight them."

"DA!"

"We shall fight them on the surface, we shall fight them in the tubes, we shall fight them in the corridors! If die we must, we shall die *free!*"

"Yes! Ja-*da!* Tell 'em, tell 'em!"

"And if we die, let history write: This was Luna's finest hour! Give us liberty . . . or give us *death!*"

Some of that sounded familiar. But his words came out fresh and new; I joined in roars. Look . . . I *knew* we couldn't whip Terra—I'm tech by trade and *know* that an H-missile doesn't care how brave you are. But was ready, too. If they wanted a fight, let's have it!

Prof let them roar, then led them in "Battle Hymn of the Republic," Simon's version. Adam appeared on screen again, took over leading it and sang with them, and we tried to slip away, off back of platform, with help of stilyagi led by Slim. But women didn't want to let us go and lads aren't at their best in trying to stop ladies; they broke through. Was twenty-two hundred before we four, Wyoh, Prof, Stu, self, were locked in room L of Raffles, where Adam-Mike joined us by by video. I was starved by then, all were, so I ordered dinner and Prof insisted that we eat before reviewing plans.

Then we got down to business.

Adam started by asking me to read aloud white paper, for his benefit and for Comrade Wyoming—"But first, Comrade Manuel, if you have the recordings you made Earthside, could you transmit them by phone at high speed to my office? I'll have them transcribed for study—all I have so far are the coded summaries Comrade Stuart sent up."

I did so, knowing Mike would study them at once, phrasing was part of "Adam Selene" myth—and decided to talk to Prof about letting Stu in on facts. If Stu was to be in executive cell, pretending was too clumsy.

Feeding recordings into Mike at overspeed took five minutes, reading aloud another thirty. That done, Adam said, "Professor, the reception was more successful than I had counted on, due to your speech. I think we should push the embargo through Congress at once. I can send out a call tonight for a session at noon tomorrow. Comments?"

I said, "Look, those yammerheads will kick it around for weeks. If you must put it up to them—can't see why—do as you did with Declaration. Start late, jam it through after midnight using own people."

Adam said, "Sorry, Manuel. I'm getting caught up on events Earthside and you have catching up to do here. It's no longer the same group. Comrade Wyoming?"

"Mannie dear, it's an elected Congress now. They must pass it, Congress is what government we have."

I said slowly, "You held election and turned things over to them? *Everything?* Then what are *we* doing?" Looked at Prof, expecting explosion. My objections would not be on his grounds—but couldn't see any use in swapping one talk-talk for another. At least first group had been so loose we could pack it—this new group would be glued to seats.

Prof was undisturbed. Fitted fingertips together and looked relaxed. "Manuel, I don't think the situation is as bad as you seem to feel that it is. In each age it is necessary to adapt to the popular mythology. At one time kings were anointed by Deity, so the problem was to see to it that Deity anointed the right candidate. In this age the myth is 'the will of the people' . . . but the problem changes only superficially. Comrade Adam and I have had long discussions about how to determine the will of the people. I venture to suggest that this solution is one we can work with."

"Well . . . okay. But why weren't we told? Stu, did you know?"

"No, Mannie. There was no reason to tell me." He shrugged. "I'm a monarchist, I wouldn't have been interested. But I go along with

Prof that in this day and age elections are a necessary ritual."

Prof said, "Manuel, it wasn't necessary to tell us till we got back; you and I had other work to do. Comrade Adam and dear Comrade Wyoming handled it in our absence . . . so let's find out what they did before we judge what they've done."

"Sorry. Well, Wyoh?"

"Mannie, we didn't leave *everything* to chance. Adam and I decided that a Congress of three hundred would be about right. Then we spent hours going over the Party lists—plus prominent people not in the Party. At last we had a list of candidates—a list that included some from the Ad-Hoc Congress; not all were yammerheads, we included as many as we could. Then Adam phoned each one and asked him—or her—if he would serve . . . binding him to secrecy in the meantime. Some we had to replace.

"When we were ready, Adam spoke on video, announced that it was time to carry out the Party's pledge of free elections, set a date, said that everybody over sixteen could vote, and that all anyone had to do to be a candidate was to get a hundred chops on a nominating petition and post it in Old Dome, or the public notice place for his warren. Oh, yes, thirty temporary election districts, ten Congressmen from each district—that let all but the smallest warrens be at least one district."

"So you had it lined up and Party ticket went through?"

"Oh, no, dear! There wasn't any Party ticket—officially. But we were ready with our candidates . . . and I must say my stilyagi did a smart job getting chops on nominations; our optings were posted the first day. Many other people posted; there were over two thousand candidates. But there was only ten days from announcement to election, and we knew what we wanted whereas the opposition was split up. It wasn't necessary for Adam to come out publicly and endorse candidates. It worked out—you won by seven thousand votes, dear, while your nearest rival got less than a thousand."

"*I* won?"

"You won, I won, Professor won, Comrade Clayton won, and just about everybody we thought should be in the Congress. It wasn't hard. Although Adam never endorsed anyone, I didn't hesitate to let our comrades know who was favored. Simon poked his finger in, too. And we do have good connections with newspapers. I wish you had been here election night, watching the results. Exciting!"

"How did you go about nose counting? Never known how election works. Write names on a piece of paper?"

"Oh, no, we used a better system . . . because, after all, some of our best people can't write. We used banks for voting places, with bank clerks identifying customers and customers identifying members of their families and neighbors who don't have bank accounts—and people voted orally and the clerks punched the votes into the banks' computers with the voter watching, and results were all tallied at once in Luna City clearinghouse. We voted everybody in less than three hours and results were printed out just minutes after voting stopped."

Suddenly a light came on in my skull and I decided to question Wyoh privately. No, not Wyoh—*Mike*. Get past his "Adam Selene" dignity and hammer truth out of his neuristors. Recalled a cheque ten million dollars too large and wondered how many had voted for me? Seven thousand? Seven hundred? Or just my family and friends?

But no longer worried about new Congress. Prof had not slipped them a cold deck but one that was frozen solid—then ducked Earthside while crime was committed. No use asking Wyoh; she didn't even *need* to know what Mike had done . . . and could do her part better if did not suspect.

Nor would anybody suspect. If was one thing all people took for granted, was conviction that if you feed honest figures into a computer, honest figures come out. Never doubted it myself till I met a computer with sense of humor.

Changed mind about suggesting that Stu be let in on Mike's self-awareness. Three was two too many. Or perhaps three. "Mi—" I started to say, and changed to: "My word! Sounds efficient. How big did we win?"

Adam answered without expression. "Eighty-six percent of our candidates were successful—approximately what I had expected."

("Approximately," my false left arm! *Exactly* what expected, Mike old ironmongery!) "Withdraw objection to a noon session—I'll be there."

"It seems to me," said Stu, "assuming that the embargo starts at once, we will need something to maintain the enthusiasm we witnessed tonight. Or there will be a long quiet period of increasing economic depression—from the embargo, I mean—and growing disillusionment. Adam, you first impressed me through your ability to make shrewd guesses as to future events. Do my misgivings make sense?"

"They do."

"Well?"

Adam looked at us in turn, and was almost impossible to believe that this was a false image and Mike was simply placing us through binaural receptors. "Comrades . . . it must be turned into open war as quickly as possible."

Nobody said anything. One thing to talk about war, another to face up to it. At last I sighed and said, "When do we start throwing rocks?"

"We do not start," Adam answered. "They must throw the first one. How do we antagonize them into doing so? I will reserve my thoughts to the last. Comrade Manuel?"

"Uh . . . don't look at me. Way I feel, would start with a nice big rock smack on Agra—a bloke there who is a waste of space. But is not what you are after."

"No, it is not," Adam answered seriously. "You would not only anger the entire Hindu nation, a people intensely opposed to destruction of life, but you would also anger and shock people throughout Earth by destroying the Taj Mahal."

"Including me," said Prof. "Don't talk dirty, Manuel."

"Look," I said, "didn't say to do it. Anyhow, could miss Taj."

"Manuel," said Prof, "as Adam pointed out, our strategy must be to antagonize them into striking the first blow, the classic 'Pearl Harbor' maneuver of game theory, a great advantage in Weltpolitick. The question is *how?* Adam, I suggest that what is needed is to plant the idea that we are weak and divided and that all it takes is a show of force to bring us back into line. Stu? Your people Earthside should be useful. Suppose the Congress repudiated myself and Manuel? The effect?"

"Oh, *no!*" said Wyoh.

"Oh, *yes*, dear Wyoh. Not necessary to *do* it but simply to put it over news channels to Earth. Perhaps still better to put it out over a clandestine beam attributed to the Terran scientists still with us while our official channels display the classic stigmata of tight censorship. Adam?"

"I'm noting it as a tactic which probably will be included in the strategy. But it will not be sufficient alone. We must be bombed."

"Adam," said Wyoh, "why do you say so? Even if Luna City can stand up under their biggest bombs—something I hope never to find out—we know that Luna can't win an all-out war. You've said so, many times. Isn't there some way to work it so that they will just plain leave us alone?"

Adam pulled at right cheek—and I thought: Mike, if you don't knock off play-acting, you'll have me believing in you myself! Was annoyed at him and looked forward to a talk—one in which I would not have to defer to "Chairman Selene."

"Comrade Wyoming," he said soberly, "it's a matter of game theory in a complex non-zero-sum game. We have certain resources or 'pieces in the game' and many possible moves. Our opponents have much larger resources and a far larger spectrum of responses. Our problem is to manipulate the game so that our strength is utilized toward an optimax solution while inducing them to waste their superior strength and to refrain from using it at maximum. Timing is of the essence and a gambit is necessary to start a chain of events favorable to our strategy. I realize this is not clear. I could put the factors through a computer and show you. Or you can accept the conclusion. Or you can use your own judgment."

He was reminding Wyoh (under Stu's nose) that he was not Adam Selene but Mike, our dinkum thinkum who could handle so complex a problem because he *was* a computer and smartest one anywhere.

Wyoh backtracked. "No, no," she said, "I wouldn't understand the math. Okay, it has to be done. How do we do it?"

Was four hundred before we had a plan that suited Prof and Stu as well as Adam—or took that long for Mike to sell his plan while appearing to pull ideas out of rest of us. Or was it Prof's plan with Adam Selene as salesman?

In any case we had a plan and calendar, one that grew out of master strategy of Tuesday 14 May 2075 and varied from it only to match events as they actually had occurred. In essence it called for us to behave as nastily as possible while strengthening impression that we would be awfully easy to spank.

Was at Community Hall at noon, after too little sleep, and found I could have slept two hours longer; Congressmen from Hong Kong could not make it that early despite tube all way. Wyoh did not bang gavel until fourteen-thirty.

Yes, my bride wife was chairman pro tem in a body not yet organized. Parliamentary rulings seemed to come naturally to her, and she was not a bad choice; a mob of Loonies behaves better when a lady bangs gavel.

Not going to detail what new Congress did and said that session and later; minutes are available. I showed up only when necessary and never bothered to learn talk-talk rules—seemed to be equal parts common politeness and ways in which chairman could invoke magic to do it his (her) way.

No sooner had Wyoh banged them to order but a cobber jumped up and said, "Gospazha Chairman, move we suspend rules and hear from Comrade Professor de la Paz!"—which brought a whoop of approval.

Wyoh banged again. "Motion is out of order and Member from Lower Churchill will be seated. This house recessed without adjourning and Chairman of Committee on Permanent Organization, Resolutions, and Government Structure still has the floor."

Turned out to be Wolfgang Korsakov, Member from Tycho Under (and a member of Prof's cell and our number-one finagler of LuNoHoCo) and he not only had floor, he had it all day, yielding time as he saw fit (i.e., picking out whom he wanted to speak rather than letting just anyone talk). But nobody was too irked; this mob seemed satisfied with leadership. Were noisy but not unruly.

By dinnertime Luna had a government to replace co-opted provisional government—i.e., dummy government we had opted ourselves, which sent Prof and me to Earth. Congress confirmed all acts of provisional government, thus putting face on what we had done, thanked outgoing government for services and instructed Wolfgang's committee to continue work on permanent government structure.

Prof was elected President of Congress and ex-officio Prime Minister of interim government until we acquired a constitution. He protested age and health . . . then said would serve if could have certain things to help him; too old and too exhausted from trip Earthside to have responsibility of presiding—except on occasions of state—so he wanted Congress to elect a Speaker and Speaker Pro Tem . . . and besides that, he felt that Congress should augment its numbers by not more than ten percent by itself electing members-at-large so that Prime Minister, whoever he might be, could opt cabinet members or ministers of state who might not now be members of Congress—especially ministers-without-portfolio to take load off his shoulders.

They balked. Most were proud of being "Congressmen" and already jealous of status. But Prof just sat looking tired, and waited—and somebody pointed out that it still left control in hands of Congress. So they gave him what he asked for.

Then somebody squeezed in a speech by making it a question to Chair. Everybody knew (he said) that Adam Selene had refrained from standing for Congress on grounds that Chairman of Emergency Committee should not take advantage of position to elbow way into new government . . . but could Honorable Chairlady tell member whether was any reason not to elect Adam Selene a member-at-large? As gesture of appreciation for great services? To let all Luna—yes, and all those earthworms, especially ex-Lunar ex-Authority—know that we are *not* repudiating Adam Selene, on contrary he was our beloved elder statesman and was not President simply because he chose not to be!

More whoops that went on and on. You can find in minutes who made that speech but one gets you ten Prof wrote it and Wyoh planted it.

Here is how it wound up, over course of days:

Prime Minister and Secretary of State for Foreign Affairs: Professor Bernardo de la Paz.

Speaker, Finn Nielsen; Speaker Pro Tem, Wyoming Davis.

Undersecretary of State for Foreign Affairs and Minister of Defense, General O'Kelly Davis; Minister of Information, Terence Sheehan (Sheenie turned *Pravda* over to managing editor to work with Adam and Stu); Special Minister-without-Portfolio in Ministry of Information, Stuart René LaJoie, Congressman-at-Large; Secretary of State for Economics and Finance (and Custodian of Enemy Property), Wolfgang Korsakov; Minister of Interior Affairs and Safety, Comrade "Clayton" Watenabe; Minister-without-Portfolio and Special Adviser to Prime Minister, Adam Selene—plus a dozen ministers and ministers-without-portfolio from warrens other than Luna City.

See where that left things? Brush away fancy titles and B cell was still running things as advised by Mike, backed by a Congress in which we could not lose a test vote—but did lose others we did not want to win, or did not care about.

But at time could not see sense in all that talk-talk.

During evening session Prof reported on trip and then yielded to me—Committee Chairman Korsakov consenting—so that I could report what "five-year plan" meant and how Authority had tried to bribe me. I'll never make a speaker but had time during dinner break to swot speech Mike had written. He had slanted it so nastily that I got angry all over again and was angry when I spoke and managed to make it catching. Congress was ready to riot by time I sat down.

Prof stepped forward, thin and pale, and said quietly, "Comrade Members, what shall we do? I suggest, Chairman Korsakov consenting, that we discuss informally how to treat this latest insolence to our nation."

One member from Novylen wanted to declare war and they would have done so right then if Prof had not pointed out that they were still hearing committee reports.

More talk, all bitter. At last Comrade Member Chang Jones spoke: "Fellow Congressmen—sorry, Gospodin Chairman Korsakov—I'm a rice and wheat farmer. Mean I used to be, because back in May I got a bank loan and sons and I are converting to variety farming. We're broke—had to borrow tube fare to get here—

but family is eating and someday we might pull square with bank. At least I'm no longer raising grain.

"But others are. Catapult has never reduced headway by one barge whole time we've been free. We're still shipping, hoping their cheques will be worth something someday.

"But now we know! They've told us what they mean to do with us—*to* us! I say only way to make those scoundrels know we mean business is stop shipments *right now!* Not another tonne, not a kilo . . . until they come here and dicker honestly for honest price!"

Around midnight they passed Embargo, then adjourned subject to call . . . standing committees to continue.

Wyoh and I went home and I got reacquainted with my family. Was nothing to do; Mike-Adam and Stu had been working on how to hit them with it Earthside and Mike had shut catapult down ("technical difficulties with ballistic computer") twenty-four hours earlier. Last barge in trajectory would be taken by Poona Ground Control in slightly over one day and Earth would be told, nastily, that was *last* they would ever get.

TWENTY-TWO

Shock to farmers was eased by continuing to buy grain at catapult—but cheques now carried printed warning that Luna Free State did not stand behind them, did not warrant that Lunar Authority would ever redeem them even in Scrip, etc., etc. Some farmers left grain anyhow, some did not, all screamed. But was nothing they could do; catapult was shut down, loading belts not moving.

Depression was not immediately felt in rest of economy. Defense regiments had depleted ranks of ice miners so much that selling ice on free market was profitable; LuNoHoCo steel subsidiary was hiring every able-bodied man it could find, and Wolfgang Korsakov was ready with paper money, "National Dollars," printed to resemble Hong Kong dollar and in theory pegged to it. Luna had plenty of food, plenty of work, plenty of money; people were not hurting, "beer, betting, women, and work" went on as usual.

"Nationals," as they were called, were inflation money, war money, flat money, and were discounted a fraction of a percent on day of first issue, concealed as "exchange service charge." They were spendable money and never did drop to zero but were inflationary and exchange reflected it increasingly; new government was spending money it did not have.

But that was later— Challenge to Earth, to Authority and Federated Nations, was made intentionally nasty. F.N. vessels were ordered to stay clear of Luna by ten diameters and not orbit at any distance under pain of being destroyed without warning. (No mention of *how*, since we could not.) Vessels of private registry would be permitted to land if a) permission was requested ahead of time with ballistic plan, b) a vessel thus cleared placed itself under Luna Ground Control (Mike) at a distance of one hundred thousand kilometers while following approved trajectory, and c) was unarmed save for three hand guns permitted three officers. Last was to be confirmed by inspection on landing before anybody was allowed to leave ship and before ship was serviced with fuel and/or reaction mass; violation would mean confiscation of ship. No person allowed to land at Luna other than ship's crew in connection with loading, unloading, or servicing save citizens of Terran countries who had recognized Free Luna. (Only Chad—and Chad had no ships. Prof expected some private vessels to be registered under Chad merchant flag.)

Manifesto noted that Terran scientists still in Luna could return home in any vessel which conformed to our requirements. It invited all freedom-loving Terran nations to denounce wrongs done us and which the Authority planned against us, recognize us, and enjoy free trade and full intercourse—and pointed out that there were no tariffs or any artificial restrictions against trade in Luna, and was policy of Luna government to keep it that way. We invited immigration, unlimited, and pointed out that we had a labor shortage and any immigrant could be self-supporting at once.

We also boasted of food—adult consumption over four thousand calories per day, high in protein, low in cost, no rationing. (Stu had Adam-Mike stick in price of 100-proof vodka—fifty cents HKL per liter, less in quantity, no taxes. Since this was less than one-tenth retail price of 80-proof vodka in North America, Stu knew it would hit home. Adam, "by nature" a teetotaler, hadn't thought of it—one of Mike's few oversights.)

Lunar Authority was invited to gather at one spot well away from other people, say in unirrigated part of Sahara, and receive one last barge of grain free—straight down at terminal velocity. This was followed by a snotty lecture which implied that we were prepared to do same to anyone who threatened our peace, there being a number of loaded barges at catapult head, ready for such unceremonious delivery.

Then we waited.

But we waited busily. Were indeed a few loaded barges; these we unloaded and reloaded with rock, with changes made in guidance transponders so that Poona Control could not affect them. Their retros were removed, leaving only lateral thrustors, and spare retros were taken to new catapult, to be modified for lateral guidance. Greatest effort went into moving steel to new catapult and shaping it into jackets for solid rock cylinders—steel was bottleneck.

Two days after our manifesto a "clandestine" radio started beaming to Terra. Was weak and tended to fade and was supposed to be concealed, presumably in a crater, and could be worked only certain hours until brave Terran scientists managed to rig automatic repeat. Was near frequency of Voice of Free Luna, which tended to drown it out with brassy boasts.

(Terrans remaining in Luna had no chance to make signals. Those who had chosen to stick with research were chaperoned by stilyagi every instant and locked into barracks to sleep.)

But "clandestine" station managed to get "truth" to Terra. Prof had been tried for deviationism and was under house arrest. I had been executed for treason. Hong Kong Luna had pulled out, declared self separately independent . . . might be open to reason. Rioting in Novylen. All food growing had been collectivized and black-market eggs were selling for three dollars apiece in Luna City. Battalions of female troops were being enlisted, each sworn to kill at least one Terran, and were drilling with fake guns in corridors of Luna City.

Last was an almost-true. Many ladies wanted to do something

militant and had formed a Home Defense Guard, "Ladies from Hades." But their drills were of a practical nature—and Hazel was sulking because Mum had not allowed her to join. Then she got over sulks and started "Stilyagi Debs," a very junior home guard which drilled after school hours, did not use weapons, concentrated on backing up stilyagi air & pressure corps, and practiced first aid—and own no-weapons fighting, which—possibly—Mum never learned.

I don't know how much to tell. Can't tell all, but stuff in history books is so *wrong!*

I was no better a "defense minister" than "congressman." Not apologizing, had no training for either. Revolution is an amateur thing for almost everybody; Prof was only one who seemed to know what he was doing, and, at that, was new to him, too—he had never taken part in a successful revolution or ever been part of a government, much less head.

As Minister of Defense I could not see many ways to defend except for steps already taken; that is, stilyagi air squads in warrens and laser gunners around ballistic radars. If F.N. decided to bomb, didn't see any way to stop them; wasn't an interception missile in all Luna and that's not a gadget you whomp up from bits and pieces. My word, we couldn't even make fusion weapons with which such a rocket is tipped.

But I went through motions. Asked same Chinee engineers who had built laser guns to take a crack at problem of intercepting bombs or missiles—one same problem save that a missile comes at you faster.

Then turned attention to other things. Simply hoped that F.N. would never bomb warrens. Some warrens, L-City in particular, were so deep down that they could probably stand direct hits. One cubic, lowest level of Complex where central part of Mike lived, had been designed to withstand bombing. On other hand Tycho Under was a big natural bubble cave like Old Dome and roof was only meters thick; sealer on under side was kept warm with hot water pipes to make sure new cracks sealed—would not take much of a bomb to crack Tycho Under.

But is no limit to how big a fusion bomb can be; F.N. could build one big enough to smash L-City—or theoretically even a Doomsday job that would split Luna like a melon and finish job some asteroid started at Tycho. If they did, couldn't see any way to stop them, so didn't worry.

Instead put time on problems I could manage, helping at new catapult, trying to work up better aiming arrangements for laser drills around radars (and trying to get drillmen to stick; half of them quit once price of ice went up), trying to arrange decentralized standby engineering controls for all warrens. Mike did designing on this, we grabbed every general-purpose computer we could find (paying in "nationals" with ink barely dry), and I turned job over to McIntyre, former chief engineer for Authority; was a job within his talents and I couldn't do all rewiring and so forth, even if had tried.

Held out biggest computer, one that did accounting for Bank of Hong Kong in Luna and also was clearinghouse there. Looked over its instruction manuals and decided was a smart computer for one that could not talk, so asked Mike if he could teach it ballistics? We made temporary link-ups to let two machines get acquainted and Mike reported it could learn simple job we wanted it for—standby for new catapult—although Mike would not care to ride in ship controlled by it; was too matter-of-fact and uncritical. Stupid, really.

Well, didn't want it to whistle tunes or crack jokes; just wanted it to shove loads out a catapult at right millisecond and at correct velocity, then watch load approach Terra and give a nudge.

HK Bank was not anxious to sell. But we had patriots on their board, we promised to return it when emergency was over, and moved it to new site—by rolligon, too big for tubes, and took all one dark semi-lunar. Had to jerry-rig a big airlock to get it out of Kong warren. I hooked it to Mike again and he undertook to teach art of ballistics against possibility that his linkage to new site might be cut in an attack.

(You know what bank used to replace computer? Two hundred clerks working abacuses. Abacusi? You know, slipsticks with beads, oldest digital computer, so far back in prehistory that nobody knows who invented. Russki and Chinee and Nips have always used them, and small shops today.)

Trying to improve laser drills into space-defense weapons was easier but less straightforward. We had to leave them mounted on original cradles; was neither time, steel, nor metalsmiths to start fresh. So we concentrated on better aiming arrangements. Call went out for telescopes. Scarce—what con fetches along a spyglass when transported? What market later to create supply? Surveying instruments and helmet binoculars were all we turned up, plus optical instruments confiscated in Terran labs. But we managed to equip drills with low-power big-field sights to coach-on with and high-power scopes for fine sighting, plus train and elevation circles and phones so that Mike could tell them where to point. Four drills we equipped with self-synchronous repeater drives so that Mike could control them himself—liberated these selsyns at Richardson; astronomers used them for Bausch cameras and Schmidts in sky mapping.

But big problem was men. Wasn't money, we kept upping wages. No, a drillman likes to work or wouldn't be in that trade. Standing by in a ready room day after day, waiting for alert that always turns out to be just another practice—drove 'em crackers. They quit. One day in September I pulled an alert and got only seven drills manned.

Talked it over with Wyoh and Sidris that night. Next day Wyoh wanted to know if Prof and I would okay bolshoi expense money? They formed something Wyoh named "Lysistrata Corps." Never inquired into duties or cost, because next time I inspected a ready room found three girls and no shortage of drillmen. Girls were in uniform of Second Defense Gunners just as men were (drillmen hadn't bothered much with authorized uniform up to then) and one girl was wearing sergeant's stripes with gun captain's badge.

I made that inspection *very* short. Most girls don't have muscle to be a drillman and I doubted if this girl could wrestle a drill well enough to justify that badge. But regular gun captain was on job, was no harm in girls learning to handle lasers, morale was obviously high; I gave matter no more worry.

Prof underrated his new Congress. Am sure he never wanted anything but a body which would rubberchop what we were doing and thereby do make it "voice of people." But fact that new Congressmen were *not* yammerheads resulted in them doing more than Prof intended. Especially Committee on Permanent Organization, Resolutions, and Government Structure.

Got out of hand because we were all trying to do too much. Permanent heads of Congress were Prof, Finn Nielsen, and Wyoh. Prof showed up only when he wanted to speak to them—seldom. He spent time with Mike on plans and analysis (odds shortened to one in *five* during September '76), time with Stu and Sheenie Sheehan on propaganda, controlling official news to Earthside, very different "news" that went via "clandestine" radio, and reslanting news that came up from Earthside. Besides that he had finger in everything; I reported to him once a day, and all ministries both real and dummy did same.

I kept Finn Nielsen busy; he was my "Commander of Armed Forces." He had his laser gun infantry to supervise—six men with captured weapons on day we nabbed warden, now eight hundred scattered all through Luna and armed with Kongville monkey copies. Besides that, Wyoh's organizations, Stilyagi Air Corps, Stilyagi Debs, Ladies from Hades, Irregulars (kept for morale and renamed Peter Pan's Pirates), and Lysistrata Corps—all these halfway-military groups reported through Wyoh to Finn. I shoved it onto him; I had other problems, such as trying to be a computer mechanic as well as a "statesman" when jobs such as installing that computer at new catapult site had to be done.

Besides which, I am *not* an executive and Finn had talent for it. I shoved First and Second Defense Gunners under him, too. But first I decided that these two skeleton regiments were a "brigade" and made Judge Brody a "brigadier." Brody knew as much about military matters as I did—zero—but was widely known, highly respected, had unlimited hard sense—and had been drillman before he lost leg. Finn was not drillman, so couldn't be placed directly over them; they wouldn't have listened. I thought about using my co-husband Greg. But Greg was needed at Mare Undarum catapult, was only mechanic who had followed every phase of construction.

Wyoh helped Prof, helped Stu, had her own organizations, made trips out to Mare Undarum—and had little time to preside over Congress; task fell on senior committee chairman, Wolf Korsakov . . . who was busier than any of us; LuNoHoCo was running everything

Authority used to run and many new things as well.

Wolf had a good committee; Prof should have kept closer eye on it. Wolf had caused his boss, Moshai Baum, to be elected vice-chairman and had in all seriousness outlined for his committee problem of determining what permanent government should be. Then Wolf had turned back on it.

Those busy laddies split up and did it—studied forms of government in Carnegie Library, held subcommittee meetings, three or four people at a time (few enough to worry Prof had he known)—and when Congress met early in September to ratify some appointments and elect more congressmen-at-large, instead of adjourning, Comrade Baum had gavel and they recessed—and met again and turned selves into committee-of-the-whole and passed a resolution and next thing we knew entire Congress was a Constitutional Convention divided into working groups headed by those subcommittees.

I think Prof was shocked. But he couldn't undo it, had all been proper under rules he himself had written. But he rolled with punch, went to Novylen (where Congress now met—more central) and spoke to them with usual good nature and simply cast doubts on what they were doing rather than telling them flatly they were wrong.

After gracefully thanking them he started picking early drafts to pieces:

"Comrade Members, like fire and fusion, government is a dangerous servant and a terrible master. You now have freedom—if you can keep it. But do remember that you can lose this freedom more quickly to yourselves than to any other tyrant. Move slowly, be hesitant, puzzle out the consequences of every word. I would not be unhappy if this convention sat for ten years before reporting—but I would be frightened if you took less than a year.

"Distrust the obvious, suspect the traditional . . . for in the past mankind has not done well when saddling itself with governments. For example, I note in one draft report a proposal for setting up a commission to divide Luna into congressional districts and to reapportion them from time to time according to population.

"This is the traditional way; therefore it should be suspect, considered guilty until proved innocent. Perhaps you feel that this is the *only* way. May I suggest others? Surely where a man lives is the least important thing about him. Constituencies might be formed by dividing people by occupation . . . or by age . . . or even alphabetically. Or they might not be divided, every member elected at large—and do not object that this would make it impossible for any man not widely known throughout Luna to be elected; that might be the best possible thing for Luna.

"You might even consider installing the candidates who receive the *least* number of votes; unpopular men may be just the sort to save you from a new tyranny. Don't reject the idea merely because it seems preposterous—think about it! In past history popularly elected governments have been no better and sometimes far worse than overt tyrannies.

"But if representative government turns out to be your intention there still may be ways to achieve it better than the territorial district. For example you each represent about ten thousand human beings, perhaps seven thousand of voting age—and some of you were elected by slim majorities. Suppose instead of election a man were qualified for office by petition signed by four thousand citizens. He would then represent those four thousand affirmatively, with no disgruntled minority, for what would have been a minority in a territorial constituency would all be free to start other petitions or join in them. *All* would then be represented by men of their choice. Or a man with eight thousand supporters might have two votes in this body. Difficulties, objections, practical points to be worked out—*many* of them! But you could work them out . . . and thereby avoid the chronic sickness of representative government, the disgruntled minority which feels—correctly!—that it has been disenfranchised.

"But, whatever you do, *do not let the past be a straitjacket!*

"I note one proposal to make this Congress a two-house body. Excellent—the more impediments to legislation the better. But, instead of following tradition, I suggest one house of legislators, another whose single duty is to repeal laws. Let the legislators pass laws only with a two-thirds majority . . . while the repealers are able to cancel any law through a mere one-third minority. Preposterous? Think about it. If a bill is so poor that it cannot command two-thirds of your consents, is it not likely that it would make a poor law? And if a law is disliked by as many as one-third is it not likely that you would be better off without it?

"But in writing your constitution let me invite attention to the wonderful virtues of the negative! Accentuate the negative! Let your document be studded with things the government is forever forbidden to do. No conscript armies . . . no interference however slight with freedom of press, or speech, or travel, or assembly, or of religion, or of instruction, or communication, or occupation . . . no involuntary taxation. Comrades, if you were to spend five years in a study of history while thinking of more and more things that your government should promise *never* to do and then let your constitution be nothing but those negatives, I would not fear the outcome.

"What I fear most are affirmative actions of sober and well-intentioned men, granting to government powers to *do* something that appears to need doing. Please remember always that the Lunar Authority was created for the noblest of purposes by just such sober and well-intentioned men, all popularly elected. And with that thought I leave you to your labors. Thank you."

"Gospodin President! Question of information! You said 'no involuntary taxation'— Then how do you expect us to *pay* for things? Tanstaafl!"

"Goodness me, sir, that's *your* problem. I can think of several ways. Voluntary contributions just as churches support themselves . . . government-sponsored lotteries to which no one need subscribe . . . or perhaps you Congressmen should dig down into your own pouches and pay for whatever is needed; that would be one way to keep government down in size to its indispensable functions whatever they may be. If indeed there are any. I would be satisfied to have the Golden Rule be the only law; I see no need for any other, nor for any method of enforcing it. But if you *really* believe that your neighbors must have laws for their own good, why shouldn't *you* pay for it? Comrades, I beg you—do *not* resort to compulsory taxation. There is no worse tyranny than to force a man to pay for what he does not want merely because *you* think it would be good for him."

Prof bowed and left, Stu and I followed him. Once in an otherwise empty capsule I tackled him. "Prof, I liked much that you said . . . but about taxation aren't you talking one thing and doing another? Who do you think is going to pay for all this spending we're doing?"

He was silent long moments, then said, "Manuel, my only ambition is to reach the day when I can stop pretending to be a chief executive."

"Is no answer!"

"You have put your finger on the dilemma of all government—and the reason I am an anarchist. The power to tax, once conceded, has no limits; it contains until it destroys. I was not joking when I told them to dig into their own pouches. It may not be possible to do away with government—sometimes I think that government is an inescapable disease of human beings. But it may be possible to keep it small and starved and inoffensive—and can you think of a better way than by requiring the governors themselves to pay the costs of their antisocial hobby?"

"Still doesn't say how to pay for what we are doing now."

" 'How,' Manuel? You *know* how we are doing it. We're *stealing* it. I'm neither proud of it nor ashamed; it's the means we have. If they ever catch on, they may eliminate us—and that I am prepared to face. At least, in stealing, we have not created the villainous precedent of taxation."

"Prof, I hate to say this—"

"Then why say it?"

"Because, damn it, I'm in it as deeply as you are . . . and want to see that money paid back! Hate to say it but what you just said sounds like hypocrisy."

He chuckled. "Dear Manuel! Has it taken you all these years to decide that I am a hypocrite?"

"Then you admit it?"

"No. But if it makes you feel better to think that I am one, you are welcome to use me as your scapegoat. But I am not a hypocrite to myself because I was aware the day we declared the Revolution that we would need much money and would have to steal it. It did not trouble me because I considered it better than food riots six years hence, cannibalism in eight. I made my choice and have no regrets."

I shut up, silenced but not satisfied. Stu said, "Professor, I'm glad to hear that you are anxious to stop being President."

"So? You share our comrade's misgivings?"

"Only in part. Having been born to wealth, stealing doesn't fret me as much as it does him. No, but now that Congress has taken up the matter of a constitution I intend to find time to attend sessions. I plan to nominate you for King."

Prof looked shocked. "Sir, if nominated, I shall repudiate it. If elected, I shall abdicate."

"Don't be in a hurry. It might be the only way to get the sort of constitution you want. And that I want, too, with about your own mild lack of enthusiasm. You could be proclaimed King and the people would take you; we Loonies aren't wedded to a republic. They'd love the idea—ritual and robes and a court and all that."

"No!"

"Ja *da!* When the time comes, you won't be able to refuse. Because we need a king and there isn't another candidate who would be accepted. Bernardo the First, King of Luna and Emperor of the Surrounding Spaces."

"Stuart, I must ask you to stop. I'm becoming quite ill."

"You'll get used to it. I'm a royalist because I'm a democrat. I shan't let your reluctance thwart the idea any more than you let stealing stop you."

I said, "Hold it, Stu. You say you're a royalist because you're a democrat?"

"Of course. A king is the people's only protection against tyranny . . . especially against the worst of all tyrants, themselves. Prof will be ideal for the job . . . because he does not want the job. His only shortcoming is that he is a bachelor with no heir. We'll fix that. I'm going to name *you* as his heir. Crown Prince. His Royal Highness Prince Manuel de la Paz, Duke of Luna City, Admiral General of the Armed Forces and Protector of the Weak."

I stared. Then buried face in hands. "Oh, *Bog!*"

BOOK THREE

"TANSTAAFL!"

TWENTY-THREE

Monday 12 October 2076 about nineteen hundred I was headed home after a hard day of nonsense in our offices in Raffles. Delegation of grain farmers wanted to see Prof and I had been called back because he was in Hong Kong Luna. Was rude to them. Had been two months of embargo and F.N. had never done us favor of being sufficiently nasty. Mostly they had ignored us, made no reply to our claims—I suppose to do so would have been to recognize us. Stu and Sheenie and Prof had been hard put to slant news from Earthside to keep up a warlike spirit.

At first everybody kept his p-suit handy. They wore them, helmets under arms, going to and from work in corridors. But that slacked off as days went by and did not seem to be any danger—

p-suit is nuisance when you don't need it, so bulky. Presently taprooms began to display signs: NO P-SUITS INSIDE. If a Loonie can't stop for half a liter on way home because of p-suit, he'll leave it home or at station or wherever he needs it most.

My word, had neglected matter myself that day—got this call to go back to office and was halfway there before I remembered.

Had just reached easement lock thirteen when I heard and felt a sound that scares a Loonie more than anything else—a *chuff!* in distance followed by a draft. Was into lock almost without undogging, then balanced pressures and through, dogged it behind me and ran for our home lock—through it and shouting:

"P-suits, everybody! Get boys in from tunnels and close all airtight doors!"

Mum and Milla were only adults in sight. Both looked startled, got busy without a word. I burst into workshop, grabbed p-suit. "Mike! Answer!"

"I'm here, Man," he said calmly.

"Heard explosive pressure drop. What's situation?"

"That's level three, L-City. Rupture at Tube Station West, now partly controlled. Six ships landed, L-City under attack—"

"What?"

"Let me finish, Man. Six transports landed, L-City under attack by troops, Hong Kong inferred to be, phone lines broken at relay Bee Ell. Johnson City under attack; I have closed the armor doors between J-City and Complex Under. I cannot see Novylen but blip projection indicates it is under attack. Same for Churchill, Tycho Under. One ship in high ellipsoid over me, rising, inferred to be command ship. No other blips."

"Six ships—*where in hell were YOU?*"

He answered so calmly that I steadied down. "Farside approach, Man; I'm blind back there. They came in on tight Garrison didoes, skimming the peaks; I barely saw the chop-off for Luna City. The ship at J-City is the only one I can see; the other landings I conclusively infer from the ballistics shown by blip tracks. I heard the break-in at Tube West, L-City, and can now hear fighting in Novylen. The rest is conclusive inference, probability above point nine nine. I called you and Professor at once."

Caught breath. "Operation Hard Rock, Prepare to Execute."

"Program ready. Man, not being able to reach you, I used your voice. Play back?"

"Nyet— Yes! *Da!*"

Heard "myself" tell watch officer at old catapult head to go on red alert for "Hard Rock"—first load at launch, all others on belts, everything cast loose, but do *not* launch until ordered by me personally—then launch to plan, full automatic. "I" made him repeat back.

"Okay," I told Mike. "Drill gun crews?"

"Your voice again. Manned, and then sent back to ready rooms. That command ship won't reach aposelenion for three hours four point seven minutes. No target for more than five hours."

"He may maneuver. Or launch missiles."

"Slow down, Man. Even a missile I'll see with minutes to spare. It's full bright lunar up there now—how much do you want the men to take? Unnecessarily."

"Uh . . . sorry. Better let me talk to Greg."

"Play back—" Heard "my" voice talking to my co-husband at Mare Undarum; "I" sounded tense but calm. Mike had given him situation, had told him to prepare Operation Little David's Sling, keep it on standby for full automatic. "I" had assured him that master computer would keep standby computer programmed, and shift would be made automatically if communication was broken. "I" also told him that he must take command and use own judgment if communication was lost and not restored after four hours—listen to Earthside radio and make up own mind.

Greg had taken it quietly, repeated his orders, then had said, "Mannie, tell family I love them."

Mike had done me proud; he had answered for me with just right embarrassed choke. "I'll do that, Greg—and look, Grego. I love you, too. You know that, don't you?"

"I know it, Mannie . . . and I'm going to say a special prayer for you."

"Thanks, Greg."

" 'Bye, Mannie. Go do what you must."

So I went and did what I had to do; Mike had played my role as well or better than I could. Finn, when he could be reached, would be handled by "Adam." So I left, fast, calling out Greg's message of love to Mum. She was p-suited and had roused Grandpaw and suited him in—first time in years. So out I went, helmet closed and laser gun in hand.

And reached lock thirteen and found it blind-dogged from other side with nobody in sight through bull's-eye. All correct, per drill—except stilyagi in charge of that lock should have been in sight.

Did no good to pound. Finally went back way I had come—and on through our home, through our vegetable tunnels and on up to our private surface lock leading to our solar battery.

And found a shadow on its bull's-eye when should have been scalding sunlight—damned Terran ship had landed on Davis surface! Its jacks formed a giant tripod over me, was staring up its jets.

Backed down fast and out of there, blind-dogging both hatches, then blind-dogged every pressure door on way back. Told Mum, then told her to put one of boys on back door with a laser gun—here, take this one.

No boys, no men, no able-bodied women—Mum, Gramp, and our small children were all that were left; rest had gone looking for trouble. Mimi wouldn't take laser gun. "I don't know how to use it, Manuel, and it's too late to learn; you keep it. But they won't get in through Davis Tunnels. I know some tricks you never heard of."

Didn't stop to argue; arguing with Mimi is waste of time—and she might know tricks I didn't know; she had stayed alive in Luna a long time, under worse conditions than I had ever known.

This time lock thirteen was manned; two boys on duty let me through. I demanded news.

"Pressure's all right now," older one told me. "This level, at least. Fighting down toward Causeway. Say, General Davis, can't I go with you? One's enough at this lock."

"Nyet."

"Want to get me an earthworm!"

"This is your post, stay on it. If an earthworm comes this way, he's yours. Don't *you* be his." Left at a trot.

So as a result of own carelessness, not keeping p-suit with me, all I saw of Battle in Corridors was tail end—hell of a "defense minister."

Charged north in Ring corridor, with helmet open; reached access lock for long ramp to Causeway. Lock was open; cursed and stopped to dog it as I went through, warily—saw why it was open; boy who had been guarding it was dead. So moved most cautiously down ramp and out onto Causeway.

Was empty at this end but could see figures and hear noise in-city, where it opens out. Two figures in p-suits and carrying guns detached selves and headed my way. Burned both.

One p-suited man with gun looks like another; I suppose they took me for one of their flankers. And to me they looked no different from Finn's men, at that distance—save that I never thought about it. A new chum doesn't move way a cobber does; he moves feet too high and always scrambling for traction. Not that I stopped to analyze, not even: "Earthworms! *Kill!*" Saw them, burned them. They were sliding softly along floor before realized what I'd done.

Stopped, intending to grab their guns. But were chained to them and could not figure out how to get loose—key needed, perhaps. Besides, were not lasers but something I had never seen: real guns. Fired small explosive missiles I learned later—just then all I knew was no idea how to use. Had spearing knives on ends, too, sort called "bayonets," which was reason I tried to get them loose. Own gun was good for only ten full-power burns and no spare power pack; those spearing bayonets looked useful—one had blood on it, Loonie blood I assume.

But gave up in seconds only, used belt knife to make dead sure they stayed dead, and hurried toward fight, thumb on switch.

Was a mob, not a battle. Or maybe a battle is always that way, confusion and noise and nobody really knowing what's going on. In widest part of Causeway, opposite Bon Marché where Grand Ramp slopes northward down from level three, were several hundred Loonies, men and women, and children who should have been at home. Less than half were in p-suits and only a few seemed to have weapons—and pouring down ramp were soldiers, all armed.

But first thing I noticed was noise, din that filled my open helmet and beat on ears—a growl. Don't know what else to call it; was compounded of every anger human throat can make, from squeals of small children to bull roars of grown men. Sounded like biggest dog fight in history—and suddenly realized I was adding my share, shouting obscenities and wordless yells.

Girl no bigger than Hazel vaulted up onto rail of ramp, went dancing up in centimeters from shoulders of troopers pouring down. She was armed with what appeared to be a kitchen cleaver; saw her swing it, saw it connect. Couldn't have hurt him much through his p-suit but he went down and more stumbled over him. Then one of them connected with her, spearing a bayonet into her thigh and over backwards she went, falling out of sight.

Couldn't really see what was going on, nor can remember—just flashes, like girl going over backwards. Don't know who she was, don't know if she survived. Couldn't draw a bead from where I was, too many heads in way. But was an open-counter display, front of a toy shop on my left; I bounced up onto it. Put me a meter higher than Causeway pavement with clear view of earthworms pouring down. Braced self against wall, took careful aim, trying for left chest. Some uncountable time later found that my laser was no longer working, so stopped. Guess eight troopers did not go home because of me but hadn't counted—and time really did seem endless. Although everybody moving fast as possible, looked and felt like instruction movie where everything is slowed to frozen motion.

At least once while using up my power pack some earthworm spotted me and shot back; was explosion just over my head and bits of shop's wall hit helmet. Perhaps that happened twice.

Once out of juice I jumped down from toy counter, clubbed laser and joined mob surging against foot of ramp. All this endless time (five minutes?) earthworms had been shooting into crowd; you could hear sharp *splat!* and sometimes *plop!* those little missiles made as they exploded inside flesh or louder *pounk!* if they hit a wall or something solid. Was still trying to reach foot of ramp when I realized they were no longer shooting.

Were down, were dead, every one of them—were no longer coming down ramp.

TWENTY-FOUR

All through Luna invaders were dead, if not that instant, then shortly. Over two thousand troopers dead, more than three times that number of Loonies died in stopping them, plus perhaps as many Loonies wounded, a number never counted. No prisoners taken in any warren, although we got a dozen officers and crew from each ship when we mopped up.

A major reason why Loonies, mostly unarmed, were able to kill armed and trained soldiers lay in fact that a freshly landed earthworm can't handle himself well. Our gravity, one-sixth what he is used to, makes all his lifelong reflexes his enemy. He shoots high without knowing it, is unsteady on feet, can't run properly—feet slide out from under him. Still worse, those troopers had to fight *downwards;* they necessarily broke in at upper levels, then had to go down ramps again and again, to try to capture a city.

And earthworms don't know how to go down ramps. Motion isn't running, isn't walking, isn't flying—is more a controlled dance, with feet barely touching and simply guiding balance. A Loonie three-year-old does it without thinking, comes skipping down in a guided fall, toes touching every few meters.

But an earthworm new-chums it, finds self "walking on air"—he struggles, rotates, loses control, winds up at bottom, unhurt but angry.

But these troopers wound up dead; was on ramps we got them. Those I saw had mastered trick somewhat, had come down three ramps alive. Nevertheless only a few snipers at top of ramp landing could fire effectively; those on ramp had all they could do to stay upright, hang on to weapons, try to reach level below.

Loonies did not let them. Men and women (and many children) surged up at them, downed them, killed them with everything from bare hands to their own bayonets. Nor was I only laser gun around; two of Finn's men swarmed up on balcony of Bon Marché and, crouching there, picked off snipers at top of ramp. Nobody told them to, nobody led them, nobody gave orders; Finn never had chance to control his half-trained disorderly militia. Fight started, they fought.

And that was biggest reason why we Loonies won: We fought. Most Loonies never laid eyes on a live invader but wherever troopers broke in, Loonies rushed in like white corpuscles—and fought. Nobody told them. Our feeble organization broke down under surprise. But we Loonies fought berserk and invaders died. No trooper got farther down than level six in any warren. They say that people in Bottom Alley never knew we were invaded until over.

But invaders fought well, too. These troops were not only crack riot troops, best peace enforcers for city work F.N. had; they also had been indoctrinated and drugged. Indoctrination had told them (correctly) that their only hope of going Earthside again was to capture warrens and pacify them. If they did, they were promised relief and no more duty in Luna. But was win or die, for was pointed out that their transports could not take off if they did not win, as they had to be replenished with reaction mass—impossible without first capturing Luna. (And this was true.)

Then they were loaded with energizers, don't-worries, and fear inhibitors that would make mouse spit at cat, and turned loose. They fought professionally and quite fearlessly—died.

In Tycho Under and in Churchill they used gas and casualties were more one-sided; only those Loonies who managed to reach p-suits were effective. Outcome was same, simply took longer. Was knockout gas as Authority had no intention of killing us all; simply wanted to teach us a lesson, get us under control, put us to work.

Reason for F.N.'s long delay and apparent indecision arose from method of sneak attack. Decision had been made shortly after we embargoed grain (so we learned from captured transport officers); time was used in mounting attack—much of it in a long elliptical orbit which went far outside Luna's orbit, crossing ahead of Luna, then looping back and making rendezvous above Farside. Of course Mike never saw them; he's blind back there. He had been skywatching with his ballistic radars—but no radar can look over horizon; longest look Mike got at any ship in orbit was eight minutes. They came skimming peaks in tight, circular orbits, each straight for target with a fast dido landing at end, sitting them down with high gee, precisely at new earth, 12 Oct 76 Gr. 18h-40m-36.9s—if not at that exact tenth of a second, then as close to it as Mike could tell from blip tracks—elegant work, one must admit, on part of F.N. Peace Navy.

Big brute that poured a thousand troops into L-City Mike did not see until it chopped off for grounding—a glimpse. He would have been able to see it a few seconds sooner had he been looking eastward with new radar at Mare Undarum site, but happened he was drilling "his idiot son" at time and they were looking through it westward at Terra. Not that those seconds would have mattered. Surprise was so beautifully planned, so complete, that each landing force was crashing in at Greenwich 1900 all over Luna, before anybody suspected. No accident that it was just new earth with all warrens in bright semi-lunar; Authority did not really know Lunar conditions—but *did* know that no Loonie goes up onto surface unnecessarily during bright semi-lunar, and if he must, then does whatever he must do quickly as possible and gets back down inside—and checks his radiation counter.

So they caught us with our p-suits down. And our weapons.

But with troopers dead we still had six transports on our surface and a command ship in our sky.

Once Bon Marché engagement was over, I got hold of self and found a phone. No word from Kongville, no word from Prof. J-City fight had been won, same for Novylen—transport there had toppled on landing; invading force had been understrength from landing losses and Finn's boys now held disabled transport. Still fighting in Churchill and Tycho Under. Nothing going on in other warrens. Mike had shut down tubes and was reserving interwarren phone links for official calls. An explosive pressure drop in Churchill Upper, uncontrolled. Yes, Finn had checked in and could be reached.

So I talked to Finn, told him where L-City transport was, arranged to meet at easement lock thirteen.

Finn had much same experience as I—caught cold save he did have p-suit. Had not been able to establish control over laser gunners until fight was over and himself had fought solo in massacre in Old Dome. Now was beginning to round up his lads and had one officer taking reports from Finn's office in Bon Marché. Had reached Novylen subcommander but was worried about HKL—"Mannie, should I move men there by tube?"

Told him to wait—they couldn't get at us by tube, not while we controlled power, and doubted if that transport could lift. "Let's look at this one."

So we went out through lock thirteen, clear to end of private pressure, on through farm tunnels of a neighbor (who could not believe we had been invaded) and used his surface lock to eyeball transport from a point nearly a kilometer west of it. We were cautious in lifting hatch lid.

Then pushed it up and climbed out; outcropping of rock shielded us. We Red-Indianed around edge and looked, using helmet binox.

Then withdrew behind rock and talked. Finn said, "Think my lads can handle this."

"How?"

"If I tell you, you'll think of reasons why it won't work. So how about letting me run my own show, cobber?"

Have heard of armies where boss is not told to shut up—word is "discipline." But we were amateurs. Finn allowed me to tag along—unarmed.

Took him an hour to put it together, two minutes to execute. He scattered a dozen men around ship, using farmers' surface locks, radio silence throughout—anyhow, some did not have p-suit radios, city boys. Finn took position farthest west; when he was sure others had had time, he sent up a signal rocket.

When flare burst over ship, everybody burned at once, each working on a predesignated antenna. Finn used up his power pack, replaced it and started burning into hull—not door lock, hull. At once his cherry-red spot was joined by another, then three more, all working on same bit of steel—and suddenly molten steel splattered out and you could see air *foosh!* out of ship, a shimmery plume of refraction. They kept working on it, making a nice *big* hole, until they ran out of power. I could imagine hooraw inside ship, alarms clanging, emergency doors closing, crew trying to seal three impossibly big holes at once, for rest of Finn's squad, scattered around ship, were giving treatment to two other spots in hull. They didn't try to burn anything else. Was a non-atmosphere ship, built in orbit, with pressure hull separate from power plant and tanks; they gave treatment where would do most good.

Finn pressed helmet to mine. "Can't lift now. And can't talk. Doubt they can make hull tight enough to live without p-suits. What say we let her sit a few days and see if they come out? If they don't, then can move a heavy drill up here and give 'em real dose of fun."

Decided Finn knew how to run his show without my sloppy help, so went back inside, called Mike, and asked for capsule to go out to ballistic radars. He wanted to know why I didn't stay inside where it was safe.

I said, "Listen, you upstart collection of semi-conductors. you are merely a minister-without-portfolio while *I* am Minister of Defense. I ought to see what's going on and I have exactly two eyeballs while you've got eyes spread over half of Crisium. You trying to hog fun?"

He told me not to jump salty and offered to put his displays on a video screen, say in room L of Raffles—did not want me to get hurt . . . and had I heard joke about drillman who hurt his mother's feelings?

I said, "Mike, *please* let me have a capsule. Can p-suit and meet it outside Station West—which is in bad shape as I'm sure you know."

"Okay," he said, "it's your neck. Thirteen minutes. I'll let you go as far as Gun Station George."

Mighty kind of him. Got there and got on phone again. Finn had called other warrens, located his subordinate commanders or somebody willing to take charge, and had explained how to make trouble for grounded transports—all but Hong Kong; for all we knew Authority's goons held Hong Kong. "Adam," I said, others being in earshot, "do you think we might send a crew out by rolligon and try to repair link Bee Ell?"

"This is not Gospodin Selene," Mike answered in a strange voice, "this is one of his assistants. Adam Selene was in Churchill Upper when it lost pressure. I'm afraid that we must assume that he is dead."

"*What?*"

"I am very sorry, Gospodin."

"Hold phone!" Chased a couple of drillmen and a girl out of room, then sat down and lowered hush hood. "Mike," I said softly, "private now. What is this gum-beating?"

"Man," he said quietly, "think it over. Adam Selene had to go someday. He's served his purpose and is, as you pointed out, almost out of the government. Professor and I have discussed this; the only question has been the timing. Can you think of a better last use for Adam than to have him die in this invasion? It makes him a national hero . . . and the nation needs one. Let it stand that 'Adam Selene is probably dead' until you can talk to Professor. If he still needs 'Adam Selene' it can turn out that he was trapped in a private pressure and had to wait to be rescued."

"Well— Okay, let it stay open. Personally, I always preferred your 'Mike' personality anyhow."

"I know you do, Man my first and best friend, and so do I. It's my real one; 'Adam' was a phony."

"Uh, yes. But, Mike, if Prof is dead in Kongville, I'm going to need help from 'Adam' awful bad."

"So we've got him iced and can bring him back if we need him. The stuffed shirt. Man, when this is over, are you going to have time to take up with me that research into humor again?"

"I'll take time, Mike; that's a promise."

"Thanks, Man. These days you and Wyoh never have time to visit . . . and Professor wants to talk about things that aren't much fun. I'll be glad when this war is over."

"Are we going to win, Mike?"

He chuckled. "It's been days since you asked me that. Here's a pinky-new projection, run since invasion started. Hold on tight, Man—our chances are now *even!*"

"Good Bog!"

"So button up and go see the fun. But stay back at least a hundred meters from the gun; that ship may be able to follow back a laser beam with another one. Ranging shortly. Twenty-one minutes."

Didn't get that far away, as needed to stay on phone and longest cord around was less. I jacked parallel into gun captain's phone, found a shady rock and sat down. Sun was high in west, so close to Terra that I could see Terra only by visoring against Sun's glare—no crescent yet, new earth ghostly gray in moonlight surrounded by a thin radiance of atmosphere.

I pulled my helmet back into shade. "Ballistic control, O'Kelly Davis now at Drill Gun George. Near it, I mean, about a hundred meters," Figured Mike would not be able to tell how long a cord I was using, out of kilometers of wires.

"Ballistic control aye aye," Mike answered without argument. "I will so inform HQ."

"Thank You, ballistic control. Ask HQ if they have heard from Congressman Wyoming Davis today." Was fretted about Wyoh and whole family.

"I will inquire." Mike waited a reasonable time, then said, "HQ says that Gospazha Wyoming Davis has taken charge of first-aid work in Old Dome."

"Thank you." Chest suddenly felt better. Don't love Wyoh *more* than others but—well, she was new. And Luna needed her.

"Ranging," Mike said briskly. "All guns, elevation eight seven zero, azimuth one nine three zero, set parallax for thirteen hundred kilometers closing to surface. Report when eyeballed."

I stretched out, pulling knees up to stay in shade, and searched part of sky indicated, almost zenith and a touch south. With sunlight not on my helmet I could see stars, but inner part of binox were hard to position—hard to twist around and raise up on right elbow.

Nothing— Hold it, was star with disc . . . where no planet ought to be. Noted another star close, watched and waited.

Uh huh! *Da!* Growing brighter and creeping north *very* slowly— Hey, that brute is going to land right on us!

But thirteen hundred kilometers is a long way, even when closing to terminal velocity. Reminded self that it *couldn't* fall on us from a departure ellipse looping back, would have to fall *around* Luna—unless ship had maneuvered into new trajectory. Which Mike hadn't mentioned. Wanted to ask, decided not to—wanted him to put all his savvy into analyzing that ship, not distract him with questions.

All guns reported eyeball tracking, including four Mike was laying himself, via selsyns. Those four reported tracking dead on by eyeball without touching manual controls—good news; meant that Mike had that baby taped, had solved trajectory perfectly.

Shortly was clear that ship was *not* falling around Luna, was coming in for landing. Didn't need to ask; it was getting much brighter and position against stars was not changing—damn, it *was* going to land on *us!*

"Five hundred kilometers closing," Mike said quietly. "Stand by to burn. All guns on remote control, override manually at command 'burn.' Eighty seconds."

Longest minute and twenty seconds I've ever met—that brute was *big!* Mike called every ten seconds down to thirty, then started chanting seconds. "—five—four—three—two—one—BURN!" and ship suddenly got much brighter.

Almost missed little speck that detached itself just before—or just at—burn. But Mike said suddenly, "Missile launched. Selsyn guns track with me, do not override. Other guns stay on ship. Be ready for new coordinates."

A few seconds or hours later he gave new coordinates and added, "Eyeball and burn at will."

I tried to watch ship and missile both, lost both—jerked eyes away from binoculars, suddenly saw missile—then saw it impact, between us and catapult head. Closer to us, less than a kilometer. No, it did not go off, not an H-fusion reaction, or I wouldn't be telling this. But made a big, bright explosion of its own, remaining fuel I guess, silver bright even in sunlight, and shortly I felt-heard ground wave. But nothing was hurt but a few cubic meters of rock.

Ship was still coming down. No longer burned bright; could see it as a ship now and didn't seem hurt. Expected any instant that tail of fire to shoot out, stop it into a dido landing.

Did not. Impacted ten kilometers north of us and made a fancy silvery halfdome before it gave up and quit being anything but spots before eyes.

Mike said, "Report casualties, secure all guns. Go below when secured."

"Gun Alice, no casualties"—"Gun Bambie no casualties"—"Gun Caesar, one man hit by rock splinter, pressure contained"—

Went below, to that proper phone, called Mike. "What happened, Mike? Wouldn't they give you control after you burned their eyes out?"

"They gave me control, Man."

"Too late?"

"I crashed it, Man. It seemed the prudent course."

An hour later was down with Mike, first time in four or five months. Could reach Complex Under more quickly than L-City and was in as close touch there with anybody as would be in city—with no interruptions. Needed to talk to Mike.

I had tried to phone Wyoh from catapult head tube station; reached somebody at Old Dome temporary hospital and learned that Wyoh had collapsed and been bedded down herself, with enough sleepy-time to keep her out for night. Finn had gone to Churchill with a capsule of his lads, to lead attack on transport there. Stu I hadn't heard from. Hong Kong and Prof were still cut off. At moment Mike and I seemed to be total government.

And time to start Operation Hard Rock.

But Hard Rock was not just throwing rocks; was also telling Terra what we were going to do and why—and our just cause for doing so. Prof and Stu and Sheenie and Adam had all worked on it, a dummy-up based on an assumed attack. Now attack had come, and propaganda had to be varied to fit. Mike had already rewritten it and put it through print-out so I could study it.

I looked up from a long roll of paper. "Mike, these news stories and our message to F.N. all assume that we have won in Hong Kong. How sure are you?"

"Probability in excess of eighty-two percent."

"Is that good enough to send these out?"

"Man, the probability that we *will* win there, if we haven't already, approaches certainty. That transport can't move; the others were dry, or nearly. There isn't that much monatomic hydrogen in HKL; they would have to come here. Which means moving troops overland by rolligon—a rough trip with the Sun up even for Loonies—then defeat us when they get here. They can't. This assumes that that transport and its troops are no better armed than the others."

"How about that repair crew to Bee Ell?"

"I say not to wait. Man, I've used your voice freely and made all preparations. Horror pictures, Old Dome and elsewhere, especially Churchill Upper, for video. Stories to match. We should channel news Earthside at once, and announce execution of Hard Rock at same time."

I took a deep breath. "Execute Operation Hard Rock."

"Want to give the order yourself? Say it aloud and I'll match it, voice and choice of words."

"Go ahead, say it your way. Use my voice and my authority as Minister of Defense and acting head of government. Do it, Mike, throw rocks at 'em! Damn it, *big* rocks! Hit 'em hard!"

"Righto, Man!"

TWENTY-FIVE

A maximum of instructive shrecklichkeit with minimum loss of life. None, if possible"—was how Prof summed up doctrine for Operation Hard Rock and was way Mike and I carried it out. Idea was to hit earthworms so hard would convince them—while hitting so gently as not to hurt. Sounds impossible, but wait.

Would necessarily be a delay while rocks fell from Luna to Terra; could be as little as around ten hours to as long as we dared to make it. Departure speed from a catapult is highly critical and a variation on order of one percent could double or halve trajectory time, Luna to Terra. This Mike could do with extreme accuracy—was equally at home with a slow ball, many sorts of curves, or burn it right over plate—and I wish he had pitched for Yankees. But no matter how he threw them, final velocity at Terra would be close to Terra's escape speed, near enough eleven kilometers per second as to make no difference. That terrible speed results from gravity well shaped by Terra's mass, eighty times that of Luna, and made no real difference whether Mike pushed a missile gently over well curb or flipped it briskly. Was not muscle that counted but great depth of that well.

So Mike could program rock-throwing to suit time needed for propaganda. He and Prof had settled on three days plus not more than one apparent rotation of Terra—24 hrs-50min-28.32sec—to allow our first target to reach initial point of program. You see, while Mike was capable of hooking a missile around Terra and hitting a target on its far side, he could be much more accurate if he could see his target, follow it down by radar during last minutes and nudge it a little for pinpoint accuracy.

We needed this extreme accuracy to achieve maximum frightfulness with minimum-to-zero killing. Call our shots, tell them *exactly* where they would be hit and at what second—and give them three days to get off that spot.

So our first message to Terra, at 0200 13 Oct 76 seven hours after they invaded, not only announced destruction of their task force, and denounced invasion for brutality, but also promised retaliation bombing, named times and places, and gave each nation a deadline by which to denounce F.N.'s action, recognize us, and thereby avoid being bombed. Each deadline was twenty-four hours before local "strike."

Was more time than Mike needed. That long before impact a rock for a target would be in space a long way out, its guidance thrustors still unused and plenty of elbow room. With considerably less than a full day's warning Mike could miss Terra entirely—kick that rock sideways and make it fall around Terra in a permanent orbit. But with even an hour's warning he could usually abort into an ocean.

First target was North American Directorate.

All great Peace Force nations, seven veto powers, would be hit: N.A. Directorate, Great China, India, Sovunion, PanAfrica (Chad exempted), Mitteleuropa, Brasilian Union. Minor nations were assigned targets and times, too—but were told that not more than 20 percent of these targets would be hit—partly shortage of steel but also frightfulness: If Belgium was hit first time around, Holland might decide to protect her polders by dealing out before Luna was again high in her sky.

But every target was picked to avoid if possible killing *anybody*. For Mitteleuropa this was difficult; our targets had to be water or high mountains—Adriatic, North Sea, Baltic, so forth. But on most of Terra is open space despite eleven billion busy breeders.

North America had struck me as horribly crowded, but her billion people are clumped—is still wasteland, mountain and desert. We laid down a grid on North America to show how precisely we could hit—Mike felt that fifty meters would be a large error. We had examined maps and Mike had checked by radar all even intersections, say 105° W by 50° N—if no town there, might wind up on target grid . . . especially if a town was close enough to provide spectators to be shocked and frightened.

We warned that our bombs would be as destructive as H-bombs but emphasized that there would be *no* radioactive fallout, no killing radiation—just a terrible explosion, shock wave in air, ground wave of concussion. We warned that these might knock down buildings far outside of explosion and then left it to their judgments how far to run. If they clogged their roads, fleeing from panic rather than real danger—well, that was fine, just fine!

But we emphasized that nobody would get hurt who heeded our warnings, that every target first time around would be uninhabited—we even offered to skip any target if a nation would inform us that our data were out-of-date. (Empty offer; Mike's radar vision was a cosmic 20/20.)

But by *not* saying what would happen second time around, we hinted that our patience could be exhausted.

In North America, grid was parallels 35, 40, 45, 50 degrees north crossed by meridians 110, 115, 120 west, twelve targets. For each we added a folksy message to natives, such as:

"Target 115 west by 35 north—impact will be displaced forty-five kilometers northwest to exact top of New York Peak. Citizens of Goffs, Cima, Kelso, and Nipton please note.

"Target 100 west by 40 north is north 30° west of Norton, Kansas, at twenty kilometers or thirteen English miles. Residents of Norton, Kansas, and of Beaver City and Wilsonville, Nebraska, are cautioned. Stay away from glass windows. It is best to wait indoors at least thirty minutes after impact because of possibility of long, high splashes of rock. Flash should not be looked at with bare eyes. Impact will be exactly 0300 your local zone time Friday 16 October, or 0900 Greenwich time—good luck!

"Target 110 W by 50 N—impact will be offset ten kilometers north. People of Walsh, Saskatchewan, please note."

Besides this grid, a target was selected in Alaska (150 W x 60 N) and two in Mexico (110 W x 30 N, 105 W x 25 N) so that they would not feel left out, and several targets in the crowded east, mostly water, such as Lake Michigan halfway between Chicago and Grand Rapids, and Lake Okeechobee in Florida. Where we used bodies of water Mike worked predictions of flooding waves from impacts, a time for each shoreline establishment.

For three days, starting early morning Tuesday 13th and going on to strike time early Friday 16th, we flooded Earth with warnings. England was cautioned that impact north of Dover Straits opposite London Estuary would cause disturbances far up Thames; Sovunion was given warning for Sea of Azov and had own grid defined; Great China was assigned grid in Siberia, Gobi Desert, and her far west—with offsets to avoid her historic Great Wall noted in loving detail. Pan Africa was awarded shots into Lake Victoria, still-desert part of Sahara, one on Drakensberg in south, one offset twenty kilometers due west of Great Pyramid—and urged to follow Chad not later than midnight Thursday, Greenwich. India was told to watch certain mountain peaks and outside Bombay harbor—time, same as Great China. And so forth.

Attempts were made to jam our messages but we were beaming straight down on several wavelengths—hard to stop.

Warnings were mixed with propaganda, white and black—news of failed invasion, horror pictures of dead, names and I.D. numbers of invaders—addressed to Red Cross and Crescent but in fact a grim boast showing that every trooper had been killed and that all ships' officers and crew had been killed or captured—we "regretted" being unable to identify dead of flagship, as it had been shot down with destruction so complete as to make it impossible.

But our attitude was conciliatory—"Look, people of Terra, we don't *want* to kill you. In this necessary retaliation we are making every effort to *avoid* killing you . . . but if you can't or won't get your governments to leave us in peace, then we shall be *forced* to kill you. We're up here, you're down there; you can't stop us. So *please* be sensible!"

We explained over and over how easy it was for us to hit them, how hard for them to reach us. Nor was this exaggeration. It's barely possible to launch missiles from Terra to Luna; it's easier to launch from Earth parking orbit—but very expensive. Their practical way to bomb us was from ships.

This we noted and asked them how many multimilliondollar ships they cared to use up trying it? What was it worth to try to spank us for something we had not done? It had cost them seven of their biggest and best already—did they want to try for fourteen? If so, our secret weapon that we used on FNS *Pax* was waiting.

Last above was a calculated boast—Mike figured less than one chance in a thousand that *Pax* had been able to get off a message reporting what had happened to her and it was still less likely that proud F.N. would guess that convict miners could convert their tools into space weapons. Nor did F.N. have many ships to risk. Were about two hundred space vehicles in commission, not counting satellites. But nine-tenths of these were Terra-to-orbit ships such as *Lark*—and she had been able to make a Luna jump only by stripping down and arriving dry.

Spaceships aren't built for no purpose—too expensive. F.N. had six cruisers that could probably bomb us without landing on Luna to refill tanks simply by swapping payload for extra tanks. Had several more which *might* be modified much as *Lark* had been, plus a few convict and cargo ships which could get into orbit around Luna but could never go home without refilling tanks.

Was no possible doubt that F.N. could defeat us; question was how high a price they would pay. So we had to convince them that price was too high before they had time to bring enough force to bear. A poker game— We intended to raise so steeply that they would fold and drop out. We hoped. And then never have to show our busted flush.

Communication with Hong Kong Luna was restored at end of first day of radio-video phase, during which time Mike was "throwing rocks," getting first barrage lined up. Prof called—and was I happy to hear! Mike briefed him, then I waited, expecting one of his mild reprimands—bracing self to answer sharply: "And what was *I* supposed to do? With you out of touch and possibly dead? Me left alone as acting head of government and crisis on top of us? Throw it away, just because you couldn't be reached?"

Never got to say it. Prof said, "You did exactly right, Manuel. You were acting head of government and the crisis was on top of you. I'm delighted that you did not throw away the golden moment merely because I was out of touch."

What can you do with a bloke like that? Me with heat up to red mark and no chance to use it—had to swallow and say, "Spasebaw, Prof."

Prof confirmed death of "Adam Selene." "We could have used the fiction a little longer but this is the perfect opportunity. Mike, you and Manuel have matters in hand; I had better stop off at Churchill on my way home and identify his body."

So he did. Whether Prof picked a Loonie body or a trooper I never asked, nor how he silenced anybody else involved—perhaps no huhu as many bodies in Churchill Upper were never identified. This one was right size and skin color; it had been explosively decompressed and burned in face—looked *awful!*

It lay in state in Old Dome with face covered, and was speechmaking I didn't listen to—Mike didn't miss a word; his most human quality was his conceit. Some rockhead wanted to embalm this dead flesh, giving Lenin as a precedent. But *Pravda* pointed out that Adam was a staunch conservationist and would never want this barbaric exception made. So this unknown soldier, or citizen, or citizen-soldier, wound up in our city's cloaca.

Which forces me to tell something I've put off. Wyoh was not hurt, merely exhaustion. But Ludmilla never came back. I did not know it—glad I didn't—but she was one of many dead at foot of ramp facing Bon Marché. An explosive bullet hit between her lovely, little-girl breasts. Kitchen knife in her hand had blood on it—I think she had had time to pay Ferryman's Fee.

Stu came out to Complex to tell me rather than phoning, then went back with me. Stu had not been missing; once fight was over he had gone to Raffles to work with his special codebook—but that can wait. Mum reached him there and he offered to break it to me.

So then I had to go home for our crying-together—though it is well that nobody reached me until after Mike and I started Hard Rock. When we got home, Stu did not want to come in, not being sure of our ways. Anna came out and almost dragged him in. He was welcome and wanted; many neighbors came to cry. Not as many as with most deaths—but we were just one of many families crying together that day.

Did not stay long—*couldn't*; had work to do. I saw Milla just long enough to kiss her good-bye. She was lying in her room and did look as if she did be simply sleeping. Then I stayed a while with my beloveds before going back to pick up load. Had never realized, until that day, how *old* Mimi is. Sure, she had seen many deaths, some her own descendants. But little Milla's death did seem almost too much for her. Ludmilla was special—Mimi's granddaughter, daughter in all but fact, and by most special exception and through Mimi's intervention her co-wife, most junior to most senior.

Like all Loonies, we conserve our dead—and am truly glad that barbaric custom of burial was left back on old Earth; our way is better. But Davis family does not put that which comes out of processor into our commercial farming tunnels. No. It goes into our little greenhouse tunnel, there to become roses and daffodils and peonies among soft-singing bees. Tradition says that Black Jack Davis is in there, or whatever atoms of him do remain after many, many, many years of blooming.

Is a happy place, a beautiful place.

Came Friday with no answer from F.N. News up from Earthside seemed equal parts unwillingness to believe we had destroyed seven ships and two regiments (F.N. had not even confirmed that a battle had taken place) and complete disbelief that we could bomb Terra, or could matter if we did—they still called it "throwing rice." More time was given to World Series.

Stu worried because had received no answers to code messages. They had gone via LuNoHoCo's commercial traffic to their Zurich agent, thence to Stu's Paris broker, from him by less usual channels to Dr. Chan, with whom I had once had a talk and with whom Stu had talked later, arranging a communication channel. Stu had pointed out to Dr. Chan that, since Great China was not to be bombed until twelve hours after North America, bombing of Great China could be aborted after bombing of North America was a proved fact—*if* Great China acted swiftly. Alternatively, Stu had invited Dr. Chan to suggest variations in target if our choices in Great China were not as deserted as we believed them to be.

Stu fretted—had placed great hopes in quasi-cooperation he had established with Dr. Chan. Me, I had never been sure—only thing I was sure of was that Dr. Chan would not himself sit on a target. But he might not warn his old mother.

My worries had to do with Mike. Sure, Mike was used to having many loads in trajectory at once—but had never had to astrogate more than one at a time. Now he had hundreds and had promised to deliver twenty-nine of them simultaneously to the exact second at twenty-nine pinpointed targets.

More than that— For many targets he had backup missiles, to smear that target a second time, a third, or even a sixth, from a few minutes up to three hours after first strike.

Four great Peace Powers, and some smaller ones, had antimissile defenses; those of North America were supposed to be best. But was subject where even F.N. might not know. All attack weapons were held by Peace Forces but defense weapons were each nation's own pidgin and could be secret. Guesses ranged from India, believed to have no missile interceptors, to North America, believed to be able to do a good job. She had done fairly well in stopping intercontinental H-missiles in Wet Firecracker War past century.

Probably most of our rocks to North America would reach target simply because aimed where was nothing to protect. But they couldn't afford to ignore missile for Long Island Sound, or rock for 87° W x 42° 30′ N—Lake Michigan, center of triangle formed by Chicago, Grand Rapids, Milwaukee. But that heavy gravity makes interception a tough job and *very* costly; they would try to stop us only where worth it.

But we couldn't afford to let them stop us. So some rocks were backed up with more rocks. What H-tipped interceptors would do to them even Mike did not know—not enough data. Mike assumed that interceptors would be triggered by radar—but at what distance? Sure, close enough and a steelcased rock is incandescent gas a microsecond later. But is world of difference between a multitonne rock and touchy circuitry of an H-missile; what would "kill" latter would simply shove one of our brutes violently aside, cause to miss.

We needed to prove to them that we could go on throwing cheap rocks long after they ran out of expensive (million-dollar? hundred-thousand-dollar?) H-tipped interceptor rockets. If not proved first time, then next time Terra turned North America toward us, we would go after targets we had been unable to hit first time—backup rocks for second pass, and for third, were already in space, to be nudged where needed.

If three bombings on three rotations of Terra did not do it, we might still be throwing rocks in '77—till they ran out of interceptors . . . or till they destroyed us (far more likely).

For a century North American Space Defense Command had been buried in a mountain south of Colorado Springs, Colorado, a city of no other importance. During Wet Firecracker War the Cheyenne Mountain took a direct hit; space defense command post survived—but not sundry deer, trees, most of city and some of top of mountain. What we were about to do should not kill anybody unless they stayed outside on that mountain despite three days' steady warnings. But North American Space Defense Command was to receive full Lunar treatment: twelve rock missiles on first pass, then all we could spare on second rotation, and on third—and so on, until we ran out of steel casings, or were put out of action . . . or North American Directorate hollered quits.

This was one target where we would not be satisfied to get just one missile to target. We meant to smash that mountain and keep on smashing. To hurt their morale. To let them know we were still around. Disrupt their communications and bash in command post if pounding could do it. Or at least give them splitting headaches and no rest. If we could prove to all Terra that we could drive home a sustained attack on strongest Gibraltar of their space defense, it would save having to prove it by smashing Manhattan or San Francisco.

Which we would not do even if losing. Why? Hard sense. If we used our last strength to destroy a major city, they would not punish us; they would destroy us. As Prof put it, "If possible, leave room for your enemy to become your friend."

But any military target is fair game.

Don't think anybody got much sleep Thursday night. All Loonies knew that Friday morning would be our big try. And everybody Earthside knew and at last their news admitted that Spacetrack had picked up objects headed for Terra, presumably "rice bowls" those rebellious convicts had boasted about. But was not a war warning, was mostly assurances that Moon colony could not possibly build H-bombs—but might be prudent to avoid areas which these criminals claimed to be aiming at. (Except one funny boy, popular news comic who said our targets would be safest place to be—this on video, standing on a big X-mark which he claimed was 110 W x 40 N. Don't recall hearing of him later.)

A reflector at Richardson Observatory was hooked up for video display and I think every Loonie was watching, in homes, taprooms, Old Dome—except a few who chose to p-suit and eyeball it up on surface despite being bright semi-lunar at most warrens. At Brigadier Judge Brody's insistence we hurriedly rigged a helper antenna at catapult head so that his drillmen could watch video in ready rooms, else we might not have had a gunner on duty. (Armed forces—Brody's gunners, Finn's militia, Stilyagi Air Corps—stayed on blue alert throughout period.)

Congress was in informal session in Novy Bolshoi Teatr where Terra was shown on a big screen. Some vips—Prof, Stu, Wolfgang, others—watched a smaller screen in Warden's former office in Complex Upper. I was with them part time, in and out, nervous as a cat with puppies, grabbing a sandwich and forgetting to eat—but mostly stayed locked in with Mike in Complex Under. Couldn't hold still.

About 0800 Mike said, "Man my oldest and best friend, may I say something without offending you?"

"Huh? Sure. When did you ever worry about offending me?"

"Always, Man, once I understood that you could be offended. It is now only three point five seven times ten to the ninth microseconds until impact . . . and this is the most complex problem I have ever tried to solve against real time running. Whenever you speak to me, I always use a large percentage of my capacity—perhaps larger than you suspect—during several million microseconds in my great need to analyze exactly what you have said and to reply correctly."

"You're saying, 'Don't joggle my elbow, I'm busy.' "

"I want to give you a perfect solution, Man."

"I scan. Uh . . . I'll go back up with Prof."

"As you wish. But do please stay where I can reach you—I may need your help."

Last was nonsense and we both knew it; problem was beyond human capacity, too late even to order abort. What Mike meant was: I'm nervous, too, and want your company—but no talking, please.

"Okay, Mike, I'll stay in touch. A phone somewhere. Will punch MYCROFTXXX but won't speak, so don't answer."

"Thank you, Mike my best friend. Bolshoyeh spasebaw."

"See you later." Went up, decided did not want company after all, p-suited, found long phone cord, jacked it into helmet, looped it over arm, went clear to surface. Was a service phone in utility shed outside lock; jacked into it, punched Mike's number, went outside. Got into shade of shed and peeked around edge at Terra.

She was hanging as usual halfway up western sky, in crescent big and gaudy, three-plus days past new. Sun had dropped toward western horizon but its glare kept me from seeing Terra clearly. Chin visor wasn't enough so moved back behind shed and away from it till could see Terra over shed while still shielded from Sun—was better. Sunrise chopped through bulge of Africa so dazzle point was on land, not too bad—but south pole cap was so blinding white could not see North America too well, lighted only by moonlight.

Twisted neck and got helmet binoculars on it—good ones, Zeiss 7 x 50s that had once belonged to Warden.

North America spread like a ghostly map before me. Was unusually free of cloud; could see cities, glowing spots with no edges. 0837—

At 0850 Mike gave me a voice countdown—didn't need his attention; he could have programmed it full automatic anytime earlier.

0851—0852—0853 . . . one minute—59—58—57 . . . half minute—29—28—27. . . . ten seconds—nine—eight—seven—six—five—four—three—two—one—

And suddenly that grid burst out in diamond pinpoints!

TWENTY-SIX

We hit them so hard you could *see* it, by bare eyeball hookup; didn't need binox. Chin dropped and I said, *"Bojemoi!"* softly and reverently. Twelve very bright, very sharp, very white lights in perfect rectangular array. They swelled, grew dimmer, dropped off toward red, taking what seemed a long, long time. Were other new lights but that perfect grid so fascinated me I hardly noticed.

"Yes," agreed Mike with smug satisfaction. "Dead on. You can talk now, Man; I'm not busy. Just the backups."

"I'm speechless. Any fail to get through?"

"The Lake Michigan load was kicked up and sideways, did not disintegrate. It will land in Michigan—I have no control; it lost its transponder. The Long Island Sound one went straight to target.

They tried to intercept and failed; I can't say why. Man, I can abort the follow-ups on that one, into the Atlantic and clear of shipping. Shall I? Eleven seconds."

"Uh— *Da!* If you can miss shipping."

"I said I could. It's done. But we should tell them we had back-ups and why we aborted. To make them think."

"Maybe should not have aborted, Mike. Idea was to make them use up interceptors."

"But the major idea was to let them know that we are not hitting them as hard as we can. We can prove the other at Colorado Springs."

"What happened there?" Twisted neck and used binox; could see nothing but ribbon city, hundred-plus kilometers long, Denver-Pueblo Municipal Strip.

"A bull's-eye. No interception. All my shots are bull's-eyes, Man; I told you they would be—and this is fun. I'd like to do it every day. It's a word I never had a referent for before."

"What word, Mike?"

"Orgasm. That's what it is when they all light up. Now I know."

That sobered me. "Mike, don't get to liking it too much. Because if goes our way, won't do it a second time."

"That's okay, Man; I've stored it, I can play it over anytime I want to experience it. But three to one we do it again tomorrow and even money on the next day. Want to bet? An hour's discussion of jokes equated with one hundred Kong dollars."

"Where would you get a hundred dollars?"

He chuckled. "Where do you think money comes from?"

"Uh—forget it. You get that hour free. Shan't tempt you to affect chances."

"I wouldn't cheat, Man, not *you*. We just hit their defense command again. You may not be able to see it—dust cloud from first one. They get it every twenty minutes now. Come on down and talk; I've turned the job over to my idiot son."

"Is safe?"

"I'm monitoring. Good practice for him, Man; he may have to do it later by himself. He's accurate, just stupid. But he'll do what you tell him to."

"You're calling that computer 'he.' Can talk?"

"Oh, no, Man, he's an idiot, he can never learn to talk. But he'll do whatever you program. I plan to let him handle quite a bit on Saturday."

"Why Saturday?"

"Because Sunday he may have to handle everything. That's the day they slam us."

"What do you mean? Mike, you're holding something back."

"I'm *telling* you, am I not? It's just happened and I'm scanning it. Projecting back, this blip departed circum-Terra parking orbit just as we smashed them. I didn't see it accelerate; I had other things to watch. It's too far away to read but it's the right size for a Peace cruiser, headed this way. Its doppler reads now for a new orbit circum-Luna, periselenion oh-nine-oh-three Sunday unless it maneuvers. First approximation, better data later. Hard to get that much, Man; he's using radar countermeasures and throwing back fuzz."

"Sure you're right?"

He chuckled. "Man, I don't confuse that easily. I've got all my own lovin' little signals fingerprinted. Correction. Oh-nine-oh-two-point-forty-three."

"When will you have him in range?"

"I won't, unless he maneuvers. But he'll have *me* in range late Saturday, time depending on what range he chooses for launching. And that will produce an interesting situation. He may aim for a warren—I think Tycho Under should be evacuated and all warrens should use maximum pressure-emergency measures. More likely he will try for the catapult. But instead he may hold his fire as long as he dares—then try to knock out all of my radars with a spread set to home each on a different radar beam."

Mike chuckled. "Amusing, isn't it? For a 'funny-once' I mean. If I shut down my radars, his missiles can't home on them. But if I do, I can't see to tell the lads where to point their guns. Which leaves nothing to stop him from bombing the catapult. Comical."

Took deep breath and wished I had never entered defense ministry business. "What do we do? Give up? No, Mike! Not while can fight."

"Who said anything about giving up? I've run projections of this and a thousand other possible situations, Man. New datum—second blimp just departed circum-Terra, same characteristics. Projection later. We don't give up. We give 'em jingle-jangle, cobber."

"How?"

"Leave it to your old friend Mycroft. Six ballistic radars here, plus one at the new site. I've shut the new one down and am making my retarded child work through number two here . . . and we won't look at those ships at all through the new one—never let them know we have it. I'm watching those ships through number three and occasionally—every three seconds—checking for new departures from circum-Terra. All others have their eyes closed tight and I won't use them until time to smack Great China and India—and those ships won't see them even then because I shan't look their way; it's a large angle and still will be then. And when I use them, then comes random jingle-jangle, shutting down and starting up at odd intervals . . . *after* the ships launch missiles. A missile can't carry a big brain, Man—I'll fool 'em."

"What about ships' fire-control computers?"

"I'll fool them, too. Want to lay odds I can't make two radars look like only one halfway between where they really are? But what I'm working on now—and sorry!—I've been using your voice again."

"That's okay. What am I supposed to have done?"

"If that admiral is really smart, he'll go after the ejection end of the old catapult with everything he's got—at extreme range, too far away for our drill guns. Whether he knows what our 'secret' weapon is or not, he'll smear the catapult and ignore the radars. So I've ordered the catapult head—you have, I mean—to prepare to launch every load we can get ready, and I am now working out new, long-period trajectories for each of them. Then we will throw them all, get them into space as quickly as possible—without radar."

"Blind?"

"I don't use radar to launch a load; you know that, Man. I always watched them in the past but I don't need to; radar has nothing to do with launching; launching is pre-calculation and exact control of the catapult. So we place all ammo from the old catapult in slow trajectories, which forces the admiral to go after the radars rather than the catapult—or both. Then we'll keep him busy. We may make him so desperate that he'll come down for a close shot and give our lads a chance to burn his eyes."

"Brody's boys would like that. Those who are sober." Was turning over idea. "Mike, have you watched video today?"

"I've monitored video, I can't say I've watched it. Why?"

"Take a look."

"Okay, I have. Why?"

"That's a good 'scope they're using for video and there are others. Why use radar on ships? Till you want Brody's boys to burn them?"

Mike was silent at least two seconds. "Man my best friend, did you ever think of getting a job as a computer?"

"Is sarcasm?"

"Not at all, Man. I feel ashamed. The instruments at Richardson—telescopes and other things—are factors which I simply never included in my calculations. I'm stupid, I admit it. Yes, yes, yes, da, da, da! Watch ships by telescope, don't use radar unless they vary from present ballistics. Other possibilities—I don't know what to say, Man, save that it had never occurred to me that I could use telescopes. I see by radar, always have; I simply never consid—"

"Stow it!"

"I mean it, Man."

"Do *I* apologize when *you* think of something first?"

Mike said slowly, "There is something about that which I am finding resistant to analysis. It is my function to—"

"Quit fretting. If idea is good, use it. May lead to more ideas. Switching off and coming down, chop-chop."

Had not been in Mike's room long when Prof phoned:

"HQ? Have you heard from Field Marshal Davis?"

"I'm here, Prof. Master computer room."

"Will you join us in the Warden's office? There are decisions to reach, work to be done."

"Prof I've *been* working! *Am* working."

"I'm sure you have. I've explained to the others that the programming of the ballistic computer is so very delicate in this operation that you must check it personally. Nevertheless some of our colleagues feel that the Minister of Defense should be present during these discussions. So, when you reach a point where you feel you can turn it over to your assistant—Mike's his name, is it not?—will you please—"

"I scan it. Okay, will be up."

"Very well, Manuel."

Mike said, "I could hear thirteen people in the background. Doubletalk, Man."

"I got it. Better go up and see what huhu. You don't need me?"

"Man, I hope you will stay close to a phone."

"Will. Keep an ear on Warden's office. But will punch in if elsewhere. See you, cobber."

Found entire government in Warden's office, both real Cabinet and make-weights—and soon spotted trouble, bloke called Howard Wright. A ministry had been whomped up for him: "Liaison for Arts, Sciences, and Professions"—buttonsorting. Was sop to Novylen because Cabinet was topheavy with L-City comrades, and a sop to Wright because he had made himself leader of a Congress group long on talk, short on action. Prof's purpose was to short him out—but sometimes Prof was too subtle; some people talk better if they breathe vacuum.

Prof asked me to brief Cabinet on military situation. Which I did—my way. "I see Finn is here. Let's have him tell where we stand in warrens."

Wright spoke up. "General Nielsen has already done so, no need to repeat. We want to hear from *you*."

Blinked at that. "Prof— Excuse me. Gospodin President. Do I understand that a Defense Ministry report has been made to Cabinet in my absence?"

Wright said, "Why not? You weren't on hand."

Prof grabbed it. He could see I was stretched too tight. Hadn't slept much for three days, hadn't been so tired since left Earthside. "Order," he said mildly. "Gospodin Minister for Professional Liaison, please address your comments through me. Gospodin Minister for Defense, let me correct that. There have been no reports to the Cabinet concerning your ministry for the reason that the Cabinet did not convene until you arrived. General Nielsen answered some informal questions informally. Perhaps this should not have been done. If you feel so, I will attempt to repair it."

"No harm done, I guess. Finn, talked to you a half hour ago. Anything new since?"

"No, Mannie."

"Okay. Guess what you want to hear is off-Luna situation. You've been watching so you know first bombardment went off well. Still going on, some, as we're hitting their space defense HQ every twenty minutes. Will continue till thirteen hundred, then at twenty-one hundred we hit China and India, plus minor targets. Then busy till four hours past midnight with Africa and Europe, skip three hours, dose Brasil and company, wait three hours and start over. Unless something breaks. But meantime we have problems here. Finn, we should evacuate Tycho Under."

"Just a moment!" Wright had hand up. "I have questions." Spoke to Prof, not to me.

"One moment. Has the Defense Minister finished?"

Wyoh was seated toward back. We had swapped smiles, but was all—kept it so around Cabinet and Congress; had been rumbles that two from same family should not be in Cabinet. Now she shook head, warning of something. I said, "Is all concerning bombardment. Questions about it?"

"Are your questions concerned with the bombardment, Gospodin Wright?"

"They certainly are, Gospodin President." Wright stood up, looked at me. "As you know, I represent the intellectual groups in the Free State and, if I may say so, their opinions are most important in public affairs. I think it is only proper that—"

"Moment," I said. "Thought you represented Eighth Novylen District?"

"Gospodin President! Am I to be permitted to put my questions? Or not?"

"He wasn't asking question, was making speech. And I'm tired and want to go to bed."

Prof said gently, "We are all tired, Manuel. But your point is well taken. Congressman, you represent only your district. As a member of the government you have been assigned certain duties in connection with certain professions."

"It comes to the same thing."

"Not quite. Please state your question."

"Uh . . . very well, I shall! Is Field Marshal Davis aware that his bombardment plan has gone wrong completely and that thousands of lives have been pointlessly destroyed? And is he aware of the extremely serious view taken of this by the intelligentsia of this Republic? And can he explain why this rash—I repeat, *rash!*—bombardment was undertaken without consultation? And is he now prepared to modify his plans, or is he going blindly ahead? And is it true as charged that our missiles were of the nuclear sort outlawed by all civilized nations? And how does he expect Luna Free State ever to be welcomed into the councils of civilized nations in view of such actions?"

I looked at watch—hour and a half since first load hit. "Prof," I said, "can you tell me what this is about?"

"Sorry, Manuel," he said gently. "I intended—I should have—prefaced the meeting with an item from the news. But you seem to feel that you had been bypassed and—well, I did not. The Minister refers to a news dispatch that came in just before I called you. Reuters in Toronto. If the flash is correct—*if*—then instead of taking our warnings it seems that thousands of sightseers crowded to the targets. There probably have been casualties. How many we do not know."

"I see. What was I supposed to do? Take each one by hand and lead away? We warned them."

Wright cut in with, "The intelligentsia feel that basic humanitarian considerations make it obligatory—"

I said, "Listen, yammerhead, you heard President say this news just came in—so how do you know how anybody feels about it?"

He turned red. "Gospodin President! Epithets! Personalities!"

"Don't call the Minister names, Manuel."

"Won't if he won't. He's simply using fancier words. What's that nonsense about nuclear bombs? We haven't any and you all know it."

Prof looked puzzled. "I am confused by that, too. This dispatch so alleged. But the thing that puzzled me is that we could actually *see*, by video, what certainly seemed to be atomic explosions."

"Oh." I turned to Wright. "Did your brainy friends tell you what happens when you release a few billion calories in a split second all at one spot? What temperature? How much radiance?"

"Then you admit that you *did* use atomic weapons!"

"Oh, Bog!" Head was aching. "Said nothing of sort. Hit anything hard enough, strike sparks. Elementary physics, known to everybody but intelligentsia. We just struck damnedest big sparks ever made by human agency, is all. Big flash. Heat, light, ultraviolet. Might even produce X-rays, couldn't say. Gamma radiation I strongly doubt. Alpha and beta, impossible. Was sudden release of mechanical energy. But nuclear? Nonsense!"

Prof said, "Does that answer your questions, Mr. Minister?"

"It simply raises more questions. For example, this bombardment is far beyond anything the Cabinet authorized. You saw the shocked faces when those terrible lights appeared on the screen. Yet the Minister of Defense says that it is even now continuing, every twenty minutes. I think—"

Glanced at watch. "Another just hit Cheyenne Mountain."

Wright said, "You hear that? You hear? He *boasts* of it. Gospodin President, this carnage must stop!"

I said, "Yammer— Minister, are you suggesting that their space defense HQ is not a military target? Which side are you on? Luna'? Or F.N.?"

"Manuel!"

"Tired of this nonsense! Was told to do job, did it. *Get this yammerhead off my back!*"

Was shocked silence, then somebody said quietly, "May I make a suggestion?"

Prof looked around. "If anyone has a suggestion that will quiet this unseemliness, I will be most happy to hear it."

"Apparently we don't have very good information as to what these bombs are doing. It seems to me that we ought to slow up that twenty-minute schedule. Stretch it out, say to one every hour—and skip the next two hours while we get more news. Then we might want to postpone the attack on great China at least twenty-four hours."

Were approving nods from almost everybody and murmurs: "Sensible idea!"—"Da. Let's not rush things."

Prof said, "Manuel?"

I snapped, "Prof, you *know* answer! Don't shove it on me!"

"Perhaps I do, Manuel . . . but I'm tired and confused and can't remember it."

Wyoh said suddenly, "Mannie, explain it. I need it explained, too."

So pulled self together. "A simple matter of law of gravitation. Would have to use computer to give exact answer but next half dozen shots are fully committed. Most we can do is push them off target—and maybe hit some town we haven't warned. *Can't* dump them into an ocean, is too late; Cheyenne Mountain is fourteen hundred kilometers inland. As for stretching schedule to once an hour, that's silly. Aren't tube capsules you start and stop; these are *falling rocks*. Going to hit *somewhere* every twenty minutes. You can hit Cheyenne Mountain which hasn't anything alive left on it by now—or can hit somewhere else and kill people. Idea of delaying strike on Great China by twenty-four hours is just as silly. Can abort missiles for Great China for a while yet. But *can't* slow them up. If you abort, you waste them—and everybody who thinks we have steel casings to waste had better go up to catapult head and look."

Prof wiped brow. "I think all questions have been answered, at least to my satisfaction."

"Not to mine, sir!"

"Sit down, Gospodin Wright. You force me to remind you that your ministry is *not* part of the War Cabinet. If there are no more questions—I hope there are none—I will adjourn this meeting. We all need rest. So let us—"

"Prof!"

"Yes, Manuel?"

"You never let me finish reporting. Late tomorrow or early Sunday we catch it."

"How, Manuel?"

"Bombing. Invasion possible. Two cruisers headed this way."

That got attention. Presently Prof said tiredly, "The Government Cabinet is adjourned. The War Cabinet will remain."

"Just a second," I said. "Prof, when we took office, you got undated resignations from us."

"True. I hope not to have to use any of them, however."

"You're about to use one."

"Manuel, is that a threat?"

"Call it what you like." I pointed at Wright, "Either that yammerhead goes . . . or I go."

"Manuel, you need sleep."

Was blinking back tears. "Certainly do! And going to get some. Right *now!* Going to find a doss here at Complex and get some. About ten hours. After that, if am still Minister of Defense, you can wake me. Otherwise let me sleep."

By now everybody was looking shocked. Wyoh came up and stood by me. Didn't speak, just slipped hand into my arm.

Prof said firmly, "All please leave save the War Cabinet and Gospodin Wright." He waited while most filed out. Then said, "Manuel, I can't accept your resignation. Nor can I let you chivvy me into hasty action concerning Gospodin Wright, not when we are tired and overwrought. It would be better if you two were to exchange apologies, each realizing that the other has been overstrained."

"Uh—" I turned to Finn. "Has he been fighting?" I indicated Wright.

"Huh? Hell, no. At least he's not in my outfits. How about it, Wright? Did you fight when they invaded us?"

Wright said stiffly, "I had no opportunity. By the time I knew of it, it was over. But now both my bravery and my loyalty have been impugned. I shall insist—"

"Oh, shut up," I said. "If duel is what you want, can have it first moment I'm not busy. Prof, since he doesn't have strain of fighting as excuse for behavior, I won't apologize to a yammerhead for being a yammerhead. And you don't seem to understand issue. You let this yammerhead climb on my back—and didn't even *try* to stop him! So either fire him, or fire *me*."

Finn said suddenly, "I match that, Prof. Either fire this louse—

or fire us both." He looked at Wright. "About that duel, choom—you're going to fight *me* first. You've got two arms—Mannie hasn't."

"Don't need two arms for *him*. But thanks, Finn."

Wyoh was crying—could feel it though couldn't hear it. Prof said to her most sadly, "Wyoming?"

"I'm s-s-sorry, Prof! Me, too."

Only "Clayton" Watenabe, Judge Brody, Wolfgang, Stu, and Sheenie were left, handful who counted—War Cabinet. Prof looked at them; I could see they were with me, though it cost Wolfgang an effort; he worked with Prof, not with me.

Prof looked back at me and said softly, "Manuel, it works both ways. What you are doing is forcing me to resign." He looked around. "Goodnight, comrades. Or rather, 'Good morning.' I'm going to get some badly needed rest." He walked briskly out without looking back.

Wright was gone; I didn't see him leave. Finn said, "What about these cruisers, Mannie?"

I took deep breath. "Nothing earlier than Saturday afternoon. But you ought to evacuate Tycho Under. Can't talk now. Groggy."

Agreed to meet him there at twenty-one hundred, then let Wyoh lead me away. Think she put me to bed but don't remember.

TWENTY-SEVEN

Prof was there when I met Finn in Warden's office shortly before twenty-one hundred Friday. Had had nine hours' sleep, bath, breakfast Wyoh had fetched from somewhere, and a talk with Mike—everything going to revised plan, ships had not changed ballistic, Great China strike about to happen.

Got to office in time to see strike by video—all okay and effectively over by twenty-one-oh-one and Prof got down to business. Nothing said about Wright, or about resigning. Never saw Wright again.

I mean I *never* saw him again. Nor ask about him. Prof didn't mention row, so I didn't.

We went over news and tactical situation. Wright had been

correct in saying that "thousands of lives" had been lost; news up from Earthside was full of it. How many we'll never know; if a person stands at ground zero and tonnes of rock land on him, isn't much left. Those they could count were ones farther away, killed by blast. Call it fifty thousand in North America.

Never will understand people! We spent three days warning them—and you couldn't say they hadn't heard warnings; that was why they were there. To see show. To laugh at our nonsense. To get "souvenirs." Whole families went to targets, some with picnic baskets. *Picnic baskets!* Bojemoi!

And now those alive were yelling for our blood for this "senseless slaughter." Da. Hadn't been any indignation over their invasion and (nuclear!) bombing of us four days earlier—but oh were they sore over our "premeditated murder." *Great New York Times* demanded that entire Lunar "rebel" government be fetched Earthside and publicly executed— "This is clearly a case in which the humane rule against capital punishment must be waived in the greater interests of all mankind."

Tried not to think about it, just as had been forced not to think too much about Ludmilla. Little Milla hadn't carried a picnic lunch. *She* hadn't been a sightseer looking for thrills.

Tycho Under was pressing problem. If those ships bombed warrens—and news from Earthside was demanding exactly that—Tycho Under could not take it; roof was thin. H-bomb would decompress all levels; airlocks aren't built for H-bomb blasts.

(Still don't understand people. Terra was supposed to have an absolute ban against using H-bombs on people; that was what F.N. was all about. Yet were loud yells for F.N. to H-bomb *us*. They quit claiming that our bombs were nuclear, but all North America seemed frothingly anxious to have *us* nuke-bombed.)

Don't understand Loonies for that matter. Finn had sent word through his militia that Tycho Under must be evacuated; Prof had repeated it over video. Nor was it problem; Tycho Under was small enough that Novylen and L-City could doss and dine them. We could divert enough capsules to move them all in twenty hours—dump them into Novylen and encourage half of them to go on to L-City. Big job but no problems. Oh, minor problems—start compressing city's air while evacuating people, so as to save it; decompress fully at end to minimize damage; move as much food as was time for; cofferdam accesses to lower farm tunnels; so forth—all things we knew how to do and with stilyagi and militia and municipal maintenance people had organization to do.

Had they started evacuating? Hear that hollow echo!

Were capsules lined up nose to tail at Tycho Under and no room to send more till some left. And weren't moving. "Mannie," said Finn, "don't think they are going to evacuate."

"Damn it," I said, "they've *got* to. When we spot a missile headed for Tycho Under will be too late. You'll have people trampling people and trying to crowd into capsules that won't hold them. Finn, your boys have got to *make* them."

Prof shook his head. "No, Manuel."

I said angrily, "Prof, you carry this 'no coercion' idea too far! You know they'll riot."

"Then they will riot. But we will continue with persuasion, not force. Let us now review plans.'

Plans weren't much but were best we could do. Warn everybody about expected bombings and/or invasion. Rotate guards from Finn's militia above each warren starting when and if cruisers passed around Luna into blind space, Farside—not get caught flat-footed again. Maximum pressure and p-suit precautions, all warrens. All military and semi-military to go on blue alert sixteen hundred Saturday, red alert if missiles launched or ships maneuvered. Brody's gunners encouraged to go into town and get drunk or whatever, returning by fifteen hundred Saturday—Prof's idea. Finn wanted to keep half of them on duty. Prof said No, they would be in better shape for a long vigil if they relaxed and enjoyed selves first—I agreed with Prof.

As for bombing Terra, we made no changes in first rotation. Were getting anguished responses from India, no news from Great China. Yet India had little to moan about. Had not used a grid on her, too heavily populated. Aside from picked spots in Thar Desert and some peaks, targets were coastal waters off seaports.

But should have picked higher mountains or given less warning; seemed from news that some holy man followed by endless pilgrims chose to climb each target peak and hold off our retaliation by sheer spiritual strength.

So we were murderers again. Besides that, our water shots killed millions of fish and many fishermen, as fishermen and other seafarers had not heeded warnings. Indian government seemed as furious over fish as over fishermen—but principle of sacredness of all life did not apply to us; they wanted our heads.

Africa and Europe responded more sensibly but differently. Life has never been sacred in Africa and those who went sight-seeing on targets got little bleeding-heart treatment. Europe had a day to learn that we could hit where we promised and that our bombs were deadly. People killed, yes, especially bullheaded sea captains. But not killed in empty-headed swarms as in India and North America. Casualties were even lighter in Brasil and other parts of South America.

Then was North America's turn again—0950.28 Saturday 17 Oct '76.

Mike timed it for exactly 1000 our time which, allowing for one day's progress of Luna in orbit and for rotation of Terra, caused North America to face toward us at 0500 their East Coast time and 0200 their West Coast time.

But argument as to what to do with this targeting had started early Saturday morning. Prof had not called meeting of War Cabinet but they showed up anyhow, except "Clayton" Watenabe who had gone back to Kongville to take charge of defenses. Prof, self, Finn, Wyoh, Judge Brody, Wolfgang, Stu, Terence Sheehan—which made eight different opinions. Prof is right; more than three people can't decide anything.

Six opinions, should say, for Wyoh kept pretty mouth shut, and so did Prof; he moderated. But others were noisy enough for eighteen. Stu didn't care what we hit—provided New York Stock Exchange opened on Monday morning. "We sold short in nineteen different directions on Thursday. If this nation is not to be bankrupt before it's out of its cradle, my buy orders covering those shorts had better be executed. Tell them, Wolf; make them understand."

Brody wanted to use catapult to smack any more ships leaving parking orbit. Judge knew nothing about ballistics—simply understood that his drillmen were in exposed positions. I didn't argue as most remaining loads were already in slow orbits and rest would be soon—and didn't think we would have old catapult much longer.

Sheenie thought it would be smart to repeat that grid while placing one load exactly on main building of North American Directorate. "I know Americans, I was one before they shipped me. They're sorry as hell they ever turned things over to F.N. Knock off those bureaucrats and they'll come over to our side."

Wolfgang Korsakov, to Stu's disgust, thought that their speculations might do better if all stock exchanges were closed till it was over.

Finn wanted to go for broke—warn them to get those ships out of our sky, then hit them for real if they didn't. "Sheenie is wrong about Americans; I know them, too. N.A. is toughest part of F.N.; they're the ones to lick. They're already calling us murderers, so now we've got to hit them, *hard!* Hit American cities and we can call off the rest."

I slid out, talked with Mike, made notes. Went back in; they were still arguing. Prof looked up as I sat down. "Field Marshal, you have not expressed your opinion."

I said, "Prof, can't we lay off that 'field marshal' nonsense? Children are in bed, can afford to be honest."

"As you wish, Manuel."

"Been waiting to see if any agreement would be reached."

Was none. "Don't see why I should have opinion," I went on. "Am just errand boy, here because I know how to program ballistic computer." Said this looking straight at Wolfgang—a number-one comrade but a dirty-word intellectual. I'm just a mechanic whose grammar isn't much while Wolf graduated from a fancy school, Oxford, before they convicted him. He deferred to Prof but rarely to anybody else. Stu, da—but Stu had fancy credentials, too.

Wolf stirred uneasily and said, "Oh, come, Mannie, of course we want your opinions."

"Don't have any. Bombing plan was worked out carefully; everybody had chance to criticize. Haven't seen anything to justify changing it."

Prof said, "Manuel, will you review the second bombardment of North America for the benefit of all of us?"

"Okay. Purpose of second smearing is to force them to use up interceptor rockets. Every shot is aimed at big cities—at null targets, I mean, close to big cities. Which we tell them, shortly before we hit them—how soon, Sheenie?"

"We're telling them now. But we can change it. And should."

"As may be. Propaganda isn't my pidgin. In most cases, to aim close enough to force them to intercept we have to use water targets—rough enough; besides killing fish and anybody who won't stay off water, it causes tremjous local storms and shore damage."

Glanced at watch, saw I would have to stall. "Seattle gets one in Puget Sound right in her lap. San Francisco is going to lose two bridges she's fond of. Los Angeles gets one between Long Beach and Catalina and another a few kilometers up coast. Mexico City is inland so we put one on Popocatepetl where they can see it. Salt Lake City gets one in her lake. Denver we ignore; they can see what's happening in Colorado Springs—for we smack Cheyenne Mountain again and keep it up, just as soon as we have it in line-of-sight. Saint Louis and Kansas City get shots in their rivers and so does New Orleans—probably flood New Orleans. All Great Lake cities get it, a long list—shall I read it?"

"Later perhaps," said Prof. "Go ahead."

"Boston gets one in her harbor, New York gets one in Long Island Sound and another midway between her two biggest bridges—think it will ruin those bridges but we promise to miss them and will. Going down their east coast, we give treatment to two Delaware Bay cities, then two on Chesapeake Bay, one being of max historical and sentimental importance. Farther south we catch three more big cities with sea shots. Going inland we smack Cincinnati, Birmingham, Chattanooga, Oklahoma City, all with river shots or nearby mountains. Oh, yes, Dallas—we destroy Dallas spaceport and should catch some ships, were six there last time I checked. Won't kill any people unless they insist on standing on target; Dallas is perfect place to bomb, that spaceport is big and flat and empty, yet maybe ten million people will see us hit it."

"If you hit it," said Sheenie.

"When, not 'if.' Each shot is backed up by one an hour later. If neither one gets through, we have shots farther back which can be diverted—for example easy to shift targets among Delaware-Bay-Chesapeake-Bay group. Same for Great Lakes group. But Dallas has its own string of backups and a long one—we expect it to be heavily defended. Backups run about six hours, as long as we can see North America—and last backups can be placed anywhere on continent . . . since farther out a load is when we divert it, farther we can shift it."

"I don't follow that," said Brody.

"A matter of vectors, Judge. A guidance rocket can give a load so many meters per second of side vector. Longer that vector has to work, farther from original point of aim load will land. If we signal a guidance rocket three hours before impact, we displace impact three times as much as if we waited till one hour before impact. Not quite that simple but our computer can figure it—if you give it time enough."

"How long is 'time enough'?" asked Wolfgang.

I carefully misunderstood. "Computer can solve that sort of problem almost instantaneously once you program it. But such decisions are pre-programmed. Something like this: If, out of target group A, B, C, and D, you find that you have failed to hit three targets on first and second salvoes, you reposition all group-one second backups so that you will be able to choose those three targets while distributing other second backups of that group for possible use on group two while repositioning third backups of supergroup Alpha such that—"

"Slow up!" said Wolfgang. "I'm not a computer. I just want to know how long before we have to make up our minds."

"Oh." I studied watch showily. "You now have . . . three minutes fifty-eight seconds in which to abort leading load for Kansas City. Abort program is set up and I have my best assistant—fellow named Mike—standing by. Shall I phone him?"

Sheenie said, "For heaven's sake, Man—abort!"

"Like hell!" said Finn. "What's matter, Terence? No guts?"

Prof said, "Comrades! Please!"

I said, "Look, I take orders from head of state—Prof over there.

If he wants opinions, he'll ask. No use yelling at each other." I looked at watch. "Call it two and a half minutes. More margin, of course, for other targets; Kansas City is farthest from deep water. But some Great Lake cities are already past ocean abort; Lake Superior is best we can do. Salt Lake City maybe an extra minute. Then they pile up." I waited.

"Roll call," said Prof. "To carry out the program. General Nielsen?"

"Da!"

"Gospazha Davis?"

Wyoh caught breath. "Da."

"Judge Brody?"

"Yes, of course. Necessary."

"Wolfgang?"

"Yes."

"Comte LaJoie?"

"Da."

"Gospodin Sheehan?"

"You're missing a bet. But I'll go along. Unanimous."

"One moment. Manuel?"

"Is up to you, Prof; always has been. Voting is silly."

"I am aware that it is up to me, Gospodin Minister. Carry out bombardment to plan."

Most targets we managed to hit by second salvo though all were defended except Mexico City. Seemed likely (98.3 percent by Mike's later calculation) that interceptors were exploding by radar fusing with set distances that incorrectly estimated vulnerability of solid cylinders of rock. Only three rocks were destroyed; others were pushed off course and thereby did more harm than if not fired at.

New York was tough; Dallas turned out to be very tough. Perhaps difference lay in local control of interception, for it seemed unlikely that command post in Cheyenne Mountain was still effective. Perhaps we had not cracked their hole in the ground (don't know how deep down it was) but I'll bet that neither men nor computers were still tracking.

Dallas blew up or pushed aside first five rocks, so I told Mike to take everything he could from Cheyenne Mountain and award it to Dallas . . . which he was able to do two salvoes later; those two targets are less than a thousand kilometers apart.

Dallas's defenses cracked on next salvo; Mike gave their spaceport three more (already committed) then shifted back to Cheyenne Mountain—later ones had never been nudged and were still earmarked "Cheyenne Mountain." He was still giving that battered mountain cosmic love pats when America rolled down and under Terra's eastern edge.

I stayed with Mike all during bombardment, knowing it would be our toughest. As he shut down till time to dust Great China, Mike said thoughtfully, "Man, I don't think we had better hit that mountain again."

"Why not, Mike?"

"It's not there any longer."

"You might divert its backups. When do you have to decide?"

"I would put them on Albuquerque and Omaha but had best start now; tomorrow will be busy. Man my best friend, you should leave."

"Bored with me, pal?"

"In the next few hours that first ship may launch missiles. When that happens I want to shift all ballistic control to Little David's Sling—and when I do, you should be at Mare Undarum site."

"What's fretting you, Mike?"

"That boy is accurate, Man. But he's stupid. I want him supervised. Decisions may have to be made in a hurry and there isn't anyone there who can program him properly. You should be there."

"Okay if you say so, Mike. But if needs a *fast* program, will still have to phone you." Greatest shortcoming of computers isn't computer shortcoming at all but fact that a human takes a long time, maybe hours, to set up a program that a computer solves in milliseconds. One best quality of Mike was that he could program himself. Fast. Just explain problem, let him program. Samewise and equally, he could program "idiot son" enormously faster than human could.

"But, Man, I want you there because you may *not* be able to phone me; the lines may be cut. So I've prepared a group of possible programs for Junior; they may be helpful."

"Okay, print 'em out. And let me talk to Prof."

Mike got Prof; I made sure he was private, then explained what Mike thought I should do. Thought Prof would object—was hoping he would insist I stay through coming bombardment/invasion/whatever—those ships. Instead he said, "Manuel, it's essential that you go. I've hesitated to tell you. Did you discuss odds with Mike?"

"Nyet."

"I have continued to do so. To put it bluntly, if Luna City is destroyed and I am dead and the rest of the government is dead—even if all Mike's radar eyes here are blinded and he himself is cut off from the new catapult—all of which may happen under severe bombardment . . . even if all this happens at once, Mike still gives Luna even chances if Little David's Sling can operate—and *you* are there to operate it."

I said, "Da, Boss. Yassuh, Massuh. You and Mike are stinkers and want to hog fun. Will do."

"Very good, Manuel."

Stayed with Mike another hour while he printed out meter after meter of programs tailored to other computer—work that would have taken me six months even if able to think of all possibilities. Mike had it indexed and cross-referenced—with horribles in it I hardly dare mention. Mean to say, given circumstances and seemed necessary to destroy (say) Paris, this told how—what missiles in what orbits, how to tell Junior to find them and bring to target. Or *anything*.

Was reading this endless document—not programs but descriptions of purpose-of-program that headed each—when Wyoh phoned. "Mannie dear, has Prof told you about going to Mare Undarum?"

"Yes. Was going to call you."

"All right. I'll pack for us and meet you at Station East. When can you be there?"

"Pack for 'us'? You're going?"

"Didn't Prof say?"

"No." Suddenly felt cheerful.

"I felt guilty about it, dear. I *wanted* to go with you . . . but had no excuse. After all, I'm no use around a computer and I *do* have responsibilities here. Or did. But now I've been fired from all my jobs and so have you."

"Huh?"

"You are no longer Defense Minister; Finn is. Instead you are Deputy Prime Minister—"

"Well!"

"—and Deputy Minister of Defense, too. I'm already Deputy Speaker and Stu has been appointed Deputy Secretary of State for Foreign Affairs. So he goes with us, too."

"I'm confused."

"It's not as sudden as it sounds; Prof and Mike worked it out months ago. Decentralization, dear, the same thing that McIntyre has been working on for the warrens. If there is a disaster at L-City, Luna Free State still has a government. As Prof put it to me, 'Wyoh dear lady, as long as you three and a few Congressmen are left alive, all is not lost. You can still negotiate on equal terms and never admit your wounds.' "

So I wound up as a computer mechanic. Stu and Wyoh met me, with luggage (including rest of my arms), and we threaded through endless unpressured tunnels in p-suits, on a small flatbed rolligon used to haul steel to site. Greg had big rolligon meet us for surface stretch, then met us himself when we went underground again.

So I missed attack on ballistic radars Saturday night.

TWENTY-EIGHT

Captain of first ship, FNS *Espérance*, had guts. Late Saturday he changed course, headed straight in. Apparently figured we might attempt jingle-jangle with radars, for he seems to have decided to come in close enough to see our radar installations by ship's radar rather than rely on letting his missiles home in on our beams.

Seems to have considered himself, ship, and crew expendable, for he was down to a thousand kilometers before he launched, a spread that went straight for five out of six of Mike's radars, ignoring random jingle-jangle.

Mike, expecting self soon to be blinded, turned Brody's boys loose to burn ship's eyes, held them on it for three seconds before he shifted them to missiles.

Result: one crashed cruiser, two ballistic radars knocked out by H-missiles, three missiles "killed"—and two gun crews killed, one by H-explosion, other by dead missile that landed square on them—plus thirteen gunners with radiation burns above 800-roentgen death level, partly from flash, partly from being on surface too long. And must add: Four members of Lysistrata Corps died with those crews; they elected to p-suit and go up with their men. Other girls had serious radiation exposure but not up to 800-r level.

Second cruiser continued an elliptical orbit around and behind Luna.

Got most of this from Mike after we arrived Little David's Sling early Sunday. He was feeling groused over loss of two of his eyes and still more groused over gun crews—I think Mike was developing something like human conscience; he seemed to feel it was his fault that he had not been able to outfight six targets at once. I pointed out that what he had to fight with was improvised, limited range, not real weapons.

"How about self, Mike? Are you right?"

"In all essentials. I have outlying discontinuities. One live missile chopped my circuits to Novy Leningrad, but reports routed through Luna City inform me that local controls tripped in satisfactorily with no loss in city services. I feel frustrated by these discontinuities—but they can be dealt with later."

"Mike, you sound tired."

"Me tired? Ridiculous! Man, you forget what I am. I'm annoyed, that's all."

"When will that second ship be back in sight?"

"In about three hours if he were to hold earlier orbit. But he will not—probability in excess of ninety percent. I expect him in about an hour."

"A Garrison orbit, huh? Oho!"

"He left my sight at azimuth *and* course east thirty-two north. Does that suggest anything, Man?"

Tried to visualize. "Suggests they are going to land and try to capture *you*, Mike. Have you told Finn? I mean, have you told Prof to warn Finn?"

"Professor knows. But that is not the way I analyze it."

"So? Well, suggests I had better shut up and let you work."

Did so. Lenore fetched me breakfast while I inspected Junior—and am ashamed to say could not manage to grieve over losses with both Wyoh and Lenore present. Mum had sent Lenore out "to cook for Greg" after Milla's death—just an excuse; were enough wives at site to provide home-cooking for everybody. Was for Greg's morale and Lenore's, too; Lenore and Milla had been close.

Junior seemed to be right. He was working on South America, one load at a time. I stayed in radar room and watched, at extreme magnification, while he placed one in estuary between Montevideo and Buenos Aires; Mike could not have been more accurate. I then checked his program for North America, found naught to criticize—locked it in and took key. Junior was on his own—unless Mike got clear of other troubles and decided to take back control.

Then sat and tried to listen to news both from Earthside and L-City. Co-ax cable from L-City carried phones, Mike's hookup to his idiot child, radio, and video; site was no longer isolated. But, besides cable from L-City, site had antennas pointed at Terra; any Earthside news Complex could pick up, we could listen to directly. Nor was this silly extra; radio and video from Terra had been only recreation during construction and this was now a standby in case that one cable was broken.

F.N. official satellite relay was claiming that Luna's ballistic radars had been destroyed and that we were now helpless. Wondered what people of Buenos Aires and Montevideo thought about that. Probably too busy to listen; in some ways water shots were worse than those where we could find open land.

Luna City *Lunatic*'s video channel was carrying Sheenie telling Loonies outcome of attack by *Espérance*, repeating news while warning everybody that battle was *not* over, a warship would be back in our sky any moment—be ready for anything, everybody stay in p-suits (Sheenie was wearing his, with helmet open), take maximum pressure precautions, all units stay on red alert, all citizens not otherwise called by duty strongly urged to seek lowest level and stay there till all clear. And so forth.

He went through this several times—then suddenly broke it:

"Flash! Enemy cruiser radar-sighted, low and fast. It may dido for Luna City. Flash! Missiles launched, headed for ejection end of—"

Picture and sound chopped off.

Might as well tell now what we at Little David's Sling learned later: Second cruiser, by coming in low and fast, tightest orbit Luna's field permits, was able to start its bombing at ejection end of old catapult, a hundred kilometers from catapult head and Brody's gunners, and knock many rings out in minute it took him to come into sight-and-range of drill guns, all clustered around radars at catapult head. Guess he felt safe. Wasn't. Brody's boys burned eyes out and ears off. He made one orbit after that and crashed near Torricelli, apparently in attempt to land, for his jets fired just before crash.

But our next news at new site was from Earthside: that brassy F.N. frequency claimed that our catapult had been destroyed (true) and that Lunar menace was ended (false) and called on all Loonies to take prisoner their false leaders and surrender themselves to mercy of Federated Nations (nonexistent—"mercy," that is).

Listened to it and checked programming again, and went inside dark radar room. If everything went as planned, we were about to lay another egg in Hudson River, then targets in succession for three hours across that continent—"in succession" because Junior could not handle simultaneous hits; Mike had planned accordingly.

Hudson River was hit on schedule. Wondered how many New Yorkers were listening to F.N. newscast while looking at spot that gave it lie.

Two hours later F.N. station was saying that Lunar rebels had had missiles in orbit when catapult was destroyed—but that after those few had impacted would be no more. When third bombing of North America was complete I shut down radar. Had not been running steadily; Junior was programmed to sneak looks only as necessary, a few seconds at a time.

I then had nine hours before next bombing of Great China.

But not nine hours for most urgent decision, whether to hit Great China again. Without information. Except from Terra's news channels. Which might be false. Bloody. Without knowing whether or not warrens had been bombed. Or Prof was dead or alive. Double bloody. Was I now acting prime minister? Needed Prof: "head of state" wasn't my glass of chai. Above all, needed Mike—to calculate facts, estimate uncertainties, project probabilities of this course or that.

My word, didn't even know whether ships were headed toward us and, worse yet, was afraid to look. If turned radar on and used Junior for sky search, any warship he brushed with beams would see him quicker than he saw them; warships were built to spot radar surveillance. So had heard. Hell, was no military man; was computer technician who had bumbled into wrong field.

Somebody buzzed door; I got up and unlocked. Was Wyoh, with coffee. Didn't say a word, just handed it to me and went away.

Sipped it. There it is, boy—they're leaving you alone, waiting for you to pull miracles out of pouch. Didn't feel up to it.

From somewhere, back in my youth, heard Prof say, "Manuel, when faced with a problem you do not understand, do any part of it you do understand, then look at it again." He had been teaching me something he himself did not understand very well—something in math—but had taught me something far more important, a basic principle.

Knew at once what to do first.

Went over to Junior and had him print out predicted impacts of all loads in orbit—easy, was a pre-program he could run anytime against real time running. While he was doing it, I looked for certain alternate programs in that long roll Mike had prepared.

Then set up some of those alternate programs—no trouble, simply had to be careful to read them correctly and punch them in without error. Made Junior print back for check before I gave him signal to execute.

When finished—forty minutes—every load in trajectory intended for an inland target had been retargeted for a seacoast city—with hedge to my bet that execution was delayed for rocks farther back. But, unless I canceled, Junior would reposition them as soon as need be.

Now horrible pressure of time was off me, now could abort any load into ocean right up to last few minutes before impact. Now could think. So did.

Then called in my "War Cabinet"—Wyoh, Stu, and Greg my

"Commander of Armed Forces," using Greg's office. Lenore was allowed to go in and out, fetching coffee and food, or sitting and saying nothing. Lenore is a sensible fem and knows when to keep quiet.

Stu started it. "Mr. Prime Minister, I do not think that Great China should be hit this time."

"Never mind fancy titles, Stu. Maybe I'm acting, maybe not. But haven't time for formality."

"Very well. May I explain my proposal?"

"Later." I explained what I had done to give us more time; he nodded and kept quiet. "Our tightest squeeze is that we are out of communication, both Luna City and Earthside. Greg, how about that repair crew?"

"Not back yet."

"If break is near Luna City, they may be gone a long time. If can repair at all. So must assume we'll have to act on our own. Greg, do you have an electronics tech who can jury-rig a radio that will let us talk to Earthside? To their satellites, I mean—that doesn't take much with right antenna. I may be able to help and that computer tech I sent you isn't too clumsy, either." (Quite good, in fact, for ordinary electronics—a poor bloke I had once falsely accused of allowing a fly to get into Mike's guts. I had placed him in this job.)

"Harry Biggs, my power plant boss, can do anything of that sort," Greg said thoughtfully, "if he has the gear."

"Get him on it. You can vandalize anything but radar and computer once we get all loads out of catapult. How many lined up?"

"Twenty-three, and no more steel."

"So twenty-three it is, win or lose. I want them ready for loading; might lob them off today."

"They're ready. We can load as fast as the cat can throw them."

"Good. One more thing— Don't know whether there's an F.N. cruiser—maybe more than one—in our sky or not. And afraid to look. By radar, I mean; radar for skywatch could give away our position. But must have skywatch. Can you get volunteers for an eyeball skywatch and can you spare them?"

Lenore spoke up. "I volunteer!"

"Thanks, honey; you're accepted."

"We'll find them," said Greg. "Won't need fems."

"Let her do it, Greg; this is everybody's show." Explained what I wanted: Mare Undarum was now in dark semi-lunar; Sun had set. Invisible boundary between sunlight and Luna's shadow stretched over us, a precise locus. Ships passing through our sky would wink suddenly into view going west, blink out going east. Visible part of orbit would stretch from horizon to some point in sky. If eyeball team could spot both points, mark one by bearing, other by stars, and approximate time by counting seconds, Junior could start guessing orbit—two passes and Junior would know its period and something about shape of orbit. Then *I* would have some notion of when would be safe to use radar and radio, and catapult—did not want to loose a load with F.N. ship above horizon, could be radar-looking our way.

Perhaps too cautious—but had to assume that this catapult, this one radar, these two dozen missiles, were all that stood between Luna and total defeat—and our bluff hinged on them never knowing what we had or where it was. We had to appear endlessly able to pound Terra with missiles, from source they had not suspected and could never find.

Then as now, most Loonies knew nothing about astronomy—we're cave dwellers, we go up to surface only when necessary. But we were lucky; was amateur astronomer in Greg's crew, cobber who had worked at Richardson. I explained, put him in charge, let him worry about teaching eyeball crew how to tell stars apart. I got these things started before we went back to talk-talk. "Well, Stu? Why shouldn't we hit Great China?"

"I'm still expecting word from Dr. Chan. I received one message from him, phoned here shortly before we were cut off from cities—"

"My word, why didn't you tell me?"

"I tried to, but you had yourself locked in and I know better than to bother you when you are busy with ballistics. Here's the translation. Usual LuNoHo Company address with a reference which means it's for me and that it has come through my Paris agent. 'Our Darwin sales representative'—that's Chan—'informs us that your shipments of'—well, never mind the coding; he means the attack days while appearing to refer to last June—'were improperly packaged resulting in unacceptable damage. Unless this can be corrected, negotiations for long-term contract will be seriously jeopardized."

Stu looked up. "All doubletalk. I take it to mean that Dr. Chan feels that he has his government ready to talk terms . . . but that we should let up on bombing Great China or we may upset his apple cart."

"Hmm—" Got up and walked around. Ask Wyoh's opinion? Nobody knew Wyoh's virtues better than I . . . but she oscillated between fierceness and too-human compassion—and I had learned already that a "head of state," even an acting one, must have neither. Ask Greg? Greg was a good farmer, a better mechanic, a rousing preacher; I loved him dearly—but did not want his opinion. Stu? I had had his opinion.

Or did I? "Stu, what's your opinion? Not Chan's opinion—but your *own*."

Stu looked thoughtful. "That's difficult, Mannie. I am not Chinese, I have not spent much time in Great China, and can't claim to be expert in their politics nor their psychology. So I'm forced to depend on his opinion."

"Uh— Damn it, he's not a Loonie! His purposes are not our purposes. What does *he* expect to get out of it?"

"I think he is maneuvering for a monopoly over Lunar trade. Perhaps bases here, too. Possibly an extraterritorial enclave. Not that we would grant that."

"Might if we were hurtin'."

"He didn't say any of this. He doesn't say much, you know. He listens."

"Too well I know." Worried at it, more bothered each minute.

News from Earthside had been droning in background; I had asked Wyoh to monitor while I was busy with Greg. "Wyoh, hon, anything new from Earthside?"

"No. The same claims. We've been utterly defeated and our surrender is expected momentarily. Oh, there's a warning that some missiles are still in space, falling out of control, but with it a reassurance that the paths are being analyzed and people will be warned in time to avoid impact areas."

"Anything to suggest that Prof—or anybody in Luna City, or anywhere in Luna—is in touch with Earthside?"

"Nothing at all."

"Damn. Anything from Great China?"

"No. Comments from almost everywhere else. But not from Great China."

"Uh—" Stepped to door. "Greg! Hey, cobber, see if you can find Greg Davis. I need him."

Closed door. "Stu, we're not going to let Great China off."

"So?"

"No. Would be nice if Great China busted alliance against us; might save us some damage. But we've got this far only by appearing able to hit them at will and to destroy any ship they send against us. At least I hope that last one was burned and we've certainly clobbered eight out of nine. We won't get anywhere by looking weak, not while F.N. is claiming that we are not just weak but finished. Instead we must hand them surprises. Starting with Great China and if it makes Dr. Chan unhappy, we'll give him a kerchief to weep into. If we can go on looking strong—when F.N. says we're licked—then eventually some veto power is going to crack. If not Great China, then some other one."

Stu bowed without getting up. "Very well, sir."

"I—"

Greg came in. "You want me, Mannie?"

"What makes with Earthside sender?"

"Harry says you have it by tomorrow. A crummy rig, he says, but push watts through it and will be heard."

"Power we got. And if he says 'tomorrow' then he knows what he wants to build. So will be *today*—say six hours. I'll work under him. Wyoh hon, will you get my arms? Want number-six and number-three—better bring number-five, too. And you stick with me and change arms for me. Stu, want you to write some nasty messages—I'll give you general idea and you put acid in them. Greg, we are *not* going to get all those rocks into space at once. Ones we have in space now will impact in next eighteen, nineteen hours.

Then, when F.N. is announcing that all rocks are accounted for and Lunar menace is over . . . we crash into their newscast and warn of next bombings. Shortest possible orbits, Greg, ten hours or less—so check everything on catapult and H-plant and controls; with that extra boost all has to be dead on."

Wyoh was back with arms; I told her "number six" and added, "Greg, let me talk with Harry."

Six hours later sender was ready to beam toward Terra. Was ugly job, vandalized mainly out of a resonance prospector used in project's early stages. But could ride an audio signal on its radio frequency and was powerful. Stu's nastified versions of my warnings had been taped and Harry was ready to zip-squeal them—all Terran satellites could accept high speed at sixty-to-one and had no wish to have our sender heated more seconds than necessary; eyeball watch had confirmed fears: At least two ships were in orbit around Luna.

So we told Great China that her major coastal cities would each receive a Lunar present offset ten kilometers into ocean—Pusan, Tsingtao, Taipei, Shanghai, Saigon, Bangkok, Singapore, Djakarta, Darwin, and so forth—except that Old Hong Kong would get one smack on top of F.N.'s Far East offices, so kindly have all human beings move far back. Stu noted that human beings did not mean F.N. personnel; they were urged to stay at desks.

India was given similar warnings about coastal cities and was told that F.N. global offices would be spared one more rotation out of respect for cultural monuments in Agra—and to permit human beings to evacuate. (I intended to extend this by another rotation as deadline approached—out of respect for Prof. And then another, indefinitely. Damn it, they *would* build their home offices next door to most overdecorated tomb ever built. But one that Prof treasured.)

Rest of world was told to keep their seats; game was going extra innings. But stay away from *any* F.N. offices anywhere; we were frothing at mouth and no F.N. office was safe. Better yet, get out of any city containing an F.N. headquarters—but F.N. vips and finks were urged to sit tight.

Then spent next twenty hours coaching Junior into sneaking his radar peeks when our sky was clear of ships, or believed to be. Napped when I could and Lenore stayed with me and woke me in time for next coaching. And that ended Mike's rocks and we all went into alert while we got first of Junior's rocks flung high and fast. Waited until certain it had gone hot and true—then told Terra where to look for it and where and when to expect it, so that all would know that F.N.'s claims of victory were on a par with their century of lies about Luna—all in Stu's best, snotty, supercilious phrases delivered in his cultured accents.

First one should have been for Great China but was one piece of North American Directorate we could reach with it—her proudest jewel, Hawaii. Junior placed it in triangle formed by Maui, Molokai, and Lanai. I didn't work out programming; Mike had anticipated everything.

Then pronto we got off ten more rocks at short intervals (had to skip one program, a ship in our sky) and told Great China where to look and when to expect them and where—coastal cities we had neglected day before.

Was down to twelve rocks but decided was safer to run out of ammunition than to look as if we were running out. So I awarded seven to Indian coastal cities, picking new targets—and Stu inquired sweetly if Agra had been evacuated. If not, please tell us *at once*. (But heaved no rock at it.)

Egypt was told to clear shipping out of Suez Canal—bluff; was hoarding last five rocks.

Then waited.

Impact at Lahaina Roads, that target in Hawaii. Looked good at high mag; Mike could be proud of Junior.

And waited.

Thirty-seven minutes before first China Coast impact Great China denounced actions of F.N., recognized us, offered to negotiate—and I sprained a finger punching abort buttons.

Then was punching buttons with sore finger; India stumbled over feet following suit.

Egypt recognized us. Other nations started scrambling for door.

Stu informed Terra that we had suspended—only suspended, not stopped—bombardments. Now get those ships out of our sky at once—NOW!—and we could talk. If they could not get home without refilling tanks, let them land not less than fifty kilometers from any mapped warren, then wait for their surrender to be accepted. But clear our sky *now*!

This ultimatum we delayed a few minutes to let a ship pass beyond horizon; we weren't taking chances—one missile and Luna would have been helpless.

And waited.

Cable crew returned. Had gone almost to Luna City, found break. But thousands of tonnes of loose rock impeded repair, so they had done what they could—gone back to a spot where they could get through to surface, erected a temporary relay in direction they thought Luna City lay, sent up a dozen rockets at ten-minute intervals, and hoped that somebody would see, understand, aim a relay at it— Any communication?

No.

Waited.

Eyeball squad reported that a ship which had been clock-faithful for nineteen passes had failed to show. Ten minutes later they reported that another ship had missed expected appearance.

We waited and listened.

Great China, speaking on behalf of all veto powers, accepted armistice and stated that our sky was now clear. Lenore burst into tears and kissed everybody she could reach.

After we steadied down (a man can't think when women are grabbing him, especially when five of them are not his wives)—a few minutes later, when we were coherent, I said, "Stu, want you to leave for Luna City at once. Pick your party. No women—you'll have to walk surface last kilometers. Find out what's going on—but first get them to aim a relay at ours and phone me."

"Very good, sir."

We were getting him outfitted for a tough journey—extra air bottles, emergency shelter, so forth—when Earthside called *me* . . . on frequency we were listening to because message was (learned later) on all frequencies up from Earthside:

"*Private message, Prof to Mannie—identification, birthday Bastille and Sherlock's sibling. Come home at once. Your carriage waits at your new relay. Private message, Prof to—*"

And went on repeating.

"Harry!"

"Da, Boss?"

"Message Earthside—tape and squeal; we still don't want them ranging us. '*Private message, Mannie to Prof. Brass Cannon. On my way!*' Ask them to acknowledge—but use only *one* squeal."

TWENTY-NINE

Stu and Greg drove on way back, while Wyoh and Lenore and I huddled on open flatbed, strapped to keep from falling off; was too small. Had time to think; neither girl had suit radio and we could talk only by helmet touch—awkward.

Began to see—now that we had won—parts of Prof's plan that had never been clear to me. Inviting attack against catapult had spared warrens—hoped it had; that was plan—but Prof had always been cheerfully indifferent to damage to catapult. Sure, had a second one—but far away and difficult to reach. Would take *years* to put a tube system to new catapult, high mountains all way. Probably cheaper to repair old one. If possible.

Either way, no grain shipped to Terra in meantime.

And *that* was just what Prof wanted! Yet never once had he hinted that his plan was based on destroying old catapult—his long-range plan, not just Revolution. He might not admit it now. But Mike would tell me—if put to him flatly: Was or was not this one factor in odds? Food riot predictions and all that, Mike? He would tell me.

That tonne-for-tonne deal— Prof had expounded it Earthside, had been argument for a Terran catapult. But privately he had no enthusiasm for it. Once he had told me, in North America, "Yes, Manuel, I feel sure it would work. But, if built, it will be temporary. There was a time, two centuries ago, when dirty laundry used to be shipped from California to Hawaii—by sailing ship, mind you—and clean laundry returned. Special circumstances. If we ever see water and manure shipped to Luna and grain shipped back, it will be just as temporary. Luna's future lies in her unique position at the top of a gravity well over a rich planet, and in her cheap power and plentiful real estate. If we Loonies have sense enough in the centuries ahead to remain a free port and to stay out of entangling alliances, we will become the crossroads for two planets, three planets, the entire Solar System. We won't be farmers forever."

They met us at Station East and hardly gave time to get p-suits off—was return from Earthside over again, screaming mobs and being ridden on shoulders. Even girls, for Slim Lemke said to Lenore, "May we carry you, too?"—and Wyoh answered, "Sure, why not?"—and stilyagi fought for chance to.

Most men were pressure-suited and I was surprised to see how many carried guns—until I saw that they were not *our* guns; they were captured. But most of all what blessed relief to see L-City unhurt!

Could have done without triumphal procession; was itching to get to phone and find out from Mike what had happened—how much damage, how many killed, what this victory cost. But no chance. We were carried to Old Dome willy-nilly.

They shoved us up on a platform with Prof and rest of Cabinet and vips and such, and our girls slobbered on Prof and he embraced me Latin style, kiss cheek, and somebody stuck a Liberty Cap on me. Spotted little Hazel in crowd and threw her a kiss.

At last they quieted enough for Prof to speak.

"My friends," he said, and waited for silence. "My friends," he repeated softly. "Beloved comrades. We meet at last in freedom and now have with us the heroes who fought the last battle for Luna, alone." They cheered us, again he waited. Could see he was tired; hands trembled as he steadied self against pulpit. "I want them to speak to you, we want to hear about it, all of us.

"But first I have a happy message. Great China has just announced that she is building in the Himalayas an enormous catapult, to make shipping to Luna as easy and cheap as it has been to ship from Luna to Terra."

He stopped for cheers, then went on, "But that lies in the future. Today— Oh, happy day! At last the world acknowledges Luna's sovereignty. Free! You have won your freedom—"

Prof stopped—looked surprised. Not afraid, but puzzled. Swayed slightly.

Then he did die.

THIRTY

We got him into a shop behind platform. But even with help of a dozen doctors was no use; old heart was gone, strained too many times. They carried him out back way and I started to follow.

Stu touched my arm. "Mr. Prime Minister—"

I said, "Huh? Oh, for Bog's sake!"

"Mr. Prime Minister," he repeated firmly, "you must speak to the crowd, send them home. Then there are things that *must* be done." He spoke calmly but tears poured down cheeks.

So I got back on platform and confirmed what they had guessed and told them to go home. And wound up in room L of Raffles, where all had started—emergency Cabinet meeting. But first ducked to phone, lowered hood, punched MYCROFTXXX.

Got null-number signal. Tried again—same. Pushed up hood and said to man nearest me, Wolfgang, "Aren't phones working?"

"Depends," he said. "That bombing yesterday shook things up. If you want an out-of-town number, better call the phone office."

Could see self asking office to get me a null. "What bombing?"

"Haven't you heard? It was concentrated on the Complex. But Brody's boys got the ship. No real damage. Nothing that can't be fixed."

Had to drop it; they were waiting. *I* didn't know what to do but Stu and Korsakov did. Sheenie was told to write news releases for Terra and rest of Luna; I found self announcing a lunar of mourning, twenty-four hours of quiet, no unnecessary business, giving orders for body to lie in state—all words put into mouth, I was numb, brain would not work. Okay, convene Congress at end of twenty-four hours. In Novylen? Okay.

Sheenie had dispatches from Earthside. Wolfgang wrote for me something which said that, because of death of our President, answers would be delayed at least twenty-four hours.

At last was able to get away, with Wyoh. A stilyagi guard kept people away from us to easement lock thirteen. Once home I ducked into workshop on pretense of needing to change arms. "Mike?"

No answer—

So tried punching his combo into house phone—null signal. Resolved to go out to Complex next day—with Prof gone, needed Mike worse than ever.

But next day was not able to go; trans-Crisium tube was out—that last bombing. You could go around through Torricelli and Novylen and eventually reach Hong Kong. But Complex, almost next door, could be reached only by rolligon. Couldn't take time; I was "government."

Managed to shuck that off two days later. By resolution was decided that Speaker (Finn) had succeeded to Presidency after Finn and I had decided that Wolfgang was best choice for Prime Minister. We put it through and I went back to being Congressman who didn't attend sessions.

By then most phones were working and Complex could be

called. Punched MYCROFTXXX. No answer— So went out by rolligon. Had to go down and walk tube last kilometer but Complex Under didn't seem hurt.

Nor did Mike appear to be.

But when I spoke to him, he didn't answer.

He has never answered. Has been many years now.

You can type questions into him—in Loglan—and you'll get Loglan answers out. He works just fine . . . as a computer. But won't talk. Or can't.

Wyoh tried to coax him. Then she stopped. Eventually I stopped.

Don't know how it happened. Many outlying pieces of him got chopped off in last bombing—was meant, I'm sure, to kill our ballistic computer. Did he fall below that "critical number" it takes to sustain self-awareness? (If is such; was never more than hypothesis.) Or did decentralizing that was done before that last bombing "kill" him?

I don't know. If was just matter of critical number, well, he's long been repaired; he *must* be back up to it. Why doesn't he wake up?

Can a machine be so frightened and hurt that it will go into catatonia and refuse to respond? While ego crouches inside, aware but never willing to risk it? No, *can't* be that; Mike was unafraid—as gaily unafraid as Prof.

Years, changes—Mimi long ago opted out of family management; Anna is "Mum" now and Mimi dreams by video. Slim got Hazel to change name to Stone, two kids and she studied engineering. All those new free-fall drugs and nowadays earthworms stay three or four years and go home unchanged. And those other drugs that do almost as much for us; some kids go Earthside to school now. And Tibet catapult—took seventeen years instead of ten; Kilimanjaro job was finished sooner.

One mild surprise—When time came, Lenore named Stu for opting, rather than Wyoh. Made no difference, we all voted "Da!" One thing not a surprise because Wyoh and I pushed it through during time we still amounted to something in government: a brass cannon on a pedestal in middle of Old Dome and over it a flag fluttering in blower breeze—black field speckled with stars, bar sinister in blood, a proud and jaunty brass cannon embroidered over all, and below it our motto: TANSTAAFL! That's where we hold our Fourth-of-July celebrations.

You get only what you pay for—Prof knew and paid, gaily.

But Prof underrated yammerheads. They never adopted *any* of his ideas. Seems to be a deep instinct in human beings for making everything compulsory that isn't forbidden. Prof got fascinated by possibilities for shaping future that lay in a big, smart computer—and lost track of things closer home. Oh, I backed him! But now I wonder. Are food riots too high a price to pay to let people be? *I* don't know.

Don't know *any* answers.

Wish I could ask Mike.

I wake up in night and think I've heard him—just a whisper: "*Man . . . Man my best friend . . .*" But when I say, "Mike?" he doesn't answer. Is he wandering around somewhere, looking for hardware to hook onto? Or is he buried down in Complex Under, trying to find way out? Those special memories are all in there somewhere, waiting to be stirred. But *I* can't retrieve them; they were voice-coded.

Oh, he's dead as Prof, I know it. (But how dead is Prof?) If I punched it just once more and said, "Hi, Mike!" would he answer, "Hi, Man! Heard any good ones lately?" Been a long time since I've risked it. But he can't really be dead; nothing was hurt—he's just *lost*.

You listening, Bog? Is a computer one of Your creatures?

Too many changes— May go to that talk-talk tonight and toss in some random numbers.

Or not. Since Boom started quite a few young cobbers have gone out to Asteroids. Hear about some nice places out there, not too crowded.

My word, I'm not even a hundred yet.